W9-BMQ-318

Praise for Janet Dawson and TAKE A NUMBER

"Well written and entertaining ... You'll find yourself turning the pages because the victim is so deliciously despicable."
—*West Coast Review of Books*

"A welcome addition to this tough genre."
—*The New York Times Book Review*

"In recent years women private eyes have become big business, as anyone who's been following the fortunes of Sue Grafton and Sara Paretsky can attest. Thanks to their success, the way has been opened for many other women to write mysteries in voices uniquely their own. A fine example is Janet Dawson."
—*The Denver Post*

"Dawson keeps suspense and interest at high pitch."
—*Publishers Weekly*

Also by Janet Dawson
Published by Fawcett Books:

KINDRED CRIMES
TILL THE OLD MEN DIE

TAKE A NUMBER

Janet Dawson

FAWCETT CREST • NEW YORK

For my brother,
ROGER LYNN DAWSON,
in spite of the tomato worms.

A Fawcett Crest Book
Published by Ballantine Books
Copyright © 1993 by Janet Dawson

All rights reserved under International and Pan-American Copyright Conventions. Published in the United States by Ballantine Books, a division of Random House, Inc., New York, and simultaneously in Canada by Random House of Canada Limited, Toronto.

Library of Congress Catalog Card Number: 93-70008

ISBN 0-449-22183-0

Manufactured in the United States of America

First Hardcover Edition: September 1993
First Mass Market Edition: September 1994

10 9 8 7 6 5 4 3 2 1

ACKNOWLEDGMENTS

I greatly appreciate the time, expertise, and information given so freely by the following people: Sergeant Dan Mercado, Homicide, Oakland Police Department; Sergeant Charlie Dove, Auto Theft, Oakland Police Department; John Jay, Alameda County District Attorney's Office; Gail Coney, Attorney at Law; Barbara Littwin, Attorney at Law; Lincoln Mintz, Attorney at Law; Lieutenant Commander Teresa Kielhorn, United States Navy JAG Corps; Peter Beall, CPA; and Sister Carol Anne O'Marie and the women of A Friendly Place.

Fast Forward . . .

One

It was just after noon on a bright hot August Friday when I met Sam Raynor for the first—and last—time.

I watched the lunchtime crowd as I waited on the far side of the street-level fountain at City Center Square in downtown Oakland. Men in shirtsleeves and women in summer dresses sat on the edge of the fountain or on benches lining the terra-cotta-tiled pedestrian mall, eating sandwiches and salad from takeout containers. Office workers strolled among the trees, spooning up frozen yogurt as they enjoyed the sunshine and the break from work. Others lingered at the edge of the lower level fountain, where water cascaded down a series of steps near the entrance to the BART station. The splashing fountains pleased my ear as I watched this midday parade.

I looked up at the modern sculpture above the nearby fountain. Constructed of outsized metal bars in lime green, pink, orange, and red, it looked as though a giant hand had played a game of pickup sticks, tossing the multicolored lengths into the air, where they stayed, frozen in place against the cloudless blue sky, a counterpoint to the Tribune Tower on the other side of Broadway.

Raynor was late. I looked at my watch, then swept the outdoor mall with a glance. He had proposed the meeting but I had picked the spot. It was neutral territory, with plenty of people around. I'd deliberately positioned myself on the far side of the fountain so I could observe him when he arrived. I had the advantage when it came to recognition.

3

He'd never seen me before, but I'd been tailing him for days.

Minutes ticked by. Then I spotted a figure in a summer white Navy uniform, walking toward the fountain. The sun glinted off his red-gold hair, the short curls hugging his skull like a nimbus. He moved with a slow, confident strut that matched the cocky grin on his face, aware of the admiring glances he received from women as he cut through the crowd. He enjoyed the attention, basking in it like a lizard on a rock.

Raynor stopped near the fountain and waited, left hand on his hip. His right hand tossed a key ring into the air and caught it. I approached him from the right, taking my time. I knew he was twenty-eight years old and that he was a first-class petty officer in the Navy, assigned to the Naval Air Station in Alameda. Until now I'd observed him from a distance, in crowds, across busy streets, through car windshields. This was the first chance I'd had to look at him up close. Six feet tall, I guessed, broad shoulders tapering down to a slim waist and muscular thighs. His pale freckled forearms were covered with the same curly copper hair. He had long blunt-fingered hands. I particularly noticed his hands.

"Sam Raynor," I said.

He jumped slightly, as though startled by my sudden appearance. I couldn't tell if it was real or if he knew I'd been watching him. His eyebrows went up and he tilted his head to one side, a smile playing over his full sensual lips.

"You must be Jeri Howard," he said, his voice pleasant and purring as he tried hard to be disarming. "Nice to finally meet you." He stuck out his hand. I kept mine at my side.

"You wanted to talk."

He cranked up the smile a couple of watts and leaned toward me. I felt as though I were too close to a high intensity light bulb.

"I hear you're asking questions about me. So I looked you up in the phone book."

I stared at him as though I were a scientist examining

4

some alien life form slithering from a petri dish. Raynor's smile dimmed just a bit. He looked earnest and concerned.

"Look, I know you're a private detective, and my wife's lawyer hired you. You're trying to find out if I've got more money than Uncle Sam pays me. Believe me," he laughed apologetically and shook his red-gold curls, "I don't. Just an enlisted man's salary. Sorry, it doesn't stretch very far. Tell Ruth what's on the table is all there is."

"California's a community property state," I said.

"I know that. Ruth's gonna get what's coming to her. After all, we have a kid." He blinked his long red-gold lashes and his face turned sober and serious. "I do want what's best for my little girl."

"So you say."

"Ruth left me," Raynor said with an aggrieved shrug. It was a jerky movement, as though he were wired with electricity, and it didn't fit his smooth face and smoother voice. I wondered if he was high on something. "I didn't want this split. I love her, I love my kid. There are two sides to every story, you know. You can imagine how I felt when I came back from Guam and found out she'd filed for divorce. She doesn't want to see me, she doesn't even want me to see my little girl. This is hard on me too. You know how it is."

As Raynor talked, he leaned closer still. I could smell the acrid musky scent of his after-shave and see the spatter of freckles on his fair skin. His left hand moved, a slow stroke down his hip to his muscled thigh, coming to rest in too-casual proximity to the bulge in his crotch. He tilted his head again and watched me through heavy-lidded eyes, his tongue darting like a snake between those full smiling lips while his pleasant-sounding voice tried to convince me of his sincerity.

His eyes gave him away. I suppose someone once told Raynor he had bedroom eyes, whatever that means. But Raynor's eyes were a flat pale blue, like disks painted on the face of a porcelain doll, devoid of warmth and emotion. They certainly engendered no passion. When they weren't gazing at me or curtained by their lashes, those eyes flicked

5

around the courtyard, zeroing in on other women nearby. He reminded me of an actor, counting the house.

As he spoke, the fingers of Raynor's left hand played invitingly over his crotch. His right hand tossed the keys into the air, a jangling accompaniment. When he got to the line about wanting to see Ruth, to talk to her and convince her that the divorce was a mistake, I cut him off with a sharp gesture and an ice-cold voice.

"You broke her wrist last fall."

"Is that what she told you?" he said with an exasperated sigh. He held his right hand out in supplication, the keys dangling from his extended middle finger. "It was an accident, honest. It could have happened to anyone. I mean, I'm a big guy." The middle finger of the left hand stroked his equipment, implying he was big everywhere else. "Sometimes I don't know my own strength."

I looked at the hand that held the keys. His knuckles looked skinned. I surveyed his face. Those flat emotionless blue eyes made my skin crawl. "Then there was the black eye a year ago."

"What black eye?"

"Surely you remember that. Or did she just accidently run into your fist? You broke her nose, two years ago."

"Now that was an accident. She's a little clumsy. She fell off a ladder."

"You knocked her off."

"I don't know where you're getting these stories," he snapped. The air crackled around us, like an electrical charge. I sensed a change in him that put me on my guard. "Yes, I do. Ruth's feeding you a line, that little bitch, her and that damned dyke lawyer."

"Let's cut through the bullshit, Raynor." My voice turned harsh. "You beat your wife, with your fists, when you're not beating her up emotionally. Ruth's entitled to half of everything you've got. You have over a hundred thousand dollars stashed somewhere, or with someone. I don't know where you hid that money, at least not yet. But I'll find it."

He tossed the keys into the air one last time. When he caught them, his right hand balled into a fist. He shoved the

6

fist under my chin. His eyes held some emotion now. It was like staring into the blue flame on a gas stove, into the heart of a fire fueled by hatred. The hatred was directed at me, at his wife and her attorney, at women in general. I suspected it was also directed at anyone who tried to thwart Sam Raynor.

His voice dropped to a low vicious growl. "You fucking bitch."

He spewed venom at me, working his way through the alphabet, calling me all the names I'd heard and some I hadn't. He warned me to stay out of his business and threatened me with what he'd do to me if I didn't. He gave off sparks, adding to the heat of the day. But he didn't touch me. Evidently he was saving that for later.

I felt a hot flush of anger, then cold, hardening resolve. One of these days, I thought, this guy is going to kill someone. Or vice versa.

I folded my arms across my chest and stared back at him with a look I usually reserve for cockroaches, choking down the urge to lash back. Instead I let him do all the talking, if you could call it that. I had no intention of backing down, from this case or from Raynor himself, if I had to stand in this courtyard all afternoon.

No, Sam Raynor would get what was coming to him. If I could help that day arrive sooner, rather than later, I'd do so with great enthusiasm. And gain more satisfaction from that than I would if I kicked this jerk in his precious balls.

Finally he ran out of words, frustrated by his failure to stampede me. His tongue darted over his full lips again, only this time he hissed at me like some deadly snake, at bay but still able to strike. The blue eyes slashed at me, then Raynor turned and walked away.

I watched until he was out of sight. Only then did I relax, surprised at how rigid my muscles had become. I walked across the square, heading in the direction of my Franklin Street office, splashed by an errant spray from the fountain.

I felt as though I needed a bath.

7

Rewind . . .

Two

I DIDN'T WANT TO TAKE THE RAYNOR CASE.

I don't like divorce work. Maybe it's been too short a time since my own. Divorce brings to the surface intense emotion, most of it bad. Two people invest themselves and all their hopes, plans, and dreams in a relationship and decide to go down the road as a couple, sharing whatever comes along. It hurts like hell when it doesn't work out. Betrayal, pain, anger, and blame come bubbling to the surface, like a geyser that can't be stopped. Hate is the flip side of love. It's all too easy for affection to turn into hostility, for a shared life to become a battleground. I don't like battlegrounds, either as a participant or an observer.

I didn't much care for Ruth Raynor's lawyer either. Blair Castle was a thin, twitchy brown-haired woman in her forties, with a family law practice on Broadway near Fifty-first Street in Oakland. I'm all for sisterhood, but Castle's voice and mannerisms grated on me like fingernails on a blackboard.

She sensed my reluctance. In her tailored gray suit and white blouse, Castle examined me, painted fingernails drumming on her desk blotter. She mentally dismissed me, telling her client that she kept an investigator on retainer for cases like this. If that was true, I wondered why she'd bothered to contact me.

But the client had insisted on a private investigator named Jeri Howard. That piqued my curiosity. When I found out why, the reason left me with a whole new dilemma.

"My mother recommended you."

11

It was the first time Ruth Raynor had spoken, other than an indistinct murmur of greeting when I arrived. While her attorney told me that her client had recently filed for divorce and that there was a child involved, Ruth sat wordless and motionless in her chair, a small woman with large golden-brown eyes and short blond hair that surrounded her head like dandelion fluff. She wore a pale green cotton dress covered with little white flowers and kept her hands in her lap. The fingers of her left hand rubbed her right wrist, as though it were a talisman. There was something vaguely familiar about those eyes and the way they looked at me. When Ruth mentioned her mother, I looked at her carefully, my mind sifting through the recent past, through recent clients. Had I met Ruth before?

"You met my parents," she said, answering my unspoken question with a steady wide-eyed gaze. "In March, when you were working on another case. Joseph and Lenore Franklin."

Of course. I looked again at Ruth's face and saw Lenore's warm topaz eyes and her hands perpetually covered in dirt from her garden. Ruth didn't resemble her father at all, which was just as well, considering the beaked nose in his narrow face. Joe Franklin was a retired Navy admiral, a tough old autocrat with a mast for a spine. We crossed swords last spring when I was working on the Willis matter, a missing persons case that evolved into an investigation of murder, past and present. I won that skirmish. Franklin didn't like me, and I thought he was a rigid narrow-minded pain in the ass. The prospect of encountering the Admiral again was one more mark in the minus column.

But I liked Lenore Franklin. She was a truly nice person, matching most of the definitions of that word you can find in the dictionary. I regretted having disrupted her well-ordered life when I forced the Franklins to examine their past ties to the Willis family. After what happened in March, I felt as though I owed her a favor. And here she was, sending her daughter to collect.

12

"Tell me about your husband," I said to Ruth, balancing on the edge of my indecision.

She spoke in a soft monotone as she rubbed her wrist. That happened in September, nearly a year ago. They were still living on Guam. Sam was working at the Naval Air Station at Agana, and Ruth was isolated, without a car in a duplex at the naval station near the town of Agat. Dinner was leftovers that night because the refrigerator was nearly empty and she hadn't been able to get to the commissary.

It happened the way it always did. Sam started with words, calling her a lazy bitch because she hadn't walked to the commissary. Then he slapped her and punched her in the stomach. Finally he seized her wrist and bent it back until it snapped. When he took her to the Navy hospital emergency room, he joked about how his stupid wife got her wrist caught in the door.

The black eye happened the year before, when he was drinking. He was usually careful not to leave marks on her face, but not that time. He told everyone that fumble-footed Ruth had stumbled into an open kitchen cabinet door. The broken nose—well, he'd knocked her off a ladder while she was changing a light bulb, then told everyone how clumsy she was. She'd heard that line so often she'd started to believe it.

"Why did you stay with him?" I've never understood why a woman stays with a man who uses her like a punching bag. I've read the books and articles, and talked with battered wives, but it's still hard for me to understand.

"Where would I go?" She looked up at me, her brown eyes like those of a deer caught in headlights, her voice defensive, tinged with shame. "Stuck on Guam with a toddler, no car, no one to talk to, thousands of miles from home. He wasn't like that when we first married. It wasn't until after Wendy was born, after we went to Guam. And then not all the time. Sometimes he was really good to me. Then, every now and then, he'd lose control."

It sounded like a pattern, a cycle repeating itself over and over. "It's not your fault," I said suddenly, because she needed to hear it.

"I know it's not." As she said the words her head came up and her jaw tightened. I saw she'd inherited some of her father's steel. "I've been planning my escape since Christmas. When Sam got orders to the Bay Area, I told him I wanted to leave Guam early so I could spend some time with my family. It didn't matter to him. He doesn't care about anyone but himself. Wendy and I left the first week in June, a month before he did. When we arrived, I told Mom and Dad everything. I'm still a California resident, so the first thing I did was contact Blair and file for divorce. Sam was served with papers the week he arrived from Guam."

Sam Raynor's response to this fait accompli was to quickly divest himself of most of his assets. He knew Ruth could garnish the Navy paycheck that came twice a month. But she knew Sam had more than his salary.

"I found a bank statement in his desk drawer," Ruth told me now, a bitter edge to her words. "Right before Christmas, when he wouldn't give me any extra money to buy presents. We didn't even have a tree, so Wendy and I decorated the rubber plant. One night we wanted to cut up construction paper to make chains. I couldn't find the scissors in the kitchen where I usually kept them, so I looked in Sam's desk, the one I was supposed to leave alone. And there was this statement from the Bank of America in downtown Agana, in Sam's name only. It had a balance of over a hundred thousand dollars." Ruth said the words as though it were a hundred million.

"I couldn't believe it. I sat there and held that statement in my hand and just stared at it. And I got madder and madder. Where did he get that kind of money?"

Where, indeed? A hundred thousand dollars might not sound like much money to your basic Wall Street robber baron. But it's a lot of cash for a sailor to have lying around. Navy enlisted men don't make that kind of money, particularly first-class petty officers with less than eight years in the Navy, which was Sam Raynor's present status. I doubted the money had been found at the end of the rainbow or obtained by legal means. Of course, how Sam

14

Raynor acquired a hundred thousand dollars was less important than what he did with it when he returned from Guam and found out his wife had filed for divorce.

"We had a joint account at the credit union on base," Ruth was saying, her voice still tinged with bitterness, "the one I used to pay the household bills and buy groceries, the one that was overdrawn half the time. Sam was always carrying on about how his salary didn't stretch far enough to cover all our expenses, and it was my fault because I didn't manage better and I spent too much money." Two red spots burned on her cheeks as she remembered. "I couldn't even buy Christmas presents for my folks because he wouldn't give me any extra money for the holidays."

"Did he always keep you on short rations?" I asked.

Ruth nodded. "I had to beg for every penny. He hated to give me anything. The only nice things we had were mine before I married Sam. If I didn't sew, Wendy and I wouldn't have any clothes. All the time he had that money. He wouldn't even spend it on his own child."

"Was he into anything illegal while he was over there?"

Ruth shrugged. "I don't know. He wasn't home much. He was always out with his buddies. That was all right with me. I felt safer when he was gone. He'd take a few days' leave and go off to Thailand or Hong Kong or the Philippines, and I wouldn't even know until he got back. It's not that far to any of those places. When you're on Guam you're already on that side of the Pacific."

"Drugs?" I wondered aloud, thinking of Thailand and the Golden Triangle, so close that someone could pick up extra money by acting as a mule.

"I don't know," Ruth said again. "I was stuck in Navy housing with no car and a three-year-old. It was a three-mile walk to the commissary if I wanted so much as a quart of milk. If it hadn't been for my neighbors I wouldn't even have seen much of Guam. Not that there's much to see. Except for Betty, my neighbor, there was no one there I could really talk to. But finding that bank statement helped me make a decision. I knew Sam was due for orders this summer. It didn't matter where he went. I was coming back to

15

California, to get a divorce. I planned how I was going to do it. I even mailed things to my folks, things I would need. Betty mailed them for me when I couldn't get out of the house. When Sam got orders to the air station in Alameda, that just made it easier for me to get back here. I'm going to get out of this mess, Jeri. My family will help me. I hope you'll help me too."

I looked at Ruth's delicate face and made my decision. "I will."

Having said it, I turned from Ruth to her attorney. Blair Castle looked less relieved than did Ruth at my signing on for this assignment. "Did you try to freeze that account in Guam?" I asked.

"Of course," she replied, with a flash of irritation. "All the standard family law restraining orders went into effect when we filed, including the one that prevents each party from disposing of any property. But Raynor closed the account before he left Guam, which was before he was served with papers. He's hidden the money. Now he's denying he ever had it."

"I wish I'd made a copy of that statement." Ruth's hands tightened in her lap. "That would at least prove he had the money. But all I could do was write down the account number."

Blair Castle leaned back in her padded leather chair. "I'm trying to find out where he transferred the money after he closed the Bank of America account. I subpoenaed the records, his lawyer filed a motion to quash. I'm waiting for a ruling."

While the attorneys dueled with their legal documents, I'd check a few other avenues. "My guess is he moved the money from Guam to California so it would be waiting when he arrived. There are several ways to do it and they all leave a paper trail. If he's still using Bank of America, they could have done an internal transfer from Guam to any of the branches here in the Bay Area. If he's switched to another financial institution, the bank might use a wire transfer. If he withdrew it using one or more cashier's checks, those checks would eventually go back to the bank

16

in Guam with the endorsement of the depositing bank. Any way I look at it, we need those records from the bank on Guam."

"I'm working on it." Castle's words were sharper than necessary.

"I doubt he'd risk opening accounts under his own name," I said. "When you do that, you have to give the bank personal information, like a social security number."

"Which we do have," the lawyer interjected.

"That'll help. Rather than run the risk that an investigator like me can trace an account with his name and social security number, Raynor's probably stashed the cash with someone or loaned some money to a friend or family member. What about his family, Ruth? Where's he from, before the Navy?"

"He told me he grew up in San Jose, and his parents are dead. I don't know much more than that. He said he didn't like to talk about himself. So we didn't. At the time I felt sorry for him. I can't imagine not having a family. I'm so close to mine."

"Are you living with your folks?" I asked, as long as we were on the subject of families.

Ruth lifted her chin and smiled. "I did for the first few weeks. But now I have a job and an apartment. Mom and Dad are helping me financially. But that's just for now. I have to get on my own two feet, and make a home for me and my daughter."

Ruth had a job at Kaiser Hospital in Oakland. She'd started last month, working as a secretary in Records, a temporary position with the promise of permanent status later on. And she'd moved into an apartment down the street from Kaiser, at Forty-first and Howe, which meant she could walk to work. She found nearby day care for Wendy. As she talked, I sensed how important it was that she take control of her own life. And I knew that would be hard, given Lenore Franklin's protective instincts and Admiral Franklin's forceful, take-charge personality.

"Sam doesn't know where I live, of course," Ruth added.

"Absolutely not," her lawyer chimed in. "We've got a

17

stay-away order." The restraining order specified Sam Raynor must stay at least a hundred yards away from Ruth and her residence, place of work, and their daughter's day care center.

"What about custody and visitation?" I asked. Divorce always rakes the nerve endings. It's much worse when children are in the battle zone. This was certainly true in *Raynor* v. *Raynor*, judging from the indignation in Ruth's voice.

"He doesn't care anything about Wendy. He never paid any attention to her. Until now."

Castle seconded Ruth's comment. "We're asking for sole legal and physical custody, of course. As for visitation, it's the same old story. The party with no interest in the child demands custody and visitation, just to push the other party's buttons. He's only pulling this superdad routine to get back at Ruth."

Going for Ruth's soft underbelly, I thought, where he could do the most damage.

Since Sam Raynor had the right to visit his child, whether or not he cared about her, the court had granted him visitation. Due to Ruth's concern about her safety, Sam's visits were controlled and supervised, at the home of Ruth's parents, under the watchful and no doubt hostile eyes of Lenore and Joseph Franklin.

"You mentioned that your husband was always running around with his buddies on Guam," I said. "Did any of those shipmates transfer here in the last year?"

"I don't know," Ruth said. "Sam came and went as he pleased. He didn't bring friends to the house and I don't recall any names. Maybe the Korsakovs would know. Ed sometimes gave Sam a ride to the air station when our car wasn't working."

"Your neighbors? Were you good friends?"

Ruth nodded. "Oh, yes, at least with Betty. We'd have coffee together in the mornings, after her kids went off to school. She'd take me places in her car."

"Do you have a current address for them?"

"Yes, I do." Ruth picked up her shoulder bag, put it on

her lap, and pulled out a slim cloth-bound address book. She flipped through the pages to the K's.

"They left Guam a short time before I did," she said as I wrote down the address. "Ed had orders to the air station at Whidbey Island, in Washington State. That's his work address. The closest town is Oak Harbor. They're probably in Navy housing or an apartment. Betty said they were going to buy a house, but I don't imagine they've done that yet." Ruth smiled wanly. "Betty said she'd be so glad to get back to a place that has all four seasons, and no tree snakes. After she left, I felt so isolated. But I was leaving too. I held on to that. It's what got me through until June."

"Did Sam have a girl in every port?" At that stereotyped description of sailors, the red spots reappeared on Ruth's cheeks and she ducked her head.

"Of course," she said, her voice low. "Probably more than one. From the day we were married until now."

If Raynor was dating someone, his current girlfriend would be worth checking out. He could have convinced her to hide a portion of his bankroll, playing on the girlfriend's sympathy by giving her a song and dance about his greedy soon-to-be-wife trying to suck him dry and take him to the financial cleaners. Name that tune—I've heard it before.

So had Blair Castle. I could tell by the look in her eye. "We don't know where he lives," she said. "He may be in the enlisted quarters on base or an apartment somewhere. Either way, directory assistance doesn't have a number for him. My only contact with him is through his lawyer, Henry Tolliver, at one of those law firms that advertises its services as being 'divorce for men only.' As if the men needed all the help."

Judging from the attorney's sour tone, she held the opposite opinion, as well as a low regard for Mr. Tolliver, whose office was on MacArthur Boulevard.

"Sooner or later, Raynor has to visit his lawyer. When he does, I'll tail him back to where he lives. I'll need a recent photograph."

"Done." The attorney reached into the folder on her desk and pulled out a snapshot that showed the upper half of a man's torso. He was broad-shouldered and good-looking, with short curly red hair, and he wore a tropical shirt over white slacks. Standing beside a palm tree, he had a can of beer in his left hand and a big grin on his face.

"That was taken last summer at a neighborhood barbecue," Ruth said. "That's the most recent picture I have."

"It'll be enough. What kind of car is he driving?"

"A red Pontiac Trans-Am," the attorney said. "I saw him get into it after the first hearing. I got part of the license number." She handed me a slip of paper with three letters and a single number. "I assume you can get information from the Department of Motor Vehicles."

"It's getting harder as the DMV gets more concerned about privacy. This should be enough, though."

Castle looked at her watch, then fixed me with a businesslike gaze. "Jeri, we've got another hearing scheduled in three weeks. I'd like to have some ammunition on Sam Raynor's finances. He's lying about the money and I want to nail him."

"I'll do my best."

"It'll take more than your best," Castle said briskly. "I'm speaking from experience here. Finding that money won't be easy. Whoever said you can't get blood out of a stone must have been a divorced woman."

Three

My office is on the third floor of a downtown Oakland building on Franklin Street, a short walk from Chinatown, the Old Oakland redevelopment project, and City Center. I'm also shoe-leather distance to the Alameda County Courthouse and various city offices, just as well because parking downtown is a hassle. I rent a space for my Toyota in a parking lot on the same block as my building, but I fear it won't be long until a developer builds something on it.

As I came out of the stairwell, I waved a greeting to my friend Cassie, an attorney and partner in the firm of Alwin, Taylor and Chao, which occupies the front suite of offices. She was with a client, standing in front of the elevator looking very serious and lawyerly in her blue linen suit, the kind that wrinkles when I wear it and wouldn't dare wrinkle on Cassie.

I unlocked the door to my office, solid wood with gold letters proclaiming J. HOWARD INVESTIGATIONS. The long narrow room was warm so I opened the window and grabbed a bottle of cold mineral water from the little refrigerator I keep at the back. A sheet of paper had emerged from my brand new fax machine. I reached for it and read a pitch to sell me fax paper. Junk fax, the latest variation on junk mail. I crumpled the ad into a ball and tossed it into the wastebasket.

I checked the messages on my answering machine and returned some calls. Then I opened a file on the Raynor case, making notes on my computer while my meeting with Ruth and her attorney was still fresh in my mind. I added these to the folder, along with my contract and the photograph of Sam Raynor.

He looks like a cocky bastard, I thought, staring at the snapshot of Raynor. He radiated charm and self-assurance, the cheerful grin on his handsome face masking the wife batterer. Men who beat their wives and children occupy a particularly low rung on my ladder of slimeballs, not far above rapists and deviates who molest children.

I closed the file abruptly on Sam Raynor's face and tucked the folder into its alphabetical niche in a filing cabinet drawer. Then I reached for the phone and called directory assistance for Oak Harbor, Washington, hoping that Edward Korsakov was not a common name in that community. It wasn't. There was only one listing. It was nearly five. With any luck, Ed Korsakov was home from whatever

21

work he did at the Naval Air Station, Whidbey Island, and Betty Korsakov was fixing dinner.

One of the Korsakov offspring answered the phone. When I asked if one or both parents was home, the kid yelled "Mom! It's for you." I winced, holding the receiver away from my ear. A moment later an adult female voice came on the line.

"Is this Betty Korsakov?" I asked. When she confirmed this, I plunged ahead. "Mrs. Korsakov, my name is Jeri Howard. I'm an investigator in Oakland, California. I'm working for Ruth Raynor, your neighbor on Guam. She's divorcing her husband."

"Good for her," Betty Korsakov blurted. "It's about damn time."

"You don't care much for Sam Raynor."

She didn't answer right away. Despite the spontaneity of her first words, I wasn't sure I'd get much information out of Betty Korsakov. In my dealings with people in the military, I'd noticed a certain us-against-them mentality, them being anyone who was a civilian. Besides, phone calls from private investigators understandably make some people wary.

"How do I know you're who you say you are?" she asked finally. Her voice had an eastern accent, I noticed, possibly New York.

"I understand your caution, Mrs. Korsakov," I said. "I can't give you Ruth's number because it's unlisted. Her attorney, Blair Castle, can verify my identity and employment." I recited the lawyer's telephone number. "After you talk with Ms. Castle, please call me back collect." I gave her my office number. "I'd appreciate hearing from you as soon as possible."

Betty Korsakov didn't ask me to repeat either phone number, so I assumed she'd written them down. Then suddenly she said, "Wait. Wait a minute. I'll be right back."

There was a muffled clunk as she set down the phone receiver. I strained to hear sounds through hundreds of miles of telephone cable, identifying a dog's bark, the high voice of a child, a woman talking, answered by the deeper timbre of a man's voice. A moment later Mrs. Korsakov picked up the receiver again. "You say Ruth Raynor gave you my number?"

"Just your husband's work address. You left Guam only two months before Ruth did and that was the only address she had for you. I called directory assistance to get your number."

"What else did Ruth say about me?" Betty Korsakov asked. I knew I was being tested.

"You were next-door neighbors on Guam. I think you were the only friend Ruth had. The two of you would get together for coffee in the morning after your children went to school. She didn't have a car, so you gave her rides to the commissary and exchange." I paused, thinking back to that afternoon's conversation with Ruth, dredging up everything she had said about the Korsakovs.

"You mailed things for Ruth, because she didn't want to alert Sam that she'd decided to leave him. When you left Guam for Washington, you told Ruth you'd be glad to get back to a place with four seasons, and no tree snakes."

There was silence on the other end of the receiver. Then Betty Korsakov laughed. "I hated those damn tree snakes. They gave me the willies. I guess you have talked to Ruth. I told her that—about the seasons—the day the movers came to pack up our household goods. Okay, I don't need to talk to the lawyer. What do you want to know?"

"Sam Raynor had a large sum of money in a bank account on Guam," I explained. "Now that Ruth has filed for divorce, the money's disappeared. He denies ever having it. He's hiding it, so he won't have to split the cash as community property in the divorce settlement. I'm trying to locate it."

"Sounds just like him, the creep. I don't know how I can help you. If that deadbeat had any money, it's news to me." It was evident from Betty Korsakov's scathing tone that she was prepared to rake Sam Raynor over a slow fire of white-hot coals. My favorite type of interview.

"You don't like Sam?" I asked again.

"After seeing the way he treated Ruth? Good God, no.

23

He acted like she was dirt under his feet, especially when he'd been drinking. He yelled at her all the time. And he ignored that child." She sighed over the phone line.

"I knew he was hitting Ruth. Not that I ever saw him do it, but I could tell. She was so cowed when she was around him, like she was waiting for the next slap. Once Ed and I came back from a week's vacation in Japan and Ruth had a broken arm. And the black eye before that. Supposedly accidents, but I didn't buy that for a minute. I tried to talk to Ruth about it, to see if I could steer her to some counseling, but she was very heavily into denial. Then sometime after last Christmas she seemed to come to her senses. She told me when Sam got orders, she was gonna leave him. That's when I mailed those boxes to her parents. She only did that a few times, so she wouldn't tip him off."

"You mentioned Sam's drinking. Any observations?"

"He was a nasty drunk. Whenever he had too much, it was like being around a snake. Like if you made the wrong move, he'd bite whoever was handy." As Betty Korsakov spoke, my mind furnished an image of Raynor's face atop a coiled scaly body. "And he thought he was God's gift to women. I'm sure he had several women on the side. That kind usually does."

"Did he ever put the moves on you?"

"He sure as hell did." Her voice turned angry. "At a neighborhood barbecue, the first year we were on Guam. Sam got drunk and made a pass at me. He didn't take it too well when I told him to keep his damn hands to himself. Didn't want to take no for an answer until I threatened to tell my husband. After that he was really hostile, like any woman who turned down the great Sam Raynor was a bitch or crazy. He didn't want Ruth to associate with me either. I guess he was afraid I'd tell her what a loser he was. Of course, I'd been doing that since the day I met them. For all his catting around, Sam Raynor doesn't like women at all."

Betty Korsakov was probably right on target with that salvo. I've encountered more than a few men with the same problem.

24

"I haven't met him yet," I said, "but I don't think I've missed much. Ruth says their financial situation was lean."

"Sam used to poormouth all the time. He bitched about how an enlisted man's salary didn't stretch far enough. He drove a real clunker of a car. It was always breaking down. He gave Ruth barely enough to buy the necessities. I passed along my kids' hand-me-downs for Wendy. Ruth sewed, so she'd alter them. Of course, Sam was a sharp dresser. He didn't mind spending money on himself. I saw him once, at a jewelry store in Agana. He was buying a ring, gold with a big hunk of apple-green jade, had to be expensive. Of course I never saw Ruth wear it. It's probably on some other woman's finger. No, if Sam Raynor had any money stashed away, I never saw any evidence of it. He probably got it illegally."

"I had considered that. That's why I wanted to talk to someone who knew him on Guam."

"Hang on," she said. "My husband wants to talk to you."

A moment later a new voice boomed in my ear. Ed Korsakov was definitely from Brooklyn. "So you want to know about Sam Raynor. Sounds like my wife's given you an earful already."

"You and Raynor both worked at NAS Agana."

"Yeah, but he was with a different squadron. I'd give him a ride to the air station when his car broke down, but that was it. When you're in the Navy, living with all sorts of people in housing, you live and let live. But to tell you the truth, I didn't have much use for the guy. Didn't like the way he treated his wife and kid. I know he cheated on Ruth. I used to see him hanging around the clubs down on Hotel Row with a blonde."

"Any idea how Raynor came by a large chunk of money? Say, a hundred thousand?"

"Him?" Ed Korsakov sounded surprised. "He was always a dollar short. The kinda guy who borrows a twenty till payday, then never pays it back. If Raynor's got money, I'd sure as hell wonder how he got it. He used to take trips to the Philippines and Thailand. Lot of drugs get smuggled through Guam. Other stuff too, like jewelry. You should

25

talk to a buddy of mine, named Duffy LeBard. He was with the Armed Forces Police Detachment on Guam. When he left Guam he went to Treasure Island. He's the chief of police there. I bet Duffy knows a thing or two about Sam Raynor. You call Duffy, tell him Ed said hello."

Neither of the Korsakovs had anything to add. I thanked them and hung up the phone, reaching for one of the Bay Area phone directories I keep in a bookcase behind my desk. In this case it was a San Francisco directory, because the naval base at Treasure Island, in the middle of San Francisco Bay, is considered part of the city. I found the number I needed, but the patrolman who answered told me that Chief Duffy LeBard had gone home, not surprising, since it was nearly six in the evening. I left my name and phone number, adding that I'd call again tomorrow.

It was time I went home as well. I closed the window, locked my office, and took the stairs down to Franklin Street. I live in Adams Point, a hilly area near Lake Merritt and downtown Oakland, crowded with apartment buildings, condos, and the occasional turn-of-the-century house that has survived the wrecking ball. My apartment is at the rear of a U-shaped stucco building, a series of connected bungalows under one red-tiled roof, surrounded by a tall steel security fence with a gate at the top of the U. The outer walls are covered with ivy and bougainvillea, and there's a flagstone courtyard in the center, with a fountain that is now dry in deference to the drought. The lemon tree near my front porch is surviving well enough to provide me with a handful of small yellow fruit now and then.

When I first saw my cat Abigail, ten years ago, she was a little brown and silver fluffball right out of the litter, tiny enough at eight weeks to fit in the palm of my hand. Now she is fat enough around the midsection to warrant diet cat food and warning clucks from the veterinarian. She wasn't in her usual spot, lying along the back of the sofa where she looked out the window and chirruped at the humming-birds that buzz my neighbor's feeder or the mourning doves exploring the bone-dry fountain. The day had been too hot for her to lie on anything that would retain warmth.

As I unlocked the front door I spotted her raggedy yellow yarn mouse discarded on the carpet at the foot of my round oak dining table. I raised my eyes and saw the cat sprawled on the cool wooden surface of the table, half on her back, half on her side, with her striped belly exposed. She had shoved a place mat out of the way, just to make herself comfortable. I leaned over to greet her. She meowed at me, stretched and yawned, then reached out a paw and patted me on the nose.

"I see you had a strenuous day of sleeping." I hung my purse over the back of a chair. "Balanced by eating and visits to the cat box." I scratched the cat's round belly, then headed for the bedroom, where I kicked off my shoes, removed my work clothes, and put on shorts, a T-shirt, and sandals.

Northern California has experienced several drought years and I've developed some water-stingy habits, such as keeping a bucket in the shower to catch the water that runs as the heater kicks in, which in my building can sometimes take a while. Now I collected my bucket and carried it to my back door, which leads off the kitchen to my patio. The concrete square gets the afternoon sun, and I have a lawn chair and a small barbecue grill in one corner. It offers a stunning view of the apartment building in back of me, which I've masked by a tall redwood trellis and a fragrant jasmine bush.

I have decided the only way to obtain tomatoes that taste like tomatoes is to grow them myself. Four pots are arrayed in front of the trellis, each containing a tomato plant. The first two are Sweet 100s, a type of cherry tomato, small and sweet. The second pair are a larger variety known as San Francisco Fog. The plants are doing well in their containers. All four have outgrown the confines of their metal cages, branches heavy with fruit in varying stages of ripeness, and I've had to tie the foliage to the trellis. Now I stuck my fingers into the soil of each pot to see how dry it was before dipping water from the bucket. Then I harvested my crop, leaning close and searching the green leaves for bright red tomatoes.

27

Gardening is not pure reward, however, as anyone who has done it will tell you. If you grow tomatoes, you get tomato worms, and they are among God's ugliest critters. Long and smooth with horned segments, they are the same shade of green as a tomato plant, and they blend so well with the foliage that you can't spot them until they get big enough to gnaw on a lot of tomatoes. Suddenly you see them, looming at you like some rubbery monster from a Japanese horror flick.

I hate the damn things. When we were youngsters, my kid brother Brian knew of my aversion, so of course he used all available creepy-crawlies to plague me. He'd pull the fat green worms off the backyard tomato plants and throw them at me, or leave them in my dresser drawers, tucked into my neatly folded underwear. Once or twice he'd even slip one down the back of my dress, chortling with delight while I clawed and squealed.

He denies this now, especially in the presence of his own children. He prefers to concentrate on my past transgressions, like the time I pushed him out of the oak tree in the front yard of the big Victorian house in Alameda where we grew up. As I recall, he had it coming, though I don't remember why. And he didn't break any bones. Despite Brian's selective memory, tomato worms were for many years part of the tapestry of summer, woven into memory with mounds of produce from my mother's garden and Dad cranking the handle on the wooden ice cream freezer.

Today I didn't see any tomato worms munching on my tomato plants, though a half-gnawed green tomato gave evidence they'd been there. I carried my ripe red jewels back to the kitchen and rinsed them at the sink, then cut up a few to add to the big green salad I was having for dinner.

Abigail rose from her nap on the oak table, stretched and thumped down to the carpet by way of a chair, purring in anticipation of kibble. After both of us had eaten, I washed the few dishes and retired to the living room, debating between the movie I'd recorded the other night or the paperback novel I hadn't yet started. Either way, I didn't feel energetic enough to tackle housework or laundry. In the first case, my clutter threshold hadn't yet been reached, and in the second, I still had clean underwear available.

I was sprawled on my sofa with my nose in the book and Abigail on my lap when the phone rang. I stuck a bookmark between the pages and dislodged the cat, who grumbled at being moved, and went to answer the phone. It was Alex Tongco, the Navy officer I'd been dating for the past three months.

I met Alex while working on a case involving the death of his uncle, one of my father's colleagues in the history department at California State University, Hayward. Alex had pursued me with amorous intent, but now that our relationship had progressed past the initial cat-and-mouse stage, I suspected he was more interested in pursuing than in catching. I'd seen Abigail exhibit the same behavior when I teased her with one of her cat toys.

I recalled my earlier question to Ruth, whether Sam Raynor had a girl in every port. Alex certainly had in the past. It was a factor in the breakup of his marriage. So was the constant moving. Sailors—in fact, all military personnel—transfer every few years. Alex had already told me he was due for orders by year-end, probably overseas. So I wasn't viewing this as a long-term relationship. Still, Alex and I shared an interest in jazz and old movies, as well as a strong physical attraction. We might as well enjoy each other's company for the moment.

"I was out of town for a few days," Alex was saying, explaining why he hadn't called. "Got back this afternoon. Chief Yancy and I had to go to a training session down at North Island. He's the newest chief in the department, just transferred here from WestPac." WestPac was shorthand for Western Pacific. Alex had familiarized me with Navy jargon, a sometimes bewildering array of abbreviations. "How about dinner and a movie on Friday?" he asked.

Alex didn't have any preferences, so I looked at the schedules affixed with magnets to my refrigerator door, one for the U.C. Theater, a repertory house in Berkeley, and the other for the Paramount here in Oakland, an Art Deco Moderne gem that frequently shows classic movies on Friday nights. Our choice at the U.C. was an Akira Kurosawa double bill. Neither of us was in the mood for Kurosawa.

"*Dark Victory* is at the Paramount," I told him. "One of my favorite Bette Davis weepies. Though it's beyond me how any intelligent woman could chose George Brent over Humphrey Bogart."

He laughed. "Well, let's go see if she's come to her senses. Where shall we have dinner?"

"Let's try that Vietnamese place over on Clay, Le Cheval."

We agreed to meet at the restaurant, then Alex asked if I was still going to Monterey Labor Day weekend. When I answered with a terse yes, he said, "Why do I think you're not looking forward to the trip?"

I sighed. "Do you get along with your mother?"

He laughed, and I pictured his dark sardonic face. "Of course I get along with my mother. I'm a good Filipino son. I listen politely to all her advice, I go to Sunday dinner at her place once a month, and Carlos and I send her to Manila twice a year. Does this have something to do with your mother?"

My response was general rather than specific. "I haven't been down to Monterey since Christmas, and here it is August."

"I believe that's called avoidance," Alex said.

I didn't answer, which was also avoidance. My relationship with my mother has been a little shaky ever since she and my father split up. Okay, a lot shaky. She left him, returning to Monterey, where she grew up, to open a restaurant. To be honest about it, I've always felt closer to Dad, and after the divorce, I felt he needed me more than she did. They remained friends, sharing a lot of history after nearly thirty years of marriage. My brother Brian and his family went down to Monterey frequently, but Mother and I have always been like a couple of cactuses, too prickly to get close to one another.

Still, I liked visiting the large extended tribe of Doyles and Ravellas who called the Monterey peninsula home. So Labor Day weekend, the last hurrah of summer, I planned to head south and stay a week—depending on how well I got along with Mother during those seven days. Things were slow here at the end of August. Dad was on vacation with his friend and fellow professor, Isabel Kovaleski. They'd driven up the coast to Oregon and weren't due back until Labor Day. My caseload was looking short-term and routine, lightening each day as I wrapped up several assignments. The Raynor case was the newest folder in the filing cabinet, and I was sure it wouldn't take long for me to sniff out where Raynor had hidden the money.

"I'm still going to Monterey," I said. "If this new case doesn't get complicated, I'll have a clear calendar by then."

"What is the new case?"

"I can't really tell you, except that it involves a sailor."

"Then I don't want to know," Alex said firmly. He was always curious about what I did for a living but he didn't want to get involved. Nor would I ask him to aid in my search for information on Sam Raynor. As a serviceman, Alex was bound by the provisions of the Privacy Act, and he could get into serious trouble raiding personnel records.

"Then I won't tell you. *Hangang sa muli,*" I said, trying out some of my recently acquired Tagalog, which in this instance translated as "So long."

Four

DUFFY LeBARD CALLED ME THE NEXT MORNING, shortly after I arrived at my office. As a chief petty officer, no doubt LeBard had a long tenure in the Navy, probably all over the map, but those years of service had done little to alter a pronounced Southern drawl.

31

"I want to talk about Sam Raynor," I said, after telling LeBard who I was. "Ed Korsakov suggested I call."

"I'd rather do this face-to-face. In my office."

"That's fine with me, Chief LeBard." I glanced down at my desk calendar, which had very little written under today's date. "I'm free this morning, or I could do it early this afternoon."

"One o'clock. I'll leave your name with the Marine at the gate. He can tell you how to get here."

As I hung up the phone, I was certain LeBard would use the intervening time to call Korsakov to verify my story. He'd probably contact the Oakland Police Department as well, just to check my credentials.

I set the wheels rolling on a credit check on Sam Raynor, then I made several cold calls to local banks. I pretended to have a check for several thousand dollars from Raynor and asked the teller if it would clear. The method was time-consuming but sometimes effective. But this time I came up with nothing, more and more convinced that Raynor had hidden his money with someone else so it couldn't be traced to his name.

My contact at the Department of Motor Vehicles agreed to run a check on Raynor's partial license plate number, though he grumbled, as always, and warned that it would take several days. Right now it appeared that my best shot for locating Sam Raynor's residence was by tailing him. I could latch onto him when he visited his attorney. If, as Blair Castle mentioned, the Raynors had a divorce hearing scheduled in three weeks, I hoped Raynor would pay a call on his lawyer soon. Given the working hours at the air station, I figured Raynor for a late afternoon appointment. That meant staking out the lawyer's office for a few days, until I spotted the redhead who drove a red Trans-Am.

I spent the rest of the morning at the Alameda County Courthouse, doing research for another case. That done, I walked the six blocks back to my building and bought a turkey sandwich at a nearby deli before climbing the stairs to my office. I managed to eat the whole thing without interruption. Then I switched on the computer and, using the information garnered from my morning's research at the courthouse, wrote a report for my client. He lived up north, near Clear Lake, so I faxed it to him. I'm having lots of fun with my new toy, I thought, watching the sheets feed into the machine. My next scheduled big purchase is a copier. At present I'm using the one at the law firm next door, not always convenient.

At twelve-thirty I locked the office and headed for Treasure Island to keep my appointment with Duffy LeBard. After handing my buck to the toll taker at the eastern end of the Bay Bridge, I drove up the long rise to the upper deck of the bridge's cantilevered section, staying in the far left lane. I took the exit leading to Yerba Buena Island, where the road wound to the left around the rocky tree-covered cone, until a picture postcard vista of San Francisco came into view, the Ferry Building in sharp focus on the city's waterfront. The road led down to a short level causeway, and I arrived at the gate of Treasure Island, shortly before one o'clock.

While Yerba Buena is a natural island, its close neighbor is man-made, a flat expanse of landfill dredged from the bay in the late thirties. Treasure Island was the site for the 1939–40 Golden Gate International Exposition, which my father remembers with a warm glow of nostalgia. After the fair closed, the island was supposed to be the site for San Francisco's airport, but World War II intervened. The Navy covered the island with housing, offices, and warehouses. Some of the structures and statues built for the fair still survive, notably the base's administration building, which faces San Francisco; its curved facade looks like some 1930s Art Deco version of an airport terminal. Whenever I see it, I get the urge to take the Clipper to Manila.

At the gate I gave my name to a scrawny young Marine. He checked his clipboard and gave me directions to the base police office, where I cooled my heels for a few minutes because Chief LeBard was on the phone. I sat on a hard plastic chair and waited, reading a recent issue of *Navy Times*, its lead story detailing the Navy's well-publicized problems with sexual harassment. Finally I heard

33

a baritone voice with a slow drawl redolent of jambalaya and dirty rice. "Miz Howard? I'm Chief LeBard."

I stood and faced him. He was a big man, at least six-foot-three, with wide shoulders, long legs, a deep chest, and just a hint of belly at the waist of his sharply-tailored khaki uniform. He had the kind of Southern bad boy sensuality I associated with Elvis or Jerry Lee, and I could easily imagine him with his wavy black hair combed into a pompadour, his wide-lipped mouth crooning a ballad into a microphone. There were silver threads in the black, and I guessed his age at about forty.

As he shut the door to his office and waved me toward a chair, Duffy LeBard looked me over, heavy-lidded brown eyes curtained by long black lashes, and smiled. "Would you like some coffee, Miz Howard?"

"I'll bet it's got chicory in it," I said, placing his accent as I returned his smile.

"You'd be right." He raised one thick eyebrow. "You like chicory in your coffee?"

"Every now and then I give it a try." I waited while he crossed his small office to a table and picked up a coffee-pot. Then he turned and handed me a dark blue ceramic mug.

"Cream or sugar?" he inquired.

I shook my head and sat down in the chair in front of his desk, sipping the steaming black brew. "Now that's a real wake-up call," I said, as caffeine and chicory hit me full bore.

LeBard laughed and settled into his own chair, a battered wooden number that creaked with his weight. He raised his own mug to his lips and I noted the absence of rings on both hands.

"Where are you from, Chief?"

"Oh, down around Baton Rouge," he said, giving his pronunciation of the Louisiana capital a decidely French twist.

"You must have hit the Gingerbread House your first week in the Bay Area," I said, mentioning a popular Oakland restaurant famed for its Cajun and Creole cuisine.

34

"Day I got off the plane. And about once a month ever since. Now, they do make a good pot of red beans and rice, but so do I. And I truly believe mine is better." He made the words sound like an invitation to a taste test. The man was flirting with me, and I was enjoying every minute of it.

Then his manner turned crisp and businesslike. "I have an acquaintance over at the Oakland Police Department," he said, setting his mug on his desk. "He says you've got a pretty good reputation as a private investigator. I also called Ed Korsakov up at Whidbey Island. He told me why you're asking questions."

"Are you going to give me any answers?"

"Ordinarily I wouldn't." LeBard took a swallow of coffee, set the mug on his desk blotter and leaned back in his chair. "I've got no business getting involved in domestic matters. As a Navy man and a police officer, I'm restricted by certain rules and regulations."

I sipped the coffee and considered the chief's disclaimers. "If you're not going to give me any answers, why did you keep the appointment?"

"Sam Raynor," LeBard said, his voice as close to ice as it would ever get. "He's a real piece of work."

"So people tell me. I haven't met him."

"You don't want to. I've met cottonmouths and alligators I like better. And trust more."

"What else can you tell me about Sam Raynor?"

Chief LeBard didn't answer my question. Instead he asked one of his own. "You know anything about Guam, Miz Howard?"

I shrugged, pulling together the few facts I knew from school and from talking to Alex, who had been stationed there. "Guam's in Micronesia, the largest island in the Marianas chain. Its history is similar to the Philippines. Both were Spanish possessions for about three hundred years, both acquired by the U.S. during the Spanish-American War. Guam's still American territory, though, with a representative in Congress. Other than some islands

35

off the coast of Alaska, Guam was the only American soil occupied by the Japanese during World War Two."

LeBard nodded. "The Japanese treated the population pretty rough, even executed a priest. A lot of the old folks who remember the war don't look too kindly on the Japanese tourists who fly down for vacation. It's only three hours by air from Tokyo to Guam, a little farther to Manila. A lot of history out there on those islands. When the Yanks took Guam and Saipan in 1944, those were bloody battles. And of course Tinian is where the *Enola Gay* took off, headed for Hiroshima. Seems like every time they dig a trench in downtown Agana, they find unexploded ordnance from the war, and have to call the Navy to defuse the damn things. A Japanese straggler turned up back in 1972, if you can imagine that. It's a real small island, about thirty-five miles long, a figure-eight tilted to one side." He traced the island's shape in the air. "Maybe four miles wide at the narrowest point, eight miles at the widest. Takes all of three hours to drive around it. But down at the southern part there's mountains and thick jungle, with only trails leading in. So I guess a Japanese straggler hiding until the seventies isn't that surprising."

"Is the history and geography lesson leading somewhere, Chief?" I asked, sipping coffee.

LeBard picked up his mug and smiled at me over the rim. "In due time, Miz Howard, in due time. A lot of military people like Guam, enough to retire over there. Pleasant climate, right above the equator, and two seasons, wet and dry, though you have to worry about the occasional typhoon. Very American, yet just a little bit foreign. When I did my first tour over there, about fifteen years ago, my sea daddy, this old chief who'd been in the Navy since Moses was an altar boy, said to me, 'Duffy, you gonna find out what it's like to be in a minority.' And he was right."

"So Guam is American, yet not American."

"Plagued by the same problems we have stateside. Only Guam's a lot closer to the source."

"The source being the Golden Triangle," I said.

LeBard nodded. "Just a short hop from Agana to Manila,

36

Hong Kong or Bangkok. A lot of sailors come back from those trips toting a few things they weren't carrying when they left. Sam Raynor was one of them. I'll bet that's where he got that money he's so interested in hiding from his wife."

"You're telling me Raynor was smuggling drugs into Guam?"

"Drugs, and anything else he could carry onto a plane," LeBard said. "I never could prove it. I was an investigator with the Armed Forces Police Detachment, and we worked with the Drug Enforcement Agency and the Guam Department of Public Safety. The stuff was coming in on a regular schedule. The local drug kingpin used tourists and sailors as mules. I think Raynor was a mule, selling stuff on the side. He took a lot of vacations to those cities I mentioned, particularly Bangkok. He always seemed to be flush when it came to money. And there always seemed to be a lot of heroin floating around town when he got back. I got close a couple of times, but I never could catch the son of a bitch red-handed."

LeBard balled his right hand into a fist and punched the flat of his left hand several times. I could feel his frustration across the space that separated us. He'd switched from *we* to *I*. His feelings about Sam Raynor were personal.

"Raynor's smart and slick. He walked a fine line, keeping his nose clean enough not to aggravate the locals or the Navy brass. You talk to anyone who worked with him, I'm sure they'd say he was a fine example of a sailor. He's got a way of charming people. They don't see past the charm until it's too late."

That must have been how it was for Ruth, I thought, swept off her feet into a marriage with a man who was abusive and dangerous. "What's under the charm?" I asked LeBard.

"The man's a sociopath." The chief frowned, resting his fist on his desk blotter. "Raynor knew about our investigation, back on Guam. He knew I was on his trail. I could tell that by the way he'd look at me when we happened to meet. It was a 'catch-me-if-you-can' look. Only I never could. If Sam Raynor's involved in something illegal back here, I'd sure like to nail his ass."

"I'm sure you would," I told him. "But I'm less interested in where he got his money than I am in what he's done with it. If I uncover any information about Raynor's illegal activities, I'd certainly pass it along to the appropriate authorities. I would hope that those authorities would reciprocate."

"Anything's possible." LeBard laced his hands behind his head, leaned back in his creaky wooden chair and surveyed me with his heavy-lidded eyes.

"Raynor had an account at the Bank of America in Agana. He closed it before he left Guam, before he was served with divorce papers. My job is to find out what he did with that money. Mrs. Raynor's attorney has subpoenaed the bank's records, but it'll take time to get a response. In the course of your investigation on Guam, did you check into Raynor's finances?"

"Not really. I knew he had money, and I guessed where he got it. He'd spread it around, buying drinks for his buddies and presents for his string of ladies. Sounds like for all his free spending, Raynor made some regular deposits. After a couple of years he must have had quite a bit of cash stashed away."

"Enough to make a difference for Mrs. Raynor and her daughter. You mentioned Raynor's buddies on Guam. Are any of those people in the Bay Area? I hear it's a small Navy. You run into the same people at different duty stations. Does Raynor have friends or acquaintances in northern California?"

Duffy LeBard snorted. "I know of one. Raynor had a running mate on Guam, an obnoxious little squirt named Harlan Pettibone. He tagged after Raynor like a puppy. Now he's over at the air station in Alameda. Spent a week in the brig, right after he arrived last spring. Harlan's idea of recreation is to get snot-slinging drunk and fight everyone within range. That's why he's still a seaman. Every time he makes rate to petty officer, he gets busted."

38

"That means they take his promotion away from him. I'm surprised he's still in the Navy."

"Harlan's a good candidate for a bad conduct discharge," the chief said, his hand reaching for the coffee mug. "It's just a matter of time. I doubt he'll make it through his first tour. Except when he's drinking, Harlan's harmless. Exactly the kind of hanger-on I'd expect Sam Raynor to have."

"Other than Pettibone, can you give me any names?"

LeBard sipped his coffee, then set down the mug and rubbed one finger across his upper lip, furrowing his high forehead. "Can't think of anyone else. No, wait. There's a chief at Alameda who was at the air station on Guam, same time Raynor was. I met him and his wife a couple of weeks ago, at the chiefs' club here on base. His wife's an enlisted woman. Yancy, that's it. Steve and Claudia Yancy. Don't know whether they knew Raynor."

I'd heard the name Yancy before, last night in fact, during my conversation with Alex Tongco. Steve Yancy was the new chief who'd accompanied Alex down to North Island, the one who'd just transferred to Alameda from WestPac.

"I know Raynor's working somewhere on NAS Alameda," I said to LeBard. "Can you tell me which department? I'd also like to know where he lives."

"I don't know how much info I can give you," LeBard drawled.

Someone knocked, then a young Navy enlisted woman opened the door and stuck her head in. "Telephone, Chief. It's the captain."

"Thanks." LeBard straightened in his chair and reached for the phone, resting his hand on the top of the receiver. "I've got to take this call. Leave me your card and I'll be in touch with you. By the way, Miz Howard, if anyone asks, we never had this conversation, and you never sampled any of my coffee with chicory."

"Does this mean I don't get to sample any red beans and rice?" I asked as I placed one of my business cards on his desk blotter. He picked it up and glanced at it before slipping it into his breast pocket.

"That might be arranged." He grinned as he lifted the phone receiver.

Five

I HEADED BACK ACROSS THE BAY BRIDGE, MY WIN- dow rolled down to capture a breeze on this hot afternoon. Far below me the dark blue waters of San Francisco Bay shifted and glimmered. As I drove off the lower deck of the bridge, I saw the giant cranes and stacks of containers at the Port of Oakland, looming to my right. I looked toward Berkeley, at the spire of the campanile on the University of California campus, recalling the antiwar demonstrations of the sixties. Despite the definite local tilt to the left, the mil- itary presence permeated the Bay Area, and had for years. Military bases dotted the map, bringing with them people and payrolls, dollars spent at local businesses, and a tran- sient population. Downtown Oakland was bracketed by two freeways, one named for Admiral Chester Nimitz, the other for General Douglas MacArthur. Both names evoked a time when things were more clearly defined, a time long past.

I stayed on the MacArthur Freeway until I reached the Fruitvale Avenue exit, in Oakland's Dimond District. Here was MacArthur again, this time MacArthur Boulevard. I parked outside the office of Sam Raynor's attorney, but my stakeout was wasted time. I saw no sign of Raynor or his red Trans-Am. At five I went back to my office to check my messages, but there was nothing earthshaking on my machine. I turned on the computer and wrote an account of my meeting with Duffy LeBard. The printer was spitting out the pages when the phone rang.

On the other end of the receiver, Ruth's voice sounded

cheerful. "Hi, Jeri. I'm at my parents' house. I was sorting through some things I have stored here, and I found something interesting."

"Great." I reached for a pencil. "What is it?"

"Can you come over here? I can't quite describe it over the phone. Besides, Mother would like to see you, and I want you to meet Wendy. And Kevin's here on leave."

I hesitated for just a moment, looking at the round clock on the wall to my left. It was nearly six. I was tired and I wanted to go home. The only member of the family Ruth hadn't mentioned was her father, but I was sure he was also present. After our clashes last March, I had no desire to see Admiral Franklin again. But I didn't see how I could avoid it. I was now working for his daughter. Like a couple of ships in a narrow channel, Franklin and I would collide sooner or later.

Might as well get this out of the way. "Sure. I'll be there in fifteen minutes."

Alameda is an elongated island running northwest to southeast along the East Bay shore, separated from Oakland by a channel everyone calls the estuary. Driving to Alameda means crossing one of several drawbridges, which in clear sunny weather often raise to allow sailboats to pass, stalling traffic at the approaches. The other alternative is a tunnel that burrows under the estuary. The Tube, as it's called, is close to downtown Oakland, so I took that route, entering Alameda at its West End. I drove the length of the island to the East End, where the Franklins lived on a tree-lined street called Gibbons Drive. The big Spanish-style house was constructed of beige stucco, topped by a red tile roof. I got out of my car and surveyed the riot of flowers in the beds surrounding the house, testimony to Lenore Franklin's green thumb and love of digging in the dirt.

"It's so nice to see you again, Jeri," Lenore Franklin said as she opened the door. She looked cool and comfortable on this August evening, a compact woman with her silver hair cut short, wearing leather sandals and a blue cotton dress.

"I wish it were under better circumstances."

41

"So do I, but be that as it may . . ." Her warm brown eyes were friendly and so was the smile on her tanned face. "I really appreciate your helping Ruth."

"I'll do what I can."

I stepped into the foyer and followed Lenore into the living room, which reflected the Franklins' history as a career Navy family. The furniture was teak and mahogany, decorated with keepsakes that spoke of visits to exotic places all over the Pacific and Asia, places like Hong Kong and Bangkok, Saigon and Taipei, Manila and Tokyo.

A little girl sat by herself in the middle of a blue and red Oriental rug. In her lap she cradled a colorful rag doll with a bright orange costume and a grinning face topped by hair made of lengths of yellow yarn. The child crooned a wordless little tune as she rocked the doll back and forth in her arms. Red highlights tinged her curly blond hair. She was bare-legged and barefoot, clad in shorts and a Mickey Mouse T-shirt. I'd seen her picture when I was here last March, one of the many family photographs that lined the Franklins' mantel.

"This is Wendy, my granddaughter," Lenore said. The child stopped singing and stared up at us. "I'll tell everyone you're here."

As Lenore headed through the dining room to the kitchen, I knelt and stuck out my hand. "Hi, Wendy. I'm Jeri."

She had her mother's solemn brown eyes and she was wary of strangers. She didn't say anything, reserving speech as well as judgment. Finally one small hand released its grip on the doll and her fingers brushed mine.

As I straightened, Ruth Raynor entered the living room from the kitchen, followed by a tall man with close-cropped blond hair, his muscular body clad in faded blue jeans and a short-sleeved shirt. Wendy scrambled to her feet and scurried toward the grown-ups she knew, her doll tucked under one arm. When she reached her mother, she hid her face in the swirl of Ruth's green skirt. Ruth ruffled the child's strawberry-blond hair and dropped to Wendy's level to hug her. "Dinner's almost ready, sweetie. Go wash your hands now."

The little girl muttered something that sounded like "not hungry." Ruth took the child's face in her hands. "But you like barbecued ribs and corn on the cob. And for dessert Grandma has ice cream. Chocolate, your favorite. You need to eat some dinner before you have dessert. Okay? Then go wash up."

Wendy looked at her mother as though she didn't see much logic in washing her hands before smearing them with barbecue sauce and butter. Then she nodded, in agreement or resignation, and carried her doll out to the kitchen. When she'd gone, Ruth turned to me. "You must remember my brother Kevin. You both graduated the same year."

I took Kevin's hand, thinking how much he looked like his father. "Fifteen years ago."

"It's been a long time," Kevin said.

Kevin Franklin and I went to high school together, but we never ran with the same crowd. Tall and good-looking, he was the star center of the basketball team. Besides sports, he'd been president of the senior class, prom king, and major heartthrob of my female classmates. I eschewed sports of any kind in favor of the drama club, and my idea of exercise was to walk down to the beach at Alameda's south shore, smear myself with suntan lotion, and sit on the sand with my nose in a book. The only connection Kevin and I had in school was as members of the honor society. I knew he'd received an appointment to the Naval Academy, just like his father, going to Annapolis that summer after graduation, just as Joseph Franklin, then a commander, transferred to another duty station in San Diego. Kevin must have been a senior lieutenant by now, if not a lieutenant commander.

"Surface, submarine or air?" I asked.

Kevin grinned. "Surface, much to the dismay of my aviator father."

"Where are you stationed?"

"I'm on leave, in transit from San Diego to Japan. I have a couple of weeks before I'm due to report."

I turned to Ruth. "You were in my brother's class, weren't you?"

"Brian Howard. Oh, I remember him." She laughed. "We were in the same biology lab. One day when we were dissecting frogs, he put an eyeball in the teacher's coffee cup."

"Sounds like my kid brother. I haven't heard that story before. I'll have to rag him about it."

"What's he doing now?"

"Married, two kids, teaches junior high in Sonoma. I assume some of his students are doing to him what he used to do to his teachers. One would hope so, anyway." I looked past Ruth and met the hard gray gaze of Admiral Joseph Franklin, USN-Retired. "Good evening," I said, voice neutral, eyes as steady as his.

"Evening," Franklin said, his voice chilly as his chin dipped in an almost imperceptible nod. The Admiral's gray hair was thin on top and his beaked nose jutted sharply from his narrow face. Despite the fact that he was dressed casually in gray slacks and a plaid shirt, he held himself erect and squared, as though he were still wearing the dress whites and sword he wore in the retirement photo on the mantel.

When I met the Admiral and his wife in March, I'd been looking for a missing woman named Elizabeth Willis, daughter of the Franklins' long-ago next-door neighbors. As my investigation progressed, I learned that Franklin and his neighbor's wife had been more than casual friends. The last time I'd seen Franklin, his eyes had been full of rage as I confronted him about the relationship. As he looked at me now, I saw the enmity was still there, frozen like a slab of ice. I wondered how Lenore, the sweet, self-effacing Navy wife, had persuaded him to let Ruth hire me, much less let me into the Franklin house. I suspected there was steel in Lenore's spine. There would have to be, for her to put up with the Admiral for thirty-plus years of marriage. Ruth must have had some of it too, to finally leave Sam and her marriage.

I turned to my client. "Ruth, what did you want to show me?"

44

"It's back here, in my old room."

Ruth led the way down the hall to a bedroom at the front of the house. I wondered if it had changed since Ruth lived here as a schoolgirl. It looked like a room in which a teenage girl would find refuge. The furniture was white wicker, a single bed with a low headboard matched by a nightstand and a dresser with a round mirror attached to the wall above it. The bed was covered with a pink and white floral comforter, its pattern matched by the curtains on the windows. Several houseplants were arrayed around the room, on the nightstand, dresser, and windowsill. A half-dozen cardboard packing cartons were shoved against one wall and a stack of papers rested on the dresser. Ruth reached for these, handing me a single sheet torn from a spiral steno pad. It was covered with blue ink, words and figures written in no order I could discern.

"I found this with some things I mailed to my mother last April," she said. "That's Sam's handwriting. And that number at the top, with B.A. in front of it, that's the account at the Bank of America. I wrote down the account number when I found the statement last Christmas." She indicated a number preceded by a squiggle that looked like a dollar sign. "This must be the balance. He's added quite a bit to it since December."

"Puts the total well over a hundred thousand dollars. If B.A. is Bank of America, then W.F. must mean Wells Fargo Bank." I looked at the sheet of paper with new eyes, trying to make sense of the jumble. I pointed at another set of figures. "This is a phone number, in the 408 area code. Which is San Jose, Sunnyvale, and points south." I looked at her. "Maybe when Sam scribbled these notes, he was planning how to move that money from Guam to the Bay Area. The first thing I'll do is check out the phone number."

"Good. When I found it, I thought it could be important. Have you made any progress, or is it too early?"

"Too early. Ed Korsakov gave me the name of a Chief LeBard who was with the Armed Forces Police Detachment on Guam the same time you were there. Sam may

45

have been involved in smuggling drugs to Guam. If that's the case, I'm sure that's where he got the money."

Ruth sat down on the bed, her weight pressing down the frilly pink and white comforter. "I had no idea," she said, her voice somber. "But it wouldn't surprise me." She fingered the collar of her white blouse. "Ill-gotten gains."

"Ill-gotten or not," I said, studying her face, "that money's community property and you're entitled to a share of it. Chief LeBard mentioned two people who were stationed on Guam the same time Sam was. They're now in the Bay Area—a sailor named Harlan Pettibone and a chief named Yancy. Are either of those names familiar?"

Ruth thought for a moment. "Pettibone . . . no, I don't think so. Now Yancy does ring a bell. Steve and Claudia Yancy. She's in the Navy too. They both worked at the air station, like Sam. They liked to play poker, so they hosted a game at their house almost every Friday night. Sam went regularly, I think."

"Did he lose or win?"

"He never would say." Ruth shrugged and played with a fold of her skirt. "If I'd ask about it, he'd tell me to mind my own business. So I didn't ask."

A supposed gambling debt might be a way for Sam Raynor to hide some of the missing money. I'd have to check out the Yancys and see if they were still hosting poker games, and whether the stakes were nickel-dime-quarter, or something with dollar signs and lots of zeroes before the decimal point.

From the kitchen at the rear of the house I heard voices, their words indistinct, Wendy's high-pitched piping mingled with the lower tones of the adults. Then Lenore Franklin appeared in the door of the bedroom. "Dinner's ready," she said. "Jeri, will you stay and have some ribs with us?"

"No, thanks. I have some things I need to do." Besides, the prospect of sitting down to dinner with the Admiral glaring at me across the table was not particularly conducive to my appetite. I folded the paper Ruth had found and tucked it into my bag.

"I'll check out this information and be in touch," I told Ruth as we walked back up the hall to the front door.

Six

THE FOLLOWING MORNING I CONSULTED MY CRISS-cross directory for the South Bay, looking up the number Sam Raynor had written on the sheet of paper Ruth found. It was a Wells Fargo branch in downtown San Jose. Bingo, I thought, picking up my coffee mug, speculating as I sipped the black brew. Raynor had moved the money from Bank of America on Guam to Wells Fargo in San Jose. Maybe. It would be nice if it were that easy. I'd have to see if I could get any information out of the bank when it opened.

I got up and poured myself another cup of coffee. It was going to be another hot day in the Bay Area. My office window was already open, seeking a breeze. The building that had gone up just down the street now blocked my view of the Oakland waterfront and I think it blocked the air flow as well.

Back at my desk I read through that morning's edition of the Oakland *Tribune*. The Port of Oakland was losing money, businesses were in trouble all up and down Broadway and the city's budget was stretched to the limit. There had been another fatal drive-by shooting, probably drug-related, and I wondered if my ex-husband Sid Vernon, an Oakland homicide cop, was working on that one. He'd been working on a similar case last May.

I pushed the newspaper aside and checked my calendar for that day. I had an appointment at ten with a prospective client, then some work to do for an insurance company.

This afternoon I planned to watch Sam Raynor's attorney's office—again.

At nine I called the Wells Fargo bank in San Jose. I told the teller on the other end that I had a check for twenty thousand dollars given to me by Sam Raynor and I wanted to know if he had sufficient funds to cover it. He wanted to know the account number.

Damn. I punted. "I don't have it in front of me," I said, sounding like a harried executive. "I'm calling from my car phone. All I know is it's drawn on your branch. I don't want to know the man's life story, I just want to know if he's got funds to cover it. Surely you can tell me that."

"Just a moment." The teller put me on what seemed like permanent hold. For several minutes I watched the second hand of my clock go round and round. Finally he came back on the line and said, "We did have an account for a Samuel Raynor, but it's been closed."

"What?" Indignation sharpened my voice. "That thief. I trusted him. When was it opened and closed?"

"It was opened in June and closed in July."

"He said he had the money. Where did he transfer those funds?" I demanded, taking a wild shot on the remote chance the teller would drop all the details in my lap.

"I'm sorry, I can't give you that information." He stumbled a bit over the words, realizing he'd given me too much already.

After I broke the connection I sat back in my chair and sipped coffee, thinking. Someone named Samuel Raynor had opened and closed an account at the Wells Fargo branch in San Jose. Given the June-July time frame, I assumed it was the Sam Raynor I was investigating. Raynor left Guam the first week in July. Maybe he'd authorized a wire transfer before he left, so his money would be waiting for him in the Bay Area. Something else was waiting for him—divorce papers. That prompted him to close the account and hide the money. But where?

I picked up the San Jose telephone directory and made several calls to school administration offices, in an attempt to find out whether Sam Raynor had in fact attended school

48

in that city. Since it was late August, the districts were gearing up for the coming school year, but no one had the time or inclination to assist me in this particular quest.

I replaced the phone in the cradle, speculating as I swallowed the lukewarm dregs of my coffee. A suspicious nature is an asset in a private investigator, and I certainly had one. Sam Raynor had lied to Ruth about many things during their marriage. What if he wasn't from San Jose after all? Apples don't fall far from the tree, or so they say. Maybe Raynor's hometown was nearby—Milpitas, Morgan Hill, or Gilroy.

Worth a few phone calls to investigate, I decided, but right now I had other things to do. Before I left for my ten o'clock appointment, I initiated credit checks on Raynor's acquaintances, Harlan Pettibone and Chief Yancy. The phone book had addresses for both, in Alameda. I figured anyone who knew Raynor on Guam was a likely accomplice, particularly since Yancy was Sam's poker-playing buddy. I liked the theory of a gambling debt as a hiding place for part of Raynor's cash, and I wanted to explore that further.

The day went by quickly. I grabbed a salad between tasks, saving room for my dinner with Alex that night, before our movie date at the Paramount. By three I was parked outside the MacArthur Boulevard office of Sam Raynor's attorney, sipping a soda from a nearby fast food stand, one eye on a paperback and the other on the office. Please let me get lucky, I muttered, chewing on the end of the straw. It's too damn hot to be sitting in this car.

I got lucky.

Just after four a bright red Trans-Am parked on the other side of the street. Sam Raynor got out of the car and stuck a few coins into the parking meter, then walked briskly into his lawyer's office. I got out of my Toyota and jaywalked across MacArthur for a closer inspection of the Trans-Am. It was a late model, and I wrote down the license plate number as well as the number of the NAS Alameda sticker in the front window. Unfortunately the car was locked. I peered inside and saw a collection of cassette tapes scattered on the passenger seat. Raynor's taste ran to rock and country.

I returned to my own car and finished my soda while I waited. At a quarter to five Raynor left the lawyer's office. The evening rush hour was in full snarl and he had to wait for an opening in traffic. I started my own car, thinking this was going to be dicey because we were on opposite sides of the street. But Raynor pulled out of the parking place and made a quick illegal U-turn.

Go home, I muttered, moving into place a couple of cars behind Raynor. He made a right turn onto Fruitvale and drove through Oakland. After he crossed the Fruitvale Bridge into Alameda, he headed for the West End. Finally he pulled the Trans-Am into the parking lot of a two-story apartment building on Pacific Avenue near Third Street, just a few blocks from the Naval Air Station.

It was an L-shaped building of faded orange stucco, looking like so many of the cookie-cutter boxes thrown up in Alameda during the fifties. The length of the L ran deep into the lot, with the short end at the back, paralleling the street. Brown doors with no screens, and windows with venetian blinds, faced a sidewalk on the first floor and an open-air walkway on the second. Raynor parked at the short end and took the metal stairs to the second floor. He unlocked the first door he came to and entered the apartment.

I waited, but Raynor didn't come out, so I chanced a stroll into the parking lot. I counted ten units per floor. The door Raynor had opened was numbered 210, and the blinds on the window were drawn shut. I returned to my car by way of the mailboxes at the front of the building. The name on 210 was Pettibone.

So Sam Raynor was living with his friend Harlan. I sat in my car, waiting and looking at my watch. The movie was at eight, and I was supposed to meet Alex for dinner at Le Cheval at six-thirty.

Just after six Raynor left the apartment, dressed in blue jeans and a T-shirt. He started the Trans-Am and pulled out of the lot, turning left onto Pacific. I followed him across

Webster to a discount liquor store. As soon as he went through the door, I was out of my car, headed for the phone booth near the entrance, hoping I could catch Alex at home.

"I'm tailing someone. I don't know how long I'll be," I said when Alex picked up the phone. I kept one eye on the liquor store's checkout counters. So far I hadn't spotted Raynor. "If I don't meet you at the restaurant, I'll meet you at the theater."

"And if you don't meet me at the theater?" Alex inquired, his voice somewhere between disappointed and understanding.

"Then I'm sorry and we'll talk later."

As I hung up the phone, I saw Raynor wheel a cart to one of the cashiers. He stacked a case of Budweiser on the conveyor belt and followed it up with several liquor bottles, a large can of nuts, and some bags of pretzels and chips. Either he was going to a party or stocking up for the weekend. The cashier rang up the sale and bagged Raynor's purchases. By the time he'd unloaded the stuff into his Trans-Am, I was in my Toyota, the engine running, ready to follow him on the next leg of his journey.

Raynor drove back across Webster Street, through a residential section of the West End, and finally parked on Fourth Street near Marion Court. Alameda is full of little cul-de-sacs like this one, short dead-end streets tucked between blocks, lined with cottages built close together. On Marion Court they were beige stucco, probably constructed in the thirties or forties, each with a tiny porch and a postage-stamp front yard, grass going brown in the drought. There were six one-story cottages on either side of the court, and two at the back with second stories built over a garage. The narrow street was crowded with parked cars, most with two wheels on the sidewalk.

Raynor tucked the case of beer under one arm and picked up his brown paper sack with his free hand, cradling the burden against his chest. His destination was the fourth cottage on the left, the one with a large green and white spider plant hanging next to the door. He knocked and was promptly admitted.

Another car parked in front of me and two men got out, one black and one white, both with short haircuts, both edging toward forty. One carried a large bucket of take-out chicken, and the other a grocery sack similar to the one Raynor had carried. I heard one man laugh and say, "Didn't I tell you never to draw to an inside straight?" I watched them walk into Marion Court, their destination the fourth cottage. So the Friday night poker game made the transition from Guam to Alameda. I'd say the odds were good that the game's host was Chief Yancy.

I got to Le Cheval just as the waiter set Alex's dinner in front of him. He raised black eyebrows above his dark brown eyes and greeted me with his quirky smile. I glanced at the menu and ordered, glad that I'd have enough time for dinner. It had been several long hours since my salad at lunch. Fortunately the service at the Vietnamese restaurant was quick and efficient, and Alex and I were able to get to the Paramount Theater right before the show started at eight o'clock.

We bought our tickets at the box office under the Paramount's brightly lit marquee, advertising Bette Davis in *Dark Victory*, then strolled through the sumptuous green and gold lobby. In the orchestra section we found two vacant seats near the aisle and sat down, listening to the guy at the Wurlitzer organ play "Strike Up the Band."

"The tail job," Alex said, draping his arm around my shoulder, "is it the case that involves a sailor?"

"Yes." I waited a moment as the organist segued into "Night and Day." "This Chief Yancy in your department, did he just transfer here from Guam?"

Alex looked alarmed as he swiveled his head in my direction. "You're not investigating Chief Yancy?"

I shook my head. "No. Someone who knew him on Guam."

"There's another man in my department whose last duty station was Guam. Also a recent arrival."

"Sam Raynor?" I guessed.

"Damn." Alex frowned. "I don't like the sound of this."

52

Seven

SATURDAY AFTERNOON I RETURNED TO THE WEST AL-
ameda apartment building. Harlan Pettibone's name was on
the mailbox, but Sam Raynor had a key. Evidently they
were sharing the apartment. It's customary for tenants to
give landlords all sorts of personal information, including
financial. Maybe I could get a look at the rental application.

I didn't see Raynor's red Trans-Am anywhere, and the
blinds were shut at the windows of the second floor unit I'd
seen him enter yesterday, so I headed for the mailboxes
near the front of the building. Two strips of red plastic tape
with raised letters decorated the mailbox for Apartment
101, one reading MANAGER and the other TORELLI. Inside the
apartment a television set was going full blast. When I
knocked, the noise level abated, then the door swung open.

She looked very young, twenty at the most, with curly
black hair pulled back in an untidy ponytail. She wore
denim cutoffs that revealed slender legs, and a sleeveless
gray T-shirt with a U.S. Navy emblem stretched over round
little breasts. One hand held a can of soda and the other
ruffled the hair of the wide-eyed toddler who clung to her
leg, training pants riding low enough for me to see that he
was a boy.

"Mrs. Torelli?" I asked. She nodded. "Are you the manager?"

"Me and my husband," she said in a wispy little voice
that made her seem even younger. She took a sip from the
can. Her eyes assessed me over its rim. "You looking for
a place to live?"

"Actually I'd like some information."

Mrs. Torelli's brown eyes widened and she fluttered a pair of long lashes. "We're not supposed to give out information on tenants."

"I'm doing a background investigation on Mr. Pettibone in 210," I told her. "It's classified." If she was a Navy wife, the word "classified" might pry open her mouth.

"Oh, yeah? Do you have some identification?" The little-girl voice turned quite firm.

I handed her one of my business cards. "I'd appreciate it if you wouldn't tell anyone I've been here."

Mrs. Torelli turned my card over in her hand, examining it, her black eyebrows arched above her brown eyes as curiosity won over caution. "Is Hal in some kind of trouble?"

"Well, I can't really give you any details. Just that there's a large sum of money involved."

"Hal and money? To hear him tell it, he hasn't got any."

The kid set up a clamor, and Mrs. Torelli handed him the soda can. He tipped it up to his mouth, gulping noisily, a trickle of the brown liquid running down his bare chest. His mother didn't miss a beat as she reached into the pocket of her cutoffs, pulled out a tissue and mopped the spill.

"If he's borrowing money, he's a lousy credit risk. If he's coming into some cash, I'd sure like to know. He's always late with the rent."

I frowned and pulled a pen and notebook from my purse. "He doesn't pay his bills on time? Always?"

"Every month, sometimes a few days, sometimes a week or more. My husband has to lean on him to collect."

"When did he rent the apartment? Could you verify that date for me?" I asked, itching to get a look at Pettibone's rental application.

"Okay. Come on in."

I followed Mrs. Torelli into the apartment. Her rubber thong sandals slapped against the soles of her feet. On my right a small dining area held a round wooden table with three woven rattan place mats, its centerpiece a box of vanilla wafers. Beyond that was a cramped-looking kitchen with a refrigerator and stove in that avocado-green shade popular years ago. The refrigerator door was decorated with

54

an array of food coupons clipped from newspapers and magazines, all affixed to the metal surface with magnets.

In the living room the shag carpet was the same tired green as the appliances, and its surface was littered with enough toys to make walking across it a hazard. One end of the brown and gold plaid sofa held a stack of neatly folded laundry, its source a big rattan basket still full of tangled clothing. The back wall of the living room held shelves with a stereo, a VCR, and a wide-screen television set, showing a close-up of the characters of a recent and forgettable movie emoting in muted dialogue and hurt-your-eyes color.

The toddler picked up a bright red plastic gizmo and stuck it into his mouth as his mother disappeared into one of the bedrooms. She returned a moment later with a file folder in her hand, just as the toddler removed the toy he was gumming from his mouth. He offered it to me, streaked with saliva and vanilla wafer residue, a beatific grin on his round-cheeked face.

"No, thanks," I told him. "I've already had lunch."

"Don't bother the lady, honeybunch," Mrs. Torelli said, tousling his hair. Honeybunch made a chirruping noise and butted his head against her leg. She set the soda can on top of the television set, opened the folder and leafed through several sheets of paper. I moved closer, looking over her shoulder.

"Hal rented the apartment in March and moved in April first. April Fool's Day." She laughed. "More fool us. He paid first and last month's rent and a security deposit. That's the only time he paid on time. My husband told him if he was late again, he'd have to move. But it's really hard to evict people in this state, so we threaten first."

Her son was now beating the arm of the sofa with his red plastic toy, talking to himself in a litany of toddler-speak that competed with the dialogue from the television. "Honeybunch, cut that out," Mrs. Torelli said automatically. Honeybunch showed no sign of desisting.

"What about Pettibone's roommate?" I asked over the din.

"Roommate?" Mrs. Torelli frowned. She expertly re-moved the plastic toy from her son's hand and replaced it with a plush purple and green frog. The kid emitted a de-lighted screech and crushed the frog to his bare chest, then he gurgled as he waddled around the living room, training pants slipping even farther down his butt. I took advantage of his mother's temporary distraction to scan Pettibone's application.

"Well, Hal said that was a temporary arrangement. It's only a one-bedroom unit, but he's had this guy named Sam staying with him since July," she said, returning to the folder. "If it looks like Sam's gonna stay on much longer, he's gotta fill out a form. I don't want to get in Dutch with the people that own this place. My husband's too easy on these guys."

"What do you mean?" I wanted to keep her talking. But so far Mrs. Torelli didn't give any indication that she was ready to end this interview. Maybe she liked talking to an-other adult, a reaction to being cooped up all day with Honeybunch, who wasn't exactly a challenging conversa-tionalist. "Too easy on which guys?"

"Sailors. My husband keeps cutting 'em slack because they're Navy. Us Navy people gotta stick together. But let me tell you," she said sagely, as though she'd had years of experience, "you manage apartments, you gotta be careful. People take advantage of you."

"That's true. Has Pettibone ever bounced a check?"

"No," she said, frowning. "Has he done that before?"

"I'm afraid so. With the Bank of America account. Is that what he's using to pay his rent?"

"It's the credit union on base." Her index finger ran down the rental application and stopped midway. "He doesn't say anything here about an account at the Bank of America."

"I didn't know about this credit union account." I quickly wrote down the account number and as much other infor-mation pertaining to Harlan T. Pettibone as I could see on the form, including his social security number and the plate number of his car, an orange Chevy Camaro.

"Boy, my husband's not gonna like hearing that Hal writes rubber checks," Mrs. Torelli was saying.

"Maybe it's just an isolated incident." To my chagrin, Mrs. Torelli closed the folder before I could jot down anything else about Pettibone. "I mean, Pettibone's in the Navy, right? Maybe he was out to sea when the rent was due and he couldn't get to the credit union to deposit his check."

"Oh, he works in Port Services. The only thing that gets under way there is a tugboat, and they don't go much past the breakwater. I'm a Navy wife. I know when payday is. He's in port most of the time, and if he's like a lot of sailors, his check is direct-deposited at the credit union."

All of a sudden it seemed quiet in the room, despite the television set. Honeybunch had worn himself out and was now curled up on the green carpet, eyes closed, his head pillowed on his green plush frog. Mrs. Torelli crossed the living room to her son. She knelt, hands smoothing his dark hair, then she pulled a blanket from the laundry basket and covered him. With a tired sigh she sat on the sofa, slipped her feet out of the sandals and propped them up on the cluttered coffee table.

"You know, I've never actually seen Pettibone," I said, smiling at the younger woman's obvious pleasure in this one quiet moment. "What does he look like?"

She laughed. "He looks weird, but he thinks he's God's gift to women. It's always the funny-looking guys think they're studs. I mean, he's short and skinny and has that funny nose."

"What do you mean by funny?" I moved a wooden train engine from an armchair and sat down.

"Well, it kinda goes like this." Mrs. Torelli's hand sketched a vague shape in the air, enough to make me suspect that someone had punched Harlan in the hooter a time or two. "He sure as hell came on to me when he moved in. But I let him know exactly how I felt about that."

"What does he do for entertainment?"

"My husband says he spends all his time in those bars on Webster Street. Plays pool. Even has a custom-made cue."

57

"Any other problems with Pettibone, besides his being late with the rent?"

"That damned orange car with the tiger stripes. It's noisy. He likes to rev it, and it sure needs a muffler."

"Tiger stripes? You mean the paint job or the upholstery?"

"Both. The car's orange with black trim, plus he's got tiger-striped seat covers. It's so tacky." She rolled her eyes. "He says his middle name is T for Tiger. He's even got a little stuffed tiger hanging from the rearview mirror, and another one with suction-cup feet stuck to one of the side windows."

That should make Pettibone easy to locate, I thought. Just look for the tigermobile. I glanced over my notes. "Do you know anything about the roommate, Sam Raynor?"

She shrugged. "He's a first-class petty officer, in one of those aviation ratings. My husband says Sam and Hal knew each other on Guam. Sam drives a red Trans-Am. He's not here much, just to sleep. He's getting a divorce from his wife. I'll bet he's got some sweet young thing on the beach," she said using the Navy lingo for "out in town." She pulled a towel from the laundry basket and folded it, adding to the stack at her side. Then she sat up straight. "I just remembered something. Sam got beat up a couple of weeks ago."

Now that was an interesting piece of news. "How badly? Where did it happen?"

"He had a shiner and some cuts on his face. When I saw him I asked about it, and he made a joke about running into a herd of flying fish. But my husband says he got jumped by some bikers in the parking lot behind Nadine's." I knew the place, a night spot on Webster Street that played oldies.

On the floor the toddler stirred. "I've taken up enough of your time," I said, getting to my feet. "You've been very helpful, Mrs. Torelli. I would appreciate it if you didn't tell either Pettibone or Raynor I was here."

As I left, she stood in the doorway of the apartment and I felt her eyes follow me out to my car. My request for silence was probably a useless exercise. Mrs. Torelli would tell her husband that I'd been there. If he was the type to cut fellow sailors some slack, he might let Raynor or Pettibone know I'd been there asking questions. Practically speaking, it was only a matter of time before Raynor found out someone was asking questions about him. And he'd know why.

After leaving the apartment building, I drove downtown to the Alameda Police Department. I wanted a look at whatever information the cops had on the incident that earned Sam Raynor a black eye. I paid for a copy of the police report and took it back outside to my car.

The assault happened two weeks ago, on a Thursday night, as Raynor was leaving Nadine's. Raynor told the police that two men in biker garb accosted him in the parking lot, braced him against the wall and worked him over. Harlan Pettibone had followed Raynor outside a few minutes later. When he saw the attack, he joined the fray, along with two other sailors who were standing near the club's front door. Together they routed the bikers, who jumped on their Harleys and roared off down Webster Street, in the direction of Oakland and the Tube.

Raynor had given Pettibone's address as his own and claimed he didn't know why the assailants jumped him. He speculated they were after his wallet, but as I read the report, the bikers appeared to be more interested in hurting Raynor than taking his bankroll. Aside from the two sailors, who were assigned to the aircraft carrier berthed at the air station, there was another witness, a man named Agustin Lopez, evidently an employee of the club. He'd been smoking a cigarette at the rear door. According to Lopez, the bikers said something to Raynor before their fists came into play.

Interesting, I thought. Was someone sending Raynor a message?

I drove back to the West End. The nightclub was in a one-story building at the corner of Webster and Pacific, its rough stucco exterior painted a tired blue, with red and orange signs advertising the name of the joint and various brands of beer. Inside, I saw tables in front of me and to my left. On the right was a counter where patrons could order beer or food. As befitted a place named Nadine's, Chuck Berry's song of the same title blasted out of the jukebox, a big squat Rockola over in the corner. I asked the guy at the bar where I could find Lopez. He waved me toward the kitchen. Lopez wasn't much help, though. He couldn't recall anything more than what he told the cops two weeks before. In fact, he seemed hesitant. Had someone, or something, made him forget?

I returned to my car, considering what I'd learned this afternoon and the questions that knowledge raised. Why had the bikers attacked Sam Raynor? What if someone besides me was looking for Raynor's money, not the cash he had on him, but the much larger sum he had buried so deeply? If that was the case, why and who?

Eight

MONDAY AFTERNOON I SAT RESTLESSLY IN MY Toyota, opposite Raynor's apartment building. He arrived at four o'clock, wearing his uniform, got out of his Trans-Am and went upstairs. I spent the next hour thinking how excruciatingly boring tail jobs are. This whole case seemed to be at a standstill. None of the credit reports I'd requested had come in today. None of my feelers about Raynor's finances had netted any information so far. I suspected that was because he'd been back in California for such a short time he hadn't generated much of a paper trail. Besides, he was being careful not to leave any evidence about his true financial status.

I planned to talk to Chief Yancy, whose address was the

Marion Court cottage, site of the Friday night poker game. Perhaps Raynor had given some of the money to his chief, disguised as gambling losses. Other than that, I contemplated the prospect of making cold calls to every financial institution in the Bay Area to see if Sam Raynor had an account, a long and tedious process. Something had better happen soon, before I faced hours on the phone.

At five Raynor left the apartment, in slacks and a short-sleeved shirt. As the Trans-Am turned left onto Pacific, I started my Toyota. I almost lost him as he took a left onto Webster Street. I made it through the yellow light and followed him through the Tube. Once in Oakland, Raynor made a series of turns that put him on the southbound Nimitz Freeway. It was rush hour and traffic was slow, good news for me, since Raynor drove like the proverbial bat out of hell. He was a lane hopper, but as we passed the Oakland Coliseum he veered into the far right lane and stayed, despite the slower traffic. Raynor took Davis Street into San Leandro. I followed him onto Estudillo Avenue, where he turned right into the parking lot of an apartment building, so quickly that I overshot the entrance.

I circled the block. By the time I made it back to Estudillo, Raynor was climbing the stairs at the street end of the building. It was another ticky-tacky stucco box, this one painted a particularly unpleasant shade of green. Set perpendicular to the street, the structure was three stories high, with parking stalls at ground level and two floors above, each with six doors opening onto an exterior walkway fronted by flimsy-looking metal railings. Raynor was now on the top floor, knocking on the second door from this end. The only person who responded was an elderly woman in the first apartment. She opened her door and looked out at Raynor, who stuck something—a note?—in the crack between door and frame. He headed for the stairs, ignoring the old woman.

When Raynor departed, I stayed. I wanted to know who lived here. As I walked toward the building, I saw that the apartment doors were lettered rather than numbered. The unit where Raynor had left the note was H. I headed for the mailboxes. Glancing up, I saw the flick of a curtain and a white-haired figure watching me from unit G. The name slot for apartment H held a card with a name printed in block letters—Tiffany Collins.

It would be a Tiffany, I thought. So Sam Raynor did have a girlfriend. I wondered if she was short and blond, like Ruth Raynor. I'd have liked to examine whatever he'd left at Tiffany Collins's door, but I didn't want an encounter with the nosy neighbor. I returned to my car and waited.

For the next half hour AC Transit buses lumbered past on both Estudillo and Bancroft, discharging commuters on their way home. I saw several tenants arrive, collect their mail, and trudge up the stairs to their apartments. Twice the curtains in the corner unit shifted, as the old woman looked down to see if I was still there.

Just after six I heard a roar that brought the old woman back to her watching post. A Harley-Davidson turned off Estudillo into the lot. The helmeted rider parked near the hedge that separated the property from the building next door, almost even with my car. I watched as he removed the helmet and set it on the seat.

He was a biker. He wore faded blue jeans, heavy boots, and a leather vest over a white T-shirt that revealed tattoos on both forearms. He turned so that his back was to me, and I noticed some sort of insignia on his vest. I couldn't read it because it was partly covered by his lank blond ponytail. Then he shifted position, his face in profile, obscured by a beard. Medium height, early thirties, I guessed, though it was hard to judge with all that facial foliage.

The biker fired up a cigarette and looked up to the third floor, where the watchful old woman stared down from her window. He stared right back at her and blew a few smoke rings as he leaned on his bike. Was he waiting for Tiffany Collins? An old boyfriend, the kind who might attack Tiffany's new boyfriend? He slouched against the bike and smoked the cigarette down to the butt. Then he dropped it to the pavement, grinding it out with his boot. He straightened and looked toward the street.

A car purred into the parking lot, a Mercedes, several

years old, its gleaming finish the color of old gold. The driver parked the car in the slot Sam Raynor had vacated. A young woman emerged from the sedan, a handbag with a long strap swinging from her right shoulder. Her left hand grasped the handles of several shopping bags.

She was a short blonde, all right, with a mane of shoulder-length hair the color of corn silk, and a bosomy figure packed into a thigh-high blue dress that showed off a pair of shapely legs. I wondered how she could walk in those high heels, but she managed to cover ground rapidly, reaching the mailboxes just as the biker reached her. She opened the mailbox for H, pulled out a couple of envelopes and tossed them into one of her shopping bags.

Tiffany Collins? She lives in a place like this but drives a Mercedes? That dichotomy was certainly worth investigating.

The woman turned to face the biker. I couldn't see their faces clearly, but there was a lot of gesturing going on. Their decibel level was high enough for me to hear a couple of words, high enough to bring the old lady in apartment G out onto the walkway, craning for a look and a listen. She scurried for cover as Tiffany Collins stamped one high-heeled foot, stuck her nose into the air and started up the stairs. The biker, angry, judging from his body language, headed for his Harley.

I could always come back to talk to Tiffany, I reasoned, turning the key on the Toyota. Now I wanted to find out who the biker was. The Harley snarled to life. I followed it west, toward downtown San Leandro, where it pulled into the lot outside a large drugstore.

The biker parked the Harley near the entrance. He left the helmet on the seat and strode through the automatic doors. I walked over to the Harley, pulling a notebook and pen from my purse. I quickly wrote down the motorcycle's license plate number, stowed pen and paper, and turned, heading back to my car.

A hand like a vise grabbed my arm and spun me around, propelling me backward against the brick wall of the building. I felt a frisson of alarm as I looked into the sharp blue eyes in the bearded face. It wasn't so much that I feared for my safety. We were about the same height and I could fight him off if I had to. Besides, there were plenty of customers going in and out of the drugstore. But he looked a lot like one of the thugs who beat me up in an Oakland parking lot a few years ago. The resemblance put me off balance for a moment as I pushed back the past and focused on the present.

"I spotted you at the apartment," he growled, lips moving in the bearded face. "You followed me here. Why?"

I revised my estimate of his age upward. There was a lot of gray in the beard and the ponytailed hair, and the lines in his face were wrought by hard living. A mechanic, I guessed, examining the hand that gripped my arm. It was callused and scarred, with the sort of grime under the fingernails that required heavy-duty soap and a brush to remove. Above the hand a muscled forearm was tattooed with four blue letters.

"Acey. Is that what they call you?"

"Never mind what they call me. Who the fuck are you?"

"Jeri Howard. I'm a private investigator."

He didn't look impressed. "You got something proves that?"

"Let go of my arm and I'll show you my license."

He released me. I stuck my hand in my purse and pulled out the license. The blue eyes examined it, then returned to my face. "Investigating what?"

"Sam Raynor." He didn't say anything, mouth pulled down into a frown. He pulled a fresh pack of cigarettes out of his pocket, tore it open and knocked out one, lighting it with a tarnished Zippo. "You know Sam Raynor?" I asked, returning the license to my purse.

His mouth had a grim set as he blew smoke to one side. "If the motherfucker don't stay away from my sister, I'm gonna have his liver for breakfast."

I folded my arms in front of me as I revised my scenario from disgruntled boyfriend to concerned older brother. Either way, he could be useful.

"Tiffany Collins is your sister?" He nodded. "You know

anything about a couple of bikers who jumped Raynor two weeks ago in the parking lot of Nadine's in Alameda?" I got no answer. If he'd had anything to do with that incident, he wasn't copping to it. "What do you know about Raynor?"

"He's slime." Acey Collins sneered, mouth twisting as he took another hit on his cigarette. "I had his number the first time I met him."

The man in front of me looked as though he knew a thing or two about slime. "The evidence seems to point in that direction. Maybe we can help each other out."

"What's your angle? Who you working for?"

"Raynor's wife. Soon to be ex-wife. Did you know he was married?"

"Yeah. He fed Tiff some line about how his old lady took a hike and won't let him see the kid. I figure it's bullshit."

"She did leave him. She has her reasons."

"Such as?"

"He beat her up once too often."

Acey Collins's eyes narrowed into cold blue slits. "He ever lays a hand on my sister, he's dead meat."

"All the more reason for you to help me."

"What are you looking for?"

"Money. Raynor had a big bankroll on Guam. Now that it's time to divvy up the community property, he says he's broke."

Acey considered this for a moment as he puffed on his cigarette. "He spends a lot of money on Tiff, throws it around like it was water. Buys her lots of presents too. Last time it was a gold chain, must have cost five hundred."

"We're talking about a lot more money than that."

"You see that fancy car my sister's driving? A Mercedes. A few years old. Previously owned, as they say." He gave the words a sardonic twist as he folded his arms across his chest. "Hell, I know what a used Mercedes costs. It ain't cheap. Tiff can't afford a car like that. She's civil service, works on the base at Alameda, fer crissakes. That's where she met the creep."

"You think Raynor gave her the money to buy it?"

"A month ago she was driving a Japanese four-banger. I got the damn thing down at my shop, trying to sell it. No takers yet. Yeah, I think he gave her the money for the car, but she claims she borrowed it from her credit union. She's playing games with me. I hate it when she does that." He grimaced, his gray-blond eyebrows drawing together.

"Why would she hook up with a guy like Raynor?"

"Shit, I don't know. I thought she had more sense. She's usually pretty sharp when it comes to men, but this creep Raynor, he's got her—" He stopped, searching for a word. "Mesmerized. That's it. Like what a snake does to a rabbit before he eats the sucker."

"Let's hope we can keep Tiffany from being eaten," I said. "If Raynor did buy her the Mercedes, he may be using her to hide his assets from his wife. And that's fraud. It looked like the two of you were having words. What about?"

He tossed the cigarette to the pavement and crushed it out, taking his time answering. "Raynor's got another woman. Don't know who she is. But I saw them together in Oakland."

"Been keeping an eye on Sam?"

"Yeah. And I'm gonna continue to keep an eye on the bastard. Until Tiff wises up."

"How did she react when you told her about the other woman?"

Acey snorted. "Didn't believe me. Said I was lying."

"What did you see? When and where?"

"Saturday night, Lake Merritt in Oakland. Raynor met a woman in the parking lot near the boathouse. She got out of her car and they got into his backseat. It was damn clear they were more than friends."

"Did you get a good look at her and her car?" I asked.

"Yeah. Wasn't quite dark yet. Short blond hair, maybe five-four. Driving a late model Nissan, cranberry-colored, with one of those Navy stickers in the front windshield."

"Could you tell if the sticker was red or blue?" Officers like Alex had blue stickers on their cars, allowing them to

66

drive past the Marine guards at the gate of the Alameda Naval Air Station. Cars belonging to enlisted personnel bore red stickers.

Acey Collins shook his head. "No. Just know it was one of those base stickers."

I mulled this over for a moment. The woman who met Sam Raynor at the boathouse could be in the service herself, married to someone who was, or even the daughter of a military family. The base sticker meant she had access to a service member's car. Alameda was the nearest military base, but that didn't mean she had come from the air station. There were other possibilities in the Bay Area, Army and Air Force as well as Navy.

"Thanks for the information. I'll look into it. How can I get in touch with you?"

"I'll find you," Acey Collins said. "You got a card or something?"

I dug a business card out of my purse. "There's an answering machine on the phone."

I stepped back as he fired up the Harley. After he'd gone, I retraced my route to Tiffany Collins's apartment building, only to discover the gold Mercedes gone. I'd missed her while I was talking to Acey, but the information her brother gave me was worth it. Another woman in Sam Raynor's life meant another possible hiding place for Raynor's money.

Nine

THE NEXT MORNING I CALLED SERGEANT ANGIE Walters in Records at the Oakland Police Department. "I need to find out if you have a sheet on someone."

"Didn't think you were calling to exchange recipes," Angie rasped. "Who is it?"

"Collins, Acey." I spelled the name. "Blond and blue, five-eight, about thirty-five. Rides a Harley."

Angie said she'd put her ear to the ground and get back to me. I poured myself a cup of coffee, then returned to my desk to make another phone call, to a friend who worked at NAS Alameda.

Mary and I met eight years ago when we both signed up for a paralegal course in San Francisco. Back then I was a legal secretary, spending my free time playing roles with various little theater groups and wondering why I'd majored in history since I didn't want to teach. Mary was the widow of a Navy man who'd died in a shipboard accident, a boiler room explosion. Faced with a small pension and three kids to raise, she didn't have any choice but to work. Both of us thought the paralegal program might give us an edge in the job market. I had no idea I was about to meet a private investigator named Errol Seville, who would take me under his wing as an operative. All I knew was legal research looked a lot more interesting than typing and filing legal documents.

Mary stayed with paralegal work, first at an Oakland law firm, then a civil service position with the Navy, which had officers of the Judge Advocate Corps—Navy lawyers— assigned to the Naval Legal Service office at Treasure Island. She lived in Oakland and didn't care for the commute halfway across the Bay Bridge, so last year she'd transferred to a position at NAS Alameda. It wasn't legal work, but at the time, she told me she was ready for a change.

When I asked her about Tiffany Collins, Mary chuckled. "How in the world did you meet her? Is this about one of your investigations?"

"Yes, it is. Does she work in your building?"

"She does indeed. Right here in the civilian personnel office. I can see her desk from where I sit. She's not here today, though. She took a day's leave. Something about an appointment."

"Tell me about her." I shifted in my chair and reached for my coffee.

"G.S. Five clerk-typist. I'm not sure how long she's worked here, but I think it's at least four or five years. I get the impression she's been around awhile. You know how I can tell? She's got an ivy plant on her desk and it's climbed halfway up the wall. And bunnies everywhere." Mary laughed but she didn't explain the bunny remark. "Anyway, she does her job well. It's what she does outside the job that excites some comment."

"Such as?"

"Well, have you seen her?"

"From a distance. Short blonde, nice figure, great legs."

"And dresses to show it off," Mary finished. "All she has to do is stroll down the sidewalk and every sailor and Marine on this base starts salivating. It's only normal. The girl's young and attractive. The grapevine says she likes to have fun."

"What else does the grapevine say?"

"Lately?" Mary's voice dropped, and I surmised that someone had come within hearing range of her desk. "Well, rumor has it the girl's in love. She's been seen on the arm of a good-looking sailor. And she's driving a fancy car. The kind that makes me wonder how she can afford the insurance, let alone the payments. Say, Jeri, I hope she's not in some kind of trouble. She really is a nice kid. Just, well, young and foolish. We were all young and foolish once."

True, I thought, but you couldn't afford to be young and foolish around Sam Raynor. It was too dangerous.

The morning mail brought the credit check I'd initiated on Sam Raynor, which didn't tell me anything more than what I already knew. I was convinced that Raynor had stashed the money with friends. The fact that his current girlfriend was driving a car that cost forty or fifty thousand dollars waved at me like a bright red flag. That gold Mercedes was more car than the average low-level civil servant could afford.

Was the car in her name? I had a scenario in mind, in which Sam Raynor disguised some of his funds by purchasing the car and putting it in Tiffany Collins's name. If Tiffany was under Raynor's spell, she'd be ripe for the usual story about the greedy, grasping wife after revenge and money. Or perhaps the car was in fact registered to Sam Raynor, and his girlfriend was driving it, though yesterday's chat with Acey Collins made me think otherwise.

I was interrupted by a phone call from Blair Castle, Ruth Raynor's attorney. She wanted to know if I'd made any progress, and sounded impatient and abrupt when all I had for her was the information about the Wells Fargo bank in San Jose.

"You don't have an account number for Wells Fargo?"

"No. All I've got is the guy on the phone telling me that Raynor had an account, then he closed it."

"We've got a hearing in two weeks, Jeri, on Raynor's motion to quash the subpoena for the Bank of America records. I need more ammunition. I hope you can come up with something." Her tone implied that she didn't think I was moving fast enough.

"I've got some leads, but it'll take me a while to check them out." My own voice was sharp. I disliked being pressured, even though I understood the urgency of the situation.

"I'll go ahead and subpoena the Wells Fargo records," Blair was saying. "That should rattle Raynor and his lawyer, if nothing else. You call me if you find out anything."

I left my office, locking the door behind me, and walked to the suite of offices at the front of the building, the law firm of Alwin, Taylor and Chao. I waved at Bill Alwin, who looked preoccupied as he walked down the hall with a law book in his hand. Cassie Taylor was in her office, on the phone as usual, shoes off and her feet propped up on a desk drawer that had been pulled out to serve that purpose. The jacket of her gray-and-white-checked suit had been draped on a wooden hanger that now hung on the coat tree in one corner of her office.

Cassie waved me to one of the chairs in front of her desk and kept talking, one slender brown hand playing with the narrow collar of the pink silk blouse she wore. She reveled in elegant clothes and always looked bandbox fresh, tweaking me constantly about my own preference for comfortable slacks and practical shoes. I sat down and examined the crepe sole of my own footgear while she finished her phone call.

"Just the person I wanted to see," she said, hanging up the phone.

"Why?"

"Eric and I would like you and Alex to join us for dinner Saturday night. Seven o'clock, at my place."

"Are you cooking?" I asked, somewhat alarmed at the prospect. Cassie had been dating an accountant named Eric for the past few months and she was sounding increasingly domestic as the relationship progressed. But meal preparation was not her forte, which is why she was my frequent dining companion in local restaurants.

"Lord no, girl." Cassie laughed and ran her hand through her short black hair. "You know I only understand defrost, microwave, and let's go out."

"Much to your mother's dismay."

"Well, we all dismay our mothers in this life," Cassie said philosophically. I could certainly relate to that. I'd been dismaying mine since I was old enough to talk. "No, I'm not cooking. But Eric has many charms, and cooking skills are among them. All you have to bring is Alex and a couple of bottles of wine."

"Sounds good to me. I'll check with Alex to see if he's free. While we're on the subject of food, how about lunch?"

Cassie looked at her watch and her calendar, then shook her head. "Can't. I have a client coming in about twenty minutes. Maybe tomorrow. Speaking of mothers, you still going down to Monterey to see yours?"

"I'm going down to see the family. Labor Day weekend. Cannery Row will be knee-deep in tourists." I switched subjects. "What do you know about an attorney named Blair Castle?"

"Divorce lawyer," Cassie said promptly. "Is she a client? I thought you didn't take divorce cases."

"It's a long story. Yes, I'm working for her. I don't like her, but I'm working for her."

Cassie leaned back in her chair and recrossed her legs. "I've only met her a couple of times. She belongs to my women's network thing but she doesn't come to the meetings often. Skinny woman with brown hair, in her forties. A lot of nervous energy, that's my impression. What do I know about her? She was admitted to the bar less than ten years ago. I think she went to McGeorge Law School, at the University of the Pacific over in Stockton. She has a good reputation as a lawyer, but she can be abrasive."

"I've noticed," I said dryly. "She irritates me. I'm trying not to let it get to me."

Cassie's phone buzzed. She picked up the receiver, listened, then returned the instrument to its cradle. "My client's here."

I got to my feet. "Thanks for the conversation. I'll let you know about Saturday night. Ask Eric whether he wants us to bring a bottle of red or white."

Cassie laughed. "If I know Eric, he'll specify vineyard and vintage."

According to Mary, Tiffany Collins was using a vacation day to keep an appointment, so I didn't know whether I'd find her at home. When I arrived at the San Leandro apartment building, I didn't see the gold Mercedes in her parking stall. I glanced up at her apartment and saw the drapes were open to the afternoon sun. Then I saw movement inside the apartment, so I climbed the stairs to H.

When I knocked, the door opened wide and I was face-to-face with Tiffany Collins. She was a good ten years younger than her brother Acey, probably mid-twenties. Her round face was fair and smooth-skinned, with a pouty red mouth and a belligerent-looking jaw that tensed as she raked me with her blue eyes. She wore white shorts and a blue T-shirt decorated with pink rabbits. Her hands were on her hips as she glared at me, a hectoring tone in her voice.

"It's about time you got here. I stayed home from work

72

because of this. And I've been waiting since this morning. I don't like waiting."

I'll bet you don't, I thought, tilting my head to one side. "Sorry, I think you've made a mistake."

"Aren't you from the insurance company?" she demanded, running one hand through her corn-silk hair. Her earrings were rabbits too, tiny gold rabbits.

"Insurance company?"

"Yeah. Are you the insurance adjuster?" She leaned toward me as though I hadn't heard her properly. "About the car."

"What about the car?"

"Are you retarded or something?" she snapped as her hands went up in an exasperated gesture. "My car's been stolen."

"The gold Mercedes?" I asked with interest.

"My dream car," she wailed. "I only had it a month. Now it's gone. What are you going to do about it?"

"Not much I can do about it, except ask a few questions. May I come in?"

She nodded impatiently. I stepped into the apartment and immediately understood Mary's comment about bunnies. I felt as though I'd walked into a rabbit hutch.

To my right was a small dining area and kitchen. On the end of the counter I saw a ceramic cookie jar shaped like a rabbit holding a carrot. The rabbit was white, with wide blue eyes like those of Tiffany Collins. There were place mats decorated with bunnies on the round table in the dining area. On the small refrigerator I saw several rabbit-shaped magnets. In the living room to my left bunnies frolicked on the shelves of the entertainment center, peeking from all sides of the television set, VCR, and stereo system. They crowded the end tables that bracketed the sofa, upholstered in a busy floral print. Everywhere I looked I saw rabbits, made of wood and china, pottery and porcelain, crystal and brass and who knows what else, in every hue and pose. The only wall decoration was a framed watercolor of a rabbit, and I wasn't at all surprised to see a paperback copy of *Watership Down* on the low bookcase under the window, along with a complete set of the works of Beatrix Potter.

I have a friend who's the same way about cats. Makes her easy to shop for. Overdosed on bunnies, I turned my gaze back to Tiffany Collins. "When was the car stolen?"

"Last night. I had dinner with a friend, over at the San Leandro Marina. When we left the restaurant, the car was gone. God, I was pissed."

"Car theft is a built-in hazard when you drive a Mercedes."

"That's why my insurance premiums are so high," she shot back.

"Did you have an alarm system?"

"Yeah, but we didn't hear a thing."

"Who were you with last night?"

"What difference does that make?" Tiffany narrowed her blue eyes. At that moment she looked very much like her brother.

"Was it Sam Raynor?"

"You're not from the insurance company," she said flatly, light dawning. "And you're not a cop. I talked to the cops last night."

"I never said I was from the insurance company. You assumed. Assuming can get you into trouble."

Tiffany put her hands on her curvaceous hips and glared up at me. "Well, I assume you're going to tell me who you are. Then you can get the hell out of my apartment."

"Let's talk about Sam Raynor, Tiffany."

She folded her arms over the rabbits bouncing across her T-shirt. "Did my brother send you? If he did, you can tell him from me—"

"Acey didn't send me. Though we had a mutually enlightening conversation yesterday. He seems to be concerned about you."

"I don't run his life. You'd think he'd let me run mine."

"Maybe he's afraid you'll get into trouble."

"He should talk," Tiffany sneered. "Did he tell you he sent some of his biker buddies to hassle Sam? They beat him up a couple of weeks ago, and threatened to do worse

74

if he didn't stop seeing me. You tell Acey if he doesn't cut it out, his parole officer just might get a phone call."

Parole officer. My ears pricked at that. "You'd do that to your own brother?"

"Just watch me. When did you talk to him?"

"Yesterday. Right after he told you about Sam's other girlfriend."

I watched her face flush. "He made that up. Just shows what lengths he'll go to."

"You're sure about that?" Tiffany didn't answer. "So Sam doesn't know a blond woman who drives a Nissan with a Navy sticker?"

"I don't know," she said slowly, looking down at her bare feet on the beige carpet. "I asked him about it at dinner and he just laughed. He says I'm the only woman in his life."

"What about his wife? And his daughter?"

"You're working for his wife, aren't you? Well, you can just get your ass out of my apartment, right now." She marched indignantly to the door and pulled it open. "Of all the sneaky, underhanded—you tell that bitch she has a lot of nerve, after all she's put Sam through."

"What has she put Sam through?" I asked, holding my ground in the middle of the rabbit hutch.

"She walked out on him without any warning. She won't let him see their little girl. And she's trying to take him for every dime he's got."

"Sam has every right to visit Wendy," I said. "In fact, the court granted him supervised visits. California is a community property state, so Ruth is entitled to half of everything. Did Sam tell you why Ruth left?"

"She hated Guam, she hated Navy life."

"I don't know whether she hated Guam. As for Navy life, she had a whole lifetime to experience it, since she's an admiral's daughter."

"I know that. He said she was a snob, she didn't like being married to an enlisted man."

"He beat her up, Tiffany, more than once. Broken wrist, black eyes, broken nose, even a dislocated shoulder."

75

"I don't believe you," she hissed.

"I'm telling you the truth. You run the risk of getting the same kind of treatment, once the bloom's off the rose. Guys like Sam Raynor do it again and again."

"I don't believe you. He wouldn't do anything like that." Her chin tilted defiantly upward.

"You're deluding yourself, Tiffany."

Her mouth tightened and she stared at me. I caught a movement from the corner of my eye and glanced toward the hallway at the rear of the apartment. This time it was a real live bunny rabbit, a large lop-eared creature, its fur a dark rich brown. The rabbit's eyes glittered at me and its nose twitched as it slowly hopped into the living room. Tiffany knelt to scoop it into her arms. She buried her face in the rabbit's fur and made clicking noises with her tongue.

She straightened, looking at me over the rabbit's ears. "I don't believe you," she said again, but she sounded less convinced.

"Sam Raynor is using you," I told her. "He gave you the money to buy that Mercedes, didn't he?"

"What if he did?"

"He's hiding money from his wife to avoid a community property split. That makes you an accessory to fraud."

Tiffany gaped at me over the rabbit's head. The creature had tired of being cuddled. Now it kicked her in the stomach a couple of times, gently, given its powerful hindquarters, demanding to be lowered to the carpet where it could hop around on its own. Tiffany knelt and released the rabbit. Freed, nose twitching, it hopped away, toward a corner of the living room.

As Tiffany stood, I saw wheels turning in her head. I hadn't completely convinced her of Sam Raynor's venality, but I'd certainly planted a seed of doubt. Maybe if Acey and I kept watering it, the seed would sprout.

Ten

I STOPPED AT THE SAN LEANDRO POLICE DEPART-
ment for a copy of the report regarding Tiffany's stolen
Mercedes. The incident appeared to be a routine case of
auto theft. Tiffany met Sam Raynor for dinner the night before at Horatio's, near the San Leandro Marina. When they
left the restaurant at nine o'clock, the gold Mercedes was
gone. The fact that the alarm hadn't sounded indicated
some skill on the part of the car thief.

I looked up from the report, staring out my windshield as
I recalled Raynor's movements yesterday when I'd tailed
him to Tiffany's apartment. He'd left his own apartment at
five, arriving at Tiffany's place maybe twenty minutes later.
He left a note on her door, then departed. I'd hung around,
hoping to talk to Tiffany, then I'd gotten sidetracked by
Acey. When I returned to Tiffany's apartment building, I
hadn't noted the exact time, but I guessed it was about a
quarter to seven. The Mercedes wasn't there. Tiffany must
have been on her way to the restaurant.

Something nagged at the back of my mind. It was an article I'd read recently in the San Francisco *Chronicle*, about
insurance fraud. But the thrust of that article was bogus accident claims. What about that case I'd investigated a couple of years ago, over in San Mateo County? That was a
car theft scam. I tried to recall the details but they wouldn't
come. I'd have to look back through my own files.

Of course, there was always the argument that I should
give Tiffany Collins the benefit of the doubt. She seemed
legitimately upset about the theft of the car. If I'd had a

Mercedes for only a month and it had been stolen, I'd be upset too.

I leafed through the report, looking for the name of Tiffany's insurance company. It was one of the largest operating in the state of California, and I'd done some work for them earlier in the year, investigating a fraudulent accident claim. When I returned to my office, I picked up the phone and called the insurance adjuster I'd worked with on that particular case.

"Let me see who's handling that one," she said when I gave her the particulars. I was on hold for several minutes, listening to some appalling Muzak, then a man came on the line. I explained myself all over again.

"Are you telling me there's something dicey about this claim?" he asked, sounding suspicious. I wasn't sure if he was suspicious of me or if insurance adjusters were naturally wary.

"I'm not telling you anything, other than I'm curious about that Mercedes."

"To tell you the truth, so am I," the adjuster said. "The last car we insured for Ms. Collins was a Subaru hatchback. It's a big leap in premiums from that to a Mercedes. She's only had the car a month, and now it's been stolen. Drive a car like that, it's just an invitation to a rip-off."

The insurance adjuster said he'd have someone investigate the claim, but unless concrete evidence turned up indicating Tiffany had something to do with the theft of her own car, eventually the claim would be paid. He confirmed that Tiffany Collins owned the Mercedes, valued at forty-five thousand dollars.

I wrote some letters and paid a few bills. When I left my office at six, I drove through the Tube to Alameda. It was a pleasant, late August evening. The fog had not yet crept through the Golden Gate, bringing in the cool night, and the sun was still warm in the blue sky overhead. I parked my Toyota on Fourth Street and walked into the Marion Court cul-de-sac, headed for the fourth cottage on the left. There was a small red Chevy pickup parked in front, its passenger side wheels on the narrow sidewalk. On the left side of the

78

windshield I saw a red sticker denoting that the vehicle belonged to an enlisted person, the ticket for admission to the Naval Air Station.

I stepped onto the low porch, dodging the spider plant, and rang the bell. A moment later the door opened. I met the curious gaze of a man wearing brown slacks, a short-sleeved shirt, and scuffed leather sandals. He had a round fair face and short brown hair. His eyes were hazel. Older than me by a few years, I guessed, putting his age in the late thirties.

"Chief Yancy?" I asked.

"Yes," he said with a nod. "Help you with something?"

"I hope so." I introduced myself and handed him one of my business cards. "I'd like to ask you a few questions about Sam Raynor. I understand he works for you."

He turned the card over in his hand. "Yes, he does. What's this about?"

"I work for an attorney. Raynor's getting a divorce."

Yancy frowned. "I don't know if I should be talking to you."

"My questions are routine," I assured him. "We just want to confirm some information."

"Does he know you're asking questions about him?"

"I imagine he expects it," I said. If Yancy wanted to think I worked for Raynor's attorney, I was prepared to let him.

"Listen, I've got a fire to tend. Can you come out back?"

"Certainly." I stepped into a living room furnished with a lot of rattan furniture covered with flowered tropical cushions. What is it about rattan furniture and military people who've been stationed in the Pacific? They probably picked it up for a fraction of what it would cost here. The stuff was certainly lightweight and easy to move.

I followed Yancy through a small kitchen, appliances and counter on my right and an oak trestle table hugging the wall on my left. On the counter a covered glass dish held a couple of steaks marinating in reddish-brown sauce. Yancy pushed open a screen door. The backyard wasn't much bigger than the front, half filled with a makeshift patio of concrete blocks. The patio was crowded with lawn chairs, a table, and a barbecue grill which now radiated heat from the glowing coals. Yancy had left a can of beer on the table. Now he picked it up and took a swallow as he poked at the coals.

"Don't know what I can tell you about Sam," Yancy said. "I don't have any complaints about his job performance. Never have, in all the time I've known him."

"You knew him on Guam," I said, my words a statement more than a question.

"Yes, that's where I met him." Yancy set the beer down. "He didn't work for me there. We were at different commands, at NAS Agana. We played a little poker. Still do, as a matter of fact. What else can I say? Sam's a nice guy. I like him."

I heard a sound from the house. A woman appeared in the kitchen, carrying a brown paper sack which she set down on the trestle table. She began unloading the bag, pulling out romaine, bell peppers, cucumbers, celery, and a package of carrots. I watched through the screen door as she grabbed a shallow plastic colander and rinsed the vegetables, leaving them to drain in the sink. Then she turned back to the grocery sack and pulled out a bottle of salad dressing and some canned goods before she looked up and saw me on the other side of the screen door. She froze, the red label on a can of tomatoes a splash of color in her hand.

"Steve?" She set the can on the counter as she walked to the door.

"I'm out here, hon."

She pushed open the screen door and stepped out onto the patio, a slender blonde about five-foot-four. She was at least ten years younger than Yancy, maybe more, wearing shorts and a sleeveless blouse. Her straight hair was short and parted on one side, hugging her head. Her brown eyes wary, she looked me over, then darted a glance at her husband.

"This is my wife Claudia," Yancy said, putting an arm around her shoulders.

"Jeri Howard."

From what Ruth had told me, I knew Claudia Yancy was in the Navy. Both Yancys worked at the air station at Agana at the same time Sam Raynor had. As I introduced myself, I held out my hand and got a limp, noncommittal handshake in return, accompanied by a polite smile. On her right hand Claudia Yancy wore a ring with a large apple-green stone. Suddenly I recalled last week's conversation with Betty Korsakov, Ruth's neighbor on Guam. She'd told me about seeing Raynor in a jewelry store, buying just such a ring. Of course, lots of people have jade rings.

"Jeri's asking some questions about Sam Raynor."

At her husband's words, Claudia Yancy's eyes widened with alarm. Her smile disappeared. She masked it by stepping back into the kitchen, where she opened the refrigerator door. "What about Sam Raynor?" Her voice stayed steady as she pulled out a can of beer and popped the top.

I walked to the screen door and stared through the mesh, fixing the younger woman with my gaze. "How well did you know Sam Raynor when you were on Guam?"

She shrugged. "He was just another guy at the air station."

"But you weren't friends?"

She shook her head slowly behind the protective barrier of the screen door. "No. Not at all."

"Actually, Claudia's known Sam longer than I have," Steve Yancy said, turning from his grill. The heat from the coals had turned his fair face red, and I saw the shine of perspiration on his forehead. "Before we got married. We got married on Guam, two years last January. Didn't you know Sam when you were stationed at Pearl Harbor?"

"No, I didn't." Claudia bit off the words. "Whatever gave you that idea?"

"Sorry, hon," Yancy said, a placating tone in his voice. "Sam was at Pearl before Guam, and so were you."

"Pearl's a big place." Claudia had her hand clamped around the beer can as though it were a life preserver. She raised it to her lips again.

"My mistake." Yancy gazed at his wife with a smile on

his round face, obviously besotted with her. When she looked back at him, her eyes were so full of scorn I wondered at his inability to see it.

"You knew Sam better than I did," Claudia said. She saw me watching her and she hastily dropped her eyes. "After all, you guys played poker every payday."

"Yeah." The chief laughed and took another swallow of his beer. "Sam and Harlan used to clean up at those poker games. I didn't do too badly myself, though."

"You know Harlan Pettibone?" I asked. It sounded like the whole cast of characters had made the move from Guam to Alameda.

The chief laughed. "Harlan and Sam were steaming mates on Guam. He's a character."

"He's a creep," Claudia snapped. "I'm surprised they haven't thrown him out of the Navy by now."

"He's working on it," Steve said. "Couple of months ago he did some time in the brig over at Treasure Island. Something about a fight with a Marine."

"I hope the Marine beat the shit out of him." Claudia snarled the words. "I'm hungry, Steve." She set her beer down on the low table and gave me a pointed look that was meant to usher me out the door. "Are those coals ready?"

"Absolutely." Chief Yancy smiled at his wife, then at me. "Hope we were able to give you what you need, informationwise."

"You've been very helpful." I spotted a gate at the side of the house, leading to the narrow passage that separated it from the next cottage. "I'll let myself out."

I walked back to the street. A car was parked in front of the red pickup, a car that hadn't been there when I arrived. It was a cranberry-colored Nissan sedan, a red base sticker on the windshield, just like the car Acey Collins saw last week when Sam Raynor met a woman near the boathouse at Lake Merritt. A blonde, he said, in the backseat with Raynor, and they'd been doing more than talking.

Sam's taste evidently ran to short blondes, and Claudia Yancy certainly fit that description. Was her affair with Sam of recent vintage, or a replay of something that began when they were stationed on Guam, or even as far back as Pearl Harbor?

Whatever its duration, her husband would be the last to know. And how would Steve Yancy react when he found out? Would he suffer quietly—or explode?

Eleven

"ARNOLD CLAUDE COLLINS," ANGIE WALTERS SAID when I picked up the phone late the next morning.

"Known to all and sundry as Acey?" I knew from Tiffany's comment about her brother's parole officer that Acey must have a record, but I'd been waiting for Angie to get back to me with details. I'd figured it could take a while since Angie wasn't supposed to be feeding me information. She did it anyway, for reasons of her own.

"Thirty-six years old," Angie continued in her trademark raspy voice. "He's got a sheet going back fifteen years. He used to ride with a motorcycle gang but he's been out of circulation for a while, owing to a recent stretch at Folsom."

"What was he in for?"

"Receiving stolen property. Plea-bargained, sentenced to three years. Got out in two. He's on parole."

"Who's his parole officer? Do you have an address for Collins?" Angie gave me the name and two addresses.

Acey worked as a mechanic—that much I'd guessed from the condition of his hands. Both addresses were in North Oakland. The garage was located on Telegraph Avenue near the MacArthur BART station, and Acey's residence was in the Temescal neighborhood, on Miles Avenue near Forty-ninth Street. It was just after noon when I visited the garage. I didn't see the car Acey said he was selling for his sister, but I supposed that now that the Mercedes had been stolen, Tiffany would need her Subaru.

A man in oil-stained coveralls told me Acey was on his lunch break. Had Acey gone home? It was a possibility, since he lived nearby. I headed for Miles Avenue, expecting an apartment building. Instead I found a small Victorian house, painted blue with gray trim, its window boxes full of geraniums, and a bird feeder hanging from the eaves of the porch.

I parked at the curb, got out of my Toyota and looked at the house, one story built high off the ground, with a garage tucked underneath. I didn't see the Harley, but an old bronze Plymouth with California plates sat in the driveway. The lawn had been replaced by drought-resistant foliage surrounded by redwood chips.

If the flowers and the bird feeder weren't enough to intrigue me, the sound effects certainly were. Rachmaninoff's Second Piano Concerto poured through the open screen door, the volume turned up to an ear-splitting level. I climbed the steps leading to the front porch and spotted a bell to the right of the door. I pushed it, but the music was so loud it drowned out the buzzer, if that worked at all. I peered through the screen door and saw shelves on the right-hand wall, holding a stereo system and a television set.

I pounded on the door and shouted a greeting. "Hello? Anybody home?"

A woman appeared from the back of the house and saw me at the door. She picked up a small rectangle, aimed it at the shelves, and the music stopped abruptly. Compact disc remote, I realized.

"You like Rachmaninoff," I said.

"I like piano music."

She spoke in a crisp no-nonsense voice, hands on her hips as she walked up to the screen door. She was a slender woman, her long hair a straight shiny curtain down her back and shoulders, its dark brown strands touched here and there with silver. She wore black jeans, black espadrilles, and a white eyelet cotton blouse, its tail tucked into the waistband of the jeans. Gold hoops glinted in her ears. I looked at her left hand and didn't see a wedding band.

"If you're selling something, I'm not buying," she said.

"I'm looking for Acey Collins."

A pair of sharp brown eyes bored directly into mine. "Why? Who're you?"

"Jeri Howard. I need to talk with him about his sister Tiffany."

"The private investigator," she said. "He told me about you. He's not here."

"Are you Mrs. Collins?" I asked. She nodded. "May I talk with you, then?"

She thought about it for a moment, then unlocked the screen door. "My name's Genevieve. People call me Gen. We can talk for a little while. Then I've got errands to run."

The first thing I saw when I stepped into the Collins's living room was an old upright piano, its wood scarred and its ivory keys yellowed and chipped. A stack of sheet music was piled on top, and a backless stool was tucked under the keyboard. The piano stood against the wall opposite the front door, to the left of an open doorway leading to the back of the house. I walked over and played a scale. As far as I could tell, the piano was in tune.

"Do you play?" I asked.

"A little. Blues and boogie-woogie."

"And Mozart." I glanced at the sheet music on the top of the stack and saw the composer's name.

"Blues I can handle." She smiled. "Mozart's a challenge. Look, you didn't come here to talk about piano music. What's on your mind?"

I turned and looked around the room. Genevieve Collins was a casual housekeeper, but so was I. The place wasn't dirty, it was just cluttered, the kind of clutter that accumulates with day-to-day life and busy schedules, too many things and not enough places to put them. Some children's toys, a stuffed bear and a doll, had been discarded on the seat of the rocking recliner chair that stood near the front window. Books were stacked haphazardly on a low book-case under the window, as well as here and there on the shelves that held record albums, CDs, and audiotapes. The VCR rested on top of the TV set, and I saw a couple of videotapes as well.

Genevieve took the CD out of the player and replaced it in its case, then turned off the unit. She crossed the room to the old sofa. It was long with a high back, upholstered in a harvest print of squash, pumpkin, and ears of corn spilling from a cornucopia, its rust and brown and yellow fabric worn and scratched at the bottom, as though a cat had been sharpening its claws there. A crocheted afghan in the same fall colors was folded lengthwise and lay across the top of the sofa. Genevieve sat down on the sofa and be-gan straightening the magazines strewn atop the rattan chest that served as a coffee table. I pulled out the piano stool, its leg catching on the edge of the brown-and-gold-patterned rug that covered the hardwood floor. I righted the stool and sat down.

"How long have you and Acey been together?"

"Fifteen years. Married twelve. We've had our ups and downs and two kids." She looked up from the magazines. "I thought you came to talk about Tiffany."

"So tell me about Tiffany."

Genevieve didn't say anything for a moment, then she sighed. "She's the baby sister, Acey's the oldest. There's two other boys in between. One's in the Army, the other's in jail."

"Acey did some time too."

"He was set up," she snapped, the glare from her eyes hard and narrow. She didn't ask me how I knew about Acey's prison record. "Look, he stays out of trouble. We're doing all right. He's got a good job as a mechanic. He comes home every night and stays with the kids while I work nights, waiting tables. He hands me his paycheck ev-ery week and I pay the bills. We even manage to put a little money away. On weekends he gets together with his bud-dies and raises a little hell. But he stays out of trouble, because he doesn't want to go back to the joint. So don't hold that against him."

"I'm not," I said.

"Well, a lot of people do. It grinds my gears. What has this got to do with Tiffany anyway?"

"When I talked with Acey a few days ago, he made some threats against Sam Raynor."

"So Acey doesn't like Tiffany's boyfriend. I met the guy. Believe me, he's no prize."

"Raynor got roughed up a couple of weeks ago over in Alameda. Two bikers grabbed him in a parking lot outside a club on Webster Street and slapped him around. Raynor wound up with a black eye, but they could have hurt him worse. I think the whole incident was designed to get his attention."

Genevieve's mouth twisted into a bitter smile. She sat back on the sofa, crossed her legs, and folded her arms over her chest, her head tilted to one side as she challenged me. "And you figure Acey had something to do with it. Just because he's a biker and rides a Harley."

"I think it's a logical assumption. It's not because Acey's a biker. When I talked with him the other day, he seemed genuinely concerned about his sister. When it comes to protecting his family, who knows?"

Now she frowned and shook her head, the fingers of her right hand toying with one gold earring. "Acey's got a blind spot where Tiffany's concerned," she admitted. "Ever since they were kids, he gets into this big brother number. He thinks he's got to protect her all the time. I keep telling him she's a grown woman. She's twenty-five, been out on her own since she was eighteen. Tiff does all right. She's just independent."

Headstrong was the word I would have used to describe Tiffany Collins. I tempered my words, appealing to Genevieve to look at another side. "Sometimes the wrong kind of guy can turn a woman's head. Even a sensible woman who can take care of herself. Did Acey tell you why I'm investigating Raynor?"

Genevieve nodded. "He said Sam's in the middle of a divorce and he's hiding some money from the wife. He also said Sam beat up on his wife. Tiffany wouldn't put up with that. She's got too much self-respect."

"Are you sure? You said Acey has a blind spot where his sister is concerned. What if Tiffany has a blind spot and can't see Sam Raynor for what he is? I'm sure his wife didn't, at first. I'll bet if I dig deep enough, I'll find some past girlfriends with bruises. Guys who beat up the women in their lives have a pattern. It's easy to get fooled. Acey said himself he's afraid Raynor has Tiffany mesmerized. Raynor's smooth, he talks a good line. He buys Tiffany presents, takes her out to dinner. He's free with the money that he's not supposed to have. I'll bet he even had something to do with buying that Mercedes."

"That's what Acey thinks." Genevieve's frown had deepened while I talked. "Tiffany said it was her money, but she was really vague about whether it was her own savings or if she'd taken out a loan. I guess Sam actually found the car and negotiated the deal. According to Tiff, Sam picked up the car for a song, because it was several years old and needed some work. Acey checked it out, though. He said it was in good shape."

"A used Mercedes is still worth a lot of money. I'd like to know where Sam Raynor found this bargain. Did he or Tiffany happen to mention that?" She shook her head. "Is she the type to save for a rainy day?"

"She's the type to hit Nordstrom and blow a week's salary on clothes. And bunnies." Genevieve smiled as she spoke of Tiffany's penchant for rabbits. Then her face grew serious again. She shifted on the sofa, recrossing her legs. "When Acey and the other kids were growing up, they were dirt-poor, didn't have much. I think that's why Tiff spends money on herself. She's gotta have all those pretty things she didn't have when she was little."

"Does she just have her civil service salary?" I asked. "Where would she come up with the kind of money it takes to buy a Mercedes, even a used one?"

Genevieve leaned forward and tapped one finger against her knee. "When Acey's mom died last year, there was some insurance money. All four of the kids got a share. It was a good chunk of cash. Acey and I locked his share up in an IRA. I don't know what Tiff did with hers. I kept talking IRAs, but you can't preach to someone that age about retirement. They think they're gonna live forever. Tiff talked about buying a condo. Then she turned up with this flashy car that cost a bundle. I think that's why Acey was upset with her. Why put all that money into a car when she could have used it for a down payment and closing costs?"

"You know the Mercedes was stolen night before last?"

"Yeah." Genevieve shook her head. "Tiff called here yesterday. She was pissed, at the cops, the insurance company—and you. You were there in the afternoon, asking questions. She had to take BART up here to Oakland last night to get the Subaru, so she'd have something to drive. Good thing Acey hadn't sold it yet."

"Tiffany barely had the Mercedes long enough to register it," I said. "Now the insurance company is going to have to pay off a fairly large sum of money. It doesn't set right."

Genevieve stared at me, brown eyebrows raised over her dark eyes. "You think Sam had something to do with stealing the car," she said. "How do you figure?"

"I haven't yet. But this whole situation with the missing Mercedes is a little too ripe for my nose. I've done some work for insurance adjusters over the years. That means I've seen a scam or two. This reminds me of one I encountered a couple of years ago. Let me speculate for a moment."

I paused, gathered my thoughts. "Raynor has money he wants to hide from his wife, so he doesn't have to share it as community property. He claims he has nothing except his Navy salary. That's where I come in, to find the money. I look at Raynor's friends and see he's spending a lot on Tiffany. I think he gave her the money to buy that car."

"I can't believe she'd go along with it."

"She would if he's got her convinced she's doing him a favor. Sam goes to Tiffany with some song and dance about his horrible wife trying to take everything he's got. Can he stash some money with Tiffany, in her name, in her bank account? But that might be too obvious, considering everyone knows he's dating her. So he says, let's buy this expensive car and put it in your name. That makes it more difficult to trace. Sam buys the car, Tiffany registers and insures it, and lo and behold, the car gets stolen. When Tiffany gets that insurance check, she banks it, holds it until Sam's divorce is final, then gives the money back. It's no longer community property. There's a kicker to this particular scenario. Suppose Sam stole the car himself, or arranged to have it stolen? He sells it back to whoever he bought it from, and gets paid off twice."

Genevieve looked alarmed. "You think Tiffany's involved in this?"

"I hope not. If she is, it's more than just bad judgment. It's fraud." Genevieve frowned. She hadn't considered that possibility. "Look, when I talked to Tiffany, she appeared to be genuinely upset about the car. I don't think she knows anything about how it was stolen. But it's just too convenient for that Mercedes to disappear a month after she supposedly bought it. It makes me very suspicious."

We were both silent for a moment. My fingers stroked a couple of piano keys, the notes sounding in the room. Then I heard children's voices and the thump of feet on the front steps. The screen door opened and two children entered, both with Acey's dark blond hair and Genevieve's brown eyes. The younger was a little girl, about eight, scuffed knees showing under her denim shorts and pink shirt. The boy was ten or eleven, dressed in faded dusty jeans and a T-shirt decorated with dinosaurs in neon greens and yellows. School hadn't started yet, and the kids had a tousled, grubby look that indicated they were wringing the last few days of freedom and pleasure out of the summer.

When they saw me sitting on the piano stool, the children stopped their chatter and looked me over with curious eyes. "Are we gonna go shopping for school clothes?" the boy asked his mother.

"Yes, we are." Genevieve uncrossed her legs and rose from the sofa in one quick movement. "Find those library books. They're due today." As the children headed for the

90

rear of the house, she turned to me. "I can't talk anymore. I've got errands to run and I have to be at work at six."

"If you have anything to add, call me." I gave her one of my business cards.

Outside, I sidestepped two bicycles, both with shiny red paint scuffed and scratched with use, which lay against the front steps. "Put those bikes away before we leave," I heard Genevieve say as I walked to my car.

Twelve

A NAVY CHIEF ONCE TOLD ME EVERY TOWN WITH A Navy base has a "Hey, Joe Boulevard," a street full of businesses catering to the transient population of sailors in search of food, liquor, tattoos, and entertainment. Sometimes the kind of entertainment sought by sailors is not the sort sanctioned by the Navy or the local police department, but that sort thrives nevertheless. There are always consumers and suppliers, whether the desired commodity is flesh or some other substance.

Webster Street is West Alameda's shopping district, with banks, stores and restaurants, its length punctuated by AC Transit bus stops that link the island city to Oakland. Webster Street is also Alameda's "Hey, Joe Boulevard," though not to the degree you'd find in San Diego or Pearl Harbor. The Navy's presence in Alameda is smaller, but of long duration. So the street has its share of tattoo parlors, fast food joints, and funky bars full of young men whose hair is so short they are obviously members of Uncle Sam's yacht club.

Time to stir the pot, I decided Thursday afternoon. I had several leads concerning Sam Raynor's money. One was

91

Tiffany, whose stolen Mercedes would account for about a third of the money. Then there were the Yancys, Steve and Claudia. I had originally targeted Steve Yancy because of the Friday night poker games, thinking Raynor may have hidden money disguised as gambling debts. But my visit to their cottage had netted other, more interesting possibilities. Claudia Yancy was evidently having an affair with Sam Raynor. Two girlfriends, two places to stash the cash. All these people were pressure points. If Raynor had hidden his money with them, I could put pressure on Raynor through his friends.

It was time I met Raynor's roommate, Harlan Pettibone. I wasn't sure how I'd handle the encounter. What did I know about him? Duffy LeBard had described Pettibone as an obnoxious little squirt who liked to get drunk and fight. Claudia Yancy said he was a creep. Mrs. Torelli, Pettibone's landlady, said he liked to play pool, that he even had a custom-made cue. And he drove an orange Chevy Camaro—the tigermobile. He was consistently late with his rent, which indicated a certain lack of fiscal responsibility. Would Sam Raynor trust a large sum of money to a guy like that?

I circled by the apartment building on Pacific Street, but neither Raynor's Trans-Am nor Pettibone's Camaro were there. Then I cruised Webster Street, looking for an orange car with black trim, tiger-striped upholstery, decorated with stuffed tigers. It would be hard to miss such a vehicle, but I didn't see it on my first pass of Webster, or on any of the side streets feeding into the main drag. It was now late afternoon, coming-home time, and the streets were clogged with cars crawling from red light to red light. Slow-moving buses disgorged passengers and diesel fumes.

I was making little progress on wheels so I switched to shoe leather. I walked up one side of Webster and down the other, peering into doorways. Commuters picked up their laundry or bought take-out suppers at one of the restaurants along the street. In the bars, serious drinkers were getting a head start on the evening. The post office branch and the banks all had lines of last-minute customers. I saw plenty of sailors in civilian clothes, doing a variety of things at a variety of establishments, but Harlan Pettibone was not among them.

I didn't find him in any of the bars either, as I hunted through them, my eyes smarting from the smoke and the adjustment from bright daylight to dim interior. I received a number of invitations and lots of whistles. The smoke level in the bars brought on a headache. Finally I stood on a corner waiting for a green light, as passengers got off a dirty blue-and-white AC Transit bus. According to my watch, I'd been lurking around Webster Street for over an hour, and still hadn't located Pettibone. The bus roared off just as the light turned green, and at the opposite curb I spotted a bright orange car.

I hurried across the street and gave the vehicle a quick once-over. It was a late model Camaro, with Texas plates and a Naval Air Station Alameda sticker on the front windshield. I glanced inside and saw the garish tiger-striped seat covers Mrs. Torelli had described, as well as two plush tigers, the smaller hanging by a cord from the rearview mirror and a larger one upside down, affixed to the rear windshield by suction-cup feet.

The closest bar was on the corner. I'd already checked it out, maybe half an hour ago, but this time when I looked in the open doorway, I saw a short skinny sailor with an odd-looking nose. He had to be Harlan Pettibone. He wore baggy black jeans and black high-top sneakers with orange laces. His orange shirt was unbuttoned halfway down his pale hairless chest, and a gold chain decorated his neck. Under his white-blond short-back-and-sides haircut, he had a narrow rabbity face that was so fair he looked as though he'd burn to the second degree if he spent more than five minutes in the sun.

Pettibone was holding court at the far side of the pool table, his fancy cue in one hand and a bottle of Lone Star beer in the other. The jukebox was at maximum decibel, as Waylon Jennings growled a chorus of "Ramblin' Man." Pettibone laughed and shouted over the music, playing jester to a group of friends, all white guys in their early

93

twenties. They looked and sounded as though they were cut from the same bolt of Southern cloth, a bunch of cocky redneck peckerwoods. I took a deep breath of unpolluted air and walked into the bar, zeroing in on my quarry.

Pettibone's funny nose was truly a marvel. Spackled with freckles, it slanted to the left, then the tip veered off to the right. I decided he was cute in an ugly kind of way. He thought so too. When I stood in front of him, he looked me up and down with a pair of milky blue eyes screened by long sandy lashes. He greeted me with a lascivious grin and a Texas twang.

"Where you been all my life, Big Mama?"

The things I have to put up with. I couldn't decide whether I wanted to smack him or laugh down in his face. Instead I opted to follow his lead. I narrowed my eyes, tilting my aching head.

"I've been around." Disparagement flavored my words. "A lot longer than you. You're a little young for me."

Pettibone sidled closer and winked at me. "Honey, I like my women experienced."

I put my hands on my hips. "At what? Babysitting?"

He roared with laughter. So did his pool-playing buddies. "You got a mouth on you. Is it good for anything but talk?"

"Let's talk first. Then you might find out."

He laughed again. "What are you drinking?"

"Lone Star's fine with me," I said, indicating the bottle he held. While he paid for the beer, I spotted a small table at the rear of the bar, far enough from the jukebox to make conversation possible. I pulled out a chair as Waylon gave way to Willie Nelson. Pettibone plunked the Lone Star down on the table, pulled the other chair and sat down, his knee rubbing mine.

"So what's your name, honey?" He threw his left arm over the back of my chair, his hand massaging my shoulder. He leaned forward with what passed for a flirtatious look on his ugly little face.

I raised the cold beer bottle to my lips and took a long swallow. It tasted good after the time I'd spent scouring

Webster Street, looking for Pettibone. I unfastened the top button of my shirt and ran the frosted brown glass over my perspiring neck.

"Jeri," I said, lowering the bottle. "What's yours?"

"You can just call me Tiger," he purred, his blue eyes staring at my cleavage. He moved a little closer and his right hand reached for mine, stroking my wrist.

"Big talk for a little guy," I said with a downward sideways glance. Even seated, I was taller than he was. "Are you sure it's not Pussycat?"

He leered at me and pressed his leg against mine. "Honey, I just love pussy . . . cats."

"Your name is Harlan T. Pettibone." My voice cooled as I straightened, moving his arm off the chair back.

"How did you know that?" All of a sudden he looked wary instead of horny.

"Word gets around, Harlan. So the T stands for Tiger. I thought maybe it meant Texas."

"Sometimes it does. Did you come looking for me, honey? For a reason?"

"Sure did, Harlan. Only it's not the reason you think."

He shrugged, all hormones and ego, and stretched out his legs. Then he stuck a thumb in his belt, just to the right of his buckle, and let his fingers brush his fly.

"You think I'm too short for you? Honey, I got the inches where they really count. Stick around and I might let you play with 'em. You don't know what you're missin'."

"I know what I'm missing, Harlan." I leaned forward and my voice turned cold. "Ten thousand bucks. Sam Raynor owes me that money, plus interest. When I go to collect, he tells me to talk to you."

Harlan T for Tiger Pettibone proceeded to tap dance, but not very well, considering he was still sprawled in his chair waving his crotch at me. "What the fuck you talking about?" He cocked his head and furrowed his smooth brow. "Do I know anybody named Sam?"

"Harlan, don't bullshit me. You sure as hell live with him. Over on Pacific Street. Now when do I get my money? He's owed it to me since he moved here from Guam. I'm damn tired of this runaround."

Harlan straightened in his chair, all interest in sex wiped off his face. "Hey, I got nothing to do with this. You say Sam owes you money, you'll have to take that up with him."

"I already have. He claims he doesn't have any. Pretty damn convenient, since he used to be so flush on Guam. He's lying through his teeth, and I bet you are too. You must be holding some of it for him."

"Me?" Harlan looked outraged. "I'm just scraping by payday to payday, same as Sam. If he says he ain't got the dough, he ain't got it."

"Oh, yeah, sure." I slapped the table with the palm of my hand. Harlan jumped. I waved an emphatic index finger under his skewed nose. "You lying sons of bitches. Both of you. I can see what's going down here. Sam hid that cash somewhere and now he'll even deny he knows me. Well, if I don't know him, how do I know so much about him? You tell Sam he'd better ante up that money. What he got over in the parking lot at Nadine's was just a taste of what I can deliver."

I got to my feet and leaned over Harlan, menace in my voice. "If I don't get my money, I'm gonna be all over you two assholes, like fleas on a dog."

I turned and strode quickly out of the bar, adrenaline pumping, sucking in the relatively unpolluted air out on Webster Street. Then I headed for my car. If that didn't stir the pot, nothing would, I thought as I unlocked the door and slipped into the driver's seat. Maybe I'd laid it on a bit thick, but I'd certainly gotten Harlan's attention.

As it happened, I got Sam Raynor's attention too. I don't know how he got my name and office number, but somehow I wasn't surprised Friday morning when I picked up the phone and heard his voice crackle over the wire.

"This is Sam Raynor. We need to talk."

Play . . .

Thirteen

AFTER SAM RAYNOR STALKED AWAY FROM ME FRIDAY afternoon, I returned to my office, replaying our confrontation as I finished some paperwork and straightened my cluttered desk. I'd pared down my workload in anticipation of my upcoming trip to Monterey, now just a week away. My calendar was clear of all save routine matters—and one case, Ruth's case.

I tried to separate the antipathy I felt for Raynor from the frustrating facts of the case. Despite rattling cages and digging for information, I was no closer to finding the money than when I started. I had many possibilities but no definite answers. Raynor had hidden his tracks well.

Each time I thought of Raynor, I saw his contorted face and heard his voice, hissing obscenities at me. How could a woman like Ruth marry such a dangerous, violent man? Then I recalled Acey Collins's description of a snake mesmerizing a rabbit.

At four I locked my office and headed for the stairwell, reaching it as the elevator door opened. Cassie stepped out, wearing a crisp mauve linen suit, her briefcase at her side. "Are you taking what Alex would call a meritorious afternoon off?" she asked with a smile.

I shook my head as I took her place in the elevator, holding the door open. "I have to talk with a client. Anyway, it's too hot to be cooped up in my office. At least yours is air-conditioned."

"That's more than I can say for the courtroom I was in today. Don't forget dinner tomorrow night. Seven o'clock at my place. You're bringing Alex and the wine."

I drove to Forty-first and Howe, where Ruth lived in a three-story security building on the corner, close to her new job at Kaiser Hospital. It was a great setup for her, since she had yet to buy a car. She had a two-block walk in one direction to work, and Wendy's day care center was nearby, as were the grocery store and other shops on Piedmont Avenue.

When I checked the tenant list outside the double glass doors, I saw that Ruth had put Franklin opposite the buzzer for her apartment, number 303. A necessary precaution, like the security building and the stay-away order. Sam wasn't supposed to know where she lived. The only time he saw Wendy was during the court-ordered supervised visits at the Franklins' home in Alameda. He saw Ruth in court.

She wasn't home yet, so I waited for her, sitting on the edge of a low concrete planter full of bright red-orange marigolds, the afternoon sun making me warm and sleepy. The Friday afternoon procession began, as people returned from work or zeroed in on Piedmont Avenue, a block away. This Oakland neighborhood was always lively, drawing customers to its shops, restaurants or other amusements, such as the Piedmont Cinema. A bus stopped on Piedmont, then moved on, leaving a handful of shoppers in casual dress, men and women in work attire, and teenagers wearing whatever was de rigueur this summer. Walking briskly toward me was a woman in the uniform of the commuter, gray pinstriped suit with socks and sneakers, briefcase in one hand and an I. Magnin shopping bag in the other. As she strode quickly across Howe Street, walking up Forty-first, she passed a commuter of a different sort.

This second woman wore the uniform I'd seen all too often these days, the attire and accessories of the homeless. A shapeless blue dress, several sizes too big, hung loosely on her bony frame. Over this was a baggy green cardigan sweater. Like the first commuter, she wore socks and sneakers, but the elastic in the cuffs had stretched, causing the socks to slip down around her ankles. The shoes had once been blue and white, but now they were gray with dirt and sported a hole in one toe. The woman's hair was covered by a wide-brimmed straw hat with a pink sash tied under her pointed chin, a bedraggled pink cloth rose decorating the front brim.

The woman in the gray suit gave the homeless woman a wide berth and a troubled look, stepping past the grocery store shopping cart that was full of the second woman's possessions. In the cart I saw a green sleeping bag, rolled up and tied with a length of rope, a blue nylon tote bag, a large black plastic trash bag, and a wooden dowel about three feet in length, a nail affixed to the end. I'd seen homeless people use similar tools to probe refuse containers for cans and bottles to sell at the local recycling centers. But I hadn't seen many in this neighborhood. The homeless were more visible downtown.

As she approached the corner, the homeless woman stared at me from under the brim of her straw hat. The eyes that skewed my way were younger and sharper than I'd expected. I felt a chill of realization preceded by the phrase, "There but for the grace of God . . ."

She was humming, an aimless little melody punctuated by a whispered dialogue with herself. She pushed the shopping cart down the shallow curb cut at the corner and walked directly into the path of a car that had made a running stop and was now attempting to turn right. The driver yelled at her but the woman ignored him as though he were an insect buzzing around her hat.

She continued her ragged diagonal progress until she reached the opposite corner, pushing her cart up the curb cut from street to sidewalk, then onto the uneven dirt surface of a lot that wouldn't be vacant for long, judging from the construction equipment and the pile of building materials on the site. Did she sleep there? Bushes along one property border offered limited shelter. As I watched I wondered what had brought her to this life. What separated her from the commuter in suit and sneakers? Or Ruth, starting over? Or me, self-employed, stretching my income to cover rent, health insurance, car payments, and other expenses? Sometimes I think life is a big poker game. Some people get a full house and others have to fold. Mostly we just break even.

My eyes left the homeless woman and I saw Ruth walking toward me. She waved as she crossed the street, reaching into her shoulder bag for her keys. She unlocked one of the glass doors that led to the paneled foyer of her building. I followed her and waited while she checked her mailbox. "I must be on every mailing list in the world," she said, sifting through an array of junk mail before netting one bill. "And I haven't lived here that long."

"We need to talk," I said, echoing Sam Raynor's words.

"Sure. Do you mind if we do it on the fly? I have to change clothes and pick up Wendy."

Ruth's third floor unit was directly opposite the elevator, fronting on an open area about ten feet square. As we stepped out of the car, the doors to units 301 and 302 were on the left. Immediately to the right of the elevator a short hallway led back to a trash chute and the stairs, which were behind the elevator shaft. Beyond that hallway a door opened onto a narrow laundry room. As we reached Ruth's door I looked to the right and saw a longer corridor with doors on both sides, leading to the rear of the building. An elderly woman wearing a bright pink sweat suit emerged from the first apartment on the right side of this hallway, carrying an empty plastic basket, her apparent objective the laundry room.

"Hello, Mrs. Parmenter," Ruth said as she opened her door.

"How are you, dear?" the neighbor said with a smile and a sharp look at me. I had a feeling she didn't miss much. "Where is little Wendy?"

"I'm going to pick her up in just a few minutes."

I followed Ruth into her apartment. "That's Mrs. Parmenter," Ruth said with a low chuckle. "She's lived here forever and she snoops. She knows everything about everyone. Or so I would guess from talking with her."

Ruth's new home was a one-bedroom unit, all she could afford right now. Through the bedroom door I glimpsed a set of twin beds covered with matching flowered comforters. While Ruth changed out of her work clothes, I explored. It was a typical generic apartment, with medium-brown carpet to go with the plain white walls. A small walk-through kitchen with beige linoleum and countertops led to a dining area furnished with a round table and four chairs. The living room's only source of light was a sliding glass door opening onto a tiny balcony that overlooked Forty-first Street. The room seemed bare compared to my own cluttered apartment. The furniture looked new, basic and inexpensive. A plain brown sofa was enlivened with colorful toss pillows. Beyond the sofa I saw a low bookshelf holding a portable CD player and a few compact discs, as well as some books. Along the opposite wall was an oak rocking chair with a blue-flowered cushion and a low wooden cart with wheels and two shelves, holding TV and VCR.

"Not much, but it's home," Ruth said, joining me in the living room. She wore a loose-fitting pair of red cotton slacks with a blue shirt, her feet in a pair of red canvas shoes.

"It all looks new," I said.

"It is. Recently bought, or borrowed from Mom and Dad. When I left Guam, I didn't want to tip Sam off that I was leaving him, so I didn't pack much besides clothes and linens and a few personal things, like photo albums and Wendy's favorite doll. I had to leave all my kitchen stuff and furniture in the household goods shipment, which is in storage someplace. I hope I can get some of it back when we settle this."

"It'll be over soon," I told her.

"Not soon enough." We left the apartment. Ruth hit the button on the elevator, then she turned and said, "Let's take the stairs. This elevator is so pokey."

We detoured down the abbreviated corridor, pushed open the metal fire door and started down, our footsteps echoing on the concrete steps and walls of the stairwell. At the bottom another fire door opened onto the building lobby, just a few steps from the glass doors we'd entered earlier. As we crossed Howe Street, walking along Forty-first toward

Piedmont Avenue, I glanced across the street and saw the straw-hatted homeless woman with her cart and her probe, foraging through a garbage Dumpster behind the block of shops that fronted on this section of Piedmont.

"Poor thing," Ruth said, following the direction of my eyes. "I see her around here all the time. I think she lives in that lot across from me. I even left some food for her once, just like you'd leave food for a stray cat."

Talking about the homeless woman made me feel uncomfortable. Abruptly I moved the conversation to another equally disturbing subject. "Sam called me this morning. He wanted to talk, so I had the dubious pleasure of meeting him on his lunch hour."

Ruth stopped, her face alarmed. "Oh, no. He knows I've hired a private detective."

"He was bound to find out. I've been questioning his friends. No doubt one of them told him."

Ruth clutched her shoulder bag to her side and started walking again, frowning as she stared ahead of her. "Now that he knows I'm looking for the money, it will be harder to find."

She sounded so grim I tapped her on the shoulder and gave her a wide smile when she looked up at me. "Hey, I like to think I'm smarter than he is."

She smiled back. "You're right. I should have confidence in you. Mom does."

Never mind Dad, I thought, visualizing the Admiral's stern face. "It's not as though Sam's got a Swiss bank account. He's not in that league. I'm sure he's given it to friends, disguised as loans or gifts. If I can just prove it."

We waited for the light at Piedmont Avenue. It turned green and we stepped out into the crosswalk. "With everything I've found out about Sam," I said, "and after finally meeting him, I have a little trouble understanding how you wound up with him in the first place."

Ruth didn't answer until we reached the sidewalk on the other side of Piedmont. "Sometimes I wonder myself." She slowed, hand playing with the strap of her bag. "I've tried to make sense of it over the past few months. There are lots of reasons. You want to hear them all?"

"Just give me a history lesson."

"How far back?" she asked, glancing at our reflections in a store window.

"After you left home."

Ruth looked at her watch. "I guess Wendy can stay at day care a while longer. This is a long story. I don't want her to hear any of it."

We detoured to Peet's Coffee, the smell of freshly ground beans wafting out the open door. Inside, Ruth ordered a cappuccino and I asked for a caffe latte. Someone had vacated a couple of stools at the far end of the chest-high counter that ran across the front window, so we grabbed them.

Ruth sipped her cappuccino for a few minutes before she started talking. "I went to college at Parkville, Missouri. That's a small liberal arts school in a little town on the Missouri River near Kansas City. Mom and Dad are originally from Kansas City and we've still got relatives back there. After I graduated, I taught first grade in a suburb of K.C., for three years." She sighed and was silent for a while, as I inspected the layers of foamy milk in my latte.

"I was engaged. We were planning a big June wedding. A month before the wedding, he decided he wasn't ready for marriage. I heard later he'd met someone else. It really hurt. I was numb. I guess that's how I managed to make it through the rest of the school term, canceling all the wedding plans and returning wedding gifts." Ruth sighed and bit her lip.

"After I took care of all those things, the summer just loomed at me, like some big void. I was so depressed I quit my job and gave up my apartment. I couldn't bear the thought of staying in Kansas City. Mom and Dad lived in Alexandria, Virginia, then. Dad was in his last tour, at the Pentagon. I didn't want to go there. I didn't want to be with my parents. So I called my brother. Kevin was stationed at Pearl Harbor then, and he had a two-bedroom condo in Pearl City. He said I could stay as long as I wanted. I went to Hawaii. The plan was to spend a couple of months relaxing, seeing the islands, then maybe look for a job there. That's where I met Sam."

Vulnerable and on the rebound, I thought, looking at the fragile woman next to me. Sam Raynor must have circled her like a shark smelling blood in the water.

"I dated a few of Kevin's friends, young officers, all fairly respectful and nonthreatening. Then one afternoon I was at Waimea Falls on the north side of Oahu. It's very beautiful and peaceful. I was sitting by myself on a bench, looking at the gorgeous tropical flowers and listening to the waterfall. Suddenly Sam walked up and introduced himself. Sam's very charming when he wants to be. And I guess I was ready to be swept off my feet."

Ruth looked at me, brown eyes full of pain. "If I sound as though I have any insight into this, it's because I've had a lot of time to think about it over the past four years, wondering how I ever got myself into this mess. I've been going to a therapy group for battered women. Blair suggested it."

"I hope it helps," I said.

Ruth nodded. "It is helping. I'm finding out some things about myself . . . well, I won't go into that. I realize now that when I went to Hawaii, I was looking for excitement and romance. Sam provided that."

She took a sip from her cup, and her mouth twisted into a bitter smile. "We went for moonlight swims on the beach. Just like Burt Lancaster and Deborah Kerr in *From Here to Eternity.* I guess Sam saw the same movies I did."

"We all need a little romance. But why did you marry him?"

"I got pregnant, Jeri." Ruth laughed and shook her head, but there wasn't any humor in her words. Her pale face reddened and she lowered her voice.

"In this age of contraception and AIDS, I climbed into bed with Sam and didn't use any birth control. I wasn't taking pills because they caused breakthrough bleeding and messed up my cycle. Of course Sam never uses anything. He trots out that line about how condoms dull the sensation and don't feel as good. And diaphragms—well, you've got to stop in mid-embrace and go put the damn thing in. Creams and gels are so messy." Her voice roughened. "All that pillow talk about loving me and wanting to feel himself inside me. And I went along with it. Two months later I missed my period."

"You didn't have to marry him. You had other options."

"I'm the good little girl who always does the right thing." Ruth set down her cup and stared through the window. "By the time I realized I was pregnant, I was in love with Sam, or thought I was. And he wanted to get married. If he hadn't, I might have considered an abortion, though I've always been ambivalent about that. I wanted children. When I told Sam about the baby, I really thought he'd run the other way. But he surprised me and said, let's get married. So we did, a small wedding in the base chapel. Mom and Dad flew out for the ceremony."

"How did your family react?"

"Kevin was supportive. My parents are very traditional, of course. Mom was prepared to make the best of what she perceived to be a bad situation. That's the way she is. I know she was upset that I was pregnant, but she figured getting married was best for all concerned. Now Dad . . ." Ruth shook her head.

"Dad hated Sam from the start. I thought he was angry because I was marrying an enlisted man instead of an officer. I know that was part of it. Those things are important to my father. Now I know Dad realized what Sam was. But he didn't try to stop me from marrying Sam. There was the baby to consider."

"When did it turn sour?"

"On Guam. Things were fine in Hawaii. We got an apartment in Pearl City. I was all caught up in impending motherhood, decorating the nursery and buying baby clothes. My big brother was nearby, to keep an eye on me. Mom came out to stay with us when Wendy was born. So I had my family around me. Then Sam got orders to Guam and we moved, six months after Wendy was born."

"What was it like on Guam?"

"It's an island with lots of military bases. Not a very big island at that." Ruth sipped her coffee. "You can drive around it in a few hours. We just had one car and Sam needed that to get to and from work. The Navy has several housing areas. Ours was a two-bedroom duplex on the naval station. It was all right at first. Being a new mother kept me busy. Then I started to miss my family. You know, I was a Navy brat. We moved around a lot while I was growing up. But now I was the military wife. It really gave me a new perspective on what my mother went through. I don't think I handled it as well as she did."

"The circumstances were different," I told her. "Your mother wasn't in an abusive relationship." I knew from my investigation last March that Admiral Franklin had certainly coveted—and had—his neighbor's wife. But I doubted he'd ever struck Lenore. She might put up with the old man's guff, ego, and infidelity, but not that. "When did Sam start hitting you?"

"When Wendy was about a year old. We were supposed to go to a party. It was a Friday night. Sam said he had a few stops to make after work, and he'd pick me up at six. I'd made arrangements for Wendy to spend the night with a couple who lived down the street. After I took Wendy to their place, I came home and got ready. Sam didn't show up. I sat there in my fancy dress until almost eleven o'clock. Then, as I was getting ready for bed, he came in, reeking of liquor and some other woman's perfume. I flew off the handle and started screaming at him."

Ruth stopped and covered her face with her hands. After a moment she dropped her hands and leaned toward me, her voice a whisper.

"He hit me, over and over again. In the stomach and on the chest, not in the face. He shoved me back against the dresser. I had a big bruise on my back. Then he stormed out of the house. I huddled in bed most of the night and the next morning. It was so unexpected, I didn't know what to think. Saturday afternoon, after I picked up Wendy, he came home again, this time with flowers and a box of candy. He apologized and said he'd had a terrible day at work and that's why he'd been out drinking until all hours.

"I believed him, Jeri. I guess I wanted to. We got a babysitter and he took me out to dinner and we came home and made love. It was like when he was courting me in Hawaii. I thought it wouldn't happen again. But it did. Over and over again, until I realized the only way to escape was to leave. Maybe I could have left sooner, but I was afraid of him. I'm still afraid of him."

I understood why. Just standing face-to-face with the man earlier that day put me on guard.

Ruth looked at her watch and jumped off her stool, nearly upsetting it in her haste. "Oh, Jeri. I have to pick up Wendy. She gets upset when I'm too late."

We left Peet's and walked quickly down Piedmont Avenue, past Fenton's Ice Cream Parlor, which was doing its usual brisk trade. We turned onto a side street and I saw Wendy waiting at the front window of a large stucco house. I stayed on the sidewalk while Ruth went inside to collect her daughter. She came down the steps a moment later with the child, who wore a crisp blue playsuit that didn't look played in, and carried her yarn-haired rag doll clutched to her chest.

Wendy stared at me as she had that night at her grandparents' house, eyes wary. She was only four, but kids are observant. They know when something bad is going on, and I was quite sure Wendy knew things were terribly wrong between her father and mother. Perhaps she'd even seen Sam hit her mother, though Ruth didn't think so. In my first meeting with Ruth and her lawyer, Ruth said Sam was a disinterested father—until the divorce papers were served. Then he suddenly became devoted enough to demand visitation. As I looked at the little girl, she seemed to cling to her mother emotionally as she now clung to Ruth's hip.

"You remember Jeri," Ruth said when they reached me. "You met her at Grandma's house."

"You're late." Wendy's accusatory words were directed at her mother, but from the way she stared at me, I knew

109

I was being held partly responsible. She frowned and pursed her mouth, looking like a worried little old lady. "I don't like it when you're late."

Ruth knelt and put her arms around the child. "I know, honey. I'm sorry. I won't be late again."

"Can we have ice cream?" Wendy asked.

"Before dinner?" Ruth stood up and put her hands on her hips. "Oh, why not? You want to stop at Fenton's, Jeri?"

"Sure," I said. Ruth took Wendy's hand and we retraced our steps toward Piedmont. "I'm going to have toasted almond ice cream, Wendy. What are you going to have? Strawberry?" She shook her head.

"Vanilla?" I asked the little girl. "Lemon? Rocky road? Butter brickle? Peach?"

I recited the litany of flavors as we walked along, and Wendy shook her head firmly after each one. I started making up flavors, like broccoli ripple, artichoke marble, and lima bean surprise. Finally Wendy smiled. When I proposed hominy horror, she giggled, screwed up her pale little face and rewarded me with a heartfelt "Yuck!"

"I know what kind of ice cream you like," I told her, taking her other hand. "It's my favorite too. Let's get a big, big bowl of . . ."

"Chocolate," the three of us chorused in unison as we went through the door of Fenton's.

Fourteen

THE PHONE JANGLED ME INTO CONSCIOUSNESS. I struggled out of the embrace of sheets, hand groping for the lamp on my bedside table. When my fingers were finally able to switch it on, the sudden glare of light hurt my eyes.

I squinted at the clock radio as though I were staring into fog.

It was past one, too damn early Sunday morning. It had only been a few hours since Alex and I left Cassie's place, where Eric had cooked a remarkable meal and we'd indulged in two bottles of wine, plus after-dinner brandy. Beside me Alex stirred, turned over, and shaded his eyes with his hand. I picked up the receiver and the ringing stopped.

It took me a few seconds to identify the frantic, nearly incoherent voice on the other end of the line as that of Lenore Franklin. Then the Admiral took the phone away from her. His terse words were all too understandable. They propelled my feet to the floor and brought me fully awake and stone-cold sober.

"I'll meet you there in fifteen minutes." I hung up the phone, stood and reached for the clothes I'd discarded when Alex and I went to bed earlier. "I don't know when I'll be back," I told Alex. "Would you feed the cat before you leave?"

"Sure." He propped himself up on one elbow and smiled sleepily. "So this is what it feels like when someone gets up in the middle of the night and leaves. Did somebody die?"

"Yes. Sam Raynor."

When I turned onto Howe Street, I saw the pulsing red lights in front of Ruth Raynor's apartment building a couple of blocks away. There were several Oakland police cruisers, as well as an ambulance. I parked my Toyota and continued on foot, threading my way through the crowd that had gathered like metal filings on a magnet.

I spotted three faces that held more than idle curiosity. Two I recognized. Were they here by happenstance or design? The third face loomed at me from the sidewalk near the vacant lot where I'd seen the homeless woman Friday afternoon, a face unknown to me. In the red light it held such a dark glowering look that I stared at it and filed its features in my mind for future reference.

I turned toward the police line, looking for Admiral Joseph Franklin. I spotted his tall spare figure standing alone near a patrol car. He looked like he'd thrown on his clothes as quickly as I had. He was puffing on a cigarette, drawing in smoke as though it were much-needed oxygen. When he saw me, he pitched the cigarette to the pavement and ground it out with his heel as he walked briskly toward me.

"They've arrested Ruth." His thin-lipped mouth was grim.

"Start at the beginning."

"The police called. They said Sam had been shot. They wanted us to come and get Wendy. That's all they told us. When we got there, Ruth was in the back of a patrol car. They wouldn't let me talk to her." He scowled furiously and gestured in the direction of Kaiser Hospital. "They said she'd been injured, so they took her to the emergency room. From there they were going downtown, to police headquarters."

"Injured? How badly? How did it happen?"

I wouldn't have wanted to be in the Admiral's gun sights. He balled his hands into fists and his gray eyes flared with fury. The red lights of the patrol car made him look like the Devil himself.

"That bastard forced his way into her apartment, put his filthy hands around her neck, and choked her."

"What about Wendy?"

"The police had her in another patrol car, trying to calm her down. We couldn't tell if she'd been hurt, but she couldn't stop crying. Lenore and I took her down the street to Kaiser. We called you while the doctor was examining Wendy. Then Lenore took her home. I walked back up here."

"You called Ruth's attorney?"

He nodded. "Yes, right before we called you. She said she'd meet us downtown. She's a divorce lawyer, damn it. She doesn't have any experience in criminal matters."

"We'll deal with that later. Come on. My car's this way."

As we left the scene I looked up at Ruth's building, recalling my visit Friday afternoon, and her face as she told me about her disastrous marriage. And Wendy. I'd felt tri-

112

umphant when I finally got the child to laugh. That was less than thirty-six hours ago, and the whole situation had blown up in our faces, worse than I ever imagined when I took this case.

Now Sam was dead. Crime scene investigators were inside Ruth's apartment, meticulously sifting through her brave new life, looking for evidence. And Ruth herself was down at Homicide, sitting in an interview room.

I unlocked my car and Franklin folded his tall body into the passenger seat. Since Lenore had taken their car, that meant I was stuck with him for the duration. There was still no love lost between us, but he was so distracted by his daughter's predicament that he didn't say anything on our drive downtown. I parked on Seventh Street near Washington. The Admiral and I crossed the street and entered the Oakland Police Administration Building.

At this hour the elevators were locked and so were the double glass doors leading to the second-floor Criminal Investigation Division. I rapped on the glass and peered into the hallway with its garish orange walls, but no one appeared. Then a uniformed officer I knew exited through a door immediately opposite the glass doors and let us into CID. I thanked him, turned right and led the way down the hall, Franklin at my heels as I pushed open the door to Homicide.

Death was having a busy night—or morning—in Oakland. Directly in front of me I saw a disheveled white man with a cut visible in the stubble on his chin. He slumped in a chair, stinking of beer and the street, his pale blue eyes flitting around the room, until a detective in shirtsleeves hauled him to his feet and steered him toward the door the Admiral and I had just entered.

To my left, in one of the interview rooms, I saw a middle-aged black woman sobbing into a handkerchief as though her heart was already broken. Younger family members circled her anxiously, with the sheen of tears on their cheeks, caught between their own sorrow and their inability to comfort her. I heard someone shouting, the words in another language, which could have been anything from

113

Spanish to Chinese, punctuated by thuds as fists hit a wall. Cigarette smoke hovered near the ceiling, the aroma fighting with the smell of coffee from a nearby pot. Phones rang on the metal desks, receivers snatched up by the detectives, interrupting the tap of typewriter keys on paperwork.

I looked around for someone I knew and saw Sergeant Sid Vernon, my ex-husband. He stood at his desk, looming over his partner, Wayne Hobart. They look like Mutt and Jeff. Sid's tall and wide at the shoulders, his hair and moustache a dark gold, while Wayne is short, round-faced, and round-shouldered, with medium-brown hair and eyes, an average-looking guy who doesn't say much. You don't notice Wayne right away. He blends into the background, but that works to his advantage.

I crossed the dingy linoleum floor to Sid's desk, the Admiral close behind. Sid saw me and narrowed his yellow cat's eyes. "What are you doing here?"

"Who took the call on the Raynor homicide?"

"Why do you want to know?"

"Ruth Raynor's my client."

An amused smile twisted Wayne's mouth and I had my answer. Sid grimaced and raised his eyes heavenward, or more accurately, to the grimy ceiling.

"I might have known," he growled. "It's been that kind of a week."

"This is Mrs. Raynor's father, Admiral Joseph Franklin."

"I want to see my daughter." The Admiral's voice rang with authority as he stood with back ramrod straight and hawk nose jutting into the air. But his Navy rank didn't cut any ice here.

"Sir, that's not possible now." Wayne's voice was mild, level, placating. "You and Ms. Howard will have to wait."

For what or how long he didn't say.

The Admiral's control slipped just a bit and his voice shook with urgency. "But the officer at the scene said she was injured. I have to know if she's all right."

"A doctor looked her over. She's fine. We just have a few questions to ask her." Wayne put his hand on the Ad-

114

miral's arm and steered him toward the door. At that moment Franklin looked his age.

I turned to Sid. "He said Ruth was taken away in a patrol car. You must have probable cause to arrest." He didn't answer. "All I know is Sam Raynor's dead. Can't you tell me anything else?"

Sid's yellow eyes gazed at me for a long moment. "Not really. Except that Raynor took a slug in the back and we're talking to witnesses."

I had a bad feeling as I went back outside to wait with the Admiral. Sid had a look in his eye I'd seen many times before, during the three years we had been married, a look that said he and his partner were homing in on a suspect, ready to spring the trap. The evidence against Ruth Raynor must have been solid. Whether the District Attorney agreed that it was enough to charge her with murder was another matter.

In the hallway outside I stared at the walls. "I hate this orange paint," I said, more to myself than to Admiral Franklin. "One of these days I'm going to come in here with a can of nice restful blue latex and paint this damn wall."

He stared at me as though I'd taken leave of my senses. Then he pulled a pack of cigarettes from his pocket and lit one, disregarding the NO SMOKING signs posted in plain view. I don't know how long we waited, but the Admiral smoked one cigarette down to the butt and used that to fire up another. Down the hallway a sharp knock rattled the double glass doors, and I walked to the end of the corridor to see who was there. It was Blair Castle, Ruth's divorce attorney, her face pale and devoid of makeup, looking rumpled in tan slacks and an orange knit pullover that clashed with the paint on the walls.

Blair had someone with her, a tall loose-limbed lanky man whose brown hair looked like he'd combed it with his fingers. He wore dirty sneakers with no socks, faded jeans, and an Oakland A's jersey. His hazel eyes were bleary, as though he'd just gotten out of a bed he hadn't been in long. I felt an immediate kinship on that count alone.

115

"This is Bill Stanley," Blair said, making the introductions as I let them into the corridor. "He's a criminal defense attorney, one of the best."

Stanley greeted Admiral Franklin first, in a raspy voice that smoothed out as he spoke. He extended his hand as he slipped effortlessly into his lawyer persona, radiating confidence, expertise, control. He did it so well he might have been wearing a three-piece suit instead of his current grungy attire. Then he turned to me.

"We've met," I said.

Bill Stanley lifted one bushy brown eyebrow and cocked his head to one side. Up close I saw a lot of gray threaded in his brown hair. He was about ten years older than me. His eyes were a lot older.

"Jeri Howard. You worked for me on that Goldberg case. And another one, I forget the guy's name, back when you were with the Seville Agency."

I nodded. That was right before my mentor Errol Seville had a heart attack and retired. Aside from my occasional jobs for Stanley, I knew him by reputation. He was good. A bit unorthodox, but good.

"Sorry to see Errol pull the plug," Stanley said. "Hell of a guy. Okay, Blair filled me in when she phoned. Then I called Homicide, told 'em I was on my way down and to put everything on ice until I talk to Ruth." He stopped and rubbed his stubbly chin, looking past me at Joe Franklin. "I'm getting ahead of myself. Am I hired?"

The Admiral nodded vigorously. "Of course. Just get my daughter out of this mess."

"Okay, I'm gonna need a retainer up front." The defense attorney named a figure that raised my eyebrows, but Franklin was already reaching for his checkbook. He used the orange wall as a desk, quickly scribbling out the check. He signed his name with a jagged scrawl, tore the paper rectangle free and handed it to the lawyer.

"Were you able to find out anything?" Stanley asked me.

"Raynor was shot in the back. The cops are holding Ruth for questioning. They're also talking to witnesses. The

116

homicide detectives are Sid Vernon and Wayne Hobart. I should warn you that Sid and I were married once."

"Yeah, I know." Stanley didn't say how he knew. He looked from me to Blair and the Admiral. "Where'd Ruth get the gun? Did the ex bring it with him? Or was it hers?"

Admiral Franklin sighed and cleared his throat. "I bought it for her."

"Why?" I demanded, fighting down the impulse to shake him. Having a gun in the house is a lot like keeping a rattlesnake for a pet. Sooner or later the snake bites.

"For protection. She was living in Oakland." His voice was tinged with the common perception that living anywhere in Oakland is like living in a war zone. Sometimes it is, most of the time it isn't. You can say that about any city.

"I was afraid that bastard would make some move against her," the Admiral continued, "in spite of the restraining order. So I bought her a snub-nosed thirty-eight and some ammunition. All perfectly legal and aboveboard. The gun's registered to her."

"Did Ruth know how to use it?" Blair asked. From the look of dismay on her thin face, I could tell she didn't like the idea any better than I did.

"Of course." The Admiral's tone implied that everyone grew up knowing how to clean, load, and fire a gun. "I taught both Ruth and Kevin myself. I used to take them to the firing range with me."

"If it's her gun that was used to kill Sam," I said, "her prints are all over it. That's bad."

"Maybe, maybe not." Bill Stanley rubbed his chin again.

I turned to him. "Sid's got a look in his eye that says they've got a good case. They must have some strong evidence against Ruth or they wouldn't have arrested her."

Stanley laughed and narrowed his eyes, looking like a man who enjoyed a challenge, any kind of challenge. "They always want you to think that. First I need to talk to Ruth. Then we'll shake up the cops and see what falls loose."

We followed the attorney through the door into Homi-

117

cide, where Sid and Wayne were still conferring at Sid's desk. Bill Stanley greeted them as though he'd encountered them over at the Warehouse, a cop bar at the corner of Fourth and Webster.

"Who let you in?" Sid said with a grumpy snort, as though Bill Stanley's presence lowered the ambience of the joint.

"I'm here to see my client, Ruth Raynor. I know you guys got her stashed somewhere. Probably right in there." Stanley pointed one long finger at the closed door of an interview room.

"You're her lawyer?" Wayne Hobart shook his head as though unable to believe that anyone could be so foolish as to sign on Bill Stanley.

"Yeah, her old man just hired me." Stanley grinned and pointed his thumb back over his shoulder at Admiral Franklin, who looked taken aback, perhaps at being called an old man or, more likely, at the bantering tone evident in this exchange between the attorney and the detectives. I'd seen this sort of interplay often enough to know it was all part of the ritual. "I called you half an hour ago, Wayne. You've had time to roll out the red carpet. Now I'm here. Quit stalling and let me see my client."

Sid and Wayne exchanged glances in the kind of telepathy that exists between longstanding partners. "Tell Mrs. Raynor that it is in her best interest to talk with us, so we can clear up this situation."

Stanley chuckled. "Sid, you gotta get yourself a new record. That one's got too many scratches on it."

Sid shrugged and moved toward the closed door that led to the small claustrophobic room where the Oakland cops interviewed suspects. He opened it and stepped aside.

Fifteen

I SAW RUTH RAYNOR HUDDLED IN AN ORANGE PLAS-
tic chair in the far corner of the windowless room, a small
figure in a blue denim skirt, a pink blouse, and sandals. Her
back was against the graffiti-scarred blue and white walls,
and she clutched a wad of tissues. Her paper-white face
contrasted with the purple bruises visible at her neck.

She stared at us without recognition, her eyes like those
of an animal caught in a trap, waiting for rescue or death.
Her father cried out and moved toward her. Bill Stanley re-
strained him.

"Not now," Stanley ordered. "Just me and Jeri."

"I'm hired?" I asked quietly.

"Yeah. You're already in it, so everything you know is
covered by attorney-client privilege. Come see me Monday
morning and we'll hammer out details. For now I want you
to listen in. Let me do the talking."

I nodded. Stanley and I stepped into the tiny room and
he shut the door. Ruth looked up at us and she finally recognized me. "Jeri, is Wendy okay? She was crying. I
couldn't make her stop crying. The police took her away.
They said they'd call Mom and Dad. I gave them the phone
number. Is she okay?"

"She's with your mother."

Stanley positioned a plastic chair and sat down facing
Ruth. "Mrs. Raynor, I'm Bill Stanley. I'm an attorney. Your
father has retained me to defend you."

"But I didn't do anything," Ruth protested, her eyes
wide. "I told the police that."

He cut her words off with a sharp wave of his hand.

119

"You tell the police nothing. Zip, zero, *nada.* Those cops out there are the enemy. They will use anything and everything you say to put you in prison for the murder of your husband. You don't want to go to prison, Mrs. Raynor. You don't want Wendy to have to come visit her mom in prison."

Tears trickled from Ruth's brown eyes as Stanley's harsh words hit her like body blows. She dropped the wad of used tissues in her lap and reached for a fresh supply from the box on the floor.

"You understand what I'm saying?" Stanley leaned forward and his voice softened. "You don't talk to the cops. In fact, you don't talk to anybody but me. Only to me. Or Jeri. Tell me you understand."

"I understand," Ruth whispered.

"Good. Now, I want you to start from the beginning, and tell Jeri and me exactly what happened this evening. Take your time, don't leave anything out."

Ruth drew in a breath and began, her voice shaky. "We had dinner at Mom and Dad's. Kevin brought us home."

"Who's we?" Stanley asked. "Who's Kevin?"

"Wendy and me. Kevin is my older brother. He's a Navy officer. He's here on leave." Ruth took another deep breath. She appeared calmer now that she was talking. "The three of us spent the afternoon at Children's Fairyland in the park at Lake Merritt. Then we went over to Alameda, where my parents live. We had dinner. Mom and Dad and Kevin and I played cards while Wendy watched a Walt Disney video. Then Kevin brought Wendy and me home."

"What time was this?" Stanley asked.

"I'm not sure," Ruth said. "About eleven, I think. All I know is it was way past Wendy's bedtime. She fell asleep in Kevin's car. He carried her up to the apartment. We put her right to bed and—" She stopped and frowned. "Kevin left."

Why the pause? If Bill Stanley had noticed, he didn't give any indication. "What happened then?" he asked.

Ruth huddled back in the chair. "I took out the trash." When Bill Stanley asked her why, she shrugged. "I noticed

120

the garbage can under the sink was full, so I took it out to the trash chute in the hall. I left the door to my apartment open. It's only a few steps. While I was walking back to the apartment, the elevator door opened, and Sam—" She stopped and shuddered.

While Ruth composed herself, I recalled the layout of the third-floor area she'd described, from my visit on Friday afternoon. Coming out of the door of Ruth's apartment, unit 303, I had faced the short hall that led back to the trash chute and the stairwell. To the right of that hallway was the elevator door, perpendicular to the wall that held the doors to units 301 and 302.

"So he caught you in the hall," Stanley was saying.

Ruth nodded and continued her story in a halting voice. "I ran for the apartment but he got there before I could shut the door. He grabbed my arm. I broke away and got into the apartment. I tried to shut the door, but he pushed me out of the way and got in."

"He forced his way into the apartment," Stanley said. "Had he been drinking?"

Ruth nodded. "I could smell beer on him."

"What did he say? Did he threaten you, physically, verbally?"

"He said he wanted to see Wendy. I told him it's late, she's in bed, she's asleep. He's got visitation, but it's supervised, every other Saturday, at my parents' house. Plus I've got a stay-away order against him. I reminded him about that. He just laughed. He said if he wanted to come see me and Wendy, he'd just do it, and he wouldn't pay any attention to any damned court orders."

Despite my efforts to transform myself into a fly on the wall, Ruth now looked at me and said, "He was really mad about Jeri."

"About Jeri?" Stanley repeated the words and glanced over his shoulder at me.

Ruth nodded. "Sam's hiding some money, over a hundred thousand dollars. Blair and I asked Jeri to locate the money. Sam found out. He even threatened Jeri. You must be getting close. Sam was really angry. He said I'd better call off the detective or I'd be in more trouble than I already was."

"Let's get back to tonight," Stanley said. "Where were you in the apartment? The hall, the kitchen, the living room? Draw me a picture. Jeri, you got a pen and some paper?"

I quickly pulled the requested items from my bag and handed them to Ruth. She sketched her one-bedroom apartment, then used the pen as a pointer. "When he got into the apartment, he grabbed my arm again and pulled me into the living room. He looked around and said it was a dump. I told him it was my dump, and to get out. That's when he said he wanted to see Wendy."

Bill Stanley shifted in the hard plastic chair. "Okay, we know he threatened you verbally. What about physically?"

"He kept squeezing my arm. So hard I thought he'd bruise it." Ruth held out her left arm and examined it as though she'd never seen it before. On the flesh of the forearm, near the elbow, I saw faint purple marks complementing the darker ones at her throat.

"When I tried to stop him going into the bedroom where Wendy was, he slapped me. Then he shoved me away. I fell and banged my knee. Hard. It really hurt." Ruth sensed Stanley's impending question about physical evidence, so she pulled up the hem of her blue denim skirt and discovered another purple mark.

"I got to my feet. Sam was grinning. I wanted to wipe that grin off his face." Her lips clamped tightly together at the memory. "Then he said I'd better behave myself. If I didn't quit hassling him, he'd beat me bloody. If I didn't call off Jeri, he'd take Wendy and he'd hide her and I'd never see her again. He laughed. He said, 'I might even take her now.' " Ruth stopped, hands stilled in her lap.

"What did you do then?" Stanley asked.

"That's when I got the gun."

"Where did you keep it?"

"In the kitchen, in the cabinet above the refrigerator. I didn't want it when Daddy bought it for me. But he said I needed it for protection. I kept it clean and I never kept it

122

loaded, but the shells were right there next to it." Ruth sounded detached, as though she were describing something that happened to someone else.

"Sam went into the bedroom and I went to the kitchen. I pulled up the stepstool so I could reach the cabinet. I got the shells and the gun, and I loaded it, right there at the kitchen counter. Then I went out into the hallway, just outside the bedroom. When Sam came out I pointed the gun at him. I told him I'd kill him before I'd let him take my little girl."

I leaned back against the wall, folding my arms across my chest. I didn't like the way this sounded. I couldn't tell what Stanley thought about it. His face was blank, neutral, as he listened to Ruth's story.

"First he laughed," Ruth said, "and said I'd hurt myself. I told him I knew how to use a gun. Besides, at that range I couldn't miss. I backed up, toward the living room. I had the gun in my right hand. The phone's on the counter, so I picked up the telephone with my left. I told him to get out or I'd call the police. He was really angry. His face got red, almost as red as his hair. He swore at me, the way he used to do when he beat me." She took a deep ragged breath.

"He acted like he was going to leave. Then he knocked the phone out of my hand and he was trying to get the gun away from me. It happened so fast, it's all jumbled together. I know the gun went off. It was so loud, my ears were ringing and I couldn't hear anything else. His lips were moving and I couldn't hear him."

Ruth's hands moved to her bruised throat, tears in her eyes. "He had his hands around my neck. I couldn't breathe. I must have passed out. There was this red fuzziness, blurring my vision, and a rushing sensation, like I was on a train. Then I heard crying. I opened my eyes and saw the ceiling. I realized I was in the hall of my apartment. Wendy was standing there in her pajamas, crying."

Ruth stopped and covered her face with her hands. It took her a few minutes to pull herself together sufficiently to go on.

123

"I sat up," she said, "and put my arms around Wendy. My poor baby. I couldn't get her to stop crying."

"When did the police show up?" Stanley asked. "How did they get into your apartment?"

"They were there really fast. One of my neighbors must have heard the shot when the gun went off. While I had my arms around Wendy, a policeman walked into my apartment. I guess my door was open. I heard voices outside, all talking at once. The policeman had his gun drawn. That frightened Wendy. He put away his gun and asked me what was going on."

Ruth shook her head. "I'm all confused about things after that. I don't know how long I was out. I felt cold and woozy. Maybe I was in shock. I just don't know. All of a sudden there were policemen everywhere. One of them helped me to my feet, and another one took Wendy and asked if there was some relative he could call, so I gave him Mom and Dad's number. They wiped my hands with some wet cotton balls."

While Ruth looked down at her hands, Stanley and I traded glances. Gunshot primer residue was obtained by wiping the hands with nitric acid, to collect the barium and antimony left from the discharge of ammunition. Ruth had already said the gun went off during her struggle with Sam, and since it was her weapon, her fingerprints would be on the gun itself as well as the shells inside. I asked the question that had been uppermost in my mind. "Ruth, when it was over, where was your gun?"

She looked confused. "I don't know. It wasn't there on the floor beside me. The police were looking for it too. They said Sam was dead. I know they think I shot him. But I didn't. Or at least—" She stopped and her mouth formed a shocked circle. "Oh, Jeri, what if I had some of kind of blackout? What if I followed him outside the apartment and shot him? I can't remember anything between the time he choked me and when I woke up to Wendy crying."

Stanley waved his hands. "Let's not get into guessing games. Your story's fine as it is. Just remember, you talk to me or Jeri, no one else. I'll do the rest." He stood up and

124

put his hands on his hips. "Time to see what the cops have."

"I have one more question." I pushed away from the wall, fixing Ruth with a steady look. "Was there anyone with Sam? Did you see anyone else, or hear another voice?"

"I don't know," Ruth said. "When Sam stepped off that elevator, all I saw was him."

Sixteen

"YOU GUYS CALL THIS A CASE?"

Bill Stanley was perched on the corner of Sid's desk in Homicide, derision coloring his voice. Now that Ruth Raynor was represented by counsel, and counsel had advised her not to talk, there was no point in the police keeping her in the interview room. A female officer was called to escort her to jail, where she would stay until the District Attorney decided whether to charge her. That looked like a distinct probability.

Ruth looked small and delicate in her pink blouse and blue skirt, dwarfed by the taller figure of the uniformed woman beside her. As the two women left Homicide, Ruth threw a frightened look at her father. The Admiral looked stunned and haggard, a hundred years old, as he realized that events had gone beyond the point where he could make things all right again. When Ruth had gone, Stanley whispered a few words to Blair Castle. The divorce lawyer took Franklin's arm and offered to give him a ride home.

The older man straightened his slumped shoulders. He wanted to stay, but we persuaded him that there was nothing he could do here. Before leaving, he extracted my promise to come over to the Franklins' Alameda home as soon as I left police headquarters, no matter what time it was. He wasn't giving orders anymore. His words were a plea.

Now Stanley was trying to find out as much as he could about the strength of the case against Ruth. While the defense lawyer sparred with the detectives, I listened and watched, feeling like a spectator at a tennis match.

"It's her gun," Wayne pointed out, a slight smile on his face, his voice reasonable and mild.

Stanley spread his hand wide, palms up. "So where is it?"

Sid was decidedly chagrined at the sight of Stanley's butt parked on his desk. He looked as though he'd like to sweep the lawyer off its surface and into a nearby wastebasket.

"It *was* at the bottom of the trash chute," Sid said, snapping off the words. "It's now in evidence."

Score one-love for the cops, I thought. They'd found the gun. Now they'd test it to see if it had fired the slug that ended Sam Raynor's life. But there had been two shots. Ruth said the gun went off earlier, while she and Sam struggled. A positive result on the residue test was a foregone conclusion. Somewhere in the apartment, buried in a wall or a piece of furniture, was another slug, waiting to be found. Had that first shot nicked Sam? Whether it had or not, if both slugs matched, things didn't look good for Ruth, despite Bill Stanley's show of confidence.

"Any other wounds on the victim?" I asked. "Other than the fatal one?"

Sid narrowed his eyes as though wondering where I was headed. "Only one that we could see. He was shot in the back at close range. The medical examiner may find something else. We'll just have to wait for the autopsy."

"Where was the body?"

"End of the hall leading to the stairs, between the door and the trash chute. She followed him out of the apartment, plugged him in the back, tossed the gun down the trash chute and went back to the apartment."

126

"Come on." Stanley shook his head. "Look at the bruises on her throat. He damn near strangled her. She passed out."

"We have a witness," Sid said, looking implacable.

He didn't identify the witness or tell us what had allegedly been seen, but I raised the score to two-love. The more I heard, the worse it sounded. This didn't seem to bother Bill Stanley, though. He dismissed this piece of news with a wave of his hand. He didn't get much else out of Sid and Wayne, other than the information that a neighbor had called the police after hearing a gunshot. Not two, I noted, but one. Probably the same person had reported seeing Ruth drop the gun down the trash chute. But Ruth said she'd disposed of the kitchen garbage right before Sam showed up. Given the layout of the area, I doubted that anyone could have seen Ruth drop anything down the trash chute unless that person had been directly behind her, standing at the head of the short hallway.

So the witness was mistaken. Who was it? A neighbor? I recalled my visit to Ruth Friday afternoon and the elderly woman we'd seen in the hallway with her load of laundry. Ruth called her Mrs. Parmenter and said she snooped. Five'll get you ten Mrs. Parmenter is the witness, I told myself. Then an unwelcome though leapt into my mind.

"Have you talked to Wendy?" I asked.

"Of course," Sid said. That's all he said, his face maddeningly blank.

What had Wendy seen and heard? I met Bill Stanley's hazel eyes. And what had she told the police?

Sid told Stanley once again that things would go easier for Ruth if she cooperated with the police, but the lawyer slid off the corner of the desk and shook his head. "Let's just wait and see what the D.A. has to say. Then we'll talk."

The District Attorney's office had forty-eight hours from Ruth's arrest to charge the case. During that time the D.A. would examine the witness statements and get the results of various tests. Unless the coroner was backed up, the autopsy would likely be completed by then. Then we'd know what Ruth Raynor was up against.

I followed Stanley out of Homicide, down the orange hallway to the doors of CID. I didn't speak until we were outside the Police Administration Building.

"Somebody set her up," I said. "Although it's too spur-of-the-moment for a lot of planning. More like a seized opportunity. Someone else must have been with Raynor. Saw the chance, took it."

"You think so?" In the overhead glow of the street lamp, Bill Stanley's face took on a yellowish cast as his mouth curved into a world-weary grin. "Listen, Jeri, I always figure my clients are guilty. It saves time. Besides, they usually are."

Somehow I expected this. "She says she didn't kill him. I believe her."

Stanley shrugged. "Hey, my only concern is springing Ruth. Look what we got here." He ticked off the elements of the case on his fingers.

"The slimeball is an abusive husband with a restraining order against him. He breaks into his wife's building. The place has a security door, right? So he didn't push the buzzer and say, hey, honey, can I come up? He accosts Ruth in the hall, forces his way into her apartment, refuses to leave when she asks him to. He threatens to kidnap her child, then he attacks her physically. So the gun's hers—so what? Big fucking deal. It's legitimately purchased and legally registered. This creep came to her place looking for trouble, and he got it. Self-defense, piece of cake. The worst they can charge her with is voluntary manslaughter, and when I swing into action . . ." Stanley's body swayed as he swung an imaginary golf club. "She'll walk." I looked skeptical. "Jeri, trust me. I can get Ruth off."

"I don't think Ruth killed him. Which means whoever did is walking around loose."

"Sounds like the fucker had it coming," Stanley shot back. "So I don't care who killed Raynor."

"I do. It offends my sense of symmetry." Also my sense of justice. But I didn't say that. I didn't think justice was high on Bill Stanley's list of priorities.

128

"Okay, say she didn't do it," he said. "You got any candidates?"

"Sam Raynor was the biggest slug that ever oozed across my path. Anyone who wanted to kill him would have to take a number and get in line."

Stanley spread his hands wide and shrugged. "Okay, suit yourself. Look into it. Couldn't hurt. It's another line of defense."

"Another thing bothers me," I told him. "Shot in the back at close range doesn't sound like self-defense to me. It looks cold and calculated. Like murder one."

"I can get around that."

I watched him yawn and wondered at his impenetrable confidence. I guessed Stanley had to be confident to be such a successful defense attorney. It was also easy to see how he could become jaded. I knew who some of his clients were—not exactly the pick of the litter when it came to good citizens. But Stanley would be the first to tell me that everyone was entitled to a defense.

"When are you going to talk to Wendy? She may have seen something important."

"The little girl? She's what, four? Surprising what kids can retain." Stanley looked at the faint red light of dawn over the Oakland hills. "Grandma probably slapped that kid into bed as soon as she got her back to Alameda. I'll call the Franklins to set up a time. Damn, I'm tired," he said, running a hand through his already tousled hair. "I must be getting old. Need to get some rack time. You heading home?"

Rack time never sounded better, I thought, recalling my warm bed, with Alex's arms wrapped around me as we slept, and Abigail the cat staking out a spot next to my feet. Oh, well. I shook my head and looked at my watch. "I told the Admiral I'd come over."

"Yeah, the Admiral. Keep him out of my hair. He could be a real pain in the ass."

He could indeed. If I kept him out of Stanley's hair, no doubt Franklin would be in mine. The lawyer pulled his wallet from the back pocket of his jeans and fished out a

129

card. "Come by my office first thing Monday," he said, handing it to me. "I'll be there early, around eight, 'cause I gotta be in court later. We'll talk strategy. I want you to interview witnesses, especially the one who allegedly saw Ruth dump the gun."

I took the card and nodded, then watched him unlock a sleek Porsche parked on this side of Seventh. As he drove away, I walked across the street to where I'd left my Toyota. Weariness plucked at me with insistent hands, but I fought it back as I started the engine and shifted into drive, heading through the Tube to Alameda.

Despite the early hour, a light blazed on the porch of the Franklins' Gibbons Drive house. I'd hoped the Admiral had given up on me and gone to bed, but he had the front door open as I came up the walk. He held his fire until I was seated at the rectangular wooden table in the spacious kitchen, a mug of strong black coffee in front of me.

Lenore Franklin sat across the table, her topaz eyes big in her white face, pale lips seized and bitten by her teeth. She listened without a word as I repeated Ruth's account of what had happened. While I talked, pausing for sips of much-needed caffeine, Admiral Franklin paced the blue-and-white-tiled floor, hands clasped behind his back, face etched with rage. Now and again he punctuated my story with a snarl that told me if Sam Raynor wasn't already dead, Ruth's father would go after him and finish the job.

When I finished talking, I raised the coffee mug to my lips. It was nearly empty. The Franklins were silent for a long moment. Then Lenore put her hands to her temples and slowly shook her head back and forth, her voice an anguished whisper. "My God, I don't believe this is happening. This *can't* be happening."

The Admiral stopped pacing and seized the glass pot from the coffee maker near the stove. He topped off my mug and Lenore's, then poured the rest into his own. "It is happening, and we've got to deal with it. Now, what's the best plan of attack?"

"Admiral," I said, "this is not a military exercise."

"I'm aware of that, young lady. It's a war. And if you

130

think I'm going to let my daughter get railroaded for murdering that scum—"

"Calm down, Joe. Remember your blood pressure." Lenore's words came automatically. She must have been reminding him on a regular basis for over thirty years.

"My blood pressure is fine, Lenore."

He pulled the paper filter and used coffee grounds out of the basket of the coffee maker, dumped them into a trash can under the sink, and replaced them with a fresh filter and more ground coffee. He rinsed the empty glass pot, filled it with water and poured it into the receptacle at the top of the coffee maker. Soon dark brown liquid began to hiss and trickle into the pot. Above the sink a ceramic clock wreathed in yellow and white daisies told me it was close to six this Sunday morning. The sun was just coming up, but here in Alameda, near the bay, the fog would be with us until the sun grew warm enough to burn it off. The mist looked as cold and gray as I felt.

Lenore slumped tiredly in the chair across from me, but the Admiral seemed to vibrate with energy as he resumed his pacing. "We have to talk to that witness," he declared.

"What do you mean, *we*?" I said, trying not to show the alarm I felt. *God, this is all I need.* I closed my eyes against the specter of Admiral Joseph Franklin, USN-Retired, in a white dress uniform and ceremonial sword, dogging my every step as I interviewed witnesses. It was not a pretty sight. "Admiral, I think you'd better leave this to the professionals, namely me and Bill Stanley."

"I can't just do *nothing*." He stopped pacing and balled his fists in a gesture of pure frustration that carried through to his voice. "This is my daughter we're talking about."

I stood up and carried my mug to the counter, pouring in fresh coffee. "I understand that," I said, my words level and measured. "But I work best alone."

Lenore pushed her chair away from the table and got slowly to her feet. Her eyes met mine with a look that said she'd talk to him. She knelt at one of the kitchen cabinets, opened the door and took out a large ceramic bowl, a metal sifter, and an electric hand mixer.

131

"What are you doing, Lenore?" her husband asked as she straightened and set these items on the counter.

"I'm going to make some waffles," Lenore said, her voice quiet and calm as she opened a drawer and brought out a set of measuring cups and spoons. "Wendy loves waffles. It's her favorite breakfast. The way you're carrying on, she'll be awake soon."

The Admiral and I watched in silence while Lenore reached for a row of cookbooks on a little wooden shelf at the end of the counter. She selected a three-ring binder, its cover faded, stained, and well-used, and flipped expertly to the proper page. Then she pulled up the largest of a set of canisters and began measuring out flour.

"Did Wendy say anything?" I asked, leaning against the counter.

Lenore shook her head. "Nothing that I could understand. She was too upset." She searched through another cabinet until she found a bottle of cooking oil and a small tin of baking powder. "You and this lawyer will have to talk to her, won't you?"

"She was there, and the cops have already talked to her. She might have seen something important."

"She's only four years old." Lenore sighed and turned back to her waffle making.

I heard a door open at the front of the house, and a moment later Kevin Franklin walked into the kitchen, casually dressed in a pair of blue jeans and a short-sleeved knit shirt. He looked startled to see me and his parents standing in the kitchen. "What's going on?" he asked.

His father fixed him with sharp gray eyes. "Where the hell have you been?"

Kevin looked surprised. I hadn't wondered until now about Kevin's whereabouts. Ruth said she, Kevin, and Wendy spent Saturday afternoon together, before coming here for a family dinner. Kevin took Ruth home, then left her apartment building. When she said that, I assumed he'd gone back to Alameda to spend the night at his parents' home. But that was obviously not the case. Where had he gone?

132

"I spent the night at a friend's place," Kevin said, stumbling slightly on the words. Somehow I thought there was more to it than that. "What's up?"

"Sam's dead," the Admiral said. "Your sister's been arrested for murder."

Kevin's eyes widened in disbelief. His mouth opened but he couldn't get out any words. After a quick sidelong glance at her son, Lenore went to the refrigerator for a carton of milk. She measured some into the mixing bowl and returned the carton to the refrigerator. The Admiral locked eyes with Kevin. Neither parent seemed willing to explain further, so I gave him a brief account, the electric whir of Lenore's mixer in the background.

"That's crazy." Kevin pulled out a chair and sat down. "I can't believe it."

"I'm not sure how long it was after you left Ruth's building that Sam showed up. Or how he got in. As you left, did you see anyone or anything? Was the security door closed and locked?"

"Yes, the door was locked. It's one of those pneumatic-type doors, so there's a time lag when you go through. But not that long. I didn't pay any attention to whether it closed behind me. But I'd have noticed if someone was there. I'd have recognized Sam. But I didn't see him." Kevin stopped and looked around, eyes lighting on the coffee. He got up and poured himself a mug, then returned to his chair. "I just don't remember seeing anyone go in or out of the building in the short time that I was there."

I walked to the door that led out to the Franklins' patio and peered through the ruffled curtain at the fog-shrouded backyard. Then I turned back to Kevin. "Did you see a homeless woman anywhere nearby? She pushes her stuff around in a shopping cart." Kevin shook his head. "Where did you go after you left Ruth?"

Lenore shut off the electric mixer and it was suddenly very quiet in the kitchen. My question sounded like an afterthought, but Kevin's guard came up. His words were casual but careful, punctuated with an offhand shrug.

"A buddy of mine has a place over on Bayo Vista, not

133

far from Ruth. I dropped by and we had a couple of beers, got to telling sea stories. I wound up sleeping on his sofa."

Plausible, I thought, but a little too studied. I wasn't sure Kevin was telling me the truth, and I wanted to know why. "What's your friend's name?" I asked. With his parents right here, Kevin couldn't avoid answering my question.

The coffee mug he raised to his lips didn't quite mask the tight line of Kevin's mouth. "Chuck Porter. You remember Chuck, Dad. He was a year behind me at the Naval Academy. He's at RedCom Twenty over on Treasure Island."

The combination of adrenaline and caffeine that had kept me going thus far was wearing off. "I'm fading fast," I said, setting the mug in the sink. "I'd better go."

"Have some breakfast," Lenore said. "You're already here." She knelt at a cupboard and brought out a waffle iron, which she plugged into an outlet near the stove. Soon it was hot enough to sizzle when Lenore sprinkled a few drops of water onto its surface. She poured some batter onto the iron and shut the lid. Kevin set the table while the Admiral poured some maple syrup into a ceramic pitcher and zapped it in the microwave to heat it.

The four of us were seated around the table eating when Wendy padded barefoot into the kitchen, a small strawberry-blond wraith enveloped in a frilly white nightgown. She stopped, rubbed her eyes and wrinkled her nose.

"Good morning, baby," Lenore said brightly. She got up and ruffled the top of her granddaughter's fluffy head. "I made waffles for breakfast. I even have pecans to put on top, just the way you like. Are you hungry?"

The four-year-old nodded once and pulled out a chair containing a booster seat. She clambered into the seat and Lenore pushed the chair up to the table. Then Wendy looked at us and asked the question I knew she was going to ask.

"Where's Mommy?"

Seventeen

THE COFFEE I CONSUMED AT THE FRANKLINS' DID
not affect my ability to sleep. When I returned to my apartment Sunday morning, I headed straight for the bedroom
and shucked off my clothes. My much-needed slumber was
deep and dreamless, ending when the phone rang in mid-
afternoon. I roused myself and reached for the receiver.

"Did you see my note?" Alex asked.

"Note?" I looked around but I didn't see anything resembling a note. "No. Where'd you leave it?"

"On the dining room table."

"I dived right back into bed when I got home." I sat up,
propped by pillows, and pushed my hair out of my eyes.
"What did you say in your note?"

"Just that I fed the cat and I'd call you this afternoon."

The cat in question was coiled into a ball at the foot of
the bed with her nose tucked under her front paws. Under
the covers I poked my foot at her. One eye opened, then
closed again as she shifted slightly.

"The Oakland police notified the air station duty officer
about Sam Raynor," Alex said. "The duty officer called
Chief Yancy, who called his division officer, who called
me."

I pictured the Navy chain of command as Alex had once
described it, although in my mind it looked more like a big
ladder, wide at the bottom and narrow at the top. The junior
enlisted ranks, the sailors, crowded the lower rungs. Above
them were the senior enlisted supervisors—the chiefs—then
the division officers, who were junior to the department
heads, senior officers like Alex. Department heads reported

to the executive officer, who reported to the commanding officer, who ran the base and reported to some admiral down in San Diego.

"The division officer said Raynor'd been shot," Alex continued, "and the police have a suspect in custody. Who?"

"Ruth. His wife."

Alex was silent for a moment. Then he sighed. "This is a hell of a mess. Chief Yancy identified the body."

An interesting turn of events, given that I was fairly certain Sam Raynor had been having an affair with Claudia Yancy, the chief's wife. "What happens when a sailor dies? You must have procedures."

"We have to do a *JAG Manual* investigation. JAG means Judge Advocate General. Any time a service member dies of something other than natural causes, the command has to investigate, to determine whether the death was in the line of duty."

"Duty had nothing to do with this." My voice was grim. I recalled Ruth as she sat in that claustrophobic interview room at the Oakland Police Department, describing Sam Raynor's hands around her throat.

"Well, no," Alex said. "Raynor was on liberty, so the investigation will be informal rather than a board of inquiry. Usually when a sailor dies out in town, it's an accident, not murder. We have thirty days to complete the report, then it goes up the chain of command to the Judge Advocate General's office in Washington, D.C. The commanding officer will assign someone to do it, first thing tomorrow morning. Of course, we'll cooperate fully with the Oakland Police Department."

"What about cooperating with the defense attorney?"

"Which means you? You don't think she killed him?"

"No. The field's wide open, as far as I'm concerned. If I need information from the Navy, will the brass cooperate?"

"I don't see why not," Alex said finally. "We're as interested in finding out what happened to Raynor as you or the cops are."

136

But there was a difference, I thought, after I hung up the phone. The Navy merely wants an explanation of events. My first priority was proving Ruth Raynor's innocence.

I reached for Abigail, scooped her into my lap and tickled her fat round tabby belly. She purred and reached out one paw, tapping me lightly on the chin. Then I pushed aside the covers and got out of bed. After I'd showered and dressed, it was past three, but I had breakfast anyway, scrambled eggs and toast, while I glanced through the Sunday *Tribune*. I was washing dishes when the phone rang.

"The family's planning a picnic on Labor Day," my mother said cheerfully. "Are you driving down Friday night or Saturday morning?"

I stared at the calendar with dismay. Next weekend was Labor Day weekend. I was expected in Monterey for a visit with my mother and her large extended family of Doyles and Ravellas.

"I don't think I can make the trip," I said.

I got a chilly silence on the other end of the phone. "What do you mean, you can't make the trip?" Mother's voice now had an edge. "You've been planning it for weeks. You said you'd clear your calendar."

"I did clear my calendar. But something's come up."

"Something always comes up. Another case, any excuse not to visit me. What is it this time, another skip trace?"

Now she was being sarcastic. Mother never did have much use for private investigating as a profession. When I studied history in college, she assumed I was going to teach, like my brother, father, and grandfather. When I went to work as a legal secretary and paralegal, she kept asking me when I was going to law school. Teachers and lawyers are respectable. A private detective snooping around in other people's business just doesn't have the same cachet.

"My client's been arrested. It's important."

If my words were terse, hers were testy. "Of course it's important. Your work's always more important than your family."

Don't say it, I thought. I'd heard that line before and it

had prefaced a remark about it being the same way with my father. But she didn't say it.

"The whole family was looking forward to seeing you." Mother paused, as though she were having trouble with the next sentence. "So was I."

I sighed. "Look, this started out to be a routine investigation. I really thought I'd have it wrapped up in time to go to Monterey. Then the subject got shot, late last night. My client's about to be charged with murder, and I don't think she did it. It's too early to know how things are going to shake out. I'll know more in the next couple of days. I'll keep you posted but I really doubt that I can come to Monterey until later in September. I'm sorry you're disappointed, but that's the way it is."

After I hung up the phone, I stared at the residue of scrambled eggs on my plate. All the resentment I'd felt at my parents' divorce returned in force, most of it directed at my mother. How dare she walk out on my father? Of course, I'd always felt closer to him. Brian countered my "Mom liked you best" claim with a similar charge that I was always Daddy's little girl. Still was, if I admitted it to myself. Dad was still on vacation, so I couldn't call him. I decided I needed my brother's leavening to dispel my black mood, so I reached for the phone and called Brian in Sonoma.

"I guess I've pissed off Mother," I announced.

"So what else is new? What happened? C'mon, tell baby bro. You'll feel better."

I unloaded. I felt much better.

I arrived at my office at seven-thirty Monday morning, checked the messages on the answering machine and read through the Oakland *Tribune*. A sketchy article on page two described Sam Raynor's murder, adding that Ruth was being held for questioning. At ten minutes to eight I walked the few blocks to Bill Stanley's office, on the fifth floor of a building at the corner of Broadway and Nineteenth Street. I rang a buzzer outside the suite. A moment later Bill Stanley opened the door.

138

This morning the attorney was combed, shaved, and dressed in a snowy white shirt and well-cut suit trousers in a navy pinstripe. He had unbuttoned his shirt at the collar and cuffs, and loosened his tie, a vibrant floral print with splashes of yellow, orange, and magenta on a shiny blue background. He also wore a pair of bright red suspenders decorated with a repeating pattern of tiny black figures, diamonds, clubs, hearts, and spades. With this ensemble, and the gambler's glint in his hazel eyes, Bill Stanley looked like a riverboat cardsharp.

"What's this?" I pointed. "Power suspenders?"

Bill hooked his thumbs through the suspenders and grinned. "Clarence Darrow never had a pair of galluses like these. Want some coffee?"

"Sure." My feet sank into the thick forest-green carpet that covered the floor in the reception area and the hallway as I accompanied him to a combination lunchroom-kitchenette, with a microwave oven on a counter and a refrigerator in the corner. Next to the stainless steel sink a pot of coffee was already brewed. Bill took two mugs from a cupboard and filled both, handing one to me. Then he opened the refrigerator, pulled out a quart of milk, and sniffed the top of the carton to see if the contents had gone bad. Evidently it hadn't, because he splashed some into his coffee.

"This way," he said, and I followed.

Bill's corner office had the same dark green carpet as the reception area and corridor. The walls were ivory and the tall windows had pale green vertical blinds open to a view of Broadway, Oakland's main downtown thoroughfare, now busy with morning commute traffic. He also had a clear view down Nineteenth Street to Telegraph Avenue, where I saw the fading Art Deco husk of the Fox Oakland Theater. As I stared down at the old movie palace, I remembered how it looked years ago and wished someone with money and vision would rehab it into another jewel like the Paramount.

I turned from the window and looked at Bill. His desk was a wide oak rectangle, strewn with papers and files, yellow legal pads, pens and pencils in a pewter beer stein, and a notebook computer. Behind the desk I saw a swivel chair upholstered in well-worn brown leather and an oak credenza on which rested a telephone, a fat Rolodex, and an open leather briefcase. A coat tree stood in the corner, with Bill's suit jacket hanging on one hook.

Bill waved me to a couple of chairs covered with nubby green tweed, arranged in front of his desk. A low table between the chairs held this morning's Oakland *Tribune* and San Francisco *Chronicle*. I sat down and looked around, sipping my coffee. I've always wanted one of those lawyer's bookcases with the individual glass doors for each shelf, and Bill had a pair of them, on the wall to my right. Above the credenza I saw a framed poster advertising the Oakland Ballet's production of *Le Train Bleu*. Bill didn't strike me as the ballet type, I thought as the attorney settled into his leather chair and set his coffee cup on the nearest file folder.

"Heard anything from the police or the D.A.'s office?" I asked.

Bill shook his head. "Too early. I'll be over at the courthouse this morning. I'll schmooze with the D.A., see what I can find out. Cops should have test results later today."

"When's the autopsy?"

"Don't know. I'll have someone find out. Let's get the money matters out of the way first. What's your usual rate?"

I had brought a copy of my standard contract with me. Now I took it from my purse and Bill and I went over it. "Looks good to me," he said, signing it. "When Donetta gets in, I'll have her cut you a check."

"After we left police headquarters, I went over to the Franklins' house." I described my Sunday morning visit, adding that Kevin Franklin hadn't spent the night there. "I'll check his story. There's probably nothing to it, but he certainly was evasive. What about Ruth's little girl? Do you think she saw something that might help our case? I'd sure like to know what she told the police."

"We'll find out tonight," Bill said. "I've arranged with

140

the Franklins to talk to Wendy. Their place, seven o'clock. I'd like you to be there, since the kid knows you. In the meantime, start at the beginning and tell me everything about your investigation."

I gave Bill a detailed account, from the day I was hired by Ruth Raynor and Blair Castle to locate Sam Raynor's hidden assets, to my last conversation with Ruth on Friday, the day before the murder, right before she, Wendy, and I pigged out on ice cream at Fenton's. He was particularly interested in Friday's confrontation with Sam Raynor himself.

"He sounds like a jerk," Bill said. "A dangerous jerk."

"I agree. Raynor and I were out in the open with lots of people around. I can generally take care of myself. But I felt menaced. I wondered how a woman like Ruth could marry a guy like Raynor. That's why I went over to talk with her, so I could understand it better. I guess the Sam Raynors of this world are very good at hiding their true natures."

"And the women who marry them are very good at deluding themselves." Bill washed down his cynical words with coffee. "I see this happen all the time. Blair Castle handles lots of divorces involving abusive husbands. The slimeball marries some woman, beats the shit out of her and the kids, she finally gets a bellyful and leaves the guy. Blair says for every woman who leaves, there's probably four who stay." He shook his head.

"And if she does leave, the husband won't let go. I remember one case down in Fremont. Blair was frantic about it. She kept saying to me, he's gonna kill her, he's gonna kill her. So one night the ex-husband came after the ex-wife, with a shotgun. But she got him first." Bill's voice was matter-of-fact, leaving my imagination to illustrate the scene.

"Did you defend her?"

"Didn't have to." He waved his hand. "Clear-cut self-defense, lots of witnesses. D.A. didn't even charge her."

"The Raynor case isn't that cut-and-dried. I think the D.A. will charge Ruth. And I don't think she killed Sam."

He set his coffee mug down and leaned forward, elbows

141

on his desk. "What do you base that on, Jeri? Gut instinct?"

"Yes. That's what I'd call it."

"I don't fault it. I operate on guts too—instinct and gall. I'm not so sure the D.A. will charge. Let's wait for the test results and see what the cops have. Bottom line is, my job's defending Ruth Raynor. That's your job too. I'm looking at mitigating circumstances here. If you want to investigate Sam Raynor's murder, that's okay with me as long as it doesn't get in the way of defending Ruth. As I told you yesterday, anything you can find out about this guy will help our case. The more people who wanted to blow him away, the better it is for Ruth's defense. If some of those people had opportunity, even better."

I sipped my coffee as he talked, thinking about the three faces I'd seen in the pulsing red lights outside Ruth's apartment building, two that I recognized and the third that I didn't know. That face had been so full of anger that I'd made note of it. Would I ever see it again? I had a feeling that the person who belonged to that face was somehow tied into this. As for the other two, they were high on my list of people I wanted to interview. I intended to find out what they were doing at the scene of Sam Raynor's murder.

"What do you think he did with the money?" Bill asked, bringing me back to the here-and-now.

"I think Raynor had several friends open bank accounts under the friends' names. Any deposits over ten thousand get reported to the feds, so I figure he broke it into smaller increments and spread it out all over the Bay Area. That way, if I find one bank account, I might not locate the others. So far that's just a theory. I haven't been able to find a paper trail."

"It's plausible," Bill said. "Any candidates for these helpful friends and thrifty savers?"

I finished my coffee and set the mug on the low table next to me. "According to Ruth, there's no family. Looks like Raynor moved the money from Guam via a Wells Fargo branch in San Jose. He may have disguised some of the cash as gambling debts, since he was involved in a reg-

142

ular poker game. That would be easy enough to do, small amounts over a period of time. I plan to check his poker-playing buddies. Raynor lived with another sailor named Pettibone, but he's a flake. After meeting the guy, I don't know that I'd trust him with grocery money, let alone a large chunk of cash."

Bill leaned forward. "What about the girlfriend? If we're playing hide-the-cash, I'd pick the girlfriend every time."

"Raynor had two. I think he was involved with Claudia Yancy, the wife of his chief, who's also one of the poker players. The other is Tiffany Collins, a civil service employee at the air station. Last month Tiffany traded up from a Subaru. She acquired a used Mercedes 450 SEL convertible, supposedly with her own money, although I understand Mr. Raynor handled the transaction."

Bill whistled. "A car like that's worth . . ."

"According to the insurance adjuster, about forty-five thousand. The car's history, by the way. It was stolen last week. Sam Raynor's the one who bought that car, no matter who it was registered to. And my guess is that the car theft is part of Raynor's scam. The girlfriend files the claim, the insurance company pays her, and she gives the money to Raynor, which makes it a gift from her to him. Except none of this has happened yet. Too soon for the insurance company to pay the claim. Besides, I tipped off the adjuster. He's going to be very slow with the paperwork."

"Even with the car," Bill pointed out, "that doesn't account for all of Raynor's missing cash. You're probably right about him spreading it around. Do what you can to find it. But remember, our first priority is to beat this rap."

I agreed with him. Ruth's situation was of primary importance. But I had a feeling the money was the key.

"What I want you to do today," Bill said, "is go over to that apartment building and beat the bushes for anybody who saw or heard anything. The cops supposedly have a witness, a neighbor. This Mrs. Parmenter says she saw Ruth dump the gun."

Just as I'd thought. The elderly woman Ruth and I had

143

encountered in the hallway on Friday afternoon. "Not unless she was right behind Ruth."

"Yeah. I saw a sketch of the scene. Talk to the woman, find out what she saw, or thinks she saw. And what time she saw it. I want to know what happened when. If you can find another witness who can shake the neighbor's story, all the better."

"There's something you should know," I said. "I've been dating a guy named Alex Tongco, a lieutenant commander stationed over at NAS Alameda. He was Sam Raynor's department head." I told Bill about the Navy's pending *JAG Manual* investigation. Was I being overly concerned about a possible conflict with the Navy in conducting my own inquiry?

Bill shook his head. "Hell, it's not like we're asking for classified information. I've had some dealings with the air station before. Worked out fine. If the information we need is discoverable, we can get it. Do what you have to. Any problems, let me know. As for your Navy friend, I trust your judgment. If it gets in the way, we'll talk."

The door to Bill's office opened and a woman entered. She was tiny, less than five feet tall, with coffee-colored skin and short black hair sprinkled with gray. She wore a mauve silk dress with a shawl collar that showcased the gold necklace around her slender neck. Her brown eyes glanced at me briefly, but her objective was Bill.

"Bill, you're due at the courthouse in twenty minutes," she said, her voice stern.

"Yeah, I'd better get going." Bill stood up, buttoning his collar and fixing his tie. "Jeri Howard, private investigator, meet Donetta Fox, my secretary and strong right arm. Never mind the names on the letterhead. Donetta runs the place."

"Only because you need a keeper." Donetta Fox turned to me and tilted her head to one side, looking me over as I got to my feet. "Private investigator. You've worked for us before."

"You've got a good memory," I told her.

144

"That's why I run the place." Donetta turned to Bill. "Do we have a new case?"

"Ruth Raynor. Her husband got killed late Saturday night. Nasty divorce, you know the routine. Mrs. Raynor's father gave me a check. It's in my top drawer." Bill collected an armful of files and papers from his desk and transferred them to his briefcase. "I've signed Jeri's contract. She needs some money."

"I'll take care of everything."

Bill put on his jacket, grabbed his briefcase and headed for the door, tossing words over his shoulder. "Don't forget, we talk to Wendy tonight. Seven o'clock."

Eighteen

AFTER LEAVING BILL STANLEY'S OFFICE I DEPOSITED the check, then I retrieved my Toyota and headed for the Bay Bridge. I took the exit for Yerba Buena Island and Treasure Island. As I drove across the causeway, sunlight winked and shifted on the water of San Francisco Bay. In a nearby lagoon white-hulled sailboats dipped and shimmied at their moorings.

Today the gate was guarded by a ramrod-straight Marine whose semishaved head and muscled arms made him look as though he'd been carved from obsidian. I showed him my driver's license and told him I was here to see Chief LeBard at the Treasure Island police station. The Marine picked up a phone in his guard shack and punched in a number. I hadn't called to make an appointment but LeBard must have been in his office. I saw the Marine's mouth move as he spoke into the receiver. Then he hung up the

145

phone, stepped back outside, gave me a pass and waved me through.

I didn't go directly to LeBard's office. Instead I made an immediate right turn into the parking lot of the Treasure Island administration building and parked the Toyota in a visitor's slot. The first floor lobby of the curved building contains a small historical museum, but I had viewed the contents of the glass display cases before. I checked a directory sign and took a long curved staircase to the second floor. Kevin Franklin's friend, Lieutenant Commander Charles Porter, worked at RedCom 20, which was Navy talk for Readiness Command Region 20. I located the office, a large suite full of smaller offices, on the bay side of the building, the portals guarded by a civilian secretary. She was an older woman with short gray hair, wearing a stylish silky print and a lot of gold jewelry. Her eyes flicked over my blue slacks and checked shirt, and she wrinkled her nose, passing judgment on their appropriateness as attire. No doubt I came up short in her estimation.

"Jeri Howard to see Lieutenant Commander Porter," I told the secretary.

She ran a finger down her appointment book and frowned. "He has an appointment at nine-thirty, with a Lieutenant Crowell. You say your name is Howard? Is he expecting you?"

"No, but it's important." I looked around me at the desks and the open doors of various offices. Four officers, two men and two women, stood in the doorway of one cubicle, their conversation punctuated by laughter. I pointed a thumb in their direction. "Is that him over there, the tall dark one?"

"No, he's the blond one." I set off in Porter's direction, the secretary at my heels. "Commander Porter, this lady would like a word with you."

The group outside the doorway broke up, three of the officers looking at me curiously as they headed in their own directions. Charles Porter's back had been toward me. Now he turned and took a few steps toward me. He was a broad-shouldered man in a summer khaki uniform decorated with

146

the usual array of ribbons on the left breast. His skin was fair, the type that sunburns easily, and he had blue eyes in a square face. He stopped and smiled pleasantly as he surveyed me. "You're not Lieutenant Crowell."

"No, I'm not." I walked past him and paused at the doorway where he and the other officers had been standing. The desk inside the smaller office faced the door. At its front perimeter I saw a black nameplate with white letters, reading LCDR C. K. PORTER. I strolled in, past the desk to the window, which looked out at San Francisco Bay and the city beyond.

"Great view," I said, my eyes sweeping over the wide, ever-shifting surface of the water to the Ferry Building, towering at the end of Market Street. "If this were my office, I'd move the desk so I could take advantage of the window."

"Who are you? What do you want?"

I turned to face him, my hip against the windowsill. "I'm Jeri Howard, an investigator, working for Ruth Franklin Raynor. Have you talked to Kevin Franklin since Saturday?"

His jaw muscle tensed, a rhythmic play of muscles around his mouth. His eyebrows met in a point above his nose and formed worried wings as he stared at me. Porter moved toward his desk, reaching for the telephone receiver. He wore a Naval Academy ring on his right hand, just like the one I'd seen Kevin wear. "How do I know you're who you say you are? Suppose you give me one good reason why I shouldn't call the base police and have you taken into custody?"

"Ask for Chief LeBard," I shot back. "He's expecting me. Or call Admiral Franklin." I recited the phone number, but Porter made no move to call it. Instead his hand dropped away from the receiver. "Here's your one good reason, Porter. Ruth Franklin Raynor is in jail. Her husband was murdered Saturday night."

Shock and disbelief washed over Porter's face, erasing the tensing muscles at his jaw and filling his blue eyes with confusion. Evidently he had neither talked to Kevin nor heard about Sam Raynor's death, something Kevin had known since his parents and I informed him of it early Sunday morning. Surely Kevin would have picked up the phone and informed Porter of the traumatic events that had occurred while the two of them were enjoying their beers and sea stories. Unless Porter wasn't around to get the news.

"Kevin says he took Ruth home Saturday night, about eleven o'clock." My eyes bored into Porter. "Then he went to see you at your apartment on Bayo Vista. That's not far from Ruth's building, at Forty-first and Howe, so it wouldn't have taken him long to get there. According to Kevin, the two of you had a few beers, talked, and he slept on your sofa. He got back to his parents' house about six Sunday morning. Sam Raynor was killed around eleven-thirty. Was Kevin with you at that time?"

Porter's jaw tightened again and a thin film of moisture appeared on his clean-shaven upper lip. He saw me watching him and averted his eyes, looking out the window as he wiped the palm of his right hand over his chin, as though to still the movement of his facial muscles.

"Did you see Kevin Franklin late Saturday night?" I asked again. "Or any time this weekend?"

Porter took a deep breath and backed further into the corner I'd provided for him. "Kevin was at my apartment Saturday night."

"Maybe he was. I note that you don't say you actually saw him. I certainly hope you're more decisive at the helm of a ship." I stepped between Porter and the window, blocking his view of the bay.

"You're lying, Commander, and so is Kevin Franklin. I don't know why but I'll find out. Considering that Ruth Raynor may be charged with murder before the week is out, I hope you both have a damned good reason." In the long ensuing silence, I took one of my business cards from my purse and slapped it down on his desk blotter. "Call me when you figure out where your loyalties lie."

By now Lieutenant Crowell had arrived for her appointment, a tall slender woman in a service dress-blue uniform with two gold stripes around the cuffs, her dark hair scraped back into a knot under her bucket of a hat. She carried a briefcase and stood behind the secretary, who hovered at a respectful distance outside Porter's office, an anxious look on her face.

"He's all yours, Lieutenant," I said as I walked through the doorway.

I drove the few blocks to the Treasure Island police station. Duffy LeBard waited for me in his office, his height and bulk filling the room, face stern, arms folded across his broad chest. "I was about to send out a search party."

"I made a detour."

"This is my turf," he said, steel beneath his honey-soft Southern drawl. "You say you're comin' to see me, you don't make detours. Where did you go?"

I acknowledged his words with a nod. "I went to see Lieutenant Commander Charles Porter, RedCom Twenty. He's somebody's alibi, not a very good one, I might add. Sam Raynor was murdered Saturday night."

"Good riddance," the chief said with a snort. "I heard that news Sunday morning. Also heard the wife shot him."

"I don't think so."

"How does Porter figure in?" the chief asked, motioning me to a chair. He settled into his own chair, pulled out a desk drawer and propped up his feet as I told him Kevin Franklin's story. LeBard shook his head. "You don't think the brother would kill Raynor and let his sister take the heat? I sure as hell wouldn't do that to my own sister. It just doesn't make sense."

"I know it doesn't. But I also know when people are lying to me, especially if they're not good at it. Kevin Franklin and Charles Porter are both lousy poker players. Their faces telegraph every card. I want to know what and why."

"Don't know if I can help you there," LeBard said, frowning. "I got no reason to contact Porter."

"I don't expect you to. I think I shook him up pretty good this morning. He'll be on the phone to Kevin Franklin very soon, if not as we speak. Let me see what sifts out."

LeBard pursed his wide-lipped mouth and blew out an

149

audible puff of air. His chair squeaked as he leaned back and tilted his head to one side. "Now if Mrs. Raynor didn't blow ol' Sam away, who do you think did?"

"I have a few candidates. I saw a couple of faces I recognized outside Ruth's apartment early Sunday morning. I'll have to ask them what they were doing there. I'd also like to know where Harlan Pettibone was at the time."

Duffy LeBard chuckled. "I can answer that question, real easy. Ol' Harlan got himself arrested Saturday night, at the NAS enlisted club. Little bastard got likkered up and took on a couple of Marines. The jarheads kicked his sorry butt all over the floor. After the dispensary patched him up, the base cops tossed all three of them in the brig so's they could cool their jets. They're all going up in front of their respective commanding officers sometime today. The Marines claim Harlan started it. They've both got clean records, so I'm inclined to believe 'em. Harlan, on the other hand, is a miserable excuse for a human being who wouldn't know the truth if it bit him on the ass. He's looking at brig time. After that, he's about due for a bad conduct discharge. I fervently hope he gets tossed out of my Navy."

I considered this, chewing on my lip. The fight gave Harlan an alibi and made it more difficult for me to check the sailor's movements on Saturday. If Harlan's commanding officer incarcerated him for fighting, I wouldn't be able to get to him until he was released.

"What was Harlan doing before he got into that fight?" I asked. "Guess I need to talk to his pool-playing buddies, if you can get me some names."

LeBard told me he'd see what he could do about identifying Harlan's running mates. It wasn't so much Pettibone's friends I was interested in as Raynor's movements the day he died. The two men had been roommates. Surely they'd seen each other Friday night or during the day on Saturday. Maybe the landlady, the helpful Mrs. Torelli, could provide some answers.

I drove back over the Bay Bridge to Oakland, stopping at my office to check messages. There was one from a

150

Lieutenant Bruinsma at the Naval Air Station. When I returned the call, I discovered that the lieutenant had just had something dropped in her lap—the *JAG Manual* investigation on Sam Raynor.

"Why did you want to talk with me, Lieutenant?"

"I understand you had an appointment with Petty Officer Raynor on Friday. What was that concerning?"

"How did you know about that?" I asked. It felt odd to be the subject of someone else's investigation instead of the person doing the investigating.

"He wrote it on his desk calendar. Your name, phone number, and the time. He must have had some reason for contacting a private investigator."

"Not the reason you think. The meeting concerned Raynor's divorce. I'm working for Ruth Raynor."

"Ah," she said. "That explains his mood. Chief Yancy said Petty Officer Raynor was in a foul mood when he got back to work. I've talked with some of Raynor's coworkers. They said he and his wife were having an acrimonious divorce. Evidently there were some bad feelings."

"Bad feelings." My voice sharpened. "Why do you think Ruth Raynor had a restraining order against her husband? He was a wife beater. Keep in mind that I'm working for the defense in this case. And based on my one meeting with Sam Raynor, I wouldn't describe him as a prize."

The lieutenant's tone matched my own. "And keep in mind that I'm getting feedback from the people Raynor worked with. He gave them his side of the story, and for the most part they liked him. I'm trying to be objective, Ms. Howard. The only thing I'm supposed to pass judgment on is whether Petty Officer Raynor died in the line of duty."

"Fair enough," I said. I had to admit I was partisan in this matter. The lieutenant was trying to be objective, and the scope of her investigation was admittedly limited. "Just so we know which side everyone's on. Have you talked with Raynor's girlfriend yet?"

"Someone mentioned he'd been dating a civil service employee, but I don't have a name."

151

I told Lieutenant Bruinsma about Tiffany Collins, but I didn't mention Claudia Yancy. I wanted to talk with Claudia first.

"I've been looking through Raynor's service record," the lieutenant said. "He hadn't been at this command long, but his file looks clean."

During our initial interview, Duffy LeBard had indicated that he'd prefer to be an anonymous source concerning Sam Raynor. But Raynor's murder had upped the stakes. I phrased my next words carefully. "I suggest you dig deeper, Lieutenant. Chief LeBard at Treasure Island was with the Armed Forces Police on Guam. He may be able to tell you a few things about Raynor."

That piqued Lieutenant Bruinsma's interest. We ended the call with a wary agreement to cooperate with each other's investigation. After she hung up, I called my friend Mary at the Alameda air station's administrative offices. "Is Tiffany Collins at work this morning?"

"As a matter of fact," Mary told me, "she called in sick. She's a good worker, but now and then she gets a mysterious illness on Mondays, presumably after an interesting weekend. By the way, Jeri, I've been hearing some disturbing things about that guy she's been dating. Such as, he can't keep his hands to himself where women are concerned. I like Tiffany. I hope she hasn't gotten herself into a bad situation."

Considering Tiffany's current boyfriend was in the Alameda County Morgue, it had been a more interesting weekend than most, and Tiffany's situation was a big question mark. I didn't tell Mary that, however. It was a sure bet that Lieutenant Bruinsma would come looking for Tiffany. Let Mary find out that way. I depressed the button on my phone and dialed Tiffany's home number. I got a recording of Tiffany's voice, inviting me to leave a message after the tone. I hung up instead.

That doesn't mean she's not home, I thought. Maybe she was sick, in bed, not wanting to bother with the phone. Then again, maybe she wasn't.

152

Nineteen

I DROVE DOWN TO SAN LEANDRO TO SEE FOR MYSELF.
Tiffany Collins's designated parking slot at the Estudillo
Avenue apartment was empty. I went up the metal stairs at
the front end of the stucco building and knocked on Tiffany's door several times, but there was no answer. The elderly neighbor lifted her curtain and glared at me. I tapped
on her door, hoping to ask if she'd seen Tiffany, but she
wouldn't answer.

I drove back to Oakland, to the motorcycle repair shop
where Acey Collins worked. Maybe he could tell me where
his sister was. But Acey wasn't at the shop. He's off Mondays, said another mechanic. When I parked in front of the
Victorian on Miles Avenue, the old Plymouth I'd seen on
my earlier visit was in the driveway, along with Acey's
Harley.

As before, music poured out the open screen door, but
this time it was Bob Seger wailing "Night Moves." I rang
the bell, pounded on the door and called out. Finally
Genevieve Collins appeared from the back of the house, in
shorts, a T-shirt, and sandals, drying her hands on a dish
towel. She looked at me, her mouth drawn down at the corners, then crossed the living room, turned the music down
a notch, and unlocked the screen door.

"He's on the back porch," she said.

I followed her to the kitchen, a big rectangle with a
round oak table at this end, its surface scarred and stained,
four pleated cloth place mats arranged in front of four mis-
matched chairs. The counter that ran down one wall was as
old-fashioned as the house, constructed of tiny squares of

brown and white tile. Above the counter I saw tall cabinets painted white, so high that they were the reason for the metal step stool propped nearby. On the opposite wall was a big refrigerator, its door covered with papers held by magnets. The big gas stove in the far corner looked older than I was.

Genevieve dropped the dish towel onto the counter and walked to the back door, motioning me to follow. We stepped out onto the enclosed porch, about five feet square, holding a washer and dryer, with a shelf above both appliances for laundry supplies. The dryer had been pulled away from its hookup. Acey Collins sat on the bare board floor, an open toolbox within reach.

"Gen, why'd you turn down the music?" he asked. Then he looked up, saw me and scowled. "Shit. What're you doing here?"

"I'm glad to see you too, Acey. Let's talk."

He tossed a pair of pliers into the toolbox and scrambled to his feet, wiping his hands on the legs of his faded blue jeans. He wore a sleeveless white athletic shirt that revealed his muscled shoulders and arms.

"What the hell do you want?" he barked as he strode into the kitchen. He opened the refrigerator door with such force that a magnet and a child's drawing fell to the floor. He plucked both items off the linoleum and slapped them back into place. Then he seized a can of Budweiser, popped it open and took a long swallow.

"You knew I was going to turn up sooner or later," I said. "What were you doing outside Ruth Raynor's apartment building early Sunday morning?"

Acey slammed the beer can down on the counter and some of the amber brew splashed onto the tiled surface. He raised his arms toward the ceiling, palms up in angry supplication as he directed his words to his wife.

"See? See? What did I tell you?"

Genevieve sighed and looked at him with the same mixture of patience and exasperation I'd seen in her eyes the week before, when she looked at her children. She reached for a dishrag and wiped up the spilled beer, then took a sip

154

from the can as she leaned against the counter. "Don't tell me, tell her. Or you'll be talking to the cops."

By now the music had stopped and it was quiet in the house, so quiet I hoped someone would fill the silence. Acey put his hands on his hips and lowered his ponytailed head, like an angry bull that's been backed into a corner. Then he looked up at me and drew in a deep breath.

"Okay, I was there. For the same reason everybody else was. Curiosity. I heard the sirens, saw the lights, walked over to check it out. Hell's bells, I didn't know Raynor's old lady lived there till I read about it in the paper."

"You walked over from where? What were you doing on Piedmont that night?"

"A buddy of mine owns a bar on Piedmont, between Forty-first and Linda. It's called the Royal Flush." I nodded. I'd seen the place, a neighborhood tavern with a stained-glass window and a wooden door, its neon sign decorated with the five cards of that particular poker hand. "I had a few beers and played darts," Acey continued. "You got a problem with that?"

"Since Sam Raynor was murdered a block away, maybe I do. Just tell me everything you did that night, especially from eleven o'clock on."

"The paper said the cops have the wife in custody," Genevieve said. "Ruth, isn't that her name? You don't think she shot him?"

"She says no. I think she was set up, by someone who saw an opportunity to kill Sam Raynor and let Ruth take the blame. My guess is that person was with Sam when he went up to Ruth's apartment. Maybe a friend, a person he trusted. Someone he'd turn his back on."

"That lets me out," Acey said. "Raynor knew how I felt about him. Wouldn't've turned his back on me."

"Especially since you sent your buddies to rough him up in the parking lot at Nadine's. That was your doing, wasn't it?"

He took the beer from Genevieve's hand and raised the can to his mouth. As he did, a look passed between husband and wife. "Yeah, that was me," he admitted after he'd

155

swallowed a mouthful. "Bastard didn't scare like I thought he would. But I didn't kill him. Sam Raynor's not worth going to jail for."

"So where were the two of you Saturday night?"

"I was working," Genevieve said.

"And Acey was at the bar? Where were the kids?"

"Sleep-over at my sister's. She and her husband took all the kids to Marine World on Sunday so Acey and I could have a day to ourselves."

"Where do you work?"

"New Sunshine Pizza on Piedmont."

"Let me take a wild guess," I said, my eyes moving from Genevieve to Acey. "Sam came into the restaurant Saturday night. With Tiffany." Neither of them said anything. "You know, Tiffany called in sick this morning. She's not at work. I just went by her apartment. She's not there either, or she's not answering the phone or the doorbell. Any idea where she is?"

Acey swore under his breath. "No, I don't. I tried to get her on the phone all day yesterday. Kept getting that damn answering machine." He shook his head. "She can't be involved in all this. She just can't."

"But she was with Sam Saturday night."

Genevieve walked to the table, pulled out a chair and sat down. "They came into the restaurant about nine and ordered a pizza. It wasn't my table, so I didn't wait on them. When I spotted Tiffany, I called Acey over at the Royal Flush."

"Why?"

"Because I knew he wanted to talk to his sister. I thought since Acey was just down the street, he could sort of drop in by accident, to see me, you know? Except Tiffany knows I work there. I didn't know if she'd buy it."

"And the reason for this brotherly concern?" I asked, turning to Acey.

"You," he said, shooting me an outraged look. "You told me Raynor'd been beating up on his wife. I never laid a hand on my wife and I sure as hell don't want anybody slapping my sister around. I told Tiff that the last time I saw her, on Friday. She said she didn't believe me. I said, you ask that guy straight out if he's ever hit his wife and you look at his face when he answers. That's what I wanted to talk to her about. That, and the car."

"Why the car?"

"This whole business with that goddamn Mercedes stinks to high heaven." Acey leaned against the counter and folded his arms across his chest. "When Tiff told me she and Raynor bought this fancy car, I thought, this jerk took her money, kept most of it and bought some junker. But I looked the Mercedes over and it was in good shape, nothing wrong. So I figure maybe Raynor's up to something else, like a VIN switch."

I looked blank, and Acey proceeded to explain. "VIN—vehicle identification number. Every car's got one. Some guy buys a junker for a coupla hundred bucks, for the VIN and the license plate, which he puts on a stolen car. Then he can turn over the hot car legit."

Since Acey had done some time in Folsom, I saw no reason to doubt that he knew what he was talking about. "So you assumed all along the Mercedes was hot."

"Absolutely," Acey said. "Tiff said they bought it from some guy who advertised in the classifieds. It's not like going to some car lot where you can check the pedigree." He rubbed his chin and took another sip of beer. "Thing was, I couldn't get all the pieces to fit. I thought Raynor was after Tiff's money. Then you come along and tell me he's trying to hide money from his wife. The scam's going the other way. Except I'm not sure what the scam is. Then the damn car gets stolen. I know Raynor had something to do with it. Tiff said she didn't believe that either. But she was having trouble with the insurance claim, bitching up one side and down the other about the adjuster dragging his heels. I told her to think about that too."

I pulled out a chair and joined Genevieve at the table. "You talked to Tiffany after she'd talked to the insurance company?"

"Yeah, Friday afternoon," Acey said. "She'd had words with the adjuster that morning. Then she and I had words."

"So between the two of us," I said, "we'd planted a few seeds of doubt. You wanted to talk with her again, to see if any of those seeds starting growing."

"That sums it up real good." Acey finished off the beer, crumpled the can and tossed it into a cardboard box next to the trash can, filled with other cans as well as bottles and jars. "Tiff's like that. You give her something to chew on and sooner or later she makes up her mind. I've been hoping she'd see what a shitheel Raynor was and blow him off." He stopped and looked horrified at his choice of words. "But she wouldn't shoot him, fer crissakes."

I cocked my head in Genevieve's direction. "You saw them at the restaurant. Was the bloom off the rose?"

"They looked like they were arguing," she conceded. "But I didn't hear anything. You'll have to ask Zeke, the guy that waited on them."

"I will. What time did they leave?"

She shrugged. "Don't know. I was in the kitchen. When I came out they were gone."

I looked up at Acey. "Where were you?"

"When Gen called me, I decided my best shot was to waylay Tiff when they left the restaurant. So I walked up from the Royal Flush and waited across the street."

"What time was that?"

He shook his head. "Not sure. It was maybe nine-thirty when I left the bar, and it's about a five-minute walk to the restaurant. I had time for a couple of cigarettes. There were a lot of people on the avenue, probably the movie crowd let out from the Piedmont Theater. So I'm guessing it was ten or after when I spotted Tiff and Raynor coming out of the pizza place. They hung a right and started walking up Piedmont toward Fortieth. I followed 'em. They went to that parking lot behind the shops, between Fortieth and Forty-first." I nodded. It was the same lot that bordered Howe Street, barely half a block from Ruth's apartment. "They stopped right in back of Tiff's Subaru. It was parked near the street, near Fortieth. Didn't see Raynor's Trans-Am. They must've been in separate cars, 'cause Tiff drove off by herself."

"What happened before Tiffany left? Did you ever talk to her?"

Slowly he shook his head. "No. I kept hoping Raynor would leave, so I could have a word with her. I stayed back about thirty paces, trying to keep out of sight and wishing I could hear what they were saying. 'Cause they were having an argument for sure. Tiff was mad. I could tell."

Acey shook his head again. "This Caddy came rolling by, blasting rap music. I turned my head, just for a second. When I turned back, Tiff was in her Subaru, backing it out of the parking space. And Raynor went walking off fast, toward Forty-first Street." He smacked one fist hard into the open palm of his other hand. "I saw Tiff drive out of the parking lot, damn it. She made a left on Howe Street and hauled ass. She couldn't have had anything to do with Raynor getting shot."

"Maybe, maybe not." I considered what he had told me. The fact that Tiffany had driven away from the parking lot did seem to alibi her, but she could have returned. Now, at least, I had an idea of Sam's movements shortly before his death. Had he met anyone else on Piedmont Avenue that night? "I'd like to know what they were fighting about."

"If I can find her, we'll both ask her," Acey said glumly. "But I sure as hell don't know where she is."

Twenty

I LEFT THE COLLINS'S HOUSE AND HEADED FOR PIED-mont Avenue. I parked in the lot where Acey had seen his sister and Sam Raynor on Saturday night and walked the aisles, looking for Raynor's red Trans-Am. Eventually, I found it, parked on Howe Street, three cars down from the construction site on the corner. Ruth's apartment building was on the opposite corner. Time had expired in more ways than one. A parking ticket was stuck under one of the wiper blades on the front windshield.

The car was locked. I examined the exterior and peered inside, searching for something that would tell me where Sam went and who he saw after he and Tiffany Collins parted company in the parking lot Saturday night. But the dark red upholstery gave up no secrets.

Raynor must have gone somewhere else after Tiffany drove away and before he showed up at Ruth's apartment. He and Tiffany left the restaurant just after ten. Ruth said she didn't get home from her parents' until eleven. Besides, Acey said his sister's car backed out of a space on the side of the parking lot closest to Fortieth Street. If Sam Raynor had been heading for his car—or Ruth's building—there was a parking lot exit on Howe Street, a few car lengths to the rear of the Trans-Am. But he hadn't gone that way, according to Acey. Raynor had walked toward Forty-first Street.

Maybe that doesn't mean anything, I told myself. Maybe he was angry with Tiffany and didn't care which direction he walked. Maybe he went to a bar. Ruth said she'd smelled beer on him. Maybe I was reaching when I wondered if he'd met someone later. But there was an hour, more or less, of Raynor's life unaccounted for that night.

I grabbed a sandwich and a soda at a nearby deli. While I ate I speculated about Raynor's movements that night. Then I tossed the debris into a waste can and left the deli by the rear door, passing the Dumpster where Ruth and I had seen the homeless woman Friday afternoon, probing the refuse for cans and bottles. I walked past the construction site and crossed Howe Street.

Today there was a large hand-printed sign on one of the apartment building's glass doors, admonishing residents and guests to close the door immediately on entering and not to prop it open for any reason. I ran my finger down the tenant list, past R. Franklin in 303 to M. Parmenter in 304. I pressed the button. A moment later a disembodied voice answered, coming out of the square intercom speaker, sounding tinny and full of static. "Yes? Who is it?"

"Mrs. Parmenter, my name is Jeri Howard. I'm an investigator. I'd like to talk to you about the shooting on Saturday night."

"I've already talked to the police."

"I'm a private investigator, Mrs. Parmenter. I work for Ruth Franklin Raynor."

"Well," she said, her tone letting me know exactly what she thought of my credentials. "How do I know that?"

"You can call Mrs. Raynor's attorney. His name is Bill Stanley. Or my attorney, Cassie Taylor, at Alwin, Taylor and Chao. Both can vouch for me." I gave her the phone numbers and she asked me to repeat them, which I did, slowly.

"You just wait," she said.

The speaker went dead. I could understand her caution, born of necessity to survive the urban environment, underscored by the murder that took place in this building. While I waited, my eyes went down the list of tenants on the third floor. Next to the number 301 was the legend "L. Copeland," while the same space next to unit 302 was empty. I wanted to talk with the tenants of these apartments. Both units were at the front of the apartment building, their doors opening on the wall just to the left of the elevator, sharing with Ruth Raynor's apartment the wide hallway outside the laundry room. If they had been home the night of the murder, maybe they'd heard or seen something.

I took a seat on the concrete planter where I'd waited for Ruth on Friday afternoon. I looked across the street at the construction site occupying the lot on the corner of Forty-first and Howe but I didn't see the homeless woman. Fifteen minutes crawled by. It was the middle of the afternoon, too early for the working crowd to come home from their Monday labors. Aside from the activity at the construction site and at Kaiser Hospital, two blocks away, the neighborhood seemed to be taking a siesta.

I stood up, impatient, and debated punching Mrs.

Parmenter's intercom button again. I walked to the double glass doors that barred my entry into the building and peered into the lobby just in time to see two people step off the elevator. One was the elderly woman Ruth and I had encountered in the hallway Friday afternoon. She wore white sneakers, lime-green sweatpants, and a lemon-yellow T-shirt. Her white hair was short and stylish. She held the arm of a muscular young man who wore garish neon pink and orange shorts and a purple tank top. The two of them were so bright they lit up the dark paneled walls of the building foyer. They moved slowly toward the front door, he slowing his sandaled feet to her pace. He opened the door and they both stared at me. Her eyes were blue, sharp and suspicious; his were brown, curious and amused.

"Mrs. Parmenter?" Up close she looked as though she was past seventy. She didn't give any sign that she recognized me.

"Yes. And this is Brett. He lives down the hall. We want to see some identification."

I reached into my purse and brought out my license. Mrs. Parmenter and Brett examined it. "Looks okay to me," he said, tilting his head down to her. His curly blond hair was cut short, save for a wispy tail down the back of his neck, and he wore a tiny gold hoop in his left ear.

"I don't hold much truck with lawyers," Mrs. Parmenter told me, "so I called the police instead. Sergeant Hobart said you were okay."

I mentally thanked Wayne Hobart for putting in a good word about me, or at least a neutral one. If she'd gotten Sid on the phone instead, I was sure he'd have given her an earful.

Mrs. Parmenter motioned me into the building. She was shorter than me, skinny and a bit creaky with age, her movements abrupt and jerky. She reminded me of the egrets and herons I saw along the bay shore. In the elevator I asked Brett for his last name and he told me it was Steiner. He lived in the apartment at the far end of the hall, the last door on the left, and he had lived in this building for four years. Mrs. Parmenter had been here longer, ever since her husband died ten years ago.

When the elevator door opened on the third floor, I saw the front door of Ruth's apartment, number 303. The yellow crime scene tape had been removed. As we stepped out of the elevator, I glanced to my left, at the door of 301, where a wreath of dried flowers hung above the number. I didn't think the wreath had been there Friday. The door of 302 was bare.

"Who lives in these apartments?" I asked, a sweep of my hand indicating both units.

"Lena's in 301," Brett Steiner said. "The other one's empty."

"Yes," Mrs. Parmenter added, "and poor Mr. Sullivan is worried about renting it, now that a murder has happened, right here in the building." She clucked and shook her head, averting her head from the hallway next to the laundry room, where Sam Raynor met his death.

We walked past Ruth's apartment, toward the other doors ranged down the long corridor that ran the length of the building with odd numbers on the left, even on the right. While Mrs. Parmenter opened the door of unit 304, I turned and glanced back, guessing the distance to Ruth's door, on the opposite wall, as about twenty feet. Then I followed the old woman into her apartment.

"Martha wants me to sit in," Brett said, bringing up the rear.

"That's fine. I may have some questions for you too."

He shrugged. "I can't tell you anything. I was out. Didn't get home until well after the excitement started."

Mrs. Parmenter led the way into her living room. Her unit had two bedrooms rather than Ruth's one, but it was similar in the layout of the kitchen, dining area, and living room. She had some lovely antiques among the furnishings, including an intricately carved walnut secretary and a large lamp table with corkscrew legs and eagle claw feet resting on glass balls. Mrs. Parmenter seemed to have a thing about ginger jars. I saw them everywhere, cloisonné and porcelain, in all sizes and colors. They stood next to the family photographs scattered here and there throughout the living room, on the counter that separated the kitchen from the living room, on the end table and the coffee table in front of the sofa. The array of furniture and accompanying dust catchers gave the room an overstuffed feeling, as though Mrs. Parmenter had once lived in a larger house and crammed her possessions and memories into this smaller space after her husband's death.

The sofa and wing chair were upholstered in matching floral chintz, both scattered with solid-color pillows in pastel shades. My hostess plumped the pillows on the sofa and sat down, settling herself comfortably. There was a wide-bottomed oak rocker next to the TV set on the wall opposite the sofa, its seat and back covered with a frilly flowered pad. Brett slouched into it, crossing one tanned leg over the other as he rocked gently back and forth. That left me the wing chair. I shoved a couple of pillows out of the way and sat down. They both looked at me expectantly. As I took my notebook and pen from my purse, I felt as though I were about to conduct a class.

"How well do you know Ruth? Or did you know her at all?"

"Just to speak to, in the hall or the laundry room," Mrs. Parmenter said. "I've seen her several times over at the Piedmont Grocery, when I was doing my marketing. I knew she lived there with her little girl. Seems to be a sweet little child, though very quiet. Her parents came to visit her from time to time, a short woman and a tall gray-haired man. I saw you visiting Ruth too. On Friday afternoon, when she got home from work. Brett told me Ruth works down the street at Kaiser. Didn't you, dear?"

"Yeah, that's what she said." His head bobbed up and down.

"I assumed Ruth was divorced or a widow," Mrs. Parmenter continued, "since I didn't see any evidence of a man about the place. She certainly didn't discuss that with me. The police told me it was her husband she shot."

"Estranged husband," I said. "And I'm not convinced she shot him. I wonder how he got in. It's a security build-

164

ing. I saw the sign about making sure the door's closed and not propping it open."

"Mr. Sullivan, the manager, put that sign up Sunday. Closing the barn door after the horse is long gone. But he's fussy about such things."

"Yeah." Brett grinned. "He and Lena, the woman in 301, had a disagreement about her propping the door open, right after she moved in."

"I suppose he has a point," Mrs. Parmenter said. "That must be how Ruth's husband got into the building. Obviously the front door wasn't closed properly. I do hope Lena didn't prop it open again."

"Or maybe someone let him in, someone who was just leaving the building." I looked from Brett to the old woman. "Mrs. Parmenter, please tell me what you saw and heard Saturday night."

"I was watching a video." Mrs. Parmenter gestured at the VCR on top of her television set. "I think it was about eleven, because it was the second video. Sometimes I rent two and have a double feature. I watched the first one, then I started watching the second one around ten. I'm sure I was midway through it."

I glanced at the VCR. As was usually the case, it had a digital clock readout on the front. "You're not sure of the time?"

"I think I glanced at the clock once or twice, but no, I'm not certain it was eleven. Well, I stopped the video and got up to make myself a cup of tea. That's when I heard the voices. It sounded like two people arguing. For some reason, when I'm in the kitchen I can hear people talking in that hall outside the elevator. It's just the other side of that wall." She pointed toward the far wall of her dining area.

"You say it sounded as though they were arguing. Could you make out what they were saying?"

Mrs. Parmenter shook her head. "No. It just had that tone to it, if you know what I mean. So I went to the front door and opened it and stuck my head out." From the rocking chair, Brett flashed a sudden grin. Both Mrs. Parmenter and I spotted it. The old lady tilted her chin upward with a defiant jerk. "Well, I am a nosy old biddy. I admit it."

"Martha knows everything that goes on in this building," Brett said, nodding his blond head.

"Go on, Mrs. Parmenter. What did you see?"

"I saw Ruth. She was having words with a young man, right in front of the door to her apartment. His back was to me so I didn't see his face. But I'd say he was tall with fair hair."

That description would fit Sam Raynor—and a lot of other men. "What was he wearing?"

"Blue jeans. And a short-sleeved shirt."

I frowned. This was no help to Ruth. The night of his murder, Sam Raynor had been wearing blue jeans and a short-sleeved pullover shirt, a pale green knit. But when Kevin Franklin arrived at his parents' house early Sunday morning, he was dressed in jeans and a light blue knit pullover. Both men were tall and fair-haired.

"Once you looked out," I said, "could you hear what they were saying?"

"No." She shook her head again, this time regretfully. "But I'm sure they were arguing. I could tell from their gestures and the look on Ruth's face. I didn't want them to see me, so I shut the door and locked it. Then I put the tea-kettle on. While I was waiting for the water to boil I got a handful of cookies out of the jar, and I was carrying them back to the living room when I heard this loud bang. It startled me so much I dropped the cookies. I knew it was a gun. I've heard guns before. My late husband used to go to the firing range to shoot his pistol. I picked up the phone and called 911. The young woman said that they would send a patrolman around to check on it."

According to the preliminary information Bill Stanley had obtained from the Oakland police, Mrs. Parmenter's call came in at 11:14 P.M. A patrol car arrived at the Howe street address at 11:27 P.M. The patrolmen had buzzed Mrs. Parmenter's apartment and she let them in. When they reached the third floor, they found Sam Raynor's body in the hallway in front of the stairwell door. Then Wendy's

166

cries led them through the open door of apartment 303, to Ruth, lying on the floor in her own living room. I had to find out what had happened in that critical thirteen minutes between Mrs. Parmenter's call and the arrival of the police.

"You told the police you saw Ruth Raynor drop something down the trash chute," I said. "When?"

"Right after I called the police. I heard a door open and I wanted to see if anyone else had heard the shot. That's when I saw her. She had something in her hand and she dropped it down the trash chute, then turned around and went right back into her apartment, before I could say anything to her."

"You can't see the trash chute from your door," I pointed out.

"I know that, young lady." Mrs. Parmenter sounded huffy. "But she had something in her right hand. She walked straight out of her apartment, in the direction of the trash chute, and straight back. It was just a matter of a few seconds. The door of the trash chute has a spring so that it closes automatically. It makes an audible thump when it swings shut. That's what I heard. So I knew she'd dropped something down the trash chute." She looked at me triumphantly, as though she'd just played her ace.

I didn't choose to debate with her. "What did you do after that?"

"I went to the bathroom," Mrs. Parmenter said, coloring slightly. "When I came out, the teakettle was whistling. I made myself a cup of tea, though my hand was shaking so much I thought I'd drop it. Then my intercom buzzed and it was the police. Things got very hectic after that."

"May I see your bathroom?" I asked.

My hostess looked surprised at this request, but she nodded. I located the bathroom and flipped on the light switch. The fixtures were beige, a round sink with a cabinet underneath, a toilet, lid down, and another ginger jar on the tank, which had a fluffy apricot cover that matched the rugs on the floor and the towels hanging on the wall rack. A clouded glass shower door was partly open, revealing Mrs.

167

Parmenter's hand wash drying on a plastic hanger suspended from the shower head.

What interested me most, however, was the whirring sound of the ventilator fan, high on the wall above the toilet. It was noisy and it switched on and off automatically when I flipped the bathroom light switch. When Mrs. Parmenter stepped out of the bathroom that night, her teakettle was whistling. Presumably it had reached the boiling point while she was in the bathroom. Could the combination of ventilator fan and shrilling teakettle have masked the sound of another gunshot?

When I returned to the living room I stood in front of the TV set and ran my hand over the VCR perched on top. It looked a lot like mine, and I wondered if it behaved the same way. "When you first got up, right before you heard the voices in the hall, did you stop the videotape?" I asked, pointing at the VCR remote on the coffee table, "or did you hit the pause button on the remote?"

"The pause button." She narrowed her eyes. Mrs. Parmenter might be a nosy old biddy, but she was also a sharp old biddy, and she knew which direction I was headed, particularly after I'd flipped that switch in the bathroom a couple of times. "When I do that, the VCR buzzes. If I don't press the pause button again in a few minutes, the VCR shuts itself off and goes to whatever's playing on the TV set. Yes, by the time I heard the gun, the TV was on. But that shot didn't come from the TV. It came from outside my apartment. I may be old but I've still got pretty good eyes and ears, young lady. I know what I saw, and I know what I heard."

It wasn't what she saw and heard that concerned me. It was what she didn't hear. There had been at least two shots fired from Ruth's gun, one inside apartment 303 and one in the corridor, the one that killed Sam Raynor. The timing was off. If Ruth had in fact killed Sam, then ditched the gun down the trash chute, Mrs. Parmenter must have heard the shot fired in the hall near the stairwell. Why hadn't she heard the one fired in the apartment? And if both shots had been fired while she was in the bathroom, what was the sound that prompted her to call the police?

If Ruth fired the shot that killed Sam, she was already in the hallway, just a few steps from the trash chute. Why not ditch the gun then? But Mrs. Parmenter said she'd seen Ruth exit and reenter the apartment. That didn't make sense. Unless Ruth had gone back inside to wipe the gun clean of prints. I sighed. I didn't have any answers, and I'd better find some quick if I intended to get Ruth out of jail.

Brett had been listening to all of this with interest. Now I turned to him. "What about you?" I asked.

"I didn't see or hear diddly," he said, shifting in the rocking chair. "I went to a party Saturday night and didn't get home till past midnight. There were cops all over the place and I couldn't get into the building. Had to sit in my car till nearly two in the morning. I can tell you right now, though, Martha's real sharp. If she says that's what happened, you can bet it did."

"Besides, dear," Mrs. Parmenter said, "if Ruth didn't shoot her husband, who did?"

I wish I knew, I thought grimly. I tucked my notebook and pen back in my purse. "Thank you for talking with me. When I was here Friday afternoon, waiting for Mrs. Raynor to come home from work, I saw a homeless woman across the street, at that construction site. Have either of you ever seen her before?"

"Rosie?" Brett said. "Somebody told me that's what she's called, because of that rose on her hat. Yeah, she hangs around here a lot. She roams around picking up cans and bottles, stashing them in that shopping cart. I guess she turns 'em in for the recycling money."

Mrs. Parmenter pursed her lips and shook her head, looking distressed. "Poor soul. She's younger than I am. To live like that, on the streets."

"Does she stay in that lot every night?"

"Not every night," Brett said. "Sometimes I don't see her for days, then she shows up again. You're thinking she saw something Saturday night?"

I answered him with another question. "Any idea where I could find her?"

He shook his head. "I only notice her when she's there. Guess you could ask around the neighborhood."

"I will. If you see her, would you give me a call?" I gave Brett and Mrs. Parmenter each one of my business cards.

Mrs. Parmenter was adamant about her version of the events on the night of the murder, I thought, exiting her apartment. I was certain she'd make a convincing witness in court. But there were a few ragged edges in the fabric of her story. Maybe I could widen those tears, enough to get Ruth Raynor through them.

Twenty-one

OUTSIDE MRS. PARMENTER'S FRONT DOOR I TURNED my head to the left, as she must have done Saturday night, when she said she looked out of her apartment and saw Ruth. All I could see was the door of 302, and just a sliver of Ruth's door, 303. I walked to the front hallway and knocked on the door of 301. No answer. I positioned myself at Ruth's front door. The space around me was rectangular, roughly eight by ten feet, and I noted locations as though they were hands on a clock. The hallway leading to the rear of the building was directly to my left, at nine o'clock. At ten o'clock was a short bare wall, the other side of Mrs. Parmenter's dining area. The laundry room was at eleven o'clock, running along Mrs. Parmenter's living room wall. On my immediate right, at three o'clock, was the door to 302, the empty unit. That would put the elevator and

Lena Copeland's apartment, 301, at one and two o'clock respectively.

At twelve o'clock, directly in front of me, I had a clear, unobstructed view of the hall that led to the trash chute and the stairwell door. I walked slowly down the hallway. The wall to my left was about twelve feet long. The right-hand wall, housing the elevator shaft, was shorter, perhaps eight feet. The hall itself was narrow, not quite three feet wide, and just being there made me feel claustrophobic. Shooting Sam Raynor in the back must have been like shooting fish in a barrel.

The crime scene tape had been removed from this area too. Someone, probably the manager, had tried to scrub out the blood that stained the beige carpet midway down the hall, but blood is hard to remove. No doubt this section of carpet would have to be replaced. I raised my eyes from the rusty brown splotch to the trash chute door, an eighteen-inch square, hinged at the bottom. The chrome handle at the top, about four feet off the floor, still showed the residue of fingerprint powder. The chute itself was directly opposite the metal fire door that led to the stairs.

Piece of cake, I told myself. So easy to do, in just a matter of seconds. Shoot Sam Raynor in the back, step over the body, drop the weapon down the trash chute to the left, and exit to the right, down the stairs to the lobby. You couldn't see anything, unless you were standing at the head of this hallway, or right in front of Ruth's apartment.

I turned and walked back up the hallway, pausing to check out the laundry room. A long table, about waist high, and two coin-operated washing machines stood on the left, the wall shared with Mrs. Parmenter's living room. Opposite them were two dryers and a large plastic trash can. One of the washing machines quivered and whirred as it went through a spin cycle, accompanied by a steady thump sound as clothes went round and round in a dryer. Between them, the two appliances made a lot of noise. Enough to muffle a gunshot?

I returned to Ruth's door, my arms crossed, looking toward the murder scene as I listened to the sounds around

171

me, filtering out some, identifying others. Someone on the floor below was playing rock music too loud. I heard several metallic growls, then a hum as the elevator moved in its shaft, the light on the indicator above the door telling me that the car had dropped from the second floor to the ground level. Once the elevator stopped, traffic noise seeped into the building. I heard the nearby squeal of brakes, an impatient car horn, the wail of a siren in the distance.

Saturday night in Oakland can be noisy, especially in this neighborhood, bordered by well-traveled arteries like Piedmont Avenue, MacArthur Boulevard, and Broadway. There must have been plenty of background noise the night Sam Raynor was killed, including Mrs. Parmenter's television set. The elderly tenant had to be mistaken about the timing of the shot she said she heard, as well as Ruth's supposed trip to the trash chute to dump the murder weapon. If I believed Ruth when she denied killing Sam—and mostly I did.

Ruth's story was that she had taken a bag of garbage to the chute right before Sam got off the elevator. Given the location of Mrs. Parmenter's front door, and her own statement that she'd simply poked her head out the door rather than stepping into the hall, the elderly woman could not have seen Ruth at the trash chute. She'd only seen Ruth walk out her front door, with something in her hand, then return to her apartment. According to Ruth that was before the gun went off. But Mrs. Parmenter said after.

If Ruth shot Sam, she could have wiped the gun on her clothes, then dropped it down the chute. There was no logical reason for her to go back to the apartment, then dump the gun. So Mrs. Parmenter must have seen her earlier, when she'd dumped the garbage. But that was when Sam got off the elevator, surprising Ruth in the hall. Why hadn't Mrs. Parmenter seen Sam? She also said Ruth had been arguing with a man outside her apartment, *before* Ruth made her trip to the trash chute. If the man Mrs. Parmenter had seen wasn't Sam, who was it? Kevin Franklin, who'd

172

driven his sister and niece home that night? Another question to ask Kevin.

I shook my head. Someone was confused—or lying—about the sequence of events late Saturday night. Was it Mrs. Parmenter, or Ruth Franklin Raynor?

I worked my way through all three floors of the building, knocking on doors and talking to those tenants I could find at home. It was a useless exercise. Of those who had been home, only one had heard anything resembling a gunshot, and she thought it was a backfire from a car out on the street. The tenants I spoke with were uneasy, appalled that murder had soiled their building, their refuge from the world. Not safe anywhere, even at home—I heard the words over and over again. Even though these people lived behind the locked doors in a supposedly secure building, they didn't feel safe, in their homes, on the street, in their neighborhood.

I retraced my steps to that short hallway on the third floor, staring at the murder scene, wishing for enlightenment. The elevator dinged and I heard the door open. As I rounded the corner, I saw a woman in a bright red dress standing at the door of apartment 301. Lena Copeland had come home from work.

She was facing away from me. Her long black hair had been braided into cornrows, the ends decorated with colorful beads that clicked whenever she moved her head. On her left hip she balanced a brown paper sack full of groceries. As a result, her dress was hiked up on the left side, revealing the lace hem of her slip, a wide strip of pale blue under wrinkled red linen. The thin strap of her leather handbag slipped off her right shoulder, catching on the white cuff at her elbow. She stuck a key into the dead-bolt lock above the doorknob, then I heard her swear under her breath. The lock stuck and she swore again, aiming a sharp kick at the bottom of the door with the pointed toe of her red leather pump. Judging from the number of scuff marks on the lower third of the door's surface, she kicked the door frequently. The grocery sack slipped an inch or so down her outthrust hip and threatened to escape her grasp altogether.

173

"You look like you could use some help," I said, walking toward her.

Her braids flew as she whipped her head swiftly to the right, the beads clicking and rattling together, brushing the red metal hoops in her ears. I saw a long nose, a wide mouth painted bright red, and a pair of suspicious brown eyes in a coffee-brown face. She looked about twenty-five, but weariness pulled her visage into tired lines, as though she'd already worked a forty-hour week and here it was only Monday. Her low voice was decidedly unfriendly.

"I don't need any help."

She set the grocery sack on the carpet at her feet and grabbed the doorknob with her left hand, pulling it toward her while she twisted the key with her right. The lock shifted with a click. She pulled the key out of the dead bolt and stuck it into the spring lock in the doorknob itself. The door opened a few inches and she kicked it wider, bending over to shove the grocery sack inside.

"I'd like to ask you a few questions about Saturday night," I said quickly, before she could escape into the refuge of her apartment.

"I already talked to the cops," she said harshly, ready to slam the door in my face. But the grocery sack was in the way. Swearing under her breath, she kicked off her shoes and used one foot and one hand to maneuver the grocery sack into her apartment. Then she straightened and reached for the door, long red fingernails like talons as she grasped the edge.

"I'm not a cop. I'm a private investigator." I put my left hand flat on the door she was trying to shut as my right reached into my handbag. "My name's Jeri Howard. You're Lena Copeland?"

I held one of my business cards under her nose. She didn't say anything, nor did she take the card from my hand, but she didn't slam the door in my face either.

"Who you working for? Her?" She jerked her chin in the direction of Ruth's unit. The beads in her hair swayed and clicked.

"Yes. I've been talking to some of the other tenants in

174

the building, to see if anyone saw anything Saturday, the night of the shooting. No one seems to know how the victim got into the building, since the front door is always locked. Mrs. Parmenter in 304 suggested that you may have propped the door open."

Lena Copeland's red-painted mouth twisted and her voice crackled with resentment. "That nosy old bitch. Minds everybody's business but her own. I did not leave the front door open. I did once, a couple of months ago, just to move something in. That cracker manager acted like it was a federal crime. So now anything goes down in this building they all blame me."

"Hey, I don't know how it happened," I said with a placating shrug. "Nobody'll cop to letting him in. Maybe the door was propped open. Maybe he slipped in while someone was coming in or out. Doesn't really matter." It did matter, though. If Sam Raynor came through the front door while someone else was in the building lobby, that person could tell me whether or not Raynor was alone. "Either way, he's just as dead."

Lena Copeland crossed her arms over her red linen bodice and tilted her head to one side. "From what I hear, he had it coming."

"Some people seem to think so. Why do you?"

"I talked to Ruth a time or two, in the laundry room. Enough to figure out her old man had been beating up on her. She had a restraining order on him, didn't she? So he comes in here, tries to mess with her, slaps her around. I don't blame her for blowing him away."

"Maybe she didn't." An expression flitted across Lena's face, too brief for me to assess. "So you were home Saturday night?"

Her response was a humph sound that might have been a yes and might have been a no.

"You must have been, if you've talked to the police. If you were here, maybe you heard something, saw something that could be important. You're close enough to Ruth's apartment to hear most of what went on. Especially the gunshots."

Behind her a bird began to trill, coloring the silence with melody. Lena sighed and dropped her hands to her hips. "Come on in and let me shut this door. I'm not supposed to have so much as a goldfish in this apartment. If that cracker manager hears Sophie, he'll be wanting to throw me out."

I followed her into the apartment. In one corner of the living room a cage hung on a stand, occupied by a bright yellow canary that had scattered bird seed all over the carpet. As Lena Copeland approached the cage, making kissing noises, Sophie rewarded her with a burst of song. Then Lena walked to the kitchen and hoisted the bag of groceries to the counter that separated the two rooms. As she put away the contents, I walked to the living room window, which looked down on Howe Street. The drapes were open, with a row of house plants in ceramic pots at intervals along the sill. I gazed out at the construction site on the opposite corner.

"So what is it you want to know?" Lena asked as she walked from the kitchen to the living room. She sat down on her floral print sofa and massaged one nylon-clad foot, then the other.

"Did you hear the gunshots?" She nodded. "Tell me about it. Everything you can remember."

She sighed. "I wasn't sure about the first shot. I was listening to some music while I got ready for bed. I thought maybe it was something I heard on the radio. But that second shot. It was right outside my apartment. I knew what it was. I used to live in East Oakland. Lots of drive-by shootings in that neighborhood."

"What did you do?"

"I just froze," Lena said, shaking her head. "I mean, I'm standing there in my nightgown with a jar of face cream in my hand, singing along with Anita Baker. Then comes this bang, and I'm thinking, girl, you didn't hear what you just heard. That can't be coming from inside this building. It has to be out in the street. I go to the window, peek out, I don't see anything. Then I realized it must have come from out in the hall." She glanced toward the front door of her apartment and shuddered. "I was ready to crawl under the bed. The phone was right there, but it never occurred to me to call the police. All I could think about was, my God, Maurice just left."

"Who's Maurice?"

"The guy I was out with Saturday night. I was worried about him."

"What time did he leave? How long was it before you heard the gunshot, the one out in the hall?"

Lena tilted her head and narrowed her eyes. "Five, ten minutes. I'm not sure. You're thinking Maurice let the guy in?"

"I'm thinking he may have seen something, or someone."

"I called him that same night," Lena protested, "to tell him what happened and make sure he was all right. He didn't mention seeing anything strange."

"He might not have thought it was strange or out of the ordinary. When Maurice left, did he take the elevator or the stairs?"

"When I closed the door, he was waiting for the elevator. Then when I opened it again—" She stopped.

"When did you open the door again, after you heard the shot?"

"Are you crazy? For all I knew there was still some nut out there with a gun. Only time I opened the door after I heard the shot was when the cops came knocking."

There was an armchair opposite the sofa, its faded blue upholstery covered with a plaid blanket throw. I sat down and leaned toward her. "But you opened the door *after* Maurice left and *before* you heard the gunshot? Why?" She flashed me that look again, the one I'd seen when we were standing in the doorway, when I said maybe Ruth didn't kill Sam. "Come on, Lena. You must have had a reason. Don't hold out on me."

"I heard voices," she said finally. "In the hall. Yelling. Must have been when Ruth's old man busted in."

"And right after Maurice left. How long?"

"Long enough for me to get my dress off and hang it in

177

the closet," Lena said. "That elevator door is right by my front door, so when people get off the elevator I can usually hear them, but I don't pay any attention. People talking in the hall, and the elevator itself, it's background noise. I'm used to it. This was different, though. This was yelling, first in the hall, then farther away, like they'd gone into an apartment." She sighed and shook her head again. "I wondered about Ruth, 'cause I knew she was scared of her old man. I put on my robe and took a peek outside, to see where those voices were coming from. But Ruth's door was closed. When I poked my head out, I didn't hear the voices anymore."

"You didn't see anyone in the hall?"

Lena looked perplexed. "Not really."

"Either you did or you didn't."

"When I opened the door, I was looking toward Ruth's apartment." She shifted position on the sofa and pointed to her left, bringing her hands into play. Then her other hand pointed to the right. "But I had this impression that someone had moved out of sight, into the laundry room, or that hallway that leads to the stairs. Maybe I saw somebody's shoe or pant leg. It's like I saw something out of the corner of my eye." She snapped her fingers. "It was just that quick, not enough to register as a person, but someone was there. I just know it. I feel it."

"Did you tell the police this?"

"I started to," she said, "but those cops were more interested in what I actually heard or saw, not what I thought I saw. Besides, they've got themselves a pretty good suspect, don't they?"

"Ruth." I nodded. "Mrs. Parmenter says she looked out into the hall after the shooting and saw Ruth walking toward the trash chute, with something in her hand."

"That old bitch is just foolish enough to stick her head out the door and get it shot off," Lena declared. "Besides, she can't see shit from her front door. How does she know what Ruth was doing?"

I didn't have an answer to that one. Mrs. Parmenter seemed sure of her version of the facts, just as sure as Lena

178

was of her story. "You said you were listening to the radio when you heard the gun. What station, and what song?" Lena looked surprised, then rattled off the call letters of a local rhythm and blues station and the title of Anita Baker's latest hit. I could check the station playlist and find out what time the record had been aired. That could help me pinpoint the time. "I need to talk to Maurice, Lena."

She sighed again, reluctant to give me her friend's phone number. "Give me your card. I'll have him call you."

Outside Lena's apartment I walked past the elevator and turned right, intending to leave the building by the same route Sam Raynor's killer had. I was halfway to the stairwell door when I heard an imperious voice behind me.

"You! Hey, you!" I turned and saw a belligerent red face bearing down on me. "Who are you? What are you doing in this building, bothering the tenants?"

The manager, author of the printed sign on the building door. Mrs. Parmenter had said his name was Sullivan. And Lena Copeland referred to him derisively as a cracker. I took my time answering, looking him over. He was my height, about sixty, pale blue eyes topped by a gray crew cut, with a thickset body in a green shirt and a pair of brown slacks.

"Who says I'm bothering anyone?" I asked, my voice neutral. One of the tenants I'd talked with earlier must have called him.

He shook a stubby finger at me. "Don't get smart with me, honey. I know you've been ringing bells on every floor, pretending to be a cop, or some such. We've already had the cops in here. Who are you? Who let you in?"

"I'm a private investigator. You must be the manager, Mr. Sullivan."

"Private investigator," he repeated with a snort. "Sure you are, honey. How did you get in here?" He slewed his eyes in the direction of Lena Copeland's apartment. "Was it that colored girl in 301? I've had nothing but trouble since she moved in. Leaves the front door open, lets anyone in the building."

"I came to see Mrs. Parmenter. Ask her."

Sullivan looked a bit nonplussed. Mrs. Parmenter must have been on his approved list, unlike Lena Copeland. I already had him pegged as a petty tyrant whose world revolved around building rules and regulations, and now I added racist and sexist to the description. I turned my back on him and headed for the stairs.

Twenty-two

I STOPPED BRIEFLY AT MY OFFICE, CHECKING MESsages on my answering machine. The Navy had called— Duffy LeBard, Lieutenant Bruinsma, and Alex Tongco. But I didn't have time to return the calls. I was supposed to meet Bill Stanley at seven, at the Franklins', and I was behind schedule.

"You're late," the Admiral said tersely when he opened the door. He must have been waiting for me. I hadn't even made it to the front porch yet.

"I know." I didn't explain as I stepped past him into the entry hall. "How's Wendy?"

"How do you explain to a child that age that her mother's in jail?" Franklin scowled.

He had me there. It wasn't a task I would relish.

I saw Bill Stanley at the mantel in the living room, examining the Franklin family portraits. As I entered the room, so did Kevin Franklin, coming from the kitchen. Our eyes met, then his shifted quickly away. Chuck Porter must have called him after my unannounced visit to RedCom 20 that morning.

"Productive day, Jeri?" Bill asked, turning to me. He was still in his lawyer suit, but he'd removed the jacket and unbuttoned his collar and cuffs. His gambler's suspenders stood out against his white shirt, which looked considerably more wrinkled than it had this morning.

"Somewhat. I'll fill you in later. How's Ruth?"

"Bearing up. Still in shock." He didn't specify whether Ruth's condition was due to the murder or her present incarceration at the Oakland City Jail. It was probably a combination of both. I tried to imagine Ruth in a cell, and had a hard time doing it. "Coroner was supposed to do the autopsy late today," Bill said. "I'm gonna talk to the assistant D.A. tomorrow."

"Are we ready to do this?" Franklin asked, still in the doorway between the entry hall and the living room.

The lawyer looked at him, then at Kevin, near the kitchen door. "I'm ready if you are. If either of you think it will be difficult for you, leave the room. I don't want any interruptions."

Franklin's mouth tightened. He wasn't accustomed to being talked to so plainly, especially in his own house. "That won't be a problem." He walked down the hall toward the bedrooms, then returned a moment later, followed by Lenore Franklin and Wendy.

The little girl wore a crisp green playsuit. Cradled on her left arm she carried the rag doll I had seen her playing with on my visit last week. Her face looked thin and bleak below her strawberry-blond hair. As I gazed down at her, I didn't see any resemblance to either Ruth or Sam. Wendy looked like her own person, lost in her own world.

Lenore smoothed the child's hair. "Wendy, this is Mr. Stanley. He wants to talk with you."

Bill Stanley knelt, putting himself on the little girl's level, and he stuck out one big hand. "Hi, Wendy. You can call me Bill."

Wendy hugged her rag doll tighter. She stared at Bill, then she stuck out her right hand and brushed his long fingers.

"Let's have a seat," Bill said. He straightened to his full height. There were two chairs facing the sofa, a table between them. Bill sat down in the one closest to the fireplace and I took the other. Wendy perched on the edge of the

181

sofa, while Lenore sat next to her. Admiral Franklin stood behind his wife, while Kevin remained standing near the kitchen door.

Wendy looked around the room to all the adult faces and asked the question none of the grown-ups had so far answered. "Where's my mommy?"

"Your mommy's in jail," Bill told her. Lenore Franklin winced.

Wendy thought about this for a moment, then she asked, "When is she coming home?"

"We don't know yet." Bill leaned forward. "Wendy, I want to know what happened on Saturday, when the police came to your house. I know you talked to a policeman. What did you tell the policeman?"

Wendy screwed up her face, looking as though she were about to take a spoonful of bad-tasting medicine. She didn't say anything. Then she pressed her cheek to that of the rag doll and muttered, "I want my mommy."

"Your mommy can't be here right now," Bill said.

"I want my mommy!" Wendy shouted at him. There was frustration and rage behind the words, a lot of it for a four-year-old child. Lenore's hands moved toward her grandchild. The Admiral touched her shoulders and Bill shot her a narrow-eyed stare. Lenore's hands stopped in midair. She laced her fingers together so tightly her knuckles turned white. Bill's eyes moved back to Wendy.

"Wendy, the policemen took your mommy to jail. If we are going to get her out of jail, you have to tell me what happened Saturday night, after you came back from dinner at your grandma's house."

Wendy's voice took on a scathing tone far older than her years. "My daddy was there. He came and sat on my bed. I was asleep but he woke me up. He said how would I like to go away with him."

"Did he say where?" Bill asked. "Did you want to go away with him?" She shook her head in response to both questions. "What happened then?"

"I heard them yelling and I put the pillow over my

182

head." Wendy's pale face reddened and tears slipped from her brown eyes.

"Who was yelling?"

"My mommy and my daddy. When we lived on Guam, they always yelled. Then my daddy would hit my mommy and make her cry." She sniffed and wiped the back of one small hand across her face. "I don't like my daddy very much," she whispered.

Now Lenore was crying as well, tears streaming down her face. She reached into the pocket of her slacks and pulled out a tissue. Above her the Admiral's mouth worked and his gray eyes were as cold and turbulent as the Pacific during a gale. I looked past him at Kevin but I couldn't see his face. He stuck his hands deep into his pockets and turned his back on the interview, staring out the dining room window at the backyard.

I turned my gaze back to Bill Stanley, who looked steadily at Wendy as he probed. "You were still in bed?" She nodded. "What happened then?"

"I heard a bang. Really loud. It scared me."

"When did you get out of bed? Right away, or did you wait a little while?"

"I had to wait until my legs would work."

"Do you know how long you waited?" Bill asked. Wendy shook her head. "Did you hear another bang?"

"Yes. But not as close. Then it was real quiet. I called to Mommy but she didn't answer. So I got out of bed and went to find her."

"That was very brave, Wendy. I might have hidden under the bed," Bill said matter-of-factly.

Wendy wiped the tears off her cheeks. "I had to see if Mommy was okay. She was lying on the floor. I thought my daddy killed her. But she wasn't dead. She sat up and hugged me. Then a big policeman came."

"Wendy, did you see a gun?"

"The policeman had a gun."

"Did your mommy have a gun? Did you see a gun other than the policeman's gun?"

Wendy looked at him with wide brown eyes. "No," she

said finally, drawing the word out slowly. I sat back in my chair.

"Is this what you told the policeman?" Bill asked her.

"Yes. He wanted to know if I saw something."

"What was that?"

"If I saw my mommy shoot a gun. But I didn't. I only heard bangs."

Two gunshots, the one fired inside Ruth's apartment as she and Sam struggled for the gun, and the second, the fatal shot in the hallway outside. Wendy's account of what happened Saturday was close to Ruth's. Even at the age of four the child was grimly aware of her father's abusive behavior toward her mother, enough to fear that Sam might have killed Ruth.

Bill Stanley probed further but elicited nothing more from Wendy than what she'd already told us. Finally he thanked her for talking to him and motioned to Lenore, who swept her granddaughter up and took her from the living room. When Lenore returned she looked drained. I felt tired myself.

"Well?" the Admiral demanded.

Bill shrugged. "She's four years old. She didn't see anything. Evidently she told the cops the same story, and it fits with Ruth's version of what happened. I don't think we have a problem."

It looked as though I wasn't going to get an opportunity to talk to Kevin Franklin tonight. Even as the Admiral buttonholed Bill about the next phase in Ruth's defense, I saw Kevin step into the kitchen. I heard the back door open and close, then the sound of a car engine starting up. He was definitely avoiding me, but I'd catch up with him sooner or later.

I looked down at Lenore, who sat wearily on the sofa. She spoke so softly I had to lean forward to hear her. "I'm glad Mr. Stanley told Wendy her mother's in jail. I haven't been able to bring myself to do it. I just hope he can get Ruth out of jail, and soon."

I searched for something comforting to say but couldn't

184

find it. Bill Stanley tapped me on the shoulder. "C'mon, Jeri. We've got to talk."

We conferred on the curb outside, leaving the Admiral chagrined at being out of the loop. I gave Bill a rundown of my interviews with Mrs. Parmenter and Lena Copeland. He was less concerned with the possibility that someone had been with Sam the night of the murder than with what Mrs. Parmenter heard and saw and the time sequence involved. It was clear from my earlier conversation with him and the session just completed in the Franklin living room that Bill Stanley and I approached Ruth's situation from different angles. He operated from the assumption that Ruth shot Sam, that her actions were justified and that he and the District Attorney could work out a deal.

As far as Stanley was concerned, Wendy's testimony just emphasized the Raynors' abusive marriage and Sam's status as a murder victim waiting to happen. Cutting a deal would certainly be easier, I had to admit. From what I could see, the Franklins were so anguished by the whole situation, and anxious to get Ruth out of jail, that they just might go for it. But I didn't think Ruth had killed Sam. I said it again, pointing out Lena Copeland's hunch that there had been someone else in the hallway before she heard the shot.

"You gotta give me more than hunches, Jeri," the attorney told me, pulling his car keys from his pocket and tossing them into the air.

"I'm working on it. Just don't plead her right away. Let me dig around some more."

"We've got plenty of time, unless the other side gets hard-assed on me. I'll know more tomorrow. Drop by my office around three. I will have talked to the D.A. by then."

I left the Franklins' and drove to West Alameda. It was now past eight in the evening, and I hoped to find Steve and Claudia Yancy at home. But the Marion Court cottage was dark in the fading light of the summer evening. I didn't see either the red Chevy pickup or the cranberry Nissan. As I returned to my car, I wondered what time the Yancys went to work. Maybe I could catch them early tomorrow morning.

I wanted to go home. It had been a long time since lunch, and I was both tired and hungry. Instead I drove to the Pacific Avenue building where Sam Raynor and Harlan Pettibone had shared an apartment. When Mrs. Torelli answered, she was dressed as before, in cutoffs and a T-shirt. This time she had a paperback in her hand, one finger marking her place. The apartment was unnaturally quiet. Honeybunch must have been in bed.

"I remember you," she said when I reintroduced myself. "You were here asking questions about Hal and Sam. You know Sam's dead? My husband says his ex-wife shot him Saturday night."

"May I come in?" I asked, not bothering to dispute her third-hand account of Raynor's murder. She nodded, then stepped aside to let me enter. "Did you see Sam or Hal on Friday or Saturday?"

"I haven't seen Hal since he got home from work Friday afternoon. My husband says he got busted Saturday night at the club on base."

"What does Hal do on weekends?"

Mrs. Torelli set the book down on her dining room table, its pages splayed outward. "Sleeps late and plays pool. Come to think of it, when I saw Sam on Saturday, he said Hal was still in the rack. Wasn't feeling well. Probably hung over from too much booze the night before." Whether this was Sam's assessment or her own, she didn't say.

"When did you see Sam? What was he doing?"

"Must have been around noon. I was fixing lunch. I saw the mailman go by so I went out to check the box. I ran into Sam doing the same thing, so I just made conversation. Looked like he'd been to the commissary. He was carrying a couple of sacks of groceries."

"Did you see Sam any other time on Saturday?"

She nodded. "He left about seven-thirty, eight o'clock, dressed casual. I think Hal left right after that."

"I thought you said you didn't see Hal."

"Didn't exactly see him. I heard his car. I saw Sam drive out, then about five minutes later I heard the Camaro start up and peel rubber. Must've been Hal. He's the only one around here drives like that."

I heard a wail from the bedroom as Honeybunch awakened. Mrs. Torelli sighed and looked longingly at her paperback. I thanked her and went home, my stomach rumbling all the way.

As I crossed the courtyard toward my own apartment, I saw Abigail sitting on the back of the sofa, scowling at me through the front window. By the time I opened the front door she was at my feet, her tail switching back and forth. Her piercing yowl revealed Siamese genes in her basic brown tabby ancestry.

"I know I'm late," I told her. "You don't have to make a federal case out of it."

She turned and stalked to the kitchen, where she stopped at her blue ceramic food bowl and yowled at me again. If she'd been human, I think she would have stamped her foot. The bowl was devoid of so much as a crumb. I realized that in my rush to get out of the apartment that morning to meet Bill Stanley at his office, I'd neglected to fill it with the dry food that she munched on throughout the day.

"Okay, you do get to make a federal case." I apologized profusely as I fetched the bag and poured in half a bowl of crunchies. Abigail wasn't quite over her snit, however. She grumbled at me as she stuck her face into the bowl.

I opened the refrigerator and pulled out a leftover lasagna, cut a portion and zapped it in the microwave while I threw together a salad with some veggies and several tomatoes from my patio garden. By the time I'd finished my own dinner, Abigail had eaten her fill and retired to the middle of the living room for a wash. After I'd done the dishes, I followed the cat to the living room, where I sat cross-legged on the carpet and pulled her into my lap.

"Am I forgiven?" A sharp nip on my thumb provided part of the answer, followed by a sandpaper tongue and a rumbling purr. I buried my face in the soft brown fur. "A full stomach changes everything, doesn't it?"

187

Twenty-three

AT SIX-THIRTY TUESDAY MORNING I WAS OUTSIDE THE Marion Court cottage where the Yancys lived. The fog still colored the sky pale gray, but soon the August sun would burn it away and we'd have another hot blue-sky day.

I shifted position on the fender of the red pickup. The cranberry Nissan was nowhere in sight. Had Claudia gone to work early? Did she have duty, that periodic military task that required a twenty-four-hour presence on the base? Shades were drawn across the front window and I saw no lights inside, but sooner or later one or both of the Yancys had to emerge. Since Steve worked for Alex Tongco, and Alex often started work at seven, I guessed Steve would appear first.

Sure enough, at a quarter to seven, the front door of the cottage opened and Steve Yancy came out, dressed in a chief petty officer's khaki uniform. His brown hair was slicked back and the expression on his round face was a good deal more serious than on our previous encounter. He looked startled when he saw me leaning on his pickup, squinting as he tried to place me.

"Jeri Howard," I prompted. "The private investigator. I was here last week, asking questions about Sam Raynor."

"Sam's dead," he said slowly. "I had to go identify the body."

"Did you tell the police you were there? The night of the murder?"

Yancy's face reddened and his mouth opened. He had trouble forming words. "What? How ... ?"

"I saw you early Sunday morning, right outside the police line. Tell me what you were doing there."

"I was, uh . . . I heard the sirens and . . ."

"Why were you on Piedmont Avenue that night? Were you and Claudia together? Where is Claudia, by the way?"

Yancy looked as though each word stung, especially Claudia's name. Things had changed since my last visit. "Answer my questions, Chief. Or you'll be talking to the police."

The implication of my last statement sank in gradually. "You don't think I had anything to do with it," he protested, face reddening even more. "His wife . . . that's what the newspaper said."

"What about *your* wife? And Sam Raynor?"

"How do you know about that?" He ducked his head, his voice a whisper.

"I just know. Where is Claudia?"

He ran his hands through his hair. "We had a fight. She packed her bags and moved out."

"Tell me about the fight. When did you quarrel, and why?"

"Friday." He sighed, a long drawn-out gust of air that signaled his reluctance to tell me the rest. I waited. "When I got home from work. I knew something was wrong between us. I even wondered if maybe there was someone else. I ignored it for a long time, because I didn't want to know. Claudia's my second wife. We met while I was still married to my first. I should have known better. But I love her, I'd do anything to—" He stopped abruptly, ducked his head again, then took a deep breath. Now words tumbled from his mouth.

"Some guy at work, he said he saw Claudia and Sam together at the movie theater in Emeryville. It was a couple of weeks ago, the night Claudia told me she was going to a movie with her girlfriend Dana. She said they were meeting in Berkeley, dinner first, then the movie. That started me thinking, about things that happened when we were living on Guam, and since we moved here. Things that should have tipped me off, things I ignored. When I

189

got home from work, Claudia said she and Dana were going to a movie Saturday. I was sure she was lying. I just lost it."

"What happened? What did Claudia say?"

Steve Yancy gulped in some air and examined the knuckles of his right hand. "I yelled at her. I punched the wall. Knocked a picture down. Glass everywhere." He looked up at me. "She yelled right back at me. She admitted it. Said she and Sam had been involved off and on for six years, ever since they were stationed together at Pearl Harbor. Even before she and I got married."

And probably ever since Sam and Ruth had been married. "Where is she staying?"

"With Dana. Her last name is Albertson. She lives in Alameda." He gave me an address on Santa Clara Avenue. I'd have to track down Claudia there. But first I wanted a response to the question Yancy hadn't answered yet.

"Why were you in Oakland Saturday night, Chief?"

"Why do you have to know?" His voice was anguished.

"Because as far as I'm concerned, anyone who was in the vicinity of Ruth Raynor's apartment that night is a suspect in Sam Raynor's murder." The police might not think so, but I sure as hell did. "And you had a motive, didn't you, Chief Yancy? Your wife was having an affair with Sam."

"I followed them. Claudia and Dana." The admission embarrassed him. "Over to the Piedmont Theater. They did go to the movie. She wasn't lying, at least not about that." He sighed and wiped away the film of sweat that had formed on his upper lip. "I watched them buy tickets and go inside. I checked to see what time the movie got out and I went to a bar down the street. I had a burger and a couple of beers."

"Which bar?"

"It's just a block or so from the theater. Cards . . . the Royal Flush." I nodded. The same bar where Acey Collins said he spent a good part of Saturday evening. "Right before the movie let out I went back to the theater. I hung around outside until I spotted Claudia and Dana. I followed

190

them to Fenton's. There was a line out the front door, like there always is after a show. I felt pretty damned stupid for following them, and afraid they'd see me. So I went back to the bar. I stayed there till I heard the sirens. I swear, I didn't go anywhere near that apartment building. And I didn't see Sam Raynor all evening. You've got to believe me."

I wasn't sure I did. Steve Yancy seemed mild enough now, but he had described his violent physical reaction when he finally confronted Claudia about her infidelity. The man who followed his wife all Saturday evening struck me as loose cannon material. What if he had seen Sam Raynor in the parking lot, right after Tiffany left? What if Sam had met Claudia afterward? I was speculating. I wouldn't be able to pinpoint Claudia's movements until I spoke with her.

"Let's talk about the Friday night poker games, Chief."

"Poker?" Yancy looked confused. "It's every other Friday. What about it?" I grilled him about the game and his card-playing cronies. It sounded like a basic payday nickel-dime-quarter game, where everyone usually breaks even, and a big loss might be twenty or thirty bucks. Raynor won a few, lost a few, just like the other guys at the table. If he'd been hiding money through supposed gambling debts, Yancy didn't have a clue and the poker game didn't appear to be the vehicle.

I left the chief standing next to his red pickup. The apartment where Claudia was staying with her friend was on Santa Clara near Caroline, a two-story Victorian carved up into six flats. Dana Albertson lived in the first floor front unit on the right, the one with a bay window overlooking the street. The front door of the Victorian was unlocked. I stepped into a foyer with a wide staircase and knocked on the apartment door, but there was no answer. I didn't see Claudia Yancy's Nissan parked anywhere in the vicinity. She'd already left for work, which meant a return trip to Alameda tonight.

When I reached my office I made a pot of coffee and sat down at my desk with mug in hand. I called Mary at the air station, asking her if Tiffany Collins had reported for work. "No, she hasn't," Mary said. "She called in sick again. And some lieutenant named Bruinsma's been here looking for her. Jeri, is Tiffany in some kind of trouble? Do you have some reason to believe she's not ill?"

I sighed. I didn't want to give Mary too many details, but I knew I could trust her not to shoot off her mouth. "Maybe she wants to lay low for a while."

When Mary spoke again she sounded worried. "I heard that sailor she was dating was shot to death over in Oakland this weekend. Is that why you and the lieutenant want to talk with her?" I didn't say anything, but to Mary that was answer enough. "Oh, lord."

"Mary, it's probably nothing. I just want to ask Tiffany a few questions, and so far I haven't been able to locate her. Don't say anything to anybody."

"You know I won't," Mary told me. "If I find out where she is, I'll call you."

After Mary hung up, I punched in Acey Collins's home number. Genevieve answered on the second ring. "Gen, Tiffany's not at work. She called in sick again."

"Damn that girl." She was silent for a moment, and I heard piano music crescendo in the background. "Acey went by her apartment early this morning. The curtains were shut and the Subaru's gone. None of the neighbors had seen her, and yesterday's mail was still in the box."

Sounds like Acey had done everything I would have done. "What about the rabbit?" I asked, my pet owner concerns kicking in. I could leave my cat for a couple of days and she'd be okay. I wasn't sure about Tiffany's lop-ear.

"If she's going out of town, she takes it with her, in a carrying case. She can't have gone far, if she's called in sick both yesterday and today."

"As long as she's got access to a phone, she could be in Alaska," I pointed out. "If you hear from her, tell her I have to talk with her."

As I finished my coffee, I took care of some paperwork and returned several phone calls, then I left my office and walked through downtown Oakland, past the glittery fashions displayed in the window of the Emporium and I. Magnin. When I reached Grand Avenue, I turned left, heading west past Telegraph Avenue, to a plain storefront building in the shadow of the freeway.

I pushed open the door, entering a large well-lighted room filled with tables and chairs. Against the wall to my left was a long table spread with a haphazard array of food—bread for the collection of toasters grouped there, jars of peanut butter and jam, a plate of doughnuts, a grocery store coffee cake. In the corner I saw a coffee maker, sugar bowl, and an open quart of milk. I looked around the room. Most of the tables were occupied by women, talking, drinking coffee, eating the food that had been donated. At first I didn't see the woman I sought, then she walked into the room from the corridor at the rear, the one that led to the laundry facilities, the showers, and a couple of sleeping rooms.

Sister Anne is a tall big-boned woman in her forties, her short brunette hair streaked with silver. I've never seen her in a habit, and today she was wearing a typical ensemble of blue jeans, sneakers, and a red-and-white-checked shirt. Around her neck was a plain wooden cross on a red cord.

I'd met the nun through a mutual friend and been intrigued by the fact that her order operates this downtown shelter for homeless women. No men or children are allowed inside its doors. It provides temporary refuge from the street, a place where a homeless woman can get a cup of coffee and something to eat, washers and dryers and showers to clean clothing and body, or a cot and a dark room for a few hours' sleep, away from the human predators who exploit those who are weaker, with fewer defenses.

I don't know much about homeless people, except that they seem to be everywhere these days. They get talked about on television and written about in the newspapers, and no one can agree on why people are homeless or what can be done for them. Any number of reasons have been proffered to explain the burgeoning population of homeless people on Bay Area streets—the closure of the mental hospitals; the decline in affordable low-cost housing, whether apartments or single-room occupancy hotels; the times we live in; the widening gulf between rich and poor; and the enlarging holes in the safety net.

Sister Anne puts it in simpler terms when she says being homeless can result from an unlucky combination of factors, such as the loss of a job, with no savings or family to fall back on. That's a definition Jeri Howard, self-employed with a little money in the bank and family in the area, can understand and appreciate. My safety net is intact. But it wouldn't take much to rip a hole in what I often take for granted.

"Hi, Jeri, you want some coffee?" Sister Anne has a soft calm voice, but I never let the quietness of her speech fool me, not since the day I saw her face a local tough who tried to force his way into the shelter to get at his girlfriend, who was running away from him. *He* backed down, not Sister Anne.

I took the cup Sister Anne offered and followed her to two empty chairs at a table near the back of the shelter's common room. One of the other chairs was occupied by a black woman with gray hair, her face furrowed with time and hard living. On her lap was a battered leather purse with a makeshift cloth strap. She wore a blue-and-white-striped blouse over a brown skirt, and on her feet, thick-soled shoes and what looked like several pairs of socks. I particularly noticed the socks, recalling something Sister Anne once told me. Being homeless is hard on your feet because you're always moving.

"This is Emily," Sister Anne said, introducing me to our table companion.

"Hello, Emily, I'm Jeri. How are you today?"

Emily favored me with a dignified smile. "Tolerable." She had a cup of coffee and a plate in front of her, using a plastic fork to cut a wedge of coffee cake into even smaller pieces.

"I'm looking for a homeless woman and I'm not sure where to start," I told Sister Anne, describing Rosie. I could tell that Emily was listening.

194

"Piedmont Avenue is way off the usual track," Sister Anne said, sipping her coffee. "That's a more affluent neighborhood. I wonder how she wound up there. You say she's got a shopping cart and she's collecting cans and bottles. The recycling center that buys the stuff is under the freeway at Twenty-seventh. If she's coming from Forty-first and Piedmont, that's a long way to walk, pushing a cart. On the other hand, it's mostly level ground. No major hills." She thought for a moment. "You say she's white?"

I nodded. "In her late thirties, early forties."

"Interesting." Sister Anne sipped her coffee. "I haven't seen her in this shelter. I'd have noticed. I mean, look around you. Given Oakland's demographics and this particular neighborhood, most of our clients are black, with a few Hispanics and Native Americans. We don't get many white drop-ins."

"Inga's white." Emily lifted a piece of coffee cake to her mouth.

"That's right. She's much older, though." Sister Anne turned to me with a sigh. "Inga must be in her eighties. From Germany. She came over here during the Depression and worked as a domestic for a dollar a day. No social security, no pension, nothing."

"Now she lives on the streets?" The picture Sister Anne drew was horrifying, an elderly woman with no resources. That safety net suddenly became visible in my mind, a fine green mesh knit together with money and the faces of my family, with my Kaiser health insurance card tied on one corner.

"She's got a room somewhere downtown, no kitchen, has to walk down the hall to the bathroom. She eats lunch over at St. Vincent de Paul or the Salvation Army and comes here for coffee and dessert. If the weather's good, she spends the day in the park at Lake Merritt." Sister Anne sighed, then turned to the older woman who sat with us. "Emily, you've been to some of the other downtown shelters. Have you ever seen this woman with a rose on her hat?"

Emily thought about it for a long moment. I was curious

195

about her circumstances, but she had such an air of quiet dignity and resignation that I felt it would be presumptuous to ask.

"I don't think so," Emily said finally. "If she always wears the hat, I would have noticed. I got some friends who take stuff to the recycling center. I'll ask around." Emily's tired brown eyes sharpened. "Why you looking for her? She in some kinda trouble?"

"There was a murder Saturday night, in an apartment building at Forty-first and Howe. It's just a hunch, really, but I know this woman hangs out in the area. I saw her there Friday afternoon. If she was in the neighborhood Saturday, she may have seen something."

"If she did," Emily said, "she's scared. I would be. And I'd hide."

"You're probably right, Emily. But even if she's hiding, eventually she'll come out."

Emily shrugged. "If I see her, I'll get word to Sister."

I thanked Emily. Sister Anne walked me to the door of the shelter. "Thanks for bringing over that box of clothes and shoes last month, Jeri. Any time you clean out your closet we can certainly use the donation."

I looked around me, at the women sitting at tables. "It seems like such a drop in the bucket."

Sister Anne laughed. "Yes, but eventually all those little drops fill the bucket."

Twenty-four

I STEPPED OFF THE SIDEWALK ONTO DIRT, WALKING toward a prefab building at the rear of the construction site at Forty-first and Howe. As I passed some rolls of heavy

196

duty chain-link fencing, I was stopped by a middle-aged man in tan coveralls and a red hard hat. He was about my height, with a thick torso and heavily muscled forearms.

"Sorry," he said briskly. "This is a construction site. If you don't have business here, please stay out of the area."

"I need to speak with the foreman."

"I'm the foreman. What can I do for you?"

I took one of my business cards from my purse and handed it to him. "It's about the murder that occurred in that apartment building last Saturday night," I said, my thumb pointing over my shoulder at Ruth's place.

He examined me with his serious brown eyes, then tucked the card into the breast pocket of his coveralls. "Yeah, I read about that in the *Trib*. I can't tell you anything, though. None of my crew was here that time of night."

"I know. I was here Friday afternoon. I noticed a homeless woman with a shopping cart. She headed for this lot, and I got the impression she was sleeping here. If that's the case and she was here Saturday night, maybe she saw something."

"Oh, you mean Rosie," the foreman said, using the same monicker Ruth's neighbor had. He rested one hand on his hip. The fingers of his other hand stroked his moustache, which was black flecked with gray. "I don't know what her name is. Don't know if she knows. We call her Rosie, on account of that straw hat. She wouldn't be much help to you. She ain't exactly playing with a full deck."

"What can you tell me about her?"

He shook his head, and when he spoke, his words contained a mixture of exasperation and sympathy. "You're right, she does sleep here. Or did, until we started this job about a month ago. It's been a real problem. She thinks this is her turf. We've been having a war of nerves. Hell, I don't want to hurt some poor woman whose elevator doesn't go all the way to the top floor. But I've got a job to do and a schedule to meet."

He gestured toward a row of bushes separating this lot from the parking lot behind the businesses on Piedmont Avenue. "She spreads her sleeping bag under those bushes over there. My guys clean it all out, but she comes back again. She lets us know how she feels about it."

"Vandalism?" I guessed.

"If you want to put a name on it, yeah. Bags of cement ripped open, lumber strewn around. Of course, we've also had the local kids writing graffiti all over the place. I don't know who's doing what. But Rosie scratched her initial on the shed."

The foreman pointed at the door of his office. An R was scratched onto the metal surface, a crude spiky character with a long emphatic tail. "Last time we rousted her, I told her I'd call the cops," he said. "I hate to do that, though. You shouldn't lock somebody up for being homeless. So we're putting up the fence. That'll keep everybody off the site. Rosie won't like that. Hope she doesn't go after the cars again."

"She's defaced some of your vehicles?"

"Yeah. She gets real pissed off if someone blocks the curb cut." He pointed to the shallow slope leading from sidewalk to street. "She can't get her shopping cart up on the sidewalk. About two weeks ago one of my guys parked his car a little too close to the corner, and she scratched hell out of his hood. Now he's gotta get a new paint job. Boy, was he steamed."

"Have you or any of your crew seen Rosie since Friday?"

He shook his head. "Not since Thursday morning. That's when I threatened her with the cops. Let me ask the other guys." He quickly polled the members of his crew and returned with the same negative answer.

"Any idea where I can find her?"

"She hangs out in this neighborhood. I see her with that stick, digging in the Dumpsters and the trash cans for cans and bottles."

"If you see her, call me. My number's on that card."

"Will do," he said with a brief wave.

I left the construction site, stopped on the corner and stared across the street to Ruth's building, recalling the scene early Sunday morning when I had arrived. If Rosie had been here, she may have been frightened away by the commotion surrounding Sam Raynor's murder. Police cars and flashing red lights would scare her away from the lot, particularly since the foreman had threatened her with the police.

I walked over to Piedmont Avenue and visited several businesses, describing Rosie. One employee of a frozen yogurt shop told me she'd seen Rosie late Saturday afternoon, but that was the sole information my questions netted. Was I off on a wild goose chase? I didn't know for certain that Rosie had been in the area Saturday night, or if she had, whether she'd seen anything important. All I knew was that finding her was going to be a time-consuming hassle, one that would have to wait for now.

Lena Copeland's Saturday night date, Maurice Hemphill, worked in one of the new high rises recently constructed in downtown Oakland, this one a steel and glass tower on Nineteenth between Alice and Harrison. There was a bank lobby on the first floor. The building entrance faced the corner, and when I arrived at a quarter to twelve, a steady stream of office workers flowed through the bank of glass doors, the stream widening and spreading along the downtown sidewalks, across Nineteenth to Snow Park, a city-block oasis of grass and trees. Across Lakeside Drive, Lake Merritt shimmered in the warm August sunshine, its perimeter already being circled by lunchtime joggers and walkers. Other office workers had purchased their sandwiches or salads and carried them to the park, to sit on the grass, while still others eschewed lunch to run errands or shop.

When I spoke with him on the phone that morning, Hemphill told me he'd be wearing a flowered tie, evidently the prevailing sartorial style in neckwear. It seemed every man I saw had a florist's shop hanging around his neck. I stood on the corner and scanned the crowd, then I caught sight of a tall, broad-shouldered man in his late twenties, with short black hair and bronze skin. He wore a loose-fitting, well-tailored suit in a pale silvery gray, and a silky shirt of the same color, managing to look cool even on this warm day. The tie was resplendent with peonies, pink and blue and purple, anchored with a pearl tie pin. I raised my eyes to his as he inquired, "Jeri Howard?"

"Maurice Hemphill?" I held out my hand and he shook it firmly.

"I have a short lunch hour," he said, his voice crisp. "Mind if I grab a bite to eat while we talk?"

"Not at all," I said.

As we waited for the light to change, Hemphill told me that he worked for the bank that took up several floors of the building on the corner. When the walk signal flashed on, we joined a parade of pedestrians crossing the street to a quick-lunch café filled with patrons. He asked if I wanted anything and I shook my head. I snagged one of the tiny round tables crowding the sidewalk, earning a grumpy look from two women who had designs on the same table. Hemphill queued up at the salad bar and joined me at the table about five minutes later, balancing a bottle of apple juice, a fork, napkins, and a loaded plate. He sat down, dwarfing the table, loosened his peony-splashed tie, then unfolded a paper napkin and carefully spread it on one knee.

He uncapped his apple juice and I let him get a head start on his salad, recapping what I'd told him on the phone about interviewing people who had been in Ruth's apartment building the night of the murder. Evidently Lena had filled him in on our conversation of the day before.

"I don't know whether I can help you," he said as he speared cauliflower with his fork. "As I told Lena, I'm not sure I saw anything important."

"Just tell me about Saturday night and let me decide what's important. What time did you and Lena get to her place Saturday night? And what time did you leave?"

He didn't answer right away, instead foraging through his salad for a chunk of avocado. "Can't say exactly what time we got there, and I was in Lena's apartment for a while before I left. I'm fairly certain I left right after eleven."

"What did you do? Let's walk through it, in detail, from the minute you walked out Lena's door."

"I kissed her good night, and left the building."

"Elevator or stairs?"

"Stairs," he said promptly. "The elevator was on another floor, and it's pretty slow."

"Didn't see anyone in the stairwell?"

"No." He shook his head and lifted another forkful of salad to his mouth.

"The stairs exit into the building lobby. Did you see anyone there?"

He shook his head again and touched the napkin to his lips. "I couldn't see it, but I heard a ding and that sound the elevator doors make when they close. Kind of a whoosh-whump, you know. My impression was that someone had just gotten onto the elevator, to go up, because I didn't see anyone in the lobby. Of course, the elevator could have been empty. But it was on the ground floor. Well, I think it was. I didn't actually see it. The stairs are behind the elevator shaft and when you come out the door in the lobby, the elevator is to the right and forward."

"And the front door is on the left," I added. "Was the front door closed?"

"Definitely closed," he said, giving the last word emphasis. "Lena told me the manager's been on her case. I assure you, that front door was closed until I opened it on my way out."

I was quiet while Hemphill finished his lunch, picturing the double glass doors that led to the lobby of the apartment building, with a handle on the outside, a crash bar on the inside, and pneumatic tubes at the top. "Once you push through a door like that," I said, thinking out loud, "how long does it take for it to close? For the air to escape from that tube at the top, so that it latches?"

Hemphill thought about it for a moment as he chased one last olive around his plate. "Don't know. Never thought about it. Some take longer than others. You could time it, I suppose."

The possibility might be enough. "Okay, you've just

stepped outside the door of the apartment building. What next?"

He shrugged and waved his fork. "I turn right. My car's parked on Forty-first, just around the corner."

"No, no, slow down." I looked at him across the table. "You're in slow motion. You're in front of that door, standing on that pebbly sidewalk in front of the building, just before you turn to the right. Take another look, tell me what you see and hear."

Maurice Hemphill folded his hands on the table and closed his eyes, giving in to my suggestion. He was silent for a long moment, then he opened his eyes and stared directly into mine. "A car horn honking," he said, then paused. "Traffic on Piedmont Avenue. Music from somewhere, rap music. Loud, but only for a minute. Like a car went by with its windows open. Laughing and shouting. I think it's a bunch of teenagers, over toward that parking lot across the street. I can hear people talking, but it's closer, on this side of the street."

"Can you see the people who are talking?"

"Yes. It's an older couple, walking this way on Howe Street."

"How do you know they're older?"

"Just an impression," he said with a shrug. "They stop and get into a car, just up the street, and I hear the car start."

"Anyone else?"

"I look up, in the direction of those kids. There's a man coming toward me. He's stepped onto the sidewalk there at the corner and he's coming toward the building."

"What does he look like?"

"Big white guy, not as tall as me. Red hair."

"Red hair," I repeated, trying not to show my excitement. "Are you sure?"

"He's under the street lamp there on the corner," Hemphill said, still in the present tense. "The light's shining on his head. Sure looks red to me."

"Is he alone?"

Hemphill didn't answer immediately, still looking in-

202

ward, trying to pluck things from his memory. My anxiety level heightened considerably. "There's somebody a few steps behind him, following him."

"Man or woman?"

"Can't tell," he said, shaking his head in frustration. "The second person is on the sidewalk, by the planter. There's a bush in the way. By this time I'm already walking toward my car, seeing this redheaded guy on my left, out of the corner of my eye, for just a second. Then he's gone, behind me, I guess." Hemphill sighed and looked at me, his brown eyes serious. "The redheaded guy could have reached the front door of the building before it closed. That's what you wanted to know, isn't it? How he got in. He's the one who got killed, isn't he?"

"Yes. But how he got in isn't as important as who was with him."

"You think if his wife didn't shoot him," Hemphill said slowly, "this other person did. Damn, don't know. I can't even say that they were together. Just that I had an impression they were. I didn't even get a good look at whoever it was. I wish I could help you."

"You already have. Quite a bit."

Maurice Hemphill and I parted on the corner, and I walked back toward my office on Franklin Street, moving against the crowds on the sidewalk, my head down as I mulled over Hemphill's statement. He'd seen more than he thought he had, enough to tantalize me with the possibility that Sam Raynor's killer was someone who had followed him into the apartment building. That possibility certainly wasn't enough to prove anything. Still, there was a chance Maurice Hemphill had seen Sam's killer. If he had, maybe someone else had too. I'd just have to keep digging until I unearthed another witness. As it was, I felt as though I were piecing together a patchwork quilt and I didn't have enough squares to finish the project.

There were several messages on my answering machine, including one from Lieutenant Bruinsma saying she had some information for me. The last voice on the tape was that of Bill Stanley. "Jeri, it's twelve-thirty. I'll be in my office till two or thereabouts. We need to talk." His words sounded terse, bitten off, requiring a face-to-face meeting rather than a phone call. I looked at my watch—one-thirty. If I hustled, I could catch Bill at his office. The phone rang and I reached for it.

"You didn't call me back yesterday," Alex said.

"I was busy all day." I leaned against my desk, conscious of the second hand on my wall clock. "I can't talk long. I was on my way out the door. What's on your mind?"

"Chief Yancy." Alex sounded perturbed. "He was late to work this morning, missed a staff meeting. His division officer wanted to know why, so Yancy dumped the whole story. About Mrs. Yancy and Sam Raynor. Plus you, on Yancy's doorstep this morning. Jeri, why didn't you level with me about the chief?"

"And tell you what? That the guy's wife is sleeping with someone else?"

"Not just someone. Raynor worked for him, and Mrs. Yancy's at another command here on base. Adultery's against Navy regulations," Alex said glumly.

"Adultery's against a lot of people's regulations, but that never stopped anyone from doing it. Anyway, I didn't figure it was Navy business."

"It is if it interferes with the job."

"Or leads to murder," I added.

"Surely you don't think Yancy killed Raynor?"

"He was at the murder scene. He had a motive and an opportunity." So did several others, but I wasn't quite ready to dismiss Steve Yancy—or his wife.

"Did you tell Lieutenant Bruinsma about this?" Alex asked.

"No. I figured she'd find out on her own."

"Or the chief will tell her. She wants to talk with him, and right now he's in a confessional mood. It'll all wind up in her JAG report. Should make interesting reading as it goes up the chain."

"Alex, we'll talk later," I said, watching the clock. "I have to meet someone."

I locked my office and took the stairs down to street

level, thinking about Alex Tongco. Even if there was no professional conflict between the Navy's interests and mine in the Raynor investigation, it felt awkward as hell discussing the matter with Alex. I liked the man and enjoyed his company, though I didn't think the relationship was going anywhere. But I also had a job to do and I couldn't let my personal life get in the way.

As I walked to Bill Stanley's office I thought about the Raynor investigation, the original one. Find the money, a supposedly routine task that should have been easy to complete but wasn't. Now that job had been overshadowed by Raynor's death, which complicated lives all around me, like a rock dropped in water, creating a widening circle.

The biggest complication was to Ruth Raynor, awaiting the District Attorney's decision whether to charge her with murder. Arrayed against her was the evidence of her gun, her prints, and a damned good reason to want her husband dead. Too many people were willing to accept that and let Ruth take the blame.

It was more convenient that way, especially for the killer.

Twenty-five

I WAS RIGHT ABOUT THE HINT OF TROUBLE IN BILL Stanley's phone message. When I arrived at his office shortly before two, he gave me the bad news. The Alameda County District Attorney had filed a complaint against Ruth that morning, charging her with the murder of Sam Raynor.

"Sunday you told me the worst she could be charged with was voluntary manslaughter," I reminded him. "The cops must have a better case than we thought."

Bill leaned back in his worn chair and laced his fingers

together. He was wearing another flowered tie, this one a scattering of orange California poppies on a deep blue background, matching today's rather sedate pair of blue and orange suspenders.

"The cops have nothing," he said. "Circumstantial at best. I'm counting on you to poke holes in their case. Ruth will be arraigned tomorrow. She'll enter a plea and the judge will set a date for the preliminary examination." Bill ran a hand through his already tousled hair. "Anywhere between ten and sixty days, depending on how much time we need to prepare."

"What about bail?" I asked, leaning back in my chair.

"The assistant D.A. made some noise about the amount, but I told the judge she's got ties to the community—parents, the kid. Ruth's not gonna skip. Anyway, her old man put up a big hunk of cash. He took her home to Alameda."

"How is she?"

Bill shrugged. "After two days in the lockup? Shaky, worried about Wendy."

"Why did the assistant D.A. quibble about dollars? I would think a low bail is appropriate for someone like Ruth."

"We drew Maloney. He's the D.A.'s new hotshot, out to prove how tough he is on crime. I overheard him in the hall, making noise about how he's tired of broads who blow the old man away, then claim spouse abuse."

"Great. That's all we need. A Neanderthal for a prosecutor." I got up from the chair and crossed to the window, where I looked down at the intersection as Bill continued.

"The cops talked to Raynor's divorce lawyer, Tolliver. He made a big deal about Ruth asking for the restraining order and what he described as restrictive and unreasonable visitation. He implied that Sam may have been going to see the kid."

"Oh, sure," I said, hands on my hips. "He shoves his way into his estranged wife's apartment at eleven o'clock at night just so he can visit his daughter? Come on. What else did Tolliver tell the cops?"

206

"That Ruth was a greedy, grasping woman trying to wring every cent she could out of her poor, penniless sailor husband." Bill thumped his hand on a legal-sized accordian folder that I assumed contained his case file. "Although I notice Tolliver stopped short of admitting that Raynor had salted away over a hundred thou so he wouldn't have to split it in the divorce settlement. Tolliver brought up the subject of murder for financial gain. As far as I know, Raynor died intestate, which means Ruth and Wendy split the estate, assuming there is one. And since Wendy's a minor, Ruth would administer her share."

"Murder for financial gain?" I echoed. "That's a special circumstance." Which in California means a capital crime. "Bill, that's ludicrous. If Ruth shot Sam at all, it was self-defense. And I don't think for a minute that she shot him."

"You're convinced somebody else pulled the trigger?"

"I just can't see Ruth as the shooter." I shook my head. "If the gun went off when they struggled, if Sam's body had been found in the apartment, maybe. But Sam was shot in the back, in the hall. That's too cold-blooded for the Ruth I know."

"You don't know her that well," Bill pointed out.

"Okay, I only met her two weeks ago. But I'm a good judge of character. I have to be, in my business. As far as your case is concerned, I can poke holes in Mrs. Parmenter's statement. I told you that last night. I have another witness who lends some credence to my theory that someone was with Sam Raynor when he entered that building Saturday night."

Bill listened while I related the substance of my interview with Maurice Hemphill, punctuating my narrative with questions of his own. "Theories are fine," he said when I finished, "but I need warm bodies I can bring into a courtroom."

"I take it the assistant D.A.'s tough-on-crime stance precludes a plea bargain."

"Ruth says she didn't shoot Sam," Bill said. "We've gone over her story time after time and it still comes up the same. The plea is not guilty. The cops did find the second

207

slug, buried in the sofa. So Ruth's telling the truth about the gun going off when she and Sam fought over it. But I'd like to blast the D.A.'s case out of the water. Another suspect might do it. Maybe you can rustle up something in Gilroy."

"Gilroy?" I'd been moving restlessly around Bill's office. Now I stopped and stared at the attorney. "What's in Gilroy—besides the Garlic Festival?"

"Sam Raynor's funeral. Autopsy was done Monday and the body was claimed early this morning by Raynor's mother."

"Mother? Sam told Ruth his parents were dead."

Bill stuck a hand in the accordian folder and pulled out a single sheet torn from a yellow legal pad. "Well, according to Navy records, Sam Raynor's next of kin is a Mrs. Alma Raynor, Gilroy, California. He was born and raised there."

"He told Ruth he was from San Jose," I said, examining the sheet of paper Bill tossed my way. He'd scribbled notes all over it, in blue ink, and it was hard to make sense of what he'd written. "Makes me wonder what else he lied about."

"Probably everything," Bill said. "I want you to go down there and find out. I called the mortuary that picked up the body. Funeral's Wednesday morning at some church in Gilroy. The address is at the bottom of the sheet."

I walked back to my building and climbed the stairs to my third floor office. I discovered someone waiting for me outside the door. I was more than a little surprised to see who it was.

"I was just about to leave you a note." Admiral Franklin's words were as crisp as his blue slacks and plaid shirt. He tucked a small notebook and pen back into his shirt pocket.

"How's Ruth?" I asked him, taking out my keys. He didn't answer until we were inside. I took a seat at my desk and waved him to the chair opposite me.

"As well as can be expected," he said, looking more sub-

208

dued than usual. His gray eyes rested for a moment on my face. "Glad to be out of that damned jail and home with Wendy and her mother." He paused. I looked at the message light flashing on my answering machine as the silence stretched between us.

"What did you want to talk about, Admiral?" I asked finally.

"I'm very worried about Ruth." He straightened and scowled at me. Then he stood up and began pacing, which is difficult to do in an office as narrow as mine.

"Bill Stanley is one of the best criminal defense attorneys in the area," I began, but he waved away my words.

"I know that but— To sit in that courtroom this morning and hear my daughter charged with murder. She didn't kill him, and Stanley's attitude seems to be that maybe she did but he can get her off."

"Defense attorneys have a different way of looking at these situations," I said, choosing my words carefully.

"It's not a situation. It's my daughter."

Franklin's words matched the frustration etched on his face. He was a hard-shelled old hypocrite, but I did feel a flash of sympathy for him. My own father once told me you never stop being a parent, no matter how old you or your offspring get.

"I have to do something," he said, smashing one fist into the open palm of his hand. Then he glared down at me as though I were the source of his problems. "I am not a man accustomed to inaction."

I'll bet, I thought. He'd retired several years ago, after more than thirty years in the Navy, and his recent try for the state senate had gone belly up in the primary. The man could only play so much golf, and I was sure Lenore didn't want him around the house all day, particularly now, when she was occupied with caring for Ruth and Wendy. I'd known this was coming, ever since my early morning visit to the Franklins' house on Sunday.

"There must be something I can do to assist," Admiral Franklin said. "People I can interview. You know as well as I do that Raynor must have had someone with him that

209

night, someone who used Ruth's gun to shoot him. I assume you've talked to the other tenants in the building."

"On Monday." What if I sent the Admiral to face off with that martinet building manager? Now that might be worth watching.

"Miss Howard, I know that our previous encounters have been somewhat acrimonious."

"That's an apt description," I commented.

His gray eyes flashed at me, then he went on. "But my wife likes you and so does my daughter. Furthermore, they both trust you. You've worked for Mr. Stanley before and I assume you would not have been in business as long as you have if you weren't a competent investigator. So I'm asking you, please, put the past aside and let me help, in whatever way I can."

I thought about it for a long moment, wondering what task I could assign him where he would do the least harm. "All right," I said with resignation. "There is something that needs doing. It's likely to be time-consuming and I don't have time to do it right now."

The Admiral fairly snapped to attention. "What is it?"

"There's a homeless woman who camps out across the street from Ruth's apartment, in that lot where the building is going up. The people in the neighborhood call her Rosie, because she wears a straw hat with a pink cloth rose. She pushes a shopping cart filled with all her stuff, and she scavenges food, cans, and bottles from the Dumpsters of the businesses along Piedmont Avenue. I saw her on Forty-first Street Friday afternoon, the day before the murder. Someone else saw her in the area Saturday afternoon. If she was there Saturday night, she may have seen something."

"Is she lucid?" the Admiral asked, his nose twitching as though he suspected he was being dispatched on a snipe hunt.

"Maybe, maybe not. Maybe she was there, maybe she wasn't. But she hangs out in the vicinity, so that makes her a potential witness, just as much as the people who live around there."

I gave him a brief rundown of my conversations with the

foreman and the yogurt shop employee. "She scratched her initial on the door of the shed at the construction site. The foreman showed me. It looks like this." I picked up a pencil and sketched the spiky R with the long tail. "Maybe she puts her mark other places."

Admiral Franklin had pulled out his notebook and pen and was taking notes while I talked. "Good. I'll question the merchants along Piedmont Avenue, then the people who live around Howe and Forty-first."

"You don't question anyone," I told him. "You talk. You converse. You schmooze." He stared at me without comprehension. I decided to demonstrate. "Okay, pretend I'm a Piedmont Avenue shopkeeper and give me a sample."

He frowned, drew himself up to his full height, his posture ramrod straight, and barked questions at me. I interrupted him in mid-sentence. "No, no. You can't interrogate people like that, not if you want information. You're too damned intimidating." I stood up, put my hands on my hips and looked him up and down with a critical eye. "I think what we need here is a little less military bearing."

"What do you mean?" He looked confused.

"You always look like you're wearing a uniform, even though you've retired. No wonder people still call you Admiral. But this isn't the Navy. The people you're talking to aren't sailors who have to salute and obey. Forget you ever had all that gold braid on your sleeves. You're not a cop. People don't have to tell you anything. You have to persuade them. You've got to blend in with the crowd, be a regular guy, so people will be comfortable talking with you. Remember, you're asking a favor of a person who's busy running a cash register, keeping an eye out for shoplifters and answering questions from legitimate customers. You want to do it economically, but you also want to make it as easy as possible for them to respond to your questions. Here, pretend you're a sales clerk in a bakery."

Joe Franklin stared at me in utter amazement as I went into my questioning routine, trying not to think about the absurdity of my giving private eye lessons to this man I disliked. Still, he was determined to do whatever he could

211

to help his daughter, which meant I was doomed to have him underfoot. I might as well put him to work. And if he was going to do it, he had to be effective.

The expression on Franklin's face turned thoughtful. "I think I've got it," he said. "I'll have a go at Piedmont Avenue and report back to you tomorrow. What time do you get to work?"

"I'll be out of town most of the day. Bill wants me to go to Sam Raynor's funeral. Just leave a message. Here's the number."

I handed Admiral Franklin one of my business cards and watched him leave, eagerness now flashing in those gray eyes. I shook my head, wondering what sort of monster I had just unleashed on Piedmont Avenue.

I hope I don't regret this, I muttered, punching the playback button on my answering machine.

Twenty-six

GILROY MEANS GARLIC.

If you roll down your window as you drive through on U.S. 101, you can smell the stuff for miles. Each July the citizens of Gilroy celebrate the stinking rose with a festival that draws crowds from all over the state to sample everything from garlic wine to garlic ice cream. I'm as fond of garlic as the next person, but I prefer mine on pasta.

Sam Raynor's funeral was scheduled for eleven o'clock Wednesday morning, at a Methodist church located, oddly enough, at the corner of Fourth and Church streets, west of downtown Gilroy. It was a pale brown stucco building with a red tile roof. The windows were arched, as was the doorway where a small group of people clustered on the shal-

212

low front steps, waiting for the service to begin. On the north side of the church I saw a parking lot where a long black hearse had pulled up to the building's rear entrance. I parked on the opposite side of Church Street, behind a Chevy pickup. A man sat behind the wheel of the pickup, his right arm flung across the top of the seat.

I opened the door of my Toyota and got out, feeling hot and wrinkled in my gray linen dress with little pearl buttons on the bodice and cuffs. Linen doesn't travel well, particularly on a hot day in a non-air-conditioned car. Still, the gray dress would have to do. I wasn't a relative or a friend, but I wanted to look appropriately sober.

As I passed the pickup I glanced through the open window. The man in the driver's seat was not appropriately sober. In fact he seemed inappropriately jubilant, given the broad smile on his round fair face. Our eyes met. He saluted me with the bottle he held in his left hand, then raised it to his lips and took a swig. I stopped and examined the stocky figure, clad in khaki trousers and blue work shirt, open at the neck to reveal a white T-shirt underneath. He was about my age, early thirties, with short blond hair receding from a forehead beaded with perspiration.

"Good morning," I said, moving closer to the truck.

"Beautiful morning." His voice was cheerful and his blue eyes twinkled as he glanced at my gray dress. He waggled his bottle at me. "Want a bracer before you go into the church? You'll probably need it."

"A bit early in the day for me. You're not attending the Raynor funeral?"

"Hell, I'm here to make sure the son of a bitch is dead."

He chuckled as he raised his bottle again. What I'd thought was booze turned out to be grapefruit juice. He wasn't tipsy, just cheerful. He screwed the cap on the bottle and set it on the seat next to him, humming a song that sounded familiar. I finally identified it by the first line, a phrase that ran, "I'll be glad when you're dead, you rascal you."

"You don't look like his type," he said with a grin. "Curiosity seeker?"

213

"Seeking information." I took one of my business cards from my shoulder bag and handed it to him.

"Private detective." He put thumb and forefinger together and snapped the card. "Very interesting." He chuckled again.

"I'll bet you can tell me a lot about Sam Raynor."

"Lady, you'd win that bet." The words were sharp, his voice suddenly intense. His eyes narrowed and turned cagey. "Depends on who you're working for."

"Let's just say I'm trying to keep Ruth Raynor out of jail."

"She didn't plug him, huh?" I didn't answer. "Wouldn't have blamed her if she had. It was bound to happen sooner or later. Should have been sooner." He tossed my card onto the dashboard of the Chevy. "Come and see me after the funeral. Meriwell Hardware, Seventh and Monterey. Ask for Tom."

He turned the key and gunned the pickup's engine, its roar drawing looks from the group of mourners in front of the church. I stepped back as he drove away. Then I crossed the street.

I was relieved to see that the family had chosen a closed casket. I didn't want to look at Sam Raynor's dead face, prettified by a mortician's artifice. The casket sat in front of the altar with a spray of white flowers draped over its dark wood surface. Two flower arrangements on easels stood on either side, one multicolored, the other a collection of white flowers enlivened only by the yellow centers of the daisies. This was dominated by a wide white ribbon with gilt script. I squinted at it as I walked up the center aisle, finally making out the words *Beloved Son*.

I took a seat near the front, on the left side of the aisle, behind an elderly couple. A plump silver-haired woman played a series of hymns on the organ. I checked my watch. It was five minutes before eleven. There weren't many people at this funeral, and they all appeared to be middle-aged or older. The woman at the organ continued her lugubrious accompaniment until just after eleven, when the dark-suited

214

pallbearers filed in from the side entrance and sat in the front left pew. They were followed by the family members.

The first was a slender, brown-haired man of about thirty. He held the arm of a tall woman whose black dress hung on her frame. She wore a black hat with a brim and a veil. This must be Alma Raynor, Sam's mother. No Mr. Raynor, I noted, just two other women, one older and plumper, gray hair visible under a pillbox hat thirty years out of fashion. The woman who followed her was blond, much younger, probably in her early thirties. She wore no hat and her dress was short and form-fitting. As they took seats in the right-hand front pew, a man in a dark suit stepped up to the altar and the organist stopped playing.

A funeral is supposed to provide the mourners with some sort of closure and remembrance. But this funeral was business, a means of finding out more about the late Sam Raynor, and I was not a mourner but a detached observer. Not as detached as I should have been, though. The only emotion I felt for the deceased was dislike. If my gut feelings were correct, and they usually are, there wasn't much emotion at this funeral, not even from those family members across the aisle. The minister was saying the right words, but he was playing to a disinterested audience. The Sam Raynor he described bore no resemblance to the man I'd met.

The old man in front of me had a bald dome as wrinkled as his face. He was whispering to his wife, a querulous buzz that drew my attention. "I only came out of respect to Alma," he said, "and I can't hear a thing."

Alma's friends, I thought, even the pallbearers, all of them gray and elderly. There was no one here who was a contemporary of Sam Raynor, besides the brown-haired man and the blond woman. Yet Raynor had been born in this town and presumably lived here most of his life. I didn't see anyone who might have been a high school buddy, and certainly no one who looked like a Navy acquaintance. I wondered if the rest of Gilroy had the same opinion of Sam Raynor as did the man in the pickup.

It was a short funeral. The minister was the only one

215

who spoke, and he ended his remarks by saying that interment would follow at the Odd Fellows cemetery on First Street. After that, we were invited to pay our respects to the family at Alma Raynor's home on Rosanna Street. I had no desire to see Sam Raynor buried. My objective was to talk to the family, to find out as much as I could about the man who had come to such a violent end, a demise that a lot of people seemed to think he deserved. The elderly couple in front of me didn't want to go to the cemetery either, so I followed them to the house.

Alma Raynor lived about three blocks from the Methodist church, near the corner of Rosanna and Second streets, in a quiet old neighborhood lined with single-story wood-frame and stucco homes, lawns and sidewalks shaded by trees. The house was plain and white, its wood exterior in need of painting. Three shallow steps led up to a front porch on which sat a low wooden table and two old metal lawn chairs. The house sat close to the sidewalk, and its truncated front lawn was patchy and brown, due to the drought and neglect. There were no flowers or ornamental foliage visible. It didn't look welcoming.

I parked across the street, rolled down the window of my car and waited, speculating why Sam Raynor told his wife both his parents were dead. How convenient not to have a mother-in-law to tell you all about your spouse's past. But of course Sam didn't want Ruth to know anything about his past. That told me there were a few skeletons in his closet.

Despite the shade, it was warm in my car as the sun made its midday progress high in the blue sky, heading west, where it would drop behind the Gavilan Hills, looming between Gilroy and the coast. I felt sweat pooling between my breasts and my shoulder blades, dampness wrinkling the gray dress. Finally, a station wagon pulled into the driveway of Alma Raynor's house, the brown-haired man at the wheel. He and the three women got out of the car and went up the front steps, followed by the minister, who parked his car at the curb. Others joined them, people who'd gone to the cemetery, people who hadn't, like the old couple I'd followed from the church.

I heard a murmur of conversation as I came up the low steps. I tapped on the screen door. The younger man loomed up on the other side.

"Please come in. I'm Mitch Burgett, Sam's cousin. I saw you at the church."

"Jeri Howard. From Oakland."

I opened the screen door and stepped into an uncarpeted hallway, offering my hand as I examined him. I saw little resemblance to Sam. Mitch Burgett had a firm handshake, a pair of pleasant, mild brown eyes with hints of green, and a long narrow nose in an equally narrow face. In his dark gray suit his body was wiry. He was a couple of inches taller than my own five feet eight inches. His straight brown hair was a bit long at the back, brushing his collar.

"We surely do appreciate your coming," he said, his hand lightly touching my left arm as he escorted me into Alma Raynor's living room. He loosened his tie, as though he were unaccustomed to wearing a suit. "Did you know Sam well?"

As well as I'd ever want to. "Not really," I said. "We'd just met."

A big new-looking television set on a stand dominated the left side of the room, with most of the furniture grouped to my right. The carpet was an unappetizing shade of tobacco-brown, not at all helped by the squarish green and white tweed sofa and matching armchair. The flowered needlepoint pillows on the sofa were bright, garish splashes of red and orange. Above the sofa I saw an oil-painted landscape in a too-ornate brown wood frame, depicting an idyllic-looking farm with fields and orchard, hills in the distance. It was devoid of any artistry, simply a generic picture purchased to fill space on the beige wall. In the far right-hand corner stood a recliner upholstered in brown vinyl that was supposed to simulate leather. Its surface was cracked along the arms, and a green and orange crocheted afghan had been draped haphazardly over its high back.

Nearby was a bookcase that held no books. Instead, it was a shrine to Sam Raynor. Its shelves were crowded with the framed face, first a plump baby with no hair, then the

217

grinning redhead, through various stages of childhood and adolescence, and finally the adult Sam. The top shelf held a silver-framed eight-by-ten color shot of Sam in his service dress-blue Navy uniform, looking like the competent, squared-away sailor everyone thought he was. Someone had placed a single white lily next to the photograph, a sympathy card tucked into the silver foil surrounding the pot.

Beyond the living room I saw a dining room with a rectangular table and a sideboard on the far wall, next to a door that led to the kitchen. A coffeepot and cups were arrayed on the sideboard, and the table was covered with dishes of food. A few people sat in the living room, drinking coffee and eating, while others were grouped around the table, talking in low voices as they helped themselves to a variety of comestibles, ranging from salads to desserts.

"May I get you a cup of coffee?" Mitch asked, standing at my elbow.

"Yes, thank you. I take it black."

I followed him to the dining room while he fetched the cup. Just as he returned, the screen door opened and a woman crossed the living room, the youngest of the three women who sat in the front pew during the funeral. As she reached us, Mitch introduced his sister, Nancy Tate.

She smelled of cigarette smoke. Since I didn't see any ashtrays in Alma Raynor's living room, I guessed she'd stepped outside for a few puffs. Her platinum coiffure was the result of her hairdresser's skill. In her face I saw a strong resemblance to her brother, the same narrow face and brown eyes, but there wasn't any warmth in the eyes, and her red-lipped mouth had a sullen pout to it. She was about thirty-five, slim-hipped in a short navy-blue dress that showed off a respectable pair of legs.

"I have to go," Nancy told her brother abruptly, barely acknowledging my greeting. I glanced over the table and rejected the chocolate cake on the grounds that it would be too difficult to maneuver plate, fork, and coffee cup all at once. Instead I selected an oatmeal raisin cookie and nibbled it while I listened.

"I'm showing a house at one." She glanced at her watch. "There's nothing more to be done here. He's buried." The edge in her voice made me examine her face. No mourning here. In fact, Sam's cousin seemed quite satisfied to see him planted in the ground and quite ready to get on with the business of living.

The older woman who'd worn the pillbox hat entered from the kitchen. The hat had been removed and an apron tied over her black dress. "You're leaving?" she asked as Nancy dug her keys from her handbag.

"I have to work, Mother," Nancy said, mouth tight.

"Did you have something to eat?" The woman's voice was high-pitched and fretful, with a hint of Southern roots.

"I don't want anything to eat. I'll call you later."

As Nancy made her escape, Mitch smiled apologetically. "My sister's a real estate agent here in town. She's always working." I nodded as he took the older woman's plump arm. "Jeri, this is my mother, Elva Burgett. Jeri's a friend of Sam's from Oakland."

"Well, Alma will want to talk to you, then." Elva Burgett patted my hand and turned to her son with a sigh. "I tried to get her to lie down for a bit. But she's fussing around in that kitchen."

As she spoke, Alma Raynor walked through the kitchen door, a platter of sliced meats and cheeses in one hand, and a basket of crackers in the other. She set the food on the table. I downed the rest of my cookie and examined her. The shapeless black dress she wore did nothing for her tall, broad figure. She didn't look like a woman who wore clothes with any style, or even cared about such things. She looked dry and stringy, with strong work-worn hands and a short crop of iron-gray hair. Maybe it had once been red. Sam must have gotten his full sensual lips from the absent Mr. Raynor, because this woman's mouth was a thin slash in her blunt-featured face. He got his blue eyes from her, though. She looked at me across the table and her gaze was cold, flat, and unwelcoming.

"Who are you?" she asked me in a deep voice as flat as her eyes.

219

Mitch quickly introduced me. "This is Sam's friend Jeri from Oakland."

"Didn't know Sam had any friends in Oakland," Alma Raynor said. "Did you know him long?"

I shook my head. "I only just met him."

"Nice of you to come, then." Her mouth twisted down at the corners. "That's more than I can say for some in this town who knew him all their lives."

"Really?" I said, hoping she would go on.

"I saw that fat slug Tom Meriwell sitting in his truck across the street from the church." Mrs. Raynor narrowed her eyes and her voice took on an accusatory tone. "I saw you talking to him."

"The man in the pickup," I said quickly. "I asked him if I had the right church."

She nodded, reserving judgment about me, but she had no such reservations about Tom Meriwell. "Come to gloat, about my boy being dead."

I put on a wide-eyed innocent mask. "Why would he do that?"

"Lies," Alma Raynor said. "All lies. They were always picking on him." She walked into the living room and sat down heavily in the brown recliner with the cracked arms.

"You're tired." Elva Burgett patted her sister on the shoulder. "You need to rest. Put your feet up. Mitchell, get your aunt Alma a cup of coffee."

While Mitch fetched the coffee, Alma reached down and brought up the footrest of the recliner. She didn't look at all relaxed. More like a vengeful harpy, with those flat blue eyes and the bitter set of her mouth.

I moved into the living room and perched on the end of the sofa nearest to Alma. "Why did everyone pick on Sam?"

Sam's mother took the coffee her nephew brought her and raised the cup to her lips. "They needed somebody to blame. Everybody needs somebody to blame. Sam was just naturally high-spirited, like boys are. So they picked on him, all through school. I couldn't keep track of Sam every

220

minute. I'm a working woman, on my own since that worthless Raynor left me high and dry with a boy to raise."

Listening to her, I could guess who "they" were. Teachers and school administrators and Sam's classmates. Alma Raynor described her son as "high-spirited," but the man I'd met was mean-spirited. Duffy LeBard had called him a sociopath. A psychologist might concur. Such aberrations are formed early. I'm no expert, but Sam Raynor seemed to fit the pattern, with an absent father and a mother who thought her baby boy could do no wrong.

Elva Burgett sat down next to me. "I remember the time he took Ida's car and she wanted to call the police."

Alma shook her head. "Ida never did have a sense of humor. He didn't steal it, he just borrowed it. That boy of hers put him up to it."

"Ida?" I asked. I was having trouble keeping up with all these names.

"Our sister Ida," Elva said.

"Is she here?" I looked around for someone resembling the two sisters.

Elva shook her head. "No, she's gone off on a cruise to Mexico with her second husband. They left last week, before we got the news about Sam."

"I wouldn't go on no cruise to look at a bunch of Mexes," Alma said with a snort. "But Ida never did have good sense, especially when she married that no-account Ed Coffin."

With Alma, Elva, and Ida, their parents had utilized three out of the five vowels. I wondered if there were two more sisters with names starting in O and U, but I resisted the impulse to ask. There were more important questions to be answered.

"Why would this Mr. Meriwell gloat about Sam's death?"

"That slut sister of his." The words that hissed out of Alma Raynor's mouth were dipped in venom. Mitch Burgett stood in the doorway between living room and dining room and as his aunt spoke he flushed, two splotches of red coloring his cheeks. I wondered if he was embarrassed

221

at these revelations concerning his cousin, though most of the mourners had drifted into the dining room and were now gathered around the table, talking in low tones and sampling the food. Or did his sudden reaction have something to do with Tom Meriwell's sister?

Mitch saw me looking at him. "Sam was married to Denise Meriwell," he explained.

"I didn't know Sam had been married before," I said, somehow not surprised. "He mentioned that he was in the process of divorcing Ruth." I looked closely at Alma, searching for some reaction to the name of the woman who was accused of killing her son. But Mrs. Raynor was angry at the world in general. No doubt she had been angry for most of her life.

"A couple of tramps. They trapped him, both times. Got pregnant, so Sam had to do the right thing and marry them. The one that shot him, I never met her, though Sam did send me a picture of their little girl." Alma set her coffee cup on the end table and her thin mouth compressed into a tight line. "Sam said she and her family was too hoity-toity, rich people with their nose in the air because her father was some officer. They didn't want me cluttering up the wedding. Never mind that I'd like to see Hawaii. I'm just a poor working woman from Gilroy."

What would Alma Raynor think of her boy if she knew he'd told his current wife that his mother was dead? My guess was that Sam Raynor hadn't wanted his new bride to know anything about his first wife. I leaned forward, eager to learn more about Denise Meriwell Raynor.

Fortunately, Alma was more than willing to discuss her first daughter-in-law, and it was clear she had a low opinion of the woman. "A cat in heat," she said, words issuing from her mouth like a hiss. "That Denise was sleeping around all the time she was in high school. With Mexicans and colored, I wouldn't be surprised. When Sam said he was gonna marry her, I told him how could he be sure that baby was his."

"Well, it was," Elva said. "Scott had red hair from the day he was born."

"I never saw much of the boy. His mother didn't want me around. Probably because she was catting around on Sam." Alma seemed to be telling her tale with relish. I glanced up at Mitch. The red spots on his cheeks had faded but he looked as though he were biting his tongue.

"Where is Denise now?" I asked.

"She lives in—where was it, Mitch?" Elva looked up at her son. "Mitch ran into her a couple of months ago, while he was making a business call. Where was it, honey?"

Mitch's voice sounded rusty. He cleared his throat and began again. "Benicia. I saw her in a bank in Benicia. That's where she works. She's married again, to a guy named Padilla."

"A Mex," Alma said, scornful in her casual bigotry. "She likes those dark ones."

The minister came to take his leave from Mrs. Raynor, his impending departure triggering a general exodus among the funeral attendees. I homed in on Mitch Burgett, who I suspected had far warmer feelings for his cousin's first wife than did his aunt.

"So you travel on business," I said. "What line of work are you in?"

"Computers," he said, naming a company I'd heard of, headquartered in Santa Clara. "I troubleshoot software, call on clients all over the Bay Area."

"Did you ever visit Sam when you were up in the East Bay?"

"We had lunch a couple of months ago."

"It must have been a shock when the police called this weekend to tell you about his death." Briefly I entertained the notion of Mitch as a suspect in his cousin's murder. Had he been anywhere near Oakland?

"Yes, it was an awful shock," Mitch said. "But we actually didn't find out he was dead till Monday. Friday night I drove Mom and Aunt Alma down to Bakersfield to visit some Tyrone relatives, and we headed back up here Monday morning. We hadn't been back an hour when a Gilroy policeman came by to see Aunt Alma. The Navy and the Oakland police had been trying to get hold of us."

It was time for me to leave. I had a date with the man in the pickup, who I was certain would give me a far different view of Sam Raynor than his mother had. As I stood in the middle of the living room, saying good-bye to Mitch Burgett, I saw Sam Raynor's mother reach for the silver-framed photograph of her son in his Navy uniform. She stared at that cocky smiling face, compressing her thin mouth into an even tighter line. Then she pressed the frame to her broad sagging breasts. She leaned back in her chair and stared out at nothing in particular. Her flat blue eyes glittered with tears.

I felt sorry for Alma Raynor. Sam was all she had, and he wasn't much.

Twenty-seven

DOWNTOWN GILROY RUNS ALONG MONTEREY Street. Like many towns with business districts bypassed by freeways and the development that follows freeways, downtown Gilroy is struggling to hold on. The JC Penney on one corner had going-out-of-business signs in its front windows, having lost the battle to the outlet mall near the highway. But the antique business was booming, judging from the number of stores lining both sides of Monterey Street. And in the middle of the block between Fifth and Sixth, some brave soul had launched a bookstore with a flourish of "Grand Opening" banners.

Meriwell Hardware anchored the corner of Seventh and Monterey. It was an old-fashioned hardware store that looked as though it had been at the same location for years, sitting deep and wide on its corner, with high windows at the front, ledges crowded with merchandise, and, above, signs advertising specials. Inside it was dark despite the fluorescent lighting on the high ceiling. Four cash registers with counters were arrayed across the front of the store. Beyond the registers, long narrow aisles stretched back between tall shelves. The place smelled of metal, sawdust, and machine oil, a musty aroma that tickled my nose. The wooden floor creaked as I walked past the registers into the bowels of the store. A treasure trove, I thought, peering at the booty all around me.

I saw racks and bins piled with shiny brackets and hinges of brass and steel, dull metal screws, nuts and bolts, everything from minuscule tacks to heavy nails, ready for the customer's hand to plunge into the heaps, pricked by edges and points, sifting out the required amount. Stacked on shelves or hanging from pegboard were hammers, pliers, and wrenches, ratchets and screwdrivers, saw blades and drill bits, every variety of tool I could conceive of and some I couldn't. Meriwell Hardware was an adult playground, the sort of place where I could happily roam the aisles, collecting things I needed and might need and probably didn't need. I could gather an armful of extension cords, picture-hanging supplies and sandpaper, pluck light bulbs from a shelf or batteries from the revolving metal rack at the head of one aisle, find myself seduced by a matched set of metallic red flashlights in descending sizes, or that big toolbox with all the drawers and compartments.

The sales clerks were mostly men of middle age, though I saw a gray-haired woman stocking shelves in the housewares section. Two younger women staffed the cash registers. All of them wore orange canvas vests over their work clothes. On closer inspection I saw that each vest had *Meriwell Hardware* inscribed in brown yarn script on the right side of the vest, and the clerk's name on the left side. At one of the cash registers, a customer, a clerk, and the cashier were rehashing the most recent Garlic Festival and its attendant traffic and parking problems. I interrupted them, asking for Tom Meriwell.

"He's back in plumbing," the customer said, pointing toward the rear of the store.

I thanked him and headed in the direction he indicated, sidestepping a leathery man in overalls who was staring intently at a hacksaw blade, as though contemplating some higher plane. Back in the plumbing section I found Tom Meriwell using his hands and passable Spanish as he explained the fundamentals of installing washerless faucets to an elderly Hispanic man. Then he escorted the customer to the check stands at the front and I tagged along. He turned to me with a smile on his round face.

"Find out anything interesting at the funeral?" he asked, twitching his sandy eyebrows at me.

"Tom Meriwell. Brother of Denise Meriwell, formerly Denise Raynor. Alma Raynor doesn't have a very high opinion of you. Or your sister."

He laughed, removing his orange vest. Underneath it he had a white plastic liner stuck in the left pocket of his blue work shirt, filled with pens. His clothes looked rumpled on his short stocky body. He tossed the vest over a swinging wooden door that led to a cramped makeshift office furnished with a wooden desk and a battered-looking chair, its walls lined with shelves that held a variety of publications. The vest landed on the desk's cluttered surface, covering an old black dial phone.

"Alma Raynor doesn't have a high opinion of anyone," Tom Meriwell said. "Except her son. She always had a blind spot where he was concerned. You had lunch?" I shook my head. The coffee and cookie I had consumed at the house after the funeral didn't qualify. Tom Meriwell beckoned me to follow him. "I'm going to lunch, Shirley," he called to the nearest cashier as we headed out the front door. "You in the mood for Mexican food?"

"Always," I said.

We crossed Monterey at Seventh and walked north, Tom Meriwell nodding and raising his hand as he was greeted by passersby. In the middle of the next block Tom opened the door of a bright green building. We entered a café called Robledo's, with a counter and stools along one wall, and tables covered with red-and-white-checked oilcloth. Lunchtime diners crowded both counter and tables.

226

"Hey, Estella," Tom said to the waitress, a Chicano woman with gray streaking her coiled black hair. She wore a white uniform with a frilly black apron.

"Hey, Tom," she replied, pointing us toward a recently vacated table for two, near the back against the wall. As we pulled out the chairs, she quickly cleared away the remains of the previous diners' lunch. She carried the dishes to the kitchen, moving quickly in her thick-soled white shoes, and returned with a tray, setting in front of us glasses of ice water, a basket piled with warm tortilla chips, and two small bowls of salsa, one red and one green. The plastic-covered menus were already on the table, stuck between the salt and pepper shakers and the metal napkin dispenser. I studied the menu while I took a chip and dipped it in the green salsa.

"The chiles rellenos here will set you free," Tom advised me, eyes twinkling. He didn't even bother to pick up a menu.

"I don't know about setting me free, but this salsa is about to liberate my sinuses." In fact it brought tears to my eyes. I ate another tortilla chip plain and chased it with some water in an attempt to put out the fire.

Estella appeared again, carrying a tall frosted glass and a can of Tecate beer, which she set before Tom. He picked up the can and poured the brew down the side of the glass to minimize the foam. She pulled an order pad from the pocket of her apron. "You gonna have your usual?"

"Might as well be consistent." He set the can down and took a swallow of beer. Estella turned to me, order pad and pencil at the ready. I ordered the chicken enchiladas, and she told me I'd made a good choice. As she headed for the kitchen, I reached for another chip, sampling the red salsa. It was slightly less flammable than the green.

"I'd like to talk with your sister Denise," I told Tom.

He flashed a cagey grin. "Question is, will she want to talk with you?"

"I hope so. Alma Raynor's version of the story is a bit lopsided." Tom Meriwell snorted derisively, an indication of what he thought of Alma and the whole tribe. "I know you can give me some information about Denise's marriage to

227

Sam Raynor, but I want to hear it from her too. I understand there's a child, a little boy named Scott."

"If it hadn't been for Scott, she wouldn't have married the SOB," Tom said, shaking his balding blond head. "When I found out she was pregnant, I wanted to run that varmint down with my pickup truck, I was that pissed off. I should have done it. Would have saved all of us a lot of trouble."

"Where were you the night he was killed?" I asked him bluntly.

Tom Meriwell raised his beer to his lips. His smile dimmed and his blue eyes turned wintry. "I won't say I never considered it," he said when he set the glass down on the table. His words didn't come as readily as they had before, and his voice lost its bantering tone. "Especially when I found out he was beating up my sister. The night she showed up at my parents' house with her kid in her arms, a black eye, blood running from her nose—" Tom Meriwell shook his head, his fair skin coloring at the memory. "I damn near got my hunting rifle and went after him then. If my wife hadn't blocked the door, I don't know what I'd have done."

He was quiet for a moment as the heat of renewed anger faded from his flushed face. "If I was gonna kill him, I'd've done it then, not now. Saturday night I was at the San Jose Center for the Performing Arts, me and my wife and two other couples." He picked up his beer again and stared at me over the rim of his glass.

"What he did to my sister was a crime. He should have gone to jail for it. But all Denise wanted was to get out of that marriage. She told Sam she wouldn't file charges if he'd give her a divorce and custody of the boy. So that's what happened. Maybe if he'd been locked up then, he wouldn't have had a chance to get married again and hurt some other woman. When I heard he was dead, I wasn't surprised. It's a wonder somebody hadn't shot him before now."

I looked at Tom Meriwell across the table and he looked away from me, glancing first at the counter, then back toward the kitchen. Something was bothering him, and I thought I knew what it was. Where was Denise the night Sam was killed? Was he asking himself the same question?

"Has Denise had any recent contact with Sam Raynor?"

"Maybe," he said, reluctantly meeting my gaze. "I don't know."

Estella brought our lunches, and Tom dug into his chiles rellenos, plump and covered with melted cheese, bracketed by generous heaps of rice and refried beans. The portions on my plate were equally large, and I took a fork to the chicken enchiladas. They were delicious and I was hungry. As I waited for Tom to continue I glanced at his perspiring forehead and wondered if it was the chiles, or my questions, that were making him sweat. He set down his fork and pulled a paper napkin from the dispenser on the table, mopping his forehead.

"Denise left town when she left Sam. She doesn't come back much, particularly since Dad died. She's married again. Her husband's a nice fella and I guess they're happy. We call each other about once a month. Last time we talked—hell, I don't know." He crumpled the napkin and tossed it aside.

"I really need to talk with Denise."

"I'll call her tonight. I got your phone number. If she wants to talk, she'll call you. She lives in—" He stopped, then went on. "She lives in the Bay Area."

"Benicia." He looked surprised. "Mitch Burgett said he ran into Denise a couple of months ago, working in a bank in Benicia. Would he have told Sam?"

"Wouldn't have to. If he mentioned it to his mother, it'd be all over Gilroy in half an hour. Elva Burgett does like to talk."

"What about Mitch? Did he have any kind of relationship with Denise?"

"Mitch still carrying a torch?" Tom smiled. "Whenever I see him, which isn't often, he asks about her. I guess he's being more than polite. Mitch was always fond of Denise. They dated in high school, till Sam came on the scene. Mitch and Sam were in the same class, graduated a year before Denise." That surprised me. When I met Mitch, I thought he looked older than his cousin. "I'm five years older than my sister. After high school I did a hitch in the Army. Came back to Gilroy with a Korean wife who didn't speak English very well and a baby on the way, so I went to work for Dad at the store. That's about the time Denise got married. That's another thing," Tom said, waving his fork at me. "Sam joining the Navy when he did. You better talk to Pete Bruckner down at the police department. Sam Raynor was a hell-raiser from the time he took his first step. I hear he went into the service about two jumps ahead of the law. I don't know the details, but that's something you oughta look into."

"I will. Alma and Elva mentioned an incident when Sam helped himself to an aunt's car."

"He helped himself to other people's things more than once. Dad used to catch him shoplifting at the store when he was in grade school. I think he was doing it just to see if he could get away with it."

"Sam was born here in Gilroy, but Alma and Elva talk like Southerners." I pushed my plate away, the chicken enchiladas half eaten. I was stuffed and ready to concede defeat.

"We're all Okies," Tom said with a shrug, finishing the last of his chiles rellenos. "Steinbeck's people, the ones who came to California during the *Grapes of Wrath* days. Dust Bowl ran our grandparents out of Oklahoma, Arkansas, Kansas, and Texas. They came to the San Joaquin Valley and the Salinas Valley and stayed. Quite a few went back, though, after the hard times were over. And recently too. I guess you can buy a house in Oklahoma City or Amarillo for a lot less than you can anywhere in California. I got family back there, and so do Alma and Elva."

The waitress came to collect our plates, placing the check between us. I reached for it. "Business expense."

"I'm liberated," he said. "I'll let you."

I pulled some bills from my wallet and laid them on the table. "What about Mitch Burgett's sister Nancy? I met her at the house after the funeral. She seemed a bit chilly."

"Nancy Tate? She's always had her nose in the air. Nancy was two years ahead of me in high school. She was a cheerleader and I was what the kids nowadays call a nerd." He grinned. "Still am, but what the hell, it suits me. She had a couple of years of college and married some banker. They got divorced a few years back. Now she sells real estate."

"Where can I find her?" He gave me the name and address of the real estate office where Nancy Tate worked. The waitress had collected the check and now she brought my receipt and change. I counted out the tip, then Tom and I pushed back our chairs. On the walk back to Meriwell Hardware, he promised to call Denise that evening.

The real estate firm where Nancy Tate worked was on Eigleberry Street in central Gilroy, in a single-story California bungalow of pale yellow stucco which had been converted into offices. She wasn't there, but that didn't surprise me, given her remark earlier about showing a house this afternoon. The receptionist told me Nancy would be in later, but she didn't know when. I didn't leave my name.

My next stop was the Gilroy Police Department, located near Seventh and Rosanna. Tom Meriwell had suggested I talk with Pete Bruckner, who turned out to be a sergeant. He'd gone to lunch but was due back soon. I waited half an hour before he appeared in the reception area, a tall man whose light brown hair had receded, giving him a high, domed forehead. He frowned as I identified myself and told him why I was there.

"You say Tom Meriwell sent you over here?" Bruckner paused, and I could see that he was turning things over in his mind. "Private detective, huh? I can't tell you much."

"You can check me out with the Oakland Police Department if you like," I began.

"They've already called. So has some Navy lieutenant." Bruckner frowned and scratched his nose. "It was me that went over to the house on Monday, to tell Alma. You say you're working for Mrs. Raynor's defense lawyer?"

I nodded. "Look, Sergeant Bruckner, I understand your

231

position. If the information is in public records, I'll dig it out eventually. But that's time-consuming and it doesn't usually tell the whole story. I'd rather get that from you."

Bruckner shrugged. "Hell, come on back to my desk. They buried him this morning. I guess speaking ill of the dead doesn't mean a damn thing now."

Twenty-eight

ON MY SECOND VISIT TO THE REAL ESTATE OFFICE I found Nancy Tate seated at a desk near the back of the large open room, talking on the telephone, her fingers ruffling the ends of her short platinum hair. After leaving the postfuneral gathering at her aunt's house, she had enlivened her dark blue dress with a long silk scarf in shades of pink, purple, and yellow, coiled around her neck and anchored to one side with a round gold pin. As I approached the desk, she put the phone receiver down in its cradle and looked up with a slight frown, trying to place me.

"I'm Jeri Howard. We met at Alma Raynor's house after the funeral. Your brother Mitch introduced us."

Her brown eyes narrowed and filled with suspicion. "What are you doing here?"

"I'd like to find out more about Sam Raynor."

Nancy Tate's mouth twisted like she'd bit into something sour. "I don't want to talk about him. I'm busy."

She reached for the phone with her left hand, her right sifting through the cards in a large Rolodex. I sat down in the chair next to her desk and looked at her while she punched the telephone keypad. I didn't say a word. She held the receiver to her ear, trying to ignore me while she arranged an appointment to look at a three-bedroom

232

house on Vista del Sur. That done, she glared at me with hostility as she hung up the phone with more force than necessary. "Will you please go away?"

I shook my head. "I have some questions about your cousin. I need answers before I go back to Oakland."

"Why? Mitch said you were a friend of Sam's."

"Mitch assumed." I took one of my business cards from my purse and handed it to her. "I'm a private investigator."

She stared at the card for a moment, then set it down next to the phone. Picking up a pencil, she held it like a drumstick, tapping the eraser end on the surface of the desk, watching me with wary eyes while several emotions marched across her face. When she spoke, her voice was uncertain at first, then more resolute. "You must be working for the wife, or her attorney. Believe me, I don't blame her for killing him. She probably had ample reason."

"Like Denise?"

Nancy's mouth curved upward in a sardonic smile. "You've been talking to Tom Meriwell."

"He had a lot to say."

The smile vanished. "You know that old saying—you can't choose your family. Well, I didn't choose to be related to Sam Raynor. And I don't choose to talk about him." She waved one manicured hand at me, willing me to disappear. Instead I crossed my legs and got more comfortable.

"Ruth has been charged with murder," I said. "I don't think she did it. I think there are plenty of other people who had reason to kill Sam Raynor. Some of them may be here in Gilroy."

She stared at me while she considered my words. The phone rang and she shifted her gaze to the blinking light on her extension. She stared at it but made no move to answer. Finally the receptionist picked up the call with a cheery "Good afternoon" and the name of the firm. "Nancy, line two," she called.

"Take a message," Nancy said, her voice sharp.

"It's your daughter."

"Which one?"

"She didn't say."

Nancy sighed and tossed the pencil onto the desk, picking up the receiver. "Yes?" She listened for a moment to the voice on the other end, red lips compressed, red fingernails tugging at her hair. "No, you may not . . . Because I said so . . . I don't care what everybody else's mother says, I say no . . . Don't argue, we'll talk about it when I get home." She hung up the phone and put her hands on her temples, elbows on her desk, shaking her head slowly. "God, I'll be glad when school starts. One's eleven and the other is thirteen. I may not survive puberty. And it was bad enough when I went through it."

"It's rough being a single parent."

She put her hands down and leaned back in her chair. "How did you know I was divorced?"

"Tom Meriwell mentioned it."

"Tom Meriwell. Finger on the pulse of Gilroy." She shook her head again. "I can't believe he showed up at the church. Then again, maybe I can. It's just like him. Alma was fit to be tied."

"Yes, she made her feelings plain. Of course, running into Tom Meriwell outside the church was fortunate for me. I had lunch with him after I left your aunt's house."

Nancy folded her arms across the front of her blue dress. "I'll bet he gave you an earful."

"He certainly did. Of course, it's his version. I thought you might have a different one."

"I don't. My cousin Sam was every bit as bad as Tom paints him. He was an obnoxious little bastard from the day he was born. I loathed him. I'm glad he's dead. But if you tell my mother that, I'll deny it."

"How did he get to be so obnoxious at such an early age?" I asked.

Nancy crossed her shapely legs and the smile came back, a bit crooked. "If I'd paid more attention in my psychology class at San Jose State, I might have the answer. But I was too busy mooning over the man who is now my ex-husband. And savoring what turned out to be my short-lived freedom." She sighed and her fingers played with the edge of her silk scarf.

"Alma's older than my mother, the oldest of five sisters. She married late in life and not for very long. I barely remember my uncle Lou. He went on a business trip and never came back. Can't say I blame the man. If I had to live with Alma on a regular basis, I'd leave too. Anyway, Lou took a hike about three months before Sam was born. Alma divorced him. She's been perfecting her long-suffering deserted wife act ever since."

"Alma seems to have lived for her child."

"Oh, yes. Darling Sammy was her consolation prize for failing at marriage. He was her perfect little angel. He could do no wrong. She indulged him, she spoiled him rotten. He never had any discipline." Nancy shook her head, the experience of raising her own children evident in her eyes. "You can't do that with kids. You have to set limits, or they become tyrants. That's what Sam was, an absolute devil. He was mean, vicious, and cruel. How do people like that happen? Are they born that way? Or is it the way they're raised?"

I've often wondered that myself. There seem to be a lot of people like that running around loose, creating havoc for the rest of us. They go through life leaving trails of pain. Some do it with impunity, while others populate our prisons.

"Both, I think," I said. I recalled my conversations with Tom Meriwell and Sergeant Bruckner. "I hear Sam had a few brushes with the law before he joined the Navy, mostly as a juvenile."

Nancy nodded her head vigorously. "Oh, yes. From the time he started school. If there was trouble, Sam was usually behind it. Alma always called those incidents childish pranks. But there was a nasty edge to everything he did."

"Such as?"

"He set fire to his elementary school when he was eight years old," Nancy said, lowering her voice as she leaned toward me. Now that she'd started talking about Sam, she was on a roll, and I was prepared to let her talk until she had no more words left. "He torched some books in his classroom. The fire got out of hand. The room was badly

235

damaged. It's a wonder the whole school didn't go up. Sam was playing with matches, or so he said. Everyone treated it as an accident, so he got off with a scolding from the principal. Even that made Alma mad. She hated it when anyone punished Sam, though God knows she never did it herself. But that fire was no accident. Sam and Mitch were in the same class. Mitch told me the teacher disciplined Sam for hitting another student, and Sam threatened to get back at her. And that very afternoon—flames and smoke and fire engines."

Nancy grimaced, brows drawn together, hands worrying the end of the brightly colored scarf. "You see what I mean? And that's just a sample of the stunts he pulled. Sam liked to get even. In grade school kids who crossed him got tripped in the lunchroom, or shoved into walls, or pushed out of trees. Later on they got beat up. Everyone left him alone. They were afraid of him."

I knew the type. When I was growing up there was one in every school, the bully, the petty tyrant who preyed on children younger, weaker, less sure of themselves. My classmates and I soon learned to stay out of the way, as a matter of self-preservation, and hope that sometime in the future retribution would catch up with the tormenter. Sometimes the comeuppance never came, but in Sam Raynor's case it had. Raynor was a murder waiting to happen, waiting for the person with the motive and the opportunity. As far as people with motives were concerned, it looked as though the line formed on the right.

"What about later, when Sam was in high school?" I asked. "After you left Alma's house this afternoon, your mother mentioned Sam 'borrowing' a car from an Aunt Ida. Did this happen a lot?"

"I remember that. Sam and my cousin Ty from Bakersfield. Two peas in a pod, Mother used to say. Every time Ty would visit, he and Sam would raise hell and get into trouble. Car crazy, both of them. Sam started 'borrowing' people's cars when he was about fourteen. Anyone who complained usually got their trash cans overturned on their

236

front lawns, or rocks tossed through their windows. Or their pets would turn up dead."

At that, Nancy Tate took a deep ragged breath. "Sam killed my cat, when I was in junior high school. He told Alma it was an accident, but I knew he did it on purpose." I didn't ask her why. The fact that he'd done it was enough. Her brown eyes turned cold with hatred at the memory, cold enough to make me wonder where Nancy was last Saturday night.

"Tell me about Denise Meriwell," I said quietly, breaking her mood.

She looked at me, startled, then she smiled. "Oh, Denise. She was pretty and sweet. A really nice girl."

"Alma called her a slut."

"Alma would. Denise was popular. She dated a lot. As far as Alma was concerned, that meant Denise was sleeping around."

"Denise dated your brother for a while."

Nancy nodded. "Yes, for about a year. They started going out together when Mitch was a senior and Denise was a junior, and the relationship continued through the summer and into the fall. Denise was at our house quite a bit during that time. Mitch was really fond of her. I thought it was getting serious, and so did my mother. Mom was concerned because Mitch had started college in San Jose and we wanted him to finish school. Sam didn't go to college. He was working at an auto parts store here in town. Sometime after Christmas he moved in on Denise. I always thought he did it just to take her away from Mitch. Deep down inside I don't think Sam liked women."

That jibed with Betty Korsakov's comment, and with my impression of the man I had met, the day before someone shot him. "You know, when Mom told me Sam was back in the area, I was worried. About my daughters. The oldest one is starting to develop, and she's really pretty. I didn't want him anywhere near my girls." She sighed, the breath coming out tinged with relief. "I needn't have worried. He hardly ever visited Alma, unless he wanted something. But just the same, I'm glad he's dead."

So were a lot of other people I had talked with over the last few days. "I understand Denise was pregnant when she and Sam got married."

"She'd have been a lot better off if she'd gotten an abortion," Nancy said, "or tried to go it alone. Poor kid. But no, they got married, two weeks after Denise graduated from high school. Alma was furious. She didn't think Denise was good enough for her darling Sam. They lived with Alma until the baby was born. I can't imagine a worse way to start a marriage, with my aunt Alma glowering over the dinner table."

"When was the baby born?"

"Right before Christmas." So the boy was eight years old, nearly nine. "After Scott was born," Nancy said, "Sam and Denise had a tiny little apartment near the store where Sam worked. I don't know when he started beating her. Probably early on, knowing Sam. I'd heard rumors over the years about how he treated his girlfriends, a punch or a slap here and there, nothing that ever left any evidence. The fat hit the fire the night Sam broke Denise's nose. It was right before Halloween, so Scott wasn't quite a year old. Denise should have had him arrested. I don't know why she didn't. You'll have to ask her for her reasons."

"I intend to." That is, if I could find her—with or without Tom's help.

"Sam's current wife, the one they think killed him, did he beat her too?"

"Same pattern," I told her, "over a longer period of time. Did Sam have a girlfriend while he was married to Denise?"

"Several. I guess some women would consider him attractive. He certainly must have had a good line. He always had some girl swooning over him. But it was all surface. He was a rotten human being underneath. I'm not even sure he qualified as a human being."

"Sam joined the Navy eight years ago. That must have been right after Denise left him."

Nancy nodded. "I don't have any details, but I had a feeling Sam was anxious to get out of Gilroy. You never

238

know what Tom Meriwell might do when he's angry, and he was mad enough to chew every nail in that hardware store. Denise had filed for divorce, and Sam didn't fight it. He went up to San Jose and next thing I knew, he was headed for boot camp."

Tom Meriwell was still angry, I thought, reflecting on my lunch with the hardware store owner. Sam Raynor's desire to get out of Gilroy would certainly explain his sudden rush to serve his country. After all, the Navy's ads promised adventure and exotic ports of call, something that might appeal to someone who had spent his whole life in Gilroy, California. Raynor's juvenile record was legally under wraps, and what Sergeant Bruckner told me earlier that afternoon indicated Sam had been careful enough not to acquire a record as an adult—at least not in Gilroy. Would the Navy have taken him with an adult rap sheet? I didn't know the answer to that question either. I made a mental note to ask Alex or Lieutenant Bruinsma.

"Please call me if you think of anything else I should know," I said, thanking Nancy Tate. Despite her earlier resistance, she looked relieved for having let it all out.

I headed north, arriving at the edge of San Jose's urban sprawl just in time for the evening rush hour. Trapped in my Toyota, I crawled along for a few miles, one car amid many, caught in the smog and haze, the afternoon sun glaring through my windshield, sweat dampening my now thoroughly wrinkled gray linen.

Finally I got off the freeway and detoured downtown to the Santa Clara County Courthouse, where I looked through divorce decrees from eight years ago, searching for the name Raynor. I verified the date on which Denise Meriwell obtained her dissolution of marriage from Sam Raynor and wrote down the name of her attorney.

It had been a long day and I was tired and hot, not wanting to face the freeway again. I left the courthouse and walked to a building not far from the San Jose Police Department. Upstairs, in an office that looked a lot like mine, a fellow private investigator named Norman Gerrity looked bored on this hot afternoon. His face brightened when he saw me.

"Norm," I said, "I'm buying. Let's go get a cold one."

Twenty-nine

"HE SOUNDS LIKE A REAL GRADE-A SON OF A BITCH," Norm Gerrity said when I told him about Sam Raynor. "I'm surprised someone waited this long to take him out."

"That's what everyone says. I'm even saying it myself."

Norm and I were tucked into a red leather booth at a dark watering hole just down the street from his office, a place frequented by a lot of off-duty San Jose police officers. No doubt Norm feels comfortable in these surroundings. He's a retired Boston cop, a thickset man with a bulldog face, a broken nose, and a full head of curly gray hair. His gravelly voice sounds like he never left Southie. He and his wife came to California several years ago to be near their daughter and her family. But Norm got bored with retirement, so, much to his wife's dismay, he acquired an investigator's license and set up shop downtown. We met earlier in the year, when we discovered we'd both been working, at different times, on the Willis missing persons case. Since then I've learned that Norm Gerrity is a good investigator who delivers. Plus he has connections with law enforcement all over the South Bay. That was one reason I was here. The other was his perspective, which is usually right on the money.

"The only person I'm reasonably certain didn't kill him is his wife," I said, hands locked around a mug of cold Anchor Steam. "Or his mother. Believe me, she's a piece of work. She loved her son, though, even if he wasn't lovable.

240

But it looks as though there are plenty of people with motives to go around."

"How can I help?"

"Norman, you read my mind."

He grinned over his beer as he took a swallow and wiped a thin line of foam from his upper lip. "Yeah, I'm getting good at that. Besides, you're buying. I figure you want something."

"Norm," I protested, "it's the pleasure of your company."

"Jeri, my love, it's my contacts. You want to know if the murder victim ever, shall we say, came to the attention of the law in this neighborhood."

"That's a good way to put it." I raised my mug. "Sergeant Bruckner at the Gilroy Police Department was very informative. Raynor had a record as a juvenile—vandalism, shoplifting, helping himself to other people's cars. He was more careful as an adult, at least in Gilroy. He worked in an auto parts store after he got out of high school, until he joined the Navy two years later. Until then he seemed to have cleaned up his act, except for the occasional speeding ticket. However, Bruckner heard rumors that Raynor was involved in something up here in San Jose. Rumors only, nothing concrete. Raynor's former boss got busted a few months later, for running a chop shop out of his store. It seems he wasn't too picky about where he got those auto parts. That was after Raynor left Gilroy, but it makes me wonder."

"I'll check it out. Give me some details." Norm pulled out a notebook and pen, wrote down the particulars on Sam Raynor and told me he'd put out some feelers. "Now it's payback time," he said with a grin.

"You mean the beer's not enough?" We both laughed. "Name it."

"I need some information on a real estate transaction in Alameda County. If you could look it up on your next trip to the courthouse, it would save me a drive to Oakland."

"Consider it done," I said, reaching for my own notebook.

* * *

241

It was past eight Wednesday evening when I finally re-turned to my apartment, anxious to get out of the gray linen dress I'd worn all day. Abigail met me at the door, tail up and belly wobbling, loudly announcing that she'd cleaned up every last morsel in her cat food bowl. I fed her, then headed for the bathroom, where I stripped off my clothes and took a shower to wash off the day's grime. I fell into bed and a deep dreamless sleep. After what felt like a forty-eight-hour day in Gilroy, I slept in until Abigail parked her bulk on my stomach and meowed in my face. Now, as the hot water dripped through the freshly ground coffee, I grabbed a pencil and pad and played back the messages on my home answering machine. Mother had called, I noted with a disquieting twinge. Now what?

I pushed Mother's call from my mind and breakfasted on cereal and strawberries, then made sure Abigail had plenty of crunchies before I left. I drove to my office, thinking about today's agenda. I still hadn't answered all my questions about Steve Yancy, Raynor's supervisor, who had finally tumbled to the fact that Raynor was sleeping with his wife Claudia. Yancy said he'd followed Claudia and her friend Dana to the Piedmont Cinema, then spent the rest of Saturday night drinking at the Royal Flush, until the lights and sirens lured him to the scene of Raynor's murder. Plausible, but I needed to corroborate Yancy's presence at the bar.

That was the same bar where Acey Collins spent Satur-day evening, until he was alerted by a phone call from Genevieve that Sam and Tiffany were having dinner at the restaurant where Genevieve worked. Had Acey gone back to the bar after observing his sister's argument with Sam in the parking lot? Which reminded me that I still hadn't interviewed Zeke, the waiter who had served Sam and Tif-fany that night.

My office answering machine flashed its red light rap-idly, indicating numerous messages. I reached for pencil and paper, pressing the playback button. Alex Tongco had called. So had Bill Stanley and Lieutenant Bruinsma. Then there was a terse report from Admiral Franklin. "I started at the end of Piedmont and I've worked my way down one side of the street to Ridgeway. Nothing to report."

I smiled, tapping my pencil on the notepad. It sounded as though Joe Franklin was really getting into his assigned task. Good. That would keep him out of my hair, and Bill Stanley's.

The last message on the tape made me sit up and reach for the phone. It was from Genevieve Collins, informing me that her sister-in-law Tiffany had finally turned up, late Tuesday night.

"Where was she?" I asked when Gen answered the phone.

"With a girlfriend up in Citrus Heights, near Sacramento. I'm off tonight, so Tiff's coming over for dinner. She'll be here after work, about five o'clock. I figure you want to talk with her."

"You figure right."

"Okay. I won't tell her you're coming. By the way, Zeke's working the lunchtime shift at the restaurant, if you haven't already connected with him."

"I haven't. I'll get over there today." I disconnected the call, then punched in Bill Stanley's number. His secretary, Donetta Fox, told me he was in court all day, but if I was at the courthouse, I might be able to talk with him during a recess. I had to go over there anyway, to look up Norm's real estate transaction. Now I turned on the computer and wrote a detailed report of my trip to Gilroy and the people I'd talked with after Sam Raynor's funeral. That took more than an hour, during which I fielded several calls. I was about to leave my office when the phone rang again. I reached over my desk and picked up the receiver, hearing a man's voice.

"Seems to me we have a dinner date we never kept."

"Mark Willis," I said, perching on the edge of my desk. His voice brought back memories of the case I'd been working on last March and his involvement in it. "Seems to me I was detained that night, by a couple of thugs in a parking lot."

243

"Water under the bridge," he said. "I'm in town on business. Want to try again?"

I ran through my mental list of things I had to do today. "I think I can make it. Say, seven o'clock? Shall we try for the same restaurant, Ti Bacio on College?"

"I'll be there. Hey, Jeri, don't stand me up again."

At the Alameda County Courthouse I dug up the information Norm needed, then I waited outside one of the courtrooms until Bill Stanley was free. I gave him a quick overview of my day in Gilroy and the leads I planned to check out. Then I headed for Piedmont Avenue.

I caught Zeke at New Sunshine Pizza just as his lunchtime shift began. He was a slender black man who wore round wire-rimmed glasses. He removed them and rubbed the bridge of his nose as he recalled serving Sam Raynor and Tiffany Collins Saturday night. He remembered them for several reasons. It was late, just before nine, when they walked into the restaurant. Besides, he knew Tiffany on sight, because she was Genevieve's sister-in-law and she'd been in before. More importantly, Sam and Tiffany were arguing, the kind of low-voiced quarrel that attracts attention because the participants are trying so hard not to draw the eye and ear.

"Could you hear enough to figure out what it was about?" I asked Zeke.

He stuck his glasses back on his nose and nodded. "Sure. Something about a car and some insurance. She was really upset with him, like the problem was his fault. He kept saying he had nothing to do with it."

"Did they talk about anything besides the car?"

Zeke nodded. "Right before they left, she said, 'You never answered my question about Ruth.' By then the atmosphere was definitely frosty."

It sounded as though Tiffany had done as her brother suggested and asked Sam Raynor flat-out if he'd ever hit his wife. He must have denied it, or from what the waiter just said, avoided answering. Zeke confirmed that the couple left the restaurant just after ten that night, which jibed with Acey's observation. Acey had also said that the movie crowd was leaving the Piedmont Cinema at the same time he left the bar where he'd been drinking and walked up to the restaurant. I thanked Zeke and headed up the street to the Cinema at the corner of Piedmont and Linda. I checked the time card taped to the box office window. The first evening show was at seven o'clock and the late show started at nine-forty. Assuming a fifteen-minute break between features, the first show would have been over at 9:25.

I walked back along the avenue to the Royal Flush, the tavern owned by Acey's friend. The heavy wooden door was propped open with an old flatiron, and I stepped inside, momentarily blinded as my eyes adjusted from the sunny street to the interior darkness. I stood for a moment, getting my bearings. The room was long and narrow, with booths on my left and the bar itself on my right. At the back I saw a dart board, a pool table, and beyond that, a Wurlitzer jukebox. A couple of burly guys in work pants and white T-shirts were playing pool, one chalking his cue while the other leaned over the table to make his shot. All the booths were full, a mixed bag of customers having lunch and a brew. Four stools at the bar were occupied, and the bartender had his back to me as he drew a mug of beer from the tap. As I moved toward the bar, a woman in a white shirt and a short black skirt bustled by carrying an oval basket with a burger and fries nestled inside on a sheet of waxed paper. She set it in front of a man who had removed his suit jacket and loosened his tie, and asked if he wanted another beer. Suspended from the ceiling above the bar, a color television set was tuned to one of the noontime news programs, but I couldn't hear much of the sound over the din of conversation.

I took a stool at the front of the bar and waited. "What'll you have?" the bartender asked in a gruff voice. He was tall and stringy, with a thin face and a hawk nose, his sandy hair shoulder length, combed straight back off his face. I ordered an Anchor Steam, watching him as he drew it.

There was a lot of gray in his hair, and I guessed his age as past forty.

"Are you the owner?" I asked when he brought my beer.

"Who wants to know?" he asked, his blue eyes wary.

I laid a five on the bar along with my business card. The bartender's eyes flicked over both, then he picked up the five first, moving toward the cash register. He came back with my change and picked up the business card, examining it more closely. "Yeah," he said finally. "I'm the owner. Acey Collins told me to expect you."

"Did he? What else did he tell you?"

"That you'd be asking questions." The bartender reached for a pack of cigarettes behind the bar, shook one out and lit it with a disposable lighter. "He was here Saturday night. Gen called from the restaurant, and he left, about nine-thirty. Came back about ten-thirty and had another beer. He and I shot the breeze till we heard the sirens and went to see if it was a fire or something. That was 'round eleven-thirty. You want witnesses, talk to Lucy. She's my barmaid. Anything else you want to know?"

He'd looked amused during this recitation, which more or less confirmed Acey's story. "Yes, there is." I raised the beer to my lips and took a sip. "There was someone else here that night, a man about five-ten, brown hair in a short military cut, fair, with a round face." I stopped, trying to recall what Steve Yancy had been wearing when I saw him at the murder scene early Sunday morning. "Blue jeans and a light-colored striped pullover with short sleeves."

The bartender shrugged and drew in smoke, knocking ash from the end of his cigarette into a round glass ashtray. "I get a lot of customers Saturday nights. And I was busy this past Saturday." He thought for a long moment. "I don't remember what he was wearing, but there was a guy sitting about where you are. He came in about a quarter after seven. He must have stayed a couple of hours. I think he ordered a burger and nursed three or four beers. Didn't talk much, looked morose, if you know what I mean."

"I think I do." Steve Yancy would have been morose, given the fact that he'd argued with Claudia about her affair

246

and she'd packed up and moved out. "What time did he leave?"

"Before Acey got the call from Gen, and Acey left around nine-thirty. So he must have left around a quarter after nine." In time to go to the theater as the first show let out, so he could follow Claudia and her friend to Fenton's Ice Cream Parlor. But Steve Yancy said he'd been afraid Claudia would spot him as she waited in the line outside Fenton's, so he came back to the bar until he too heard the sirens.

"If he did, I don't remember," the bartender told me when I asked him if he'd seen Yancy later that night.

Before I left the Royal Flush, I asked both the bartender and Lucy about Rosie, the homeless woman with the rose on her hat. They knew who she was, since she frequently raided the bar's trash cans in search of bottles and cans, but neither had seen her on Saturday. I walked back up Piedmont. It was past noon and I was hungry. I ignored the temptations presented at several bakeries, opting instead for a sandwich shop. It was empty, save for a clerk slouched forward, elbows resting on the counter. He straightened as I glanced at the menu board on the wall in back of him, and ordered a Calistoga and a pastrami on rye.

"Coming right up," he said, taking the mineral water from a refrigerated case. I watched him as he reached for a loaf of bread and a container full of pastrami. He was young, his blond hair short and spiky in the front and long in the back, braided into a tail at the nape of his neck. A gold hoop glittered in his left ear, and he wore a black T-shirt decorated with spotches of red, green, and neon yellow, advertising some heavy metal band I'd never heard of.

"Do you have any spicy mustard?" I asked, removing the cap from the bottle of Calistoga. It was a hot day and the cold sparkling water tasted good.

He picked up a jar and waggled it at me. "This stuff'll blow off the top of your head."

"Sounds good." He began slathering mustard on a slice of rye. "Sparingly, sparingly." I reached into my purse for my wallet and one of my business cards. "By the way, I'm

247

looking for a street person called Rosie, a woman with a rose on her hat. Maybe you've seen her?"

He looked up from his sandwich-making, glanced at my business card and grinned. "Your associate was already here."

"My associate?" I took a sip from my mineral water.

"Yeah, an old guy named Joe. He had your card." The deli clerk looked at me, a question in his eyes. "He's on the level, right?"

"Yes, he is. When did he come in?"

"Yesterday afternoon, for a cup of coffee and a muffin. Things were slow, so he and I had quite a chat."

I couldn't imagine anyone chatting with the Joseph Franklin I knew, let alone this guy with his hair in a braid and an earring in one ear. Evidently the Admiral had taken to heart my advice about being less intimidating, and he'd succeeded in getting people to talk with him. But was he getting any information?

"I haven't talked to Joe today," I said as I paid for my lunch. I took a seat at a table just opposite the counter, wrapped my hands around the pastrami on rye and took a large bite. The mustard kicked in. I could feel it burning right through my tear ducts to the back of my head, and my eyes began to water. I reached for a napkin to mop the overflow. "Wow, you were right about this mustard. What did you tell Joe? Have you seen Rosie?"

"Not for a week or so," the deli clerk said. "Joe said Rosie probably liked our Dumpster because we toss so many cans and bottles, which is true. She even scratched her initial on it, like she was telling all the other street people it's hers. He asked if I knew which other places she likes to scavenge, so I gave him a couple of possibilities. Later I saw him going into stores across the street."

I finished my sandwich, amused at the thought of the starchy Admiral Franklin canvassing Piedmont Avenue in search of a homeless woman. The laugh would be on me if he actually did find Rosie. Of course, I wanted him to find her. It sounded as though Franklin was doing a thorough job of it, and he was certainly saving me the time I'd have spent at the chore. It satisfied both his desire to do something to help solve his daughter's problem and Bill Stanley's edict to keep the Admiral out of the way.

Thirty

LENORE FRANKLIN OPENED THE DOOR OF THE HOUSE on Gibbons Drive, talking in hushed tones. "I just put Wendy down for a nap," she explained as she ushered me through the living room to the kitchen. "Poor little mite hasn't been sleeping well. She's been acting up too. Before, she was well-behaved and quiet. Too quiet, really. Now she's having tantrums. Yelling and throwing things. It's all because of this, I know."

"I'd recommend some counseling." I looked past Lenore, who leaned against the counter and reached for a frosty glass of iced tea. Through the kitchen window I saw Ruth at the far corner of the Franklins' patio, sitting in a metal lawn chair, her back to the window.

"You're right," Lenore said. She set the glass down again and wiped her hands on the sides of her blue slacks. Her topaz eyes were troubled. "Joe and I have talked about it. Joe's enjoying himself, by the way. Playing detective. He was out of here early yesterday morning and didn't get home till almost seven. If he doesn't find that homeless woman, it certainly won't be for lack of trying."

"I appreciate his help. I've been busy with other things Bill Stanley wants me to do."

"I'm not being a very good host," Lenore said suddenly. "Want some iced tea? It's been so hot, I've been gulping the stuff by the quart." Even as I said yes she was moving toward the refrigerator. She clunked several ice cubes into a tall glass and filled it to the brim with tea from a pitcher on the refrigerator shelf. "Want some sugar or lemon?"

"No, I'll just take it straight." I took the glass from her. Tea threatened to splash onto her spotless kitchen floor, and I quickly drank the liquid down an inch or so.

"That was a good idea," Lenore continued, "to get Joe involved. I've got my hands full with Ruth and Wendy. Joe wants to help. He's very much a take-charge kind of person, and it frustrates him not to be able to do something. He wants to make everything all right again." She glanced over her shoulder, at her daughter, and a shadow of worry crossed her face. "I'm not sure it will ever be all right again."

"How's Ruth?" I asked.

"Not well at all." Lenore crossed her arms over her flowered cotton blouse. "She has this incredible guilt, as though the whole thing is her fault—and no one else's. Wendy's behavior, the divorce, Sam's death. Yesterday morning, before we went to the arraignment, she even wondered out loud if she had killed him, in some kind of trance after he choked her. Jeri, when we got to the courthouse, I was afraid she'd plead guilty, just to get it over with. Thank goodness she didn't. She just sat there and let Mr. Stanley handle it. But she's so passive, as though she's just going to let whatever happens, happen."

I shook my head. "I don't think she did it, Lenore. There are a lot of people with motives to kill Sam. He generated a lot of hate and anger." I sipped my tea. "Where's Kevin?"

Lenore frowned again. "I'm not sure. He left this morning, said he was going over to the air station, that he had a lunch date with a friend. He knows a lot of people in this area, so he's been visiting friends and renewing acquaintances before he flies to Japan."

"When does he leave?" I asked. If Kevin's departure was imminent, I had to confront him about his whereabouts on Saturday night—and soon.

"He was supposed to fly to Tokyo on Tuesday, but he contacted his command at Yokosuka and asked for a week's extension of leave, because of Ruth's situation." Lenore looked out the window at her daughter. When she turned back to me, her mouth was compressed into a thin line, an effort to stop her lips from quivering. Her eyes suddenly filled with tears. "She's been sitting out there since this morning. Ignoring me, ignoring Wendy. Jeri, I don't know what to do."

"Hang in there. We'll get through this," I told her, placing my hand on her shoulder. The words sounded trite, but at this point I had nothing else to offer her.

Carrying my glass, I opened the back door and stepped outside. As I crossed the patio, Ruth did not move. When I came abreast of her I saw that she had a book in her lap but she wasn't reading. Instead she stared into space, unmoving, her eyes gazing somewhere past her mother's vegetable garden. She didn't react until I pulled up another chair, its metal legs scraping the concrete patio surface.

"Jeri," Ruth said mildly, blinking her brown eyes. "I didn't hear you."

I took another sip of tea, then set the glass on the nearby picnic table. "I'm glad to see you're out of jail. I hope it wasn't too bad."

Ruth looked at my face for a moment, then her eyes dropped. When she spoke, it was in a whisper, and I had to lean closer to hear her. "They put me in a cell with a prostitute. And a drunken woman who kept shouting and throwing up. When I got home, I felt as though I'd never be clean again. I kept showering and showering, until I used up all the hot water. I don't know if I can stand to go back there."

"You won't have to. You didn't kill Sam."

"The police think I did. My lawyer thinks I did."

"He didn't say that."

"No, he didn't," Ruth said. "Not to me, anyway. But I can tell. He's very cynical, this Mr. Stanley. I guess if you defend criminals for a living, you get cynical about guilt and innocence. I'm sure the lines get blurred. Is there such a thing as innocence, Jeri? I wonder."

"What do you mean, Ruth?"

"When Sam forced his way into the apartment, I was frightened. I was angry too. At the way he'd treated me in the past, at the way he was still treating me. When he threatened to take Wendy, I knew he could. He was physically strong, and what's more, capable of doing it. When I got the gun, I felt so angry I was cold inside. At that moment I wanted to kill him. And I knew I could. Maybe I did. Maybe I pulled the trigger and I just don't remember."

"You pulled the trigger inside the apartment and the slug went into the sofa," I said. "That was before he choked you and you lost consciousness. I believe you were angry and that you wanted to protect yourself and your child. God, yes, Ruth, we're all capable of murder. But given what you've told me and my own look at the scene, I don't believe you got up from the floor, followed him out into the hall, shot him in the back—and don't remember any of it. I just don't believe that. It would make my job a whole lot easier if you don't believe it either."

Ruth sighed and her mouth moved into a crooked little smile, but she didn't say anything. "I talked to your neighbors," I continued. "What I've heard makes me think there was someone with Sam that night. I want you to close your eyes and think hard. When the elevator door opened and Sam stepped out, did you see anyone else? Did you sense another person? And later, inside the apartment. Did Sam say or do anything that might indicate there was someone out in the hall?"

Obediently she shut her eyes and was quiet for a long moment. Then she covered her face with her hands and her shoulders shook. "No," she said, dropping her hands and staring out at the yard. "No. I told you at the police station. All I saw was Sam."

I leaned back in the chair, frustrated. Then I moved in a different direction. "Mrs. Parmenter, the elderly woman who lives down the hall from you. She told me she poked her head outside right before the shooting and saw and heard you arguing with a man. Who was it?"

Now Ruth looked surprised. "That? That was Kevin. We weren't arguing. We were discussing something."

"Why would she think it was an argument? Did you raise your voices a little? What were you talking about?"

"It was private," Ruth said, hesitating.

"Your business or his?" She didn't answer. "Let me take a guess, then. Kevin's business, and you disagreed about it."

"I promised I wouldn't say anything." Her words were a soft plea.

"Ruth, you've got to be open and honest, with me and with Bill Stanley. I know Kevin didn't come home until early Sunday morning, because I was here when he arrived. He says he spent the night with a friend. I think he's lying."

"You think he came back," Ruth said, frowning. She got up from the chair and the book fell unnoticed at her feet. "And shot Sam? My big brother Kevin? Oh, Jeri, you're wrong. He wouldn't, he couldn't."

"Maybe, maybe not." I kept my voice neutral, not putting words to my suspicions as I stood. "I've been trying to ask him questions since Monday, and he's avoiding me. Tell him I need to talk with him, Ruth."

When I returned to my office, it was nearly four. The red light on my answering machine was blinking. As I reached for the playback button my office door opened and a man entered. For a moment I didn't recognize him. His face held lines of fatigue, as though he'd trudged several miles in those scuffed thick-soled brown shoes on his feet. He wore shapeless khaki pants that looked a little worn at the knees, and a plain green shirt, open at the collar. His iron-gray hair even looked a bit windblown, which is difficult with hair as short as Joe Franklin's.

"I've got some mineral water and sodas in the refrigerator," I told Franklin, pointing toward the back of the office. "Help yourself. You look like you could use it."

He nodded and moved past me, then returned a moment later with a can of soda. He sat down in the chair in front of my desk, opened it and took a long swallow.

"I just got back from Alameda," I told him.

The Admiral grimaced. "Ruth's not . . . she seems shell-shocked. And Wendy . . . well, damnation. I just want this to be over."

"I know. I had lunch at the Sandwiched Inn. I hear you've been doing a thorough job of combing Piedmont Avenue."

"That was yesterday," the Admiral said crisply. "Today I hit Howe Street." He took another long swallow from his can of soda, then set it on my desk. "I haven't found Rosie yet, but I've confirmed that she was in the area late Saturday afternoon. And she may have been in the vicinity Saturday night."

He reached into his shirt pocket and pulled out a small spiral notebook and a ballpoint pen. He flipped open the notebook, tapping the first page with his pen. "A clerk at the hardware store on Piedmont Avenue says she was in the alley behind his store about four o'clock. He took a break around that time, and went out back for a smoke. He got a good look at her, hat and all." He took another sip and turned a page.

"A woman who works at the optical shop down the street says she closed her office at five-thirty that afternoon and walked to the Lucca Delicatessen at the corner of Fortieth and Piedmont to buy a few things for dinner. As she was leaving, she thinks she saw Rosie digging in the Dumpster behind the deli. But she's not certain it was Rosie, just that it was a woman. Only saw the backside, not the face or the hat."

"That's close to the construction site," I commented.

"Right. The parking lot at the rear of that block abuts the site." Franklin shuffled through the pages of his notebook. "There seems to be a pattern to Rosie's behavior. She's something of a loner. I talked to another street person who digs in the Dumpsters on the avenue. He says Rosie doesn't like people to get too close. So she doesn't beg from people on the street. Instead she collects cans and bottles, usable clothing and whatever she can find to eat. The librarian at the branch on Forty-first told me if the weather's bad, Rosie comes into the library to get warm. She never stays long, though. Rosie spooks the library patrons and the patrons

254

spook Rosie. Apparently, enclosed spaces make her nervous. Also, she doesn't like to get very far from her shopping cart. She appears to be territorial. Several merchants on both sides of Piedmont Avenue told me that Rosie has scratched her mark various places on their Dumpsters. I saw a couple of examples. The R you sketched for me. It's very distinctive."

"Good work," I told him, and I meant it.

"Thanks," he said, looking somewhat pleased with himself as he reached for his soda. "It hasn't been easy. In fact, it's been time-consuming and tedious. I don't know how you do it all day long."

If he thought talking to people was tedious, I ought to set him to work at the courthouse, looking up records on microfilm. "Finding a few grains of wheat in all that chaff makes the difference."

"Agreed. I'm sure it helps if you're committed to what you're doing. This exercise has also been very instructive with regard to the homeless. I must say I didn't realize until now how many folks either don't notice homeless people or simply don't want to. Rosie could very well have been in the area during the time in question, and the people I'm talking to just didn't see her."

"Or looked right through her," I said, thinking of the times I had averted my own head or ignored the outstretched hand. "It's not enough to place her near Forty-first and Howe in the afternoon. I want to know if she was there that night. And if people don't see her during daylight hours, she must be practically invisible at night. But you said you had a line on that."

"No stone unturned," Franklin said, with a brief nod. "I worked my way down Howe Street today, then some of the side streets. I've seen a number of people my own age in that neighborhood, retirement age. One thing I know about being retired is that you're home a lot. I didn't lack for people to interview." He stopped for another drink. "A man who lives in an apartment building near Gilbert and Ridgeway says Rosie raids the building's recycling bin. He heard something about nine Saturday night and looked out the window. The parking lot's lighted, and he saw Rosie pulling out cans and bottles."

"Gilbert and Ridgeway." I reached for my map stash, on the shelf behind my desk, and opened an Oakland map on my desk surface. Franklin got up and joined me. "That's two long blocks from Ruth's apartment building," I said, locating the intersection with my index finger.

"It gets better," the Admiral said. He finished the soda in one long gulp and tossed the can into my own recycling box. "A woman who lives near the corner of Ridgeway and Montgomery *thinks* she saw Rosie pushing her shopping cart down Ridgeway toward Howe, about an hour later. She's not sure of the time, or even that it was Rosie. Just a homeless person pushing a shopping cart."

"If it was Rosie," I speculated, "maybe she was headed for that construction site, to bed down for the night. Keep at it, Admiral. Sometimes you have to go back over the same turf, several times."

"I know. I knocked on plenty of doors where no one answered. I'll get back on it tomorrow, and I'll call in my reports. I just took the chance you might be in your office this afternoon. I'm headed home now. Lenore's been pushing herself too hard. I think we all need to go out to dinner."

"Good idea. She did look a bit ragged."

After my new associate left, I pushed the appropriate button on my answering machine and played back my messages. "Yo, Jeri," Norman Gerrity said in his unmistakable voice. "I got something you'll be interested in. Call me."

I reached for the phone, hoping Norm was in his office. He answered on the second ring. "It's Jeri. What have you got?"

"Sergeant Bruckner in Gilroy was right," he said. "I talked to a buddy of mine on the San Jose force. He recognized Sam Raynor's name. Told me the whole story. Raynor was a minor player in an auto theft ring and chop shop operating in San Jose. You know how it works—a car gets stolen and dismantled for the parts, or gets sold to someone who's not choosy about where it came from. Or they buy junkers and pull a VIN switch. You know what that is?"

"Yes, the term has recently come to my attention," I said, recalling Acey Collins's description of how it was done.

"It was a big operation. The San Jose cops had been trying to bust it for about a year before they finally closed it down. That's how Raynor was involved. He'd steal cars in Gilroy and Morgan Hill and deliver them to San Jose. One day he blew it. He got pulled over for speeding, driving a Mercedes that belonged to somebody else. The patrolmen took him downtown and turned him over to the guys who were working the auto theft racket. They had Raynor by the short hairs, so he covered his own ass."

"He informed on his business associates."

"You got it," Norm said. "Cops busted the whole scam and arrested ten people, including the owner of the auto parts store where Raynor worked."

"Did they know Raynor turned on them?"

"My source says yes. Raynor's ex-boss figured it had to be him, since he wasn't arrested and he dropped out of sight. The boss was the one saying if he ever caught up with Raynor, he was history. That must be the reason Raynor decided to get the hell out of Dodge."

"That, and the fact that he beat his first wife bloody, around the same time."

"Well, Raynor didn't testify at any of the trials. By the time the cops went looking for him, he was in boot camp down in San Diego. They had a strong enough case without him, so they didn't figure it was worth the trouble to bring him back up here."

"Did all of the people who were arrested go to jail?"

"Yeah. Since that was eight years ago, they're out."

"Are any of them still plying their trade?"

"Probably. It's all they know how to do."

"You've increased my list of suspects, Norm."

"How would they know Raynor was back in the area?" he asked.

"If the auto parts store owner is still in Gilroy, he may have found out from Tom Meriwell or a member of

Raynor's family. Besides, Raynor bought his latest girl-friend a shiny almost new Mercedes, which subsequently got stolen. My first question is whether the car was stolen when Raynor acquired it. I also have a hunch he engineered its disappearance. It's one way for him to hide some cash, which is why I started this investigation in the first place."

Thirty-one

DESPITE THE TANTALIZING PROSPECT THAT SAM Raynor was murdered by someone from his past, I was convinced the killer had to be someone from his present, someone in whose company he was comfortable enough to let his guard down, because that person accompanied him into Ruth's apartment building. Still, Norm's information about Sam and his involvement in the auto theft ring certainly added a new angle to my investigation, one worth considering in the light of the theft of Tiffany Collins's Mercedes.

The Harley and the Plymouth were both in the driveway outside the Victorian. I parked on the street, in front of a dusty red Subaru. As I got out of my car, I noticed the Subaru had a long scrape and a dented left front fender. I walked toward the house and up the front steps, expecting to hear piano music or rock 'n' roll. Instead I heard a television set. The Collins boy answered my knock, looking through the screen door with his mother's deep brown eyes. When I asked for his mother, he hollered "Mom" over his shoulder. A moment later Genevieve appeared.

"Hi," she said, unlatching the screen door. "Tiff's in the kitchen."

Tiffany had come directly from work, wearing a light

summer dress, yellow cotton splashed with red and pink hibiscus. She had removed her high heels, and her nylon-clad feet were propped up on one of the chairs that circled the round table. A can of Budweiser and a glass with an inch of amber liquid sat in front of her. "You." Tiffany's face crinkled with disgust at the sight of me standing in the doorway. She tossed her blond head, picked up the can and poured some more beer into the glass.

"You talk to her, damn it," Acey said behind me. I turned and saw him coming out of the bathroom, drying his hands on a worn terry-cloth towel. He was stripped to the waist and a streak of soap still lingered on one shoulder. Gen took the towel from him and wiped away the lather.

Tiffany's glare encompassed all three of us. "It's not enough that Gen called you Saturday so you could come spy on us, but I've got Ms. Hotshot Detective here dogging my steps. I bet you got a spy over at NAS too. Who else told that damn Lieutenant Bruinsma about Sam and me? For all I know, you've been talking to my insurance company."

She was on target, I thought ruefully. "I do know you called in sick Monday and Tuesday."

"You think I shot Sam?" she challenged.

"You tell me."

Suddenly Tiffany seemed quite interested in the foam that topped her beer. When she spoke, her voice was quiet. "I didn't know he was dead until I got back to town and called Acey."

"So where were you?"

"I went to see my girlfriend Kelly. She lives up in Citrus Heights. Me and Mr. McGregor drove up there early Sunday morning."

"Mr. McGregor? Oh, the rabbit."

"He goes where I go." Tiffany squared her jaw. "I should stick with Mr. McGregor and forget men." Acey gave his sister a quick sidelong glance as he walked to the refrigerator. She intercepted his look and shook a finger at him. "Don't say it. Just don't say it."

Her brother sighed and opened the refrigerator door,

259

fetching his own can of Budweiser. As he was about to shut the door, Gen held it open and pulled out a plastic container, checking its contents, a cut-up chicken marinating in a pungent brown liquid. She replaced the cover, stuck it back on the shelf, then crossed to the kitchen counter and reached for a knife, a scarred wooden cutting board, and a plastic colander full of green bell peppers. Acey watched us from the back door, taking occasional sips of beer from the can he held.

Tiffany looked up at me, her red lips twisting into a wry smile. "You were right. Sam was using me. To get over on his wife."

"Is that what you argued about Saturday?" I pulled out a chair and sat down.

"Sam loaned me the money to buy the Mercedes." Tiffany sighed and raised the glass of beer to her lips. "I knew I was gonna have to buy a new car soon. Thumper's not in great shape."

"Thumper?"

"My Subaru. So I was sort of looking at cars. I've always wanted a Mercedes, and that insurance money I got when Mom died was burning a hole in my pocket. But I couldn't quite bring myself to spend it on a car. Better to save it for a down payment on a condo or something practical." She made a face. "Sam caught me at a weak moment, with his brilliant idea. He loaned me the money, interest-free. The deal was, I'd pay him back every month, in cash."

"No record of the loan or the payments," I said. "Great way to launder money."

"Yeah, that's what finally dawned on me." She shook her head. "I had this feeling he wanted to hide money from his wife. But I believed what he said about her. Then the Mercedes was stolen, and you showed up, telling me all this stuff about Sam. Now the insurance guy's giving me problems. So I started to wonder, about everything." Tiffany jerked her chin in her brother's direction. "Acey thinks Sam had something to do with stealing the Mercedes. But he seemed as mad as I was when it disappeared."

260

She looked around the room, at her brother, her sister-in-law, and me, and colored slightly. "I know, it sounds stupid. The more I think about it, the dumber I feel. But I believed what I wanted to believe. Until Saturday."

I looked at her across the table. "What else did you and Sam argue about?"

Tiffany didn't answer right away. For a moment the only sound was that of Gen chopping peppers, the knife making a dull whacking sound as it hit the wooden cutting board.

"I asked Sam if he ever hit his wife." Tiffany's voice was quiet and her blue eyes stared at me. "The first time I asked was over dinner. He didn't answer. I asked him again, in the parking lot. He just went off, talking about you and how his wife had hired you to spread lies about him. Then he started in on his wife, and what an awful bitch she is. I knew then you were right about him beating his wife. We were standing under a streetlight, and he got this terrible look on his face. He didn't look like the same guy I'd been dating. He scared me. I kept thinking of that line from Shakespeare, about protesting too much. I was afraid he'd hit me. All I wanted to do was get out of there."

"What time did you leave the restaurant?" I asked her.

"A little after ten. I didn't look at my watch. We argued all the way to the parking lot, and then it was a couple of minutes before I got into Thumper. I steamed out of there and headed for home, but—" She stopped abruptly and ran both hands through her blond mane. "I had a fender bender. At the corner of Howe and MacArthur."

"I saw your fender. How did it happen?"

"Wasn't my fault." Tiffany looked decidedly grumpy. "This sedan was making a left off MacArthur onto Howe. The light had just turned green for me, but she jumped the signal and cut the corner too close. She stopped and started to get out of her car, but I just waved her on. She was in such a hurry, I figured she must be on her way to the emergency room at Kaiser. And I just wanted to get home."

"Why didn't you report it?"

"After the business with the Mercedes getting stolen? Are you kidding? My insurance company would laugh in

261

my face. I just figured it wasn't worth the hassle. She didn't hit me that hard and I've got a high deductible on Thumper. I'll get Acey to hammer out the dent and paint the scratch."

Her brother was standing in the doorway that led to the back porch. She flashed him a crooked grin, and he muttered, "Yeah, I'll do it." He'd finished his beer and now he crumpled the can.

"Too bad you didn't report it," I said. "I'd like to verify the time of the accident. Can you describe the car and driver?"

"I can do both," Tiffany declared. "I glanced at the clock in my car. It was ten thirty-one. I have this notepad stuck to the dash, right above the clock, and I wrote down the time and the license plate number of the other car, just in case." Tiffany reached for her purse, which was sitting on the floor beside her chair. She rummaged through the contents and pulled out a slip of paper on which she'd scribbled the number.

"It was a sedan, dark, California plates. I didn't catch the make. The driver was a white woman and she was alone. I know I should have reported it, but Saturday night I just couldn't deal with anything else. I went home, called my friend Kelly, and she said come on up. So I threw some clothes in an overnight case, and me and Mr. McGregor hit the road."

Tiffany added her friend's telephone number to the slip and handed it to me. As I stood up to leave, Gen, who had worked her way through the green peppers and was now slicing tomatoes, asked if I wanted to stay for dinner. "Thanks, but I have a date," I said, checking my watch. And if I went straight home from here, I'd have time to wash up and change clothes.

"You always watch me," Mark Willis said, "like a cat watching a mouse hole."

I blinked, startled by his observation. "Have I been staring at you?"

A smile flickered across his saturnine face. He reached

262

for the bottle of chardonnay and poured some into my wineglass. "Yes, you have. Why? Do I look different?"

I tilted my head to one side and picked up my glass. Mark is a picture framer who lives in a little Gold Rush town called Cibola, up in the Sierra. We went to high school together over in Alameda, but that was a long time and another world ago. Our lives hadn't reconnected until last March, when I was working on the same case that brought me into contact with Admiral Franklin and his family. There had been a strong attraction between Mark and me then. It was still there. I could feel it when I looked into his pale blue eyes, eyes that looked back at me, challenging, a bit amused.

I examined him, a slender wiry body, a shock of dark hair. We were sitting at a table near the front window of Ti Bacio, a restaurant on College Avenue in North Oakland, our plates scraped free of the last morsels of linguine with clams. When we'd gone out before, months ago, he had smoked cigarettes, but Ti Bacio is smoke-free. Still, Mark wasn't fidgeting like so many smokers I know, who require a nicotine fix after a meal, and I didn't see a pack distorting his shirt pocket.

"You quit smoking," I guessed.

He grinned. "A worthy accomplishment after so many years. No more nicotine stains on hands and teeth, no more hacking cough. Virginia's been after me to live a healthier lifestyle. She's a vegetarian, drinks herbal teas. I won't give up coffee, though." Virginia owns the bookstore next to Mark's frame shop. She's an attractive woman, our own age, and he'd mentioned her several times during the course of dinner. I wondered if there was something between them, and why it mattered to me.

"Give up coffee? I couldn't function without it." The server cleared away the plates. "I'll have a caffe latte. And this restaurant has the most decadent chocolate mousse cake with raspberry sauce. I'll split it with you. Unless you want something else."

"Chocolate and coffee are the only appropriate way to

end a meal," he said, ordering a cappuccino. "You have something on your mind, Jeri."

"I've gotten involved in another murder case." I gave Mark an edited account of what was happening to Ruth Franklin Raynor. When we were in high school fifteen years ago, the Franklins and the Willises had lived next door to one another. In fact, Mark's father had gone to the Naval Academy with Joe Franklin, and the families had known each other for years. Still, I knew Mark didn't like to talk about his family or the past, so I broached the subject carefully.

"Kevin Franklin is holding something back," I said. "He's been evasive about where he was after he took Ruth home Saturday night. I didn't know him well in school. We didn't run with the same crowd. But you've known Kevin since you were kids."

Mark's narrow face had turned somber. He said nothing until the coffee and dessert arrived. "Kevin Franklin was always a good kid. The golden boy, the perfect son. He was frequently held up to me in contrast to my own shortcomings." He sipped his cappuccino. "We didn't have much in common. The only thing I can tell you is that when Kevin lies, he lies badly. I'm a hell of a lot better at it." He smiled and took a fork to one corner of the chocolate mousse cake.

"Well, the good kid is lying to me," I said. "And you're right, he is lying badly. I intend to confront him about it, as soon as I can find him. He's avoiding me."

"That doesn't surprise me." Mark grinned again, and the awkward moment passed. "You get very single-minded as you pursue answers. Sneaking up on me like that, during dinner."

"I'll do penance by paying the check."

"Sounds reasonable to me. I'll leave the tip. Of course, since you've obtained information during dinner, you can take it off your taxes—"

"Mark!" I reached for his hand as he cut another wedge off our dessert. "Speaking of leaving something, you'd better leave me some cake."

"So quit talking business and pick up your fork," he ad-

264

vised. "When it comes to chocolate, I can't be counted on to restrain myself."

We parted on the sidewalk in front of the restaurant, with a kiss and hug, friendly, but tinged with rekindled longings and unexplored possibilities. He didn't suggest exploring them. As I watched him walk away, I wondered what I would have done if he had made the suggestion.

It was past eight and I would have liked to go home, but I had another stop to make. Mark was right. I was always working, always analyzing the case at hand, even during dinner. Once I got started on a job, I hated to stop until I was finished, like a plow horse with the bit between its teeth. Had I been investigating insurance fraud or interviewing witnesses in a civil lawsuit, I'd keep more regular hours. But murder put a sharper point on the tack.

Dana Albertson answered my knock at the front door of the Victorian flat in Alameda, a tall, big-boned woman in her twenties, clad in mustard-colored sweatpants and a gray Navy T-shirt. Her long brown hair was curly, caught in an untidy ponytail. "Yeah, Claudia's here," she told me, one hand playing with the end of her hair as she stood in the doorway. "And your name is?"

"Jeri Howard. Claudia and I have met before."

The door opened wider, pulled by Claudia's hand. She wore shorts and a sleeveless shirt, and she stood there with one hand on the door, glaring at me, her face a mixture of hostility and resignation. "What the hell do you want?"

"Answers. And information. Like, where were you Saturday night?"

Claudia put both hands on her slender hips and tossed her straight blond hair. "Christ, do you think I shot him?"

"Did you have a motive?"

"We went to the movies," Dana protested as I stepped from the foyer into the apartment. It was small, probably one bedroom, furnished with lots of color, frills, and plants. I guessed that Claudia was sleeping on the futon, a wood-framed piece of furniture that did double duty as sofa and extra bed, its padded striped cushion serving as a mattress. To my left, at the far end of the futon, was an old blue wing chair in need of new upholstery. Farther back, toward the kitchen, I saw a small round wooden dining table with four bentwood chairs.

A large red plastic tray rested in the middle of the rattan chest that served as a coffee table, holding a matching red bowl full of popcorn and two glasses that looked as though they held lemonade. The two women had been watching television, and now Dana turned off the set. "We went to the movies," she repeated. "At the Piedmont Cinema. We were home and in bed by midnight."

"I know you went to the movies." I looked at Claudia. "Steve followed you there."

"He what? God damn it," she snapped, her fair face now suffused with red. "Why did I ever marry him?"

"I assume because you were on the rebound from Sam Raynor."

The color drained from Claudia's face. She slumped into the wing chair, her head down as she stared at the hardwood floor. Dana perched uneasily on the edge of the futon, looking at Claudia with a frown. Then she turned to me. "I never liked the guy. Sam, I mean. 'Course, he didn't pay much attention to me."

"You're not blond," I told Dana. "That was his pattern, wasn't it, Claudia? He liked women short and blond. Slender and delicate too. That made it easier for him to dominate them physically."

"You noticed that, did you?" Claudia snapped.

"I certainly did. You, Tiffany Collins, Ruth. I haven't met his first wife yet, but I'll bet I know what she looks like."

"First wife?" Claudia's head jerked up. "He was married before? That son of a bitch."

"He never mentioned his first wife?"

"No." Claudia's glare would have withered a house plant. "I knew about that little twit over in Admin. He flaunted it. Did she know about me?"

"She does now. Tell me about your relationship with Sam." I picked up one of the bentwood chairs around the

266

dining table, placed it on my side of the rattan chest and sat down.

Claudia drew her legs up onto the chair cushion and wrapped her arms around her knees, huddling, making herself as small as possible. "I think he bewitched me," she muttered.

"I gather Sam Raynor had that effect on some people, especially women who've been involved with him. Then reality comes barreling down the track, usually like a fist. Be glad you never married him. He beat both his wives."

Dana shuddered. "What a scuzzbag."

"He wanted to get married." Claudia's mouth was set in a grim line. "We met six years ago. I was just out of boot camp and apprentice training, with orders to Pearl Harbor. I was thrilled. I'd spent my whole life in the Midwest, and here I was living in Hawaii. I met Sam at the Navy Exchange. I was looking at stereo equipment and I didn't have a clue what kind to buy. So here's this tall good-looking redheaded guy who started telling me about woofers and tweeters. Then he asked me to dinner."

She shook her head. "I should have run the other way. But Sam was so different from the other guys I'd been dating. He treated me like I was the only woman in the world. He was so goddamn romantic. Orchids and fancy dinners down in Waikiki. Picnics in tropical rain forests, complete with champagne and pâté."

"Midnight swims at the beach?" I asked, thinking of Ruth. "Like Burt Lancaster and Deborah Kerr in *From Here to Eternity*?"

"How did you know?" Claudia demanded.

"Just a wild guess. When did he start talking marriage?"

"After a few months. He said he wanted to settle down, wanted me to be the mother of his children. But I'd just turned nineteen. I didn't want to get married." Claudia paused and reached for her glass of lemonade. After she'd drained half of it, she went on. "So I called off the romance. I guess I had a lucky escape. Only the escape wasn't that complete." She raised the glass to her face and rubbed its frosted surface across her forehead. I noticed she

267

still wore her wedding ring, and on the other hand, the jade ring. She set the glass back on the tray.

"I heard he got married. By then Hawaii had palled. When you get right down to it, islands are confining. Little ones, anyway." Claudia sighed. "So when it came time for orders to my next duty station, I requested someplace bigger, exotic, exciting. Japan, Australia, Europe. And where does the Navy send me? Guam! Another dinky damn island! You think Oahu's small, you ought to see Guam."

"At least it's warm," Dana commented. "Try Adak, Alaska. It's small—and cold."

"Where did you meet Steve?" I asked. The background was interesting but I wanted to move Claudia's narrative forward.

"Guam. I was assigned to the naval station, he was at the air station. Some guy invited me to a dance at the chiefs' club and I met Steve there. He was separated from his first wife. After he got his divorce, he asked me to marry him. He's a nice guy, steady, kind, the type my mother said I should marry. But I shouldn't have. I thought I loved him, but I don't. I got restless, started thinking about divorce. Then who should show up on Guam with a wife and kid but Sam Raynor."

"Let me speculate," I said. "Sam told you his marriage was a mistake and he'd never quite gotten over you, because you were really the only woman in the world for him."

"And I bought it," Claudia said, "every damn word. The same damn routine, with the flowers and romantic dinners. Only this time we had to sneak around, because we were both married to other people. We even managed to go away for a weekend, to a hotel on Saipan. I told Steve I was going with a girlfriend. I don't know what Sam told Ruth." With the fingers of her left hand she twisted the jade ring on her right. "Sam bought me this ring, when we were on Guam. He called it an engagement ring, because he was going to leave Ruth for me. But he didn't. Here I am, still married to Steve—and you think I killed Sam."

Dana protested again that she and Claudia had been

268

home and in bed by midnight. I raised a hand, shifting on the small chair. "Let Claudia tell me. Start with Friday, when you and Steve had a fight."

Claudia ran both hands through her hair. "Steve had been real quiet for a couple of days, like he was brooding. When he got home Friday night, he asked why I hadn't fixed dinner. Well, he usually plays poker every other Friday night. He and a bunch of guys rotate between houses and they bring food. I got the Fridays mixed up. I told him I figured he was going to play cards that night. Then I said Dana and I were going to a movie Saturday night. Steve just went ballistic. He said I was lying, that someone he knew had seen me with Sam a couple of weeks ago. Steve hollered at me and hit the wall. I thought he was going to hit me. All of a sudden I yelled back. I was tired of lying. So I told him it was true. I told him all about Sam and me, and that I wanted a divorce. Then I packed some things and came over here to Dana's."

"And Saturday?" I asked.

"We went to the seven o'clock show at the Piedmont Cinema. It was a long movie. I think we left the theater around nine-thirty." Claudia looked at her friend, and Dana nodded in agreement. "We walked down to Fenton's for some ice cream. There was a line out the door, of course, there always is Saturday night, especially after the movie crowd shows up. I don't know how long we had to wait for a table."

"Twenty minutes at least," Dana chimed in.

Claudia shrugged. "I didn't notice the time. Dana and I just stood and talked and inched our way forward until we got inside the building."

"You didn't see Steve?"

"If I had, I'd've given him another piece of my mind. Following me like that." Claudia shook her head. "Inside Fenton's we took a table at the back. That must have been around ten o'clock. We shared a banana split, but we couldn't finish the whole thing. I remember thinking, it's late and if I eat all this ice cream I won't be able to sleep."

"What time did you leave Fenton's?" Claudia looked at

Dana for help. They both guessed ten-thirty. "Did you see Sam Raynor at all that night?"

"The last time I saw Sam was earlier in the week, on Wednesday. I didn't see anybody I knew—" Claudia stopped. "Yes, I did. Harlan came in."

"Pettibone?" Now that caught my attention. "You're sure? What time?"

"Of course I'm sure. Harlan's hard to miss. He always wears black and orange. Besides, he's loud and obnoxious, and Saturday night wasn't any different. He was with some of his bozo friends and he was acting like an idiot, as usual. He and his friends got a table just as Dana and I went to the cash register to pay the check at the same time." Claudia illustrated their movements with her hands. I've had enough hot fudge sundaes at Fenton's over the years to be intimately acquainted with the layout of the place. "I was hoping he wouldn't see me."

So Harlan T for Tiger Pettibone was at Fenton's on Piedmont Avenue at ten-thirty Saturday night, shortly before his friend and roommate Sam Raynor was shot to death two blocks away. Yet on my Monday morning visit to Treasure Island, Chief Duffy LeBard told me Harlan had been arrested Saturday night at the Naval Air Station enlisted club, for fighting with two Marines.

Obviously Harlan had witnesses who could place him both at Fenton's Ice Cream Parlor, then at the club. His flamboyant behavior made him noticeable, and provided him with a damned convenient alibi. Had he gone straight from one venue to the other? Or made a stop in between? I sure wanted to know when that fight at the club began. But Harlan was in the brig, out of my reach.

Thirty-two

WHEN I CALLED HIM EARLY FRIDAY MORNING, DUFFY LeBard told me Harlan Pettibone would be out of the brig on Tuesday of the following week. "He went to Captain's Mast last Monday and the C.O. gave him seven days. But this coming Monday is Labor Day, so they won't cut him loose till Tuesday."

"What time did Harlan get involved in that fight at the club? And who started it?" Duffy wanted to know the reason for my questions, so I told him. "Harlan was seen at Fenton's Ice Cream Parlor on Piedmont at ten-thirty Saturday night. That's two blocks from the building where Sam Raynor was killed."

"Cool your jets," Duffy drawled, and put me on hold. A few minutes later he came back on the line. "Don't know exactly when the altercation started or who jumped who. But the manager of the club called the dispatcher at eleven-fifty."

"What time did Harlan get to the club?"

"Hell if I know," Duffy said. "Why is it important?"

"I want to know if he made any stops between Fenton's and the club. Or if he saw his roommate. Any chance I can talk with Harlan?"

"While he's in the brig? I don't know, Jeri. If you were a cop, with official clout, maybe. But a private investigator? I might be able to talk my captain into it, but the fight happened over at the air station. Not my turf."

"Come on, Duffy. I have a feeling your turf extends anywhere you want it to. If I can't talk to Harlan, I'll take the club manager. Or the Marines involved in the fight."

271

"I'll see what I can do," Duffy said. "I'll talk to a few people, but I'm not making any promises."

I hung up the phone and got up to freshen my cup of coffee. I updated my computer file with the information I'd obtained from last night's interview with Claudia Yancy, then I called my contact at the Department of Motor Vehicles. The state of California has rules about giving out driver information to private investigators and other nosy people, but such details can be had if you talk to the right clerk. I had to be judicious about asking for favors, though, and not press my contact too hard or too often.

I gave him the license plate number of the car Tiffany Collins struck last Saturday night, after she had left Sam Raynor in the parking lot behind Piedmont Avenue. "Any chance of getting a name and address today?" I asked, with the proper note of supplication in my voice. He grumbled at me, said he'd just helped me out with another case a couple of weeks ago, told me how busy he was, then informed me he was taking the next week off. "That makes it all the more important. This is a murder case. I can't wait a week."

"All right," he groused, "but you're pushing your luck with me, Jeri."

I thanked him profusely and disconnected the call, then I waited for a dial tone and called Meriwell Hardware in Gilroy. It had been two days since Sam Raynor's funeral and Tom Meriwell's promise to contact his sister Denise. She hadn't called me. I suspected she didn't want to talk to me. When I had Tom on the line he confirmed this.

He didn't say anything at first. In the background I heard laughter and conversation and the noise of the cash register ringing up a sale. "I called Wednesday night. She said she'd think about it."

"It's important."

"I told her that." He sounded both glum and apologetic. "I laid it out for her, gave her your phone number, and she said she'd think about it. It's up to her. I can't force her to talk to you. Look, she's been through a lot. I guess she just

272

doesn't want to dredge it all up again. Can't say as I blame her. And Ruben was definitely against it."

As I hung up the phone, I catalogued what I knew about Denise Meriwell. According to Mitch Burgett, she worked in a bank in Benicia and had married a man named Padilla. Tom had just provided me with his first name. I turned to the shelf behind my desk, which held an assortment of phone directories from all over northern California. There were a couple of Padillas in Benicia with no address listed, but calls to both numbers netted no answer. I rifled through the yellow pages and listed the addresses of all the financial institutions in and around Benicia, including banks, savings and loans, and credit unions. I didn't know what Denise Padilla looked like, but I hoped there was some family resemblance to her brother. Besides, if she'd been involved with Sam Raynor, she had to be short and blond.

I took Highway 24 east, through the Caldecott Tunnel to Contra Costa County. The hills on either side of the freeway were brown and gold, the oaks and evergreens providing patches of green. Everything looked parched and tinder-dry, the result of late summer heat and below normal rainfall. Off to the east Mount Diablo poked its summit into the hazy blue sky, its dun-colored slopes looking dry as that bone everyone always talks about.

I crossed the toll bridge over the Carquinez Strait and exited the freeway at East Second Street. I started my rounds of the banks in the area, hitting the big ones first, like Bank of America and Wells Fargo, and hoping I wouldn't have to go through the entire list. It took about an hour to find Denise Padilla, at a small bank on the corner of First and J Street in downtown Benicia. It was just past noon and the white tiled lobby was full of customers conducting business at the three teller windows. I looked around and saw two desks on a section of pale blue carpet, one with a sign that read: DENISE PADILLA, BANKING SERVICES REPRESENTATIVE. There was no one seated at the desk. Then a woman walked from one of the offices at the far side of the bank lobby and sat down at the desk.

As I suspected, Denise was short in stature, and her hair

was blond, a mass of curls that brushed the collar of the short-sleeved red-and-white-striped cotton dress she wore. In her round face I saw a hint of her brother, and, from what little I glimpsed of her before she sat down, she had his tendency to gain weight in the torso.

I removed one of my business cards from my purse and walked across the carpet to Denise's desk. She looked up at me and smiled. "Hello. How may I help you?"

"Talk to me," I said, handing her my business card.

Her eyes were a clear blue-gray, and they widened with alarm as she read my business card. They flicked to either side, as though she were looking for help or an escape route. Then she looked directly at me. "Go away," she whispered urgently. "Leave me alone."

"I can't. It's vital that I talk with you. Surely your brother told you that."

"I told him I'd think about it."

"Ruth Raynor's been arraigned for Sam's murder. I don't have time for you to think about it."

She glanced at a large clock on the wall above the teller line and then down at my card. She took a deep breath. "All right. But not here."

She reached down and pulled open one of the desk drawers, removing a red shoulder bag that matched her low-heeled red pumps. She told the woman at the other desk she was going to lunch. Then she stood and walked toward the double glass doors leading out to First Street. The reason for her weight gain was now obvious. Denise Padilla was pregnant.

"I have forty-five minutes for lunch," she said grimly, as though she were going to the dentist.

"Where shall we go?"

"There's a little place down the street."

I opened the door for her and we set off down the sidewalk in the direction of the shimmering water of the Strait. A couple of blocks farther down First Street was Mabel's Cafe, its decor out of the fifties, bright with chrome, with leather-seated stools along a counter on one side of the narrow room and tables on the other. Someone had just vacated a table near the front window, and we took it. We scanned the menu without speaking. When the waitress came over, Denise ordered iced tea and a spinach salad. I asked for mineral water and decided to try the eggplant sandwich. After the waitress left, Denise stared past me toward the front window, as though the foot traffic on First Street was fascinating. The waitress brought our drinks. I poured mineral water over the ice in the glass and watched the bubbles. Denise seemed preoccupied by the lemon in her tea. She used the long spoon protruding from the glass to fish out the yellow wedge, then she squeezed out some juice and pulp. She dropped the lemon back into the tea and wiped her hands on a paper napkin.

"How did you find out about me?" she asked finally. "Tom didn't say."

"At the funeral. Mitch Burgett mentioned that he'd seen you, here in Benicia."

"Damn Mitch Burgett anyway." Sudden passion flashed in her gray-blue eyes. "I asked him not to tell anyone he'd seen me. So of course he told his mother. Elva's got the biggest mouth in Gilroy. That must be—" She stopped abruptly and reached for her glass, silencing herself by taking a drink.

"How Sam found you?" I finished. Her silence and the flicker of something in her eyes confirmed my hunch. I voiced my speculation of how the chain of events occurred. "Mitch ran into you a couple of months ago. He said something to his mother. Elva told Alma, and Alma told Sam. Then Sam came to see you. What did he want?"

"That bastard," Denise said. Her eyes turned cold and angry. "He came into the bank, just like you did, walked right up to my desk and said he wanted to talk. Could he buy me a cup of coffee? 'I'll throw it in your face,' I told him. 'You got something to say, say it right here, in front of witnesses with a desk between us.' I didn't want to be alone with him. So he trots out this line about how he wants to reestablish a relationship with his son, now that he's back in the Bay Area. I told him I'd see him in hell first. And he said, 'I'll just have to take you to court.' "

275

"What happened then?"

She shook her head, the short blond curls flying. "I'm not sure. I was so mad I couldn't see straight. I think I told him to get out before I called the security guard and accused him of trying to rob the bank. He just laughed at me and strolled out like he didn't have a care in the world. If I'd had a gun I would have—"

She stopped suddenly, as if she'd just realized what she'd said and how it sounded. It had been less than a week since a gunshot ended Sam Raynor's life. I thought her next words might be an assurance that she had not, in fact, murdered her ex-husband. But she didn't say anything. The silence stretched on the table between us. She wrapped both hands around her glass of iced tea and stared past me at the street.

The waitress brought our lunches. I tasted my eggplant sandwich and judged it a good choice. Denise ignored her salad. "How long had it been since Sam Raynor saw Scott?"

"Not since the night I walked out." Denise's eyes burned like those of a tigress protecting her cub. I'd seen the same fire in Ruth Raynor's eyes when she'd described Sam's threat to take Wendy. Maybe that protective instinct goes with the territory when you have a child. But not always. There are too many people who don't give a damn about their children, and I was certain Sam Raynor was one such person. He used his children as weapons to bludgeon their mothers.

"Scott wasn't even a year old when I left," Denise said. "Ever since I remarried, Scott thinks Ruben is his dad, and that's just the way I want it. Reestablish a relationship with his son! What a load of bullshit! Sam Raynor never had a relationship with *my* son. He never had the slightest interest in that kid. He was only doing it to get back at me." She picked up her fork and speared spinach leaves with sudden savagery.

"Where is Scott now?"

"In a safe place." Her eyes narrowed and turned wary. "But not with you."

She finished a mouthful of salad before answering, considering whether or not she trusted me. "When I got home from work that day, Ruben and I took Scott to stay with Ruben's family in Salinas."

"How safe is that?"

She smiled briefly, wielding her fork again. "Ruben has a big family. Of course, now that Sam's dead, it's safe to bring Scott back. We'll go down to get him this weekend."

"Did Sam contact you again?"

"Yes. A couple of weeks after he showed up at the bank, he called the house. So I got an unlisted number."

"What is your phone number?" I asked. She hesitated. "Just in case I need to get in touch with you. It's better that I call you at home rather than at work."

"All right." She rattled off the number. I scribbled it in my notebook. "After that, one of our neighbors told me someone had been by the house, asking questions about Scott. The way she described him, I knew it was Sam. Who could miss that red hair? That really frightened me. I talked to the head of security and to my supervisor at work. They said I should contact the police. I hadn't done that yet, but I was going to. Then Tom called to tell me Sam was dead. I never felt so relieved in my life."

Looking at her, I was sure it would take more than Sam Raynor's death to exorcise his demon. Two red spots burned on her cheeks, below the wide gray-blue eyes. "You know why I'm here," I said.

Denise hesitated. "According to my brother, you work for Ruth Raynor's attorney. She didn't kill him?"

"I don't think so, although the evidence is against her. There seem to be plenty of people with motives to kill Sam Raynor."

"Including me," she said with a defiant lift of her chin.

"Including you. And just about everyone who ever knew him. I'd really like to know how the two of you wound up married."

A wave of pain passed over her face. I realized that for all her bravado, Denise was as vulnerable as Ruth. She set her fork down on the table, suddenly devoid of appetite.

"How do any of us wind up in a mess?" she asked, as though she'd thought about it a lot over the years and might have figured out some of the answers. "I don't know. Well, maybe I do."

Denise took a deep breath. Despite her earlier reluctance to talk, words tumbled from her now, as though she was confessing her sins and I had the power to absolve her.

"I was seventeen. I wanted—whatever it is that teenage girls want. Excitement, I guess. It got me a reputation."

"Alma Raynor had a few things to say about that, when your name came up at the funeral," I said, recalling how Sam's mother had described her former daughter-in-law.

Her mouth twisted. "I'll bet she did. That dried-up old hag. She thought I was a whore. Said as much to my face." She shook her head, her eyes older than her face. "I was no virgin, I admit that. I went out with a lot of guys in high school and I slept with some of them. I wanted to be popular with the boys. I thought the way to do that was to offer them my body. Looking back, I don't think I liked myself, or I wouldn't have let them treat me like a piece of meat."

She gave a short bitter laugh. "I remember this one jock, a football player. I was so thrilled when he asked me out. Then he said he wouldn't go out with me again because I was ugly, I had such big thighs. That sure as hell didn't bother him the night before, when he was between them, pumping away." She took a drink from her glass as though to wash away the bad taste. "When I started going out with Mitch, I couldn't believe he was so nice to me. He'd kiss me good night on the front steps instead of trying to get into my pants. Then Sam came along and made this play for me and I got sucked in. And I got pregnant."

She shook her head. "It happened because I was stupid. Before Sam I was always careful to use those damn foams and gels, and make the guy wear a condom. But with Sam, it was, let's be spontaneous and get carried away and do it right here in the grass. You know what he used to say when I asked him to wear a condom?" She lowered her voice and hissed the words in a mocking tone, her lips drawn

278

away from her teeth in mockery. " 'Oh, honey, I want to come inside you. I want you to feel my love.' "

Her face held such loathing, of herself and of Sam, that I reached across the table and touched her hand. She pulled it away as though my flesh scorched hers. "If it's any consolation, it happened the same way with Ruth."

Denise's eyes burned at me, then her lips curved in a wan smile. Her voice quavered, but her words held a flash of gallows humor. "We can form our own group. The Sam Raynor Survivors. We can compare scars. I've got plenty. I'll bet she does too." By now Denise had drained her glass of iced tea. She waved the waitress over to the table and ordered another, then picked up her fork and took another mouthful of salad. When the waitress brought the tea, Denise repeated her lemon wedge routine.

"When did he start beating her?" she asked. "Did he wait until after her baby was born? Or did he slap her around while she was pregnant? That's what he did to me. He forced me to have sex, late in the pregnancy. I was terrified Scott would be born too soon. His mother was no help. She figured if he was hitting me, I deserved it. Oh, he always apologized. Then it would start all over again."

She didn't say anything for a long moment. "I had a rough labor and delivery. After the baby was born, the doctor told me not to have sex for a while. But that didn't stop Sam. He threw me on the bed and raped me." Denise's face was white and stark. Her hands gripped the edge of the table and it shook. "God damn him. I hate him. I hate him for what he did to me. I'm glad he's dead. I hope he rots in hell."

The glass of iced tea tipped and fell, ice and brown liquid splashing over the table's white surface and onto Denise's candy-striped dress. The yellow lemon wedge skittered across the floor. The waitress hurried over with extra napkins and a rag to mop up the spill. Denise mopped at her dress, her face flushed crimson, as the café patrons seated nearby looked at us curiously.

"No, I don't want anything else," she told the waitress. "Take the salad away, please."

279

When we were alone again, she balled up a wet napkin, dropping it on the table as she leaned forward and covered her face with her hands. When she finally removed the protective screen and looked at me, her face had returned to a more normal color. "I'm sorry."

"You don't have to apologize to me," I told her. "I'm sorry to make you relive it."

"I thought I'd buried all of these feelings, over the years, when I made a new life for myself, and Scott. Then Sam showed up at the bank. I've felt like a hunted animal ever since." Her fingers plucked at the wet paper napkin. "I suppose you want to know why I stayed with him as long as I did. That's what my divorce lawyer kept asking."

"You were just out of high school with a baby to take care of and you didn't have anywhere to go."

Denise nodded. "Except to my parents. Right after Scott was born, my dad was diagnosed with liver cancer. He was going through treatment. We were all worried about him and I didn't want to burden my family with my problems. I kept thinking, well, it'll get better. And it did, for a while, once we moved out of Alma's house and got a place of our own. Looking back, I think it was because Sam was gone a lot, on his job. He had to make deliveries, he said, in San Jose. And I'm pretty sure he had a girlfriend there too. I played this game with myself. If I kept the apartment clean and had dinner on the table when he got home from work, then he wouldn't hit me. If he did, somehow it was my fault for giving him a reason. I was pretty good at it. Even had myself fooled, until the night he broke my nose."

"That was in October, wasn't it?"

Denise nodded. "The week before Halloween. I'd carved a jack-o'-lantern for Scott. He was ten months old."

"What led to the beating? Can you recall any change in his behavior, something he said or did?" I knew from my recent conversation with Norm Gerrity that in early October, the San Jose police caught Raynor driving a stolen car and used that as leverage to turn him into an informer. This incident must have triggered the violent attack on Denise.

"I don't know," Denise said. "I didn't pay much attention

280

to what Sam did, other than try to make sure he didn't hit me. I was all wrapped up in my little boy, and worried about my dad having cancer. When he beat me up that night, it just seemed to come out of the blue. I knew I had to leave. When he went into the bathroom to take a shower, I grabbed the car keys and the baby and got the hell out of there. I didn't file charges. My family and my lawyer said I should have, but I just wanted out. I used the beatings as leverage, though, so Sam wouldn't contest the divorce or the custody arrangements. But at the time, he acted like he didn't care, like he wanted out as much as I did."

"And after the divorce, you moved up here to the Bay Area?"

Denise nodded. "My father died a month before the final decree. Dad left me some money in his will, so I decided to make a fresh start. I moved to Concord, got a job in a bank, and found a support group for battered wives. I went to church and I sang in the choir. I met Ruben there." Denise smiled and touched the wedding ring on her left hand. "He was going to meetings at the church, the same night I had choir practice. One night he asked me if I wanted to go out for coffee. I told him I had a little boy in the church nursery. He said that was fine with him. We got married three years ago. We're going to have a baby."

"Congratulations. Things are going well for you."

"They were." Her smile vanished. "Until my past showed up."

I pushed aside the sympathy I felt for her and posed one more question. "Where were you and your husband Saturday night?"

"Home," she said, too quickly. Her eyes slewed away from me and she looked out the window, teeth catching her lower lip. "Just a typical Saturday night. I don't even remember what we did after we had dinner." She glanced at her watch. "Oh, God, look at the time. I've got to get back to work." She turned in her chair, looking for the waitress.

"I'll take care of the check," I said.

She turned back to look at me, without a word, then pushed her chair away from the table. She clutched her red

281

purse and walked quickly out the front door of the café, heading up First Street toward the bank. I pulled several bills from my wallet.

Denise Padilla had a lot going for her. A second husband who evidently was the antithesis of her first, and a baby on the way. Would she risk it all by killing her ex-husband? He'd invaded her safe new life, tormenting her, threatening to take her child from her and bringing back memories of a horrific past she'd tried to bury.

It was a powerful motivation for murder. And I didn't quite believe her when she said she and Ruben Padilla had been home Saturday night.

Thirty-three

My answering machine contained Joe Franklin's latest update of his efforts to find Rosie, the homeless woman. He said he'd come by my office later in the afternoon. I had hoped for a message from my contact at the Department of Motor Vehicles with information on the car that hit Tiffany Collins's Subaru the night of the murder, but he hadn't called. The phone rang as I rewound the message tape. I picked it up.

"I guess we need to talk." Kevin Franklin sounded subdued. In the background I heard people talking and guessed he was in a phone booth somewhere.

"Yes, we do. Where are you?"

"Scott's Seafood, at the foot of Broadway."

"I'll meet you in front of the restaurant, in ten minutes."

I found a vacant parking spot near the corner of Broadway, where the railroad tracks ran down the middle of the Embarcadero, and walked the short block to Jack London

Square. Over the past few years, the Port of Oakland has built up this section of the waterfront. The restaurants lure people, but many of the commercial buildings are as yet untenanted. At the foot of Broadway a series of shallow steps lead to the estuary. Next to the steps an observation pier juts out over the water, with benches along the side and at the end.

As I looked at the scene, I thought about a night back in March, punctuated by gunshots, when I pursued a killer onto the pier and both of us wound up in the cold dark water. Just thinking about it made me shiver, although the day was warm, here where the sun glinted off the estuary.

The patio tables at Scott's Seafood were filled with people lingering over a Friday lunch. Kevin Franklin paced in front of the restaurant, hands stuck deep into the pockets of his gray slacks. When he saw me, he altered course. We met at the foot of the tall flagpole, where the stars and stripes hung motionless in the still air.

"I don't know where to start," he began, shaking his head.

"Let's walk." I set off in the direction of the marina, farther south. To my right was a commercial building with several empty storefronts, and on my left a landscaped plaza, trees and flowers brightening an elevated expanse of concrete and tile. We passed a young couple in business attire, seated on one of the benches facing the plaza. They sat close together, holding hands, their dark heads bowed. I glanced at them and realized they were saying grace before consuming their take-out sandwiches.

Kevin and I passed the marina, which was opposite a Mexican restaurant with umbrella-covered tables on a tiled patio. Farther along, a square log cabin had been plunked down on the concrete next to a large round planter holding the mast of the long-decommissioned USS *Oakland*. A large yellow plaque affixed to the outer wall of the cabin advised that a Yukon historical society had authenticated the cabin as one Jack London lived in while he was prospecting in the Klondike. As we approached the cabin, three middle-aged women in straw hats and pastel dresses asked me if I'd take their picture. I nodded and took the camera they offered, snapping a couple of shots as they posed in front of the cabin. They thanked me and headed off in the direction of the Italian restaurant next to the marina, drawn by the scent of garlic.

"Suppose you tell me what's going on," I said as Kevin and I walked past the First and Last Chance Saloon, another log cabin, this one with a tilted floor and country music blaring from within. "You're conveniently absent whenever I'm at the house. You say you went to Chuck Porter's apartment after you left Ruth. That may be true. But I've talked with Porter and I don't think he was there Saturday night. Who were you with?"

He didn't answer until we were on the path that ran along the parking lot, headed for Jack London Village, another development of shops and restaurants, this one constructed of grayed, weathered lumber.

"I don't think I've been operating on all cylinders." He shook his head. "I just can't fathom that my sister's been arrested for murder. It's like a bad movie, and I can't get out of the theater. My little sister Ruth—when we were kids she couldn't even kill a spider. She used to make me carry the damn things out to the backyard. Ruth murder her husband? I don't even believe she could shoot him in anger. No, no, it's ridiculous. I thought the cops were crazy. I thought the D.A. would laugh them out of his office. I guess it didn't really hit home until Ruth was arraigned on Wednesday."

"Did you know Sam was a wife beater?"

"Not until she left him," Kevin said as we stepped onto the plank flooring of the village. His blue eyes grew cold. At that moment he looked a lot like his father.

"If you'd seen him attack your sister, what would you have done?"

"I'd have killed the son of a bitch." He stopped and stared at me, face intense and incredulous. "You think I killed my brother-in-law? And let my sister take the rap?"

"It has a certain convoluted logic—if the D.A. had seen

284

it as self-defense or involuntary manslaughter, instead of murder. Still might, if Ruth gets off."

"You think I could kill someone?" he demanded.

"That's an odd question, coming from a military man. You could kill someone in a war. Why not on the street, or in an apartment building? We're all capable of murder, Kevin, if we get pushed past that point where reason acts as a deterrant."

He stared at me in silence, digesting this, then looked away, at the houseboats on the Alameda side of the estuary. We walked through the village, then out onto the asphalt path that ran along the bank of the estuary. To our left was a flat expanse of dirt and gravel dotted here and there with clumps of scrubby weeds and the occasional resting sea gull. On the right were thick pilings and chunks of rock and concrete, placed there to keep the shoreline from eroding. The tide was out. Below us the rocks and gravel were wet and coated with algae, giving off a sour stink. The dark water had tossed up the detritus of an urban throwaway society, a bald tire, ripped plastic bags that once held garbage, plastic cups and bottles, aluminum cans and broken glass, a plastic-covered chair cushion, a discarded hat and one lone shoe, smeared torn paper and splintered wood.

I turned my gaze from the debris and gave Kevin a hard look. "The police have a witness, Ruth's neighbor. She says she saw Ruth arguing with a man outside Ruth's apartment. Then she heard a shot. Then saw Ruth come out of the apartment, headed for the trash chute. That sequence makes it look like Ruth argued with Sam, shot him, then ditched the gun. I think I can shake the witness's timing on the shot. Ruth says she took the kitchen garbage to the trash chute after you left. But when it comes to Ruth outside her door with a man, we've got two choices. Sam, or you. You'd just brought Ruth and Wendy home from your parents' house. Ruth claims the two of you had a discussion. But she won't say what about. So you tell me. Because I think it has something to do with where you went after you left Ruth's place."

Kevin balled his hands into fists. "I'm involved with a

married woman," he said abruptly. "It's been going on about a year. I'd fly up from San Diego on weekends to see her. Now I'm going to Japan. I'm not going to see her for three years. I should end it. It's not something I want my parents to know."

At the edge of the path something caught my eye. It was a discarded condom, pale yellow in color, heedlessly tossed onto the gravel. I looked up at the flat barren wasteland and couldn't think of a bleaker spot for a sexual encounter. I moved my gaze to Kevin's equally bleak face, reserving comment on his revelation, wondering at the irony of his wanting to keep this affair from his parents, in light of Joe Franklin's long-term relationship with his neighbor's wife.

"I told Ruth," Kevin continued, "because she figured something was bothering me. On Saturday she urged me to break it off. But I can't. That's what we were talking about. Chuck Porter was out of town last weekend and he gave me the keys to his apartment. My friend and I spent the night there Saturday."

"What time did you arrive at Ruth's apartment, and what time did you leave? Sam may have approached or entered the building around the same time you left."

"I didn't see him," Kevin said. "If I had, I certainly wouldn't have left Ruth."

"You may have seen something you don't realize you saw. When you left Ruth, did you take the elevator or the stairs? Who or what did you see on your way out of the building? Think about it before you answer. Play it back in your mind before you tell me."

By now we had reached the rear of the three-story building that housed the offices and television studio of Channel 2. We turned and retraced our steps, headed back toward the village.

"We got there a little before eleven," he said. "Wendy fell asleep in the car on the way back from Alameda. I carried her up to Ruth's apartment. Ruth wanted me to stay and talk, and I said no, I had to be somewhere. That's when I told her about my friend and we had our . . . discussion. I think it was maybe ten after eleven when I left." He paused and ran a hand through his short blond hair. "I took the stairs down. That elevator in Ruth's building is slow, and it was on the first floor. Didn't see anyone on my way out of the building."

"What about after you left the building? Where did you park your car?"

"On Howe Street between Fortieth and Forty-first, about half a block from Ruth's place, pointing toward MacArthur. I'd driven in the opposite way, saw the parking space and did a quick U-turn in the middle of the intersection to grab the spot." His eyes took on a distant look as he played the scene over in his mind. "I crossed the street heading for my car, walked down the sidewalk, took the keys out of my pocket to unlock it. Then I heard voices, loud voices. There were two people across the street, close to the intersection. I'd walked past them but they didn't register until I reached my car. They were arguing."

"How do you know it was an argument?"

"When I looked across the street, they were in each other's faces. Just something about the way they were standing. I couldn't hear what they were saying but they kept interrupting each other. Then one of them shouted and slapped his hand on the hood of the car."

"Both men? Or a man and a woman?"

"Couldn't tell," Kevin said with a shrug, as we walked through the village toward the parking lot. "I think two men, but one shorter than the other, so it could have been a man and a woman. They were between the cars, so I couldn't tell what they were wearing. At that point I was at my car door, sticking the key into the lock, sort of looking at them over my right shoulder. Just a curious glance in the direction of the noise. I didn't want to pry."

"What about the cars? Can you describe them?"

Kevin wrinkled his forehead, then shook his head, saying again that details just hadn't registered. When we reached Broadway, Kevin told me he'd had lunch today with his friend, who'd agreed to talk with me to confirm his whereabouts Saturday night.

"She works for the Port of Oakland." He pointed toward

the new port building, a block or so away on Water Street, and handed me a business card. "She's waiting for you to call."

After he left, I ducked inside Scott's and found a phone. Then I went back outside and walked down Water Street, which was less a street than a narrow passageway between buildings. At the foot of Washington Street I passed a fountain cascading water and the entrance to the old Boatel, now remodeled into the Waterfront Plaza. Just beyond, the Port of Oakland's new building spanned the block between Washington and Clay streets, its entrance facing the estuary.

Kevin's lover met me just outside the double glass lobby doors to the lobby. Her name was Kamali and she looked as exotic as it sounded, a slender woman in an apricot silk dress that caressed her body and set off her smooth, flawless café au lait skin. Her oval face had an Asian cast and her voice a West Indian lilt.

Although she had told Kevin she would talk to me, Kamali looked nervous, as though afraid our conversation might be overheard. She moved away from the doors and I followed her to the edge of a grassy lawn that brightened the space between the street and a parking lot at the shore of the estuary. The Oakland–Alameda–San Francisco ferry terminus was at the foot of Clay Street. Beyond it I saw the enormous black hull of a container ship, tall white letters identifying it as the *Chongyang Chance*, out of Inchon. It was being loaded with containers, set in place by an enormous white motorized crane that loomed over the ship like some dreadful monster from a science fiction movie.

Kamali stared at the estuary as she spoke, her voice barely above a whisper, brushing back a lock of her curly black hair with her left hand. I noticed the wide gold wedding ring, flashing in the afternoon sun. She confirmed that she and Kevin had arranged to spend the night together and that Kevin had met her outside Chuck Porter's apartment building just past eleven. She had noted the time because he'd told her he would be there by eleven and he was a few minutes late. Finally she finished her story, but still she didn't look at me. Instead she shifted her gaze from the water to the Franklin Delano Roosevelt pier, jutting out over the estuary at the foot of Clay Street, and the City of Oakland fire boat tied up at Fire Station No. 2.

As she talked, I'd watched her face, assessing her veracity. I believed her. Kevin's story about the two people arguing near the parked cars on Howe Street was ultimately more important. He had described their interchange as acrimonious, their tone and body language carrying across the street even if their words did not. Had the taller one been Sam Raynor? That would have been about the time he'd entered Ruth's apartment building, about the time Lena Copeland's friend Maurice had stepped out of the lobby headed for his own car and seen a man matching Sam's description stepping from the street to the curb. If it had been Sam, who was his companion? Sam and Tiffany had words that evening, but Acey said they'd argued in the parking lot, not on Howe Street. Perhaps Sam met someone after Tiffany left. There were a lot of people who had bones to pick with Sam Raynor, and several had been in the area the night he was murdered.

I'd just returned to my office when someone pushed open the door with more force than necessary. I looked up and saw a short, stocky Chicano with a crop of coarse black hair over a dark square-jawed face, pugnacious and hostile. He wore khaki pants and a work shirt, with a photo ID clipped to his left breast pocket. The large print at the top told me he worked at one of the oil refineries that dot the hills above Martinez, just this side of the Carquinez Strait. The smaller print below it told me his name was Ruben C. Padilla.

"You Jeri Howard?" he growled.

"Yes, I am." I motioned to the chair in front of my desk. "Have a seat, Mr. Padilla. Let's talk."

He glared at me with angry brown eyes, hands on his hips, thick black eyebrows swooping together like birds of prey. "What I got to say to you, I can say standing up. Where do you get off hassling my wife? You leave Denise alone."

"She seemed all right when I left her." I kept my voice low and neutral, examining his face.

"The hell she did." His right hand flew off his hip and he shook his fist at me. "I went by the bank this afternoon and she was upset. When I asked how come, she burst into tears, right there in the lobby. Had to calm her down before she could even talk about it. God damn you, don't you go bothering my wife again. I don't care if you are a woman, I'll teach you one hell of a lesson."

"You're a real hothead, Mr. Padilla. Suppose you cool off and tell me what you were doing outside an apartment building at Forty-first and Howe at one-thirty Sunday morning."

The wind left Ruben Padilla's sails with an almost audible gust. His dark glowering face blanched. He tried, but failed, to regain his bluster. "I don't know what the hell you're talking about."

"Bullshit." I stood up and leaned toward him. He opened his mouth to deny it again but I waved away his protest. "I was there, near the police line. I saw you. You were on the sidewalk by the construction site. You wore blue jeans and a denim jacket. You were glaring at the building where Sam Raynor was shot to death, just like you were glaring at me a minute ago. I noticed you because you looked so angry. Why were you angry, Mr. Padilla? Does Denise know you were there?"

Padilla's mouth clamped shut. He narrowed his eyes and I watched as he made a perceptible shift from hot to cold, considering his options. When he finally spoke, his words were as cold as his stare. "I don't have to tell you jack shit. Except to leave me and Denise alone."

He turned and hauled open my office door, unbalancing Joe Franklin, who had just reached for the handle on the other side. "Who was that?" Franklin asked, watching the departing Mr. Padilla.

"A man with something to hide. Have a seat."

He sat down. Fatigue had deepened the lines on his hawk face and drawn dark circles under his gray eyes. His nondescript clothing was similar to what he'd worn earlier in the week. "I'm on my way home. I feel as though I've neglected Lenore and the rest of the family these past few days." He rubbed the bridge of his nose and shifted in the chair. "Still no sign of Rosie, but I did talk to a guy named Stubbs. He lives in his truck, parks it various places in North Oakland. He knows Rosie. Says she used to have money and a house in that neighborhood. Then she lost it all—he doesn't know how—and now she lives on the streets. I don't know if his story's true, but . . ."

His voice trailed off. In the ensuing silence, I thought about Sister Anne over at the homeless shelter and what she'd said about the little things that rip apart the safety net.

Joe Franklin roused himself and spoke again. "Every couple of weeks he takes her and some other homeless people over to the recycling center under the freeway so they can sell their cans and bottles."

"I wondered how she got down there. Piedmont Avenue to Twenty-seventh is a long way to push a shopping cart."

"I don't know if Stubbs collects a percentage for the use of his truck," Franklin said. "Maybe he just does it out of the goodness of his heart. He seemed like that kind of guy. All I can say is, based on what I've found out about Rosie over the past few days, I don't think she'd get into his truck if she didn't trust him."

"Good point. Has he seen Rosie since the murder?"

Franklin shook his head. "Not since the last time he took her to the recycling center. Stubbs hasn't seen her at all. He says lately there have been some attacks on homeless people in the neighborhood. Rosie and the others may be less visible right now, for that reason. He thought she might be camping out in the bushes near the Piedmont Avenue School, but I took a look at the area. There isn't that much cover. Besides, school starts soon. I think the cemetery at the end of Piedmont Avenue might be a possibility, though. I'll check it out tomorrow."

"It's Labor Day weekend," I said, thinking how tired he looked. "Why don't you take a few days off?"

"Are you going to put your investigation on hold until Tuesday?" he asked as he got to his feet.

"No," I admitted.

"Then neither will I." He favored me with a rare smile and sketched a salute in the air as he went out the door. I picked up the phone and punched in a number in the 408 area code. After a couple of rings the phone was answered in the village of Carmel on the coast about two hours south. "Hi, Minna. It's Jeri. Is Errol there?"

I waited while Minna Seville went out into her garden to fetch Errol. He was my mentor, a well-respected Bay Area private investigator with years in the business and lots of contacts. I had worked for him for five years, until a heart attack forced him into retirement. When Errol came on the line, he asked if I were still coming down to the Monterey area this weekend to see my mother and other relatives. "That's been postponed. I'm involved in a murder investigation. Have you got any juice with the Salinas police?"

"Of course," he said, as if there were no other answer. He didn't ask for details. "What do you need?"

"I need to know if someone has a record. Ruben C. Padilla. He's from Salinas." I gave Errol a description of Padilla, and he said he'd get back to me in a couple of days.

I looked at my watch. It was nearly four-thirty and I hadn't heard from my DMV contact, who said he was taking next week off. I had to talk with him before he left. Just as I reached for the phone again, it rang. It was Duffy LeBard.

"No go on talking to Harlan," he said. "But he'll be out of the brig Tuesday morning. Can it wait till then?"

"I guess it'll have to."

"You can talk to the Marines, though." He gave me the names of the two Marines Harlan had fought with last Saturday night and an address on San Antonio Avenue in Alameda. I replaced the receiver and the phone rang again.

"If you'd get off the damn phone," my DMV contact said, his voice irritated. "I've been trying to call you for fifteen minutes. Here's the information you want. Don't be calling me for a while unless you plan to buy me dinner."

After he'd hung up, I leaned back in my chair, pencil in

292

hand, and examined the name and address of the owner of the red Buick sedan that struck Tiffany Collins's Subaru the night of Sam Raynor's murder.

"Well, well," I said out loud, a smile playing on my lips as I considered this development. "What do you know?"

Thirty-four

"WE DON'T HAFTA TALK TO YOU," TONY LOPEZ, INformed me as he pulled a box of laundry detergent and a plastic bottle of fabric softener from the canvas tote bag he carried. He and Domingo Herrera then emptied their pockets in search of quarters, which they piled on top of one of the big double-load washers.

"I know you don't," I said patiently, "but it would help me if you did."

Tony and Domingo were the two Marines who, along with Harlan Pettibone, had been arrested at the Naval Air Station enlisted club for fighting last Saturday night. In my experience, enlisted Marines seem to come in two varieties. The first are the grizzled gunnery or master sergeants who've been in the Corps twenty or thirty years and look as though they eat leather for breakfast.

The second variety of Marine are the fresh-faced youngsters with no lines and no hair, who look as though they're not old enough to shave the section of their faces that the Corps leaves to their discretion. Tony and Domingo were definitely of the second variety. As I looked at them, both with smooth brown faces and equally smooth pates, I kept hearing that song called "Soldier Boy," by one of those sixties girl groups whose names I can never get straight.

It was just past nine on Saturday morning. We were in a

Laundromat called the Washboard, at the intersection of San Jose Avenue and Park Street near downtown Alameda. It was filling up with customers pursuing that hated but necessary chore, washers and dryers whirring and thumping, accompanied by a radio station blasting oldies to the whole room.

I had followed Tony and Domingo here from the apartment they shared, a couple of blocks away on San Antonio Avenue. Just as I pulled up to the curb, craning my neck to check house numbers, I saw them emerge from the building, both shouldering the big duffels known as seabags, one lugging the additional burden of the canvas tote. They walked to the Laundromat. After trying to find a parking space in the vicinity, I understood why.

By the time I wedged my Toyota into a tiny space farther down San Jose Avenue and doubled back to the two-room Laundromat, the Marines had established a beachhead in the front section, pulling soiled clothing, sheets, and towels from their seabags and sorting it into piles in three of the low wide carts with wheels which had been provided for the Laundromat's customers. I approached them, business card in hand, and introduced myself, asking them about last Saturday's incident. They both looked wary. That's when Tony advised me that he didn't have to talk with me. I appealed to them as Domingo fed a five dollar bill into the Laundromat's change machine and scooped up the quarters that clattered forth. He added the change to the pile they'd already started.

"What the hell, man," Domingo said, poking his friend in the side with an elbow. "We got no reason not to tell her."

"Okay, but I gotta have some breakfast first." Tony picked up a quarter and tossed it into the air. "Call it."

"Heads," Domingo said.

Tony caught the quarter in his right hand and slapped it onto the top of his left. "Tails. I buy, you fly." He shoved some bills into Domingo's hand, then turned to me. "You want some coffee or a bagel, ma'am?"

"Coffee would be fine. I take it black."

I reached for my wallet but Tony shook his head. "No, ma'am, I buy, Dom flies. That's the routine."

I nodded and watched Domingo go out the door. He crossed Park Street with the light, then waited to cross San Jose, headed for the bagel shop halfway down the block. Having now decided I was okay, Tony began to talk, telling me that he and his friend were both lance corporals. They'd known each other all their lives—in fact, their families lived next door to one another back in Carlsbad, New Mexico. Right after graduating from high school they'd joined up, going through recruit training in San Diego, then a tour of duty in Okinawa before coming back stateside.

Tony finished sorting the laundry and positioned the carts in front of several washers, ready for the assault. Just then Domingo returned, bearing two brown paper sacks. He set them on top of one of the washers and examined the carts critically, poking through the contents. He sighed and shook his head.

"Man, you do it every time," Domingo said, pulling a bright red shirt from one cart. "You wash this shirt with that stuff, it'll run all over the place."

I watched them work as a fine-tuned team, shoving laundry into several front loaders, Tony measuring out powdered detergent while Domingo brought up the rear with the liquid fabric softener. Then they positioned their quarters into the coin slots, checked temperature controls and started the cycles on each washer. While the washers filled with water, they retired to a bench near the Laundromat's front window.

I remained standing, leaning against a waist-high table next to the bench, as they opened the sacks. The first contained three large cups of coffee. Tony handed me one and I removed the lid. The other sack held two fat and fragrant onion bagels wrapped in paper, sliced in the middle and spread so thickly with cream cheese that it oozed from the sides. The bagels looked delicious and I wished I'd ordered one. But it's a little hard to interview someone with cream cheese smeared on your chin.

295

"So what happened Saturday night?" I asked, sipping my coffee.

They both started talking at once, and I had to wave my free hand at them to bring some order to the proceedings. They were proud of the fact that neither of them had ever been in trouble before last Saturday, and the demise of their perfect records rankled them.

"Never been up in front of the C.O. before," Domingo growled, swallowing a mouthful of bagel, "not since recruit depot. Till Monday morning."

"Yeah, but he believed us when he said it wasn't our fault." Tony punctuated his words with his index finger. "That's why we're walking around and that little rat bastard's in the brig."

"Do you know Harlan Pettibone?"

They shook their heads and Domingo muttered something in Spanish. I knew enough of the language to translate, and the appellation was worse than rat bastard.

"Never saw him before," Domingo said, reaching for his coffee. "He came steaming into the club while me and Tony were sitting at a table having a beer. He started a fight."

"Right out of the blue? With no provocation?" I asked. Both Marines nodded vigorously. "Tell me everything you remember. What time did you get to the club? What time did you first see Harlan?"

Tony took another bite of his bagel and chewed, his eyes fixed on the washers, as clothes and suds whirled round and round. He set down the bagel and used both hands to illustrate. "We got there about eleven, had one round, talked with some buddies, played the jukebox. I think we got the second round about eleven-forty. We'd just gone back to the table when all of a sudden I look up and this Harlan guy is standing there, grinning at us. He had on black jeans and an orange T-shirt, looked like a Halloween spook. And he had this look in his eye. He said he was a Texas tiger, then he starts calling us names."

"Like what?"

Domingo's dark eyes smoldered and his lips twisted as

296

he repeated the slurs. "Beaner, spic, wetback." This last one particularly incensed him. "Wetback! Shit, my family's been in New Mexico three hundred goddamn years. My grandma's a Mescalero Apache."

"So he just walked up to your table and started calling you names. Was he drunk?"

Tony shook his head. "I don't think so. It was something in the way he said it, that look in his eye, the way he was standing. It was like he was trying to pick a fight. When we got to fist city, I could smell beer on his clothes, real strong, like he'd spilled it on himself. But his eyes, they didn't look drunk."

"You keep mentioning his eyes. How did they look?"

"They had this sparkle," Tony said, hesitating as he searched for words. "A glint. I remember thinking, this guy's not drunk. Drunk is red nose and watery eyes. I wondered if he was wired on something, like speed or coke. My guess is that he was fighting for the hell of it. I don't know why. There were two of us. We'd have taken him apart if the club manager hadn't called in reinforcements."

Domingo chimed in. "Besides, if he'd been drinking or doing drugs, he did it someplace else. I think I saw him come in, when Tony and I were walking away from the bar. He came in alone, stood at the entrance and looked around the room, like he was looking for some friends. It wasn't but a few minutes before he came over to our table and started calling us names."

"What time did the fight start? Do you have any idea?"

"Eleven forty-five," Tony declared.

"You sound sure."

"We are sure," Domingo said, wiping some cream cheese from his mouth with a crumpled paper napkin. Just then I heard an electronic beep and Domingo raised his right arm, bagel in hand, and pointed with his left index finger at the elaborate watch he wore. The digital readout informed me that it was nine-thirty. "This sucker beeps every fifteen minutes. And it beeped when the fight started."

I set my coffee on the table and recalled what Duffy LeBard had told me yesterday. The club manager called the

297

base police at eleven-fifty, five minutes after the brawl began. More importantly, Claudia Yancy told me Thursday that she'd seen Harlan and his friends come into Fenton's Ice Cream Parlor around ten-thirty Saturday night. They'd headed for a table just as Claudia and Dana left. So Harlan could have been out of Fenton's by eleven or a little after.

Somehow I didn't think overindulging in ice cream would provide the wired look Tony had just described. What about drugs? Had Harlan had a snort or a toke before he picked a fight with the Marines? In his first mention of the fight, however, Duffy LeBard described Harlan as "likkered up." Booze was evidently the little Texan's recurring problem, enough for everyone to assume Harlan had been drinking that night. Yet it would have been easy for him to spill beer on himself and feign intoxication. I wondered if the Navy had done a blood alcohol test on Harlan. I'd have to call Duffy for an answer, if he had one.

The fact was, it simply wasn't all that unusual for Harlan Pettibone to act obnoxious, and the fight on the night of Sam Raynor's murder might just be another example of the behavior that would eventually get Harlan thrown out of the Navy. But suppose Harlan left the ice cream parlor around eleven. The Marines said he showed up at the club shortly before the fight started at 11:45. He'd been with a group of friends at Fenton's, yet, if what Domingo said was true, Harlan was alone when he got to the club. What had he been doing in between? Had he somehow connected with Sam Raynor during that time? I wouldn't be able to ask him that question until the Navy let him out of the brig Tuesday.

I left Tony and Domingo to their bagels and rinse cycles and drove back to my apartment in Oakland. I ignored Abigail's plaintive meows, advising her that there was still food in her bowl, perfectly acceptable food even if it was low-calorie and had been sitting there all morning. She finally gave up winding herself around my shins, plopped down at the food bowl and crunched a mouthful or two before going off to wash herself in the living room. While all this was going on, I picked up the phone and called Duffy's number at Treasure Island, only to discover that the chief had gone away for the weekend. Then I called the unlisted number I'd pried out of Denise Padilla. There was no answer, not surprising. Yesterday she told me she and Ruben were planning to go down to Salinas this weekend to bring her son Scott home to Benicia.

Watching the two young Marines doing their laundry spurred me to do something about the pile of dirty clothes stashed in the large basket at one end of my closet. While I was at it, I did some long-neglected housecleaning chores. I might as well have gone to Monterey, I thought as I ran the vacuum cleaner, its noise, as usual, sending Abigail to hide in the bedroom closet. I wasn't going to get much work done on the investigation. Denise and Ruben Padilla were presumably in Salinas, and Harlan was out of reach until Tuesday. Nor would I have the opportunity to do much socializing here. My father and his friend Isabel Kovaleski had not yet returned from their jaunt up the Oregon coast, though they were due back sometime this weekend. My brother Brian and his family had gone to visit his in-laws in Eureka. Cassie and her new love Eric were off on another of their romantic weekends, I forgot where. And Alex hadn't called. In fact I hadn't heard from him in a couple of days. When I called his apartment, I got his answering machine. Maybe he had duty today.

Finally bored with housework and laundry, I checked the movie listings and headed for Berkeley, where I had a solitary meal at an Indian restaurant and saw a movie I'd been wanting to catch. I got home at ten-thirty. My answering machine held nothing but a couple of hang-ups. I fed Abigail and was propped up in bed with a book on my lap when the phone rang. When I picked up the receiver, I heard Joe Franklin's voice, radiating impatience. "Where the hell have you been? I've been calling you for hours."

In the background I heard music, a loud guffaw of laughter, the buzz of talk.

"Where are you?" I asked, looking at my bedside clock. It was just after eleven.

"The Kings X bar on Piedmont. Get over here. I think I've found Rosie."

Thirty-five

IT WAS NEARLY ELEVEN-THIRTY WHEN I PARKED MY car in front of a now-closed florist's shop near the intersection of Piedmont Avenue and Pleasant Valley Road. I crossed the street at the light and entered the Kings X. Joe Franklin was hunched over the bar smoking a cigarette. At his elbow was a tall glass with an inch of amber liquid at the bottom.

When he saw me, Franklin ground out his cigarette in an ashtray, tossed back the rest of whatever he was drinking, and rose from his bar stool. He wore blue jeans, a dark blue shirt, his gray windbreaker, an old pair of sneakers on his feet. I was dressed for movement and comfort myself, in black sweatpants, black T-shirt, and running shoes. In my pocket I carried only my ID, car keys, and a small flashlight. Neither of us said anything until we were out on the sidewalk.

"I think Rosie's in the cemetery," Franklin said.

I nodded and we both walked in that direction. Piedmont Avenue dead-ends at Mountain View Cemetery, a large green oasis spread over the lower slopes of the Oakland hills. A series of roads wind up grassy knolls dotted with oaks and pines. Interspersed with the trees are graves and crypts, mostly simple ones decorated with flowers and plants, the names carved on the stones reflecting the Bay Area's ethnic diversity. The top of one central hill of the cemetery, with a panoramic view of the bay and its cities, is studded with elaborate monuments to the wealthy and socially prominent. Charles Crocker, Frank Norris, and Julia Morgan are up there, and one large crypt bears the name of Samuel Merritt, for whom Lake Merritt near downtown Oakland was named. Most of these ornate tombs were built in the Gilded Age of the late nineteenth century. Whenever I look at them, I wonder about the need for extending ostentation into the afterlife. A prime location, but the residents aren't there for the view.

I'd been to the cemetery before, always during the day. Now as we approached it, I looked at the gate, closed across the entrance, and the darkness beyond, remembering two funerals in the chapel located just up the drive on the other side of the cemetery gate. The first took place my second year in college, when my grandfather died. The second was a few years ago when my grandmother joined him in that plot marked by a single marble stone marked "Howard," perched on one of those hills. Sometimes I went there with my father, and left flowers on the earth where it joined the marble.

Joe Franklin's voice brought me into the present. "This afternoon I talked to a guy who carves headstones." He pointed to the left, at two businesses providing the monuments with which the living commemorate the dead. "He says some of the homeless people in the neighborhood have been camping out inside the cemetery."

"Makes sense. From what you told me, they've been harassed lately. And Rosie's been driven away from the construction site by the workers. The cemetery is as far as she can go up Piedmont and still stay in the neighborhood." We stopped at the entrance to the cemetery. I stepped out into the middle of the street and surveyed the high iron gate that now barred entry. "Has this guy actually seen her go in or come out? How does she get in there after hours with a shopping cart?"

"The gate's open till five," Franklin said, gesturing at the sign. "Anybody can come in or out, on foot or in a car. The stonecutter says people like to walk in the cemetery. It's quiet and pleasant, like a park with gravestones. I figure Rosie pushes her cart inside and hides until dark. He's sure

301

it's Rosie. A woman in a straw hat with a pink rose. He saw her pushing her cart out the gate early yesterday morning."

I looked at the gate and tried to recall the layout of roads, buildings, and other points of interest just inside the cemetery entrance. To the left was a little pond with a steep slope beyond it, then the Jewish section of the cemetery. Not much cover there. Directly ahead was a road that led to the chapel. On the right were several administration buildings, arrayed along the fence that separated the cemetery from the houses along a short street called Ramona Avenue. There were lots of trees and bushes along the property line. As far as I could tell, that was the best place for Rosie to hide.

"Let's do it," I said.

On either side of the iron gate closed across the cemetery entrance were concrete walls, chest high. I took a short run at the right-hand wall and easily hauled myself to the top. Franklin did the same, with more agility than I expected from a man his age. Must be all that golf. We jumped down to the sidewalk on the other side and stopped to get our bearings. Outside, on Piedmont Avenue, we'd had the benefit of street lamps. Now that we were inside the cemetery, there was some lighting on the main road that ran in front of the buildings, but where we were going, into the foliage along the fence, it was very dark.

There's something about a cemetery at night that brings a chill to the base of the spine and makes me recall all those ghost stories told around a summer campfire when I was a kid. My grandmother's brother, Woodrow, a mining engineer in the Sierra Gold Country near Jackson, would tell us bloodcurdling tales of Gold Rush bandits come back to haunt the living. And down in Monterey, my mother's Italian fishermen relatives had their own set of tales about ghosts and empty boats plying the rugged dark sea. I pushed back the specters and focused on reality, telling myself that even if I was sneaking into a cemetery in the middle of the night, most of the residents were dead and presumably couldn't hurt me.

302

My eyes were becoming accustomed to the darkness, but the tangle of trees and bushes to the right looked impenetrable. I shone the flash briefly, just enough to discern a narrow path leading back to some kind of shed. I led the way along the path, Franklin close behind me, both silent as we skirted the bushes along the fence line. It was a still night, no wind. My heart and the sound of my breathing seemed loud, as did the rustle of leaves as Franklin and I pushed past the bushes. From a house somewhere on Ramona Avenue I heard music. In the background was the ever-present tempo of the city.

I held the flash low and used it only when absolutely necessary, for fear its light might spook Rosie. We found her under an overgrown tangle of bushes along the boundary, about thirty yards from the cemetery gate. We might have missed her had I not seen a sudden movement from the corner of my eye, the sway of a low-hanging branch, revealing the dull gleam of metal. I stopped dead in my tracks, listening, and so did Joe Franklin. Then I moved slowly in the direction of the bushes. The motion I saw could have been caused by anything from a stray cat to a raccoon, but as we closed in on the foliage, I pointed my flash at the metal object. It was the shopping cart. It contained a dark plastic bag that bulged, full of bottles and cans. On top of the bag was a straw hat with a cloth rose.

Rosie stood behind the cart, in front of her rolled-out sleeping bag, her eyes wide and wild in her white face. She had armed herself against possible attack. Her right hand gripped the nail-studded stick. Her left was wrapped around the long neck of a corkless wine bottle, ready to use it as a club.

I put both my hands up in the air and slowly knelt in the grass. Joe Franklin followed suit.

"I'm not going to hurt you, Rosie," I told her. "I want to talk with you."

She didn't say anything. The three of us stared at each other. Once again I was struck by how young she looked. This was no little old lady whose pension didn't stretch far

303

enough. Rosie was close to my own age, and that in itself chilled me. Could what happened to her also happen to me?

Joe Franklin's right hand moved slowly to the inside of his unzipped jacket. He pulled out two clear plastic freezer bags and held them up so she could see them.

"Are you hungry?" he asked her. "You like cookies? My wife makes wonderful chocolate chip cookies." He tossed one packet toward Rosie and it fell at her feet, on the folds of the sleeping bag. "And this is dried fruit, apricots and figs and prunes, all mixed together." He tossed the second packet and it fell slightly to her right.

"I had dinner already." Her voice sounded rusty from disuse. She glanced quickly down at the plastic bags, and speared one, then the other, with the nail-studded stick, raising them to eye level. She scanned the contents, plopped the wine bottle on top of her bundle and pulled the plastic bags off the nail. "Somebody gave me half a burrito. Beans and cheese and chicken and rice. It was good. I like cookies, though."

"My name's Jeri. This is Joe. We've been looking for you."

"I know. Somebody told me." She lay her nail-studded stick across the shopping cart, careful to keep it within reach. Then she wiped the back of her left hand, the one that held the plastic bags, across the lower part of her face. "You cops?"

I shook my head. "No, I'm a private investigator. Joe's a friend. We just want to talk with you."

"I haven't done anything bad," the woman said with a defiant tilt of her chin. "Some people don't like it when I scratch my mark, but I only do it on things that are mine. And when they deserve it."

"I understand. I know you haven't done anything bad. I just wondered—"

"I saw you before," Rosie interrupted. "You were sitting on a wall." She pulled open one of the bags and jammed a cookie into her mouth. She chewed noisily and swallowed. "These are good. I used to bake, long time ago."

"Yes, that was me, sitting on the wall." I was surprised

that she'd remembered our brief seconds of eye contact at the corner of Howe and Forty-first. The woman was savvier than I'd assumed. "It was a Friday afternoon, two weeks ago. I was sitting on the wall in front of the apartment building, kitty-corner from the lot where you like to sleep."

Rosie's voice was garbled as she chewed on another bite of cookie, but resentment came through loud and clear. "Not anymore. Somebody's building stuff there. I had to find another place. I was at the school for a while but it wasn't safe. This is safe." She gestured in the direction of her neighbors, the ones at rest under their gravestones. "Good thing I don't mind dead people." She laughed, a startling wheeze ended by a cough as she aspirated cookie crumbs.

"You okay, Rosie?" She thumped her chest with one hand and nodded. "I'd like to know if you saw something important on Saturday, the day after you saw me sitting on the wall. Late at night, not during the day. A man was killed inside that apartment building."

"I didn't have anything to do with that," Rosie said, hand brushing her stick, as though for reassurance. "Anybody says I did is lying." She pulled open the second plastic pouch and fished around inside, shooting a sharp look at Joe Franklin. "I hope these prunes are pitted. My teeth can't take any surprises." Startled, he assured her that they were. She popped some of the dried fruit into her mouth, chewed, then stopped suddenly. "Was that the night the cop cars came?"

Excitement surged and I leaned closer. "Yes. You were there. You saw them."

"I thought they were after me." In the dim light Rosie looked a bit sheepish.

"Why?" Franklin asked. I shot him a warning look.

"I scratched my mark on two cars." Rosie snickered. "One of 'em was fancy, lotsa chrome. I'll bet somebody was pissed to see that. They don't always see it right away, 'cuz I put it low down on the back of the car, on the side where the driver doesn't sit." She laughed again, pleased with herself.

Low right rear fender, I thought. "Did the cars deserve it?" I asked.

"Damn straight." Rosie's face assumed an aggrieved expression. "The way some people park. Honest to God. They were blocking both the curb cuts. I couldn't get my cart up to the sidewalk. I had to go down to the parking lot driveway and double back. So I scratched 'em good. Soon as I got bedded down for the night, the cop cars came."

Rosie stopped and wiped her hand across her mouth. "I thought somebody saw me and called 'em. Coulda been that guy in charge of building stuff. He threatened to call the cops on me after I scratched my mark on that little house they put up. So I hightailed out of there. Been laying low since. I heard on the street somebody got killed, but I didn't have anything to do with it. Scratching stuff is about as far as I go. A'course, if somebody attacks me, like those damn kids, I got to defend myself." She patted the nail-studded stick.

I'd been kneeling on my legs so long I could feel them prickling from the weight of my body. I shifted position, trying to get more comfortable. "I know you didn't have anything to do with the murder, Rosie, but since you were there, you might have seen something important, that would help us find out who killed that man."

Rosie was munching on another cookie. Now she reached down into the cart's depths, pulling out a bottle of something that looked like cheap fortified wine. She unscrewed the cap and took a long swallow, then offered the bottle to me and Joe Franklin. I shook my head, my stomach lurching at the smell of the bottle's contents. Franklin reached for the container and took a quick sip. As he handed the bottle back to the homeless woman, his mouth struggled to mask a grimace.

"You mean before I scratched the cars?" Rosie asked, stashing the bottle in her cart. She still didn't trust us enough to sit down. Instead she leaned on her cart, one hand resting on her stick. "Somebody was arguing."

There were a lot of somebodies in Rosie's life, I thought.

Were these particular somebodies important to the Raynor case?

"Tell us about it," I said, trying not to show my eagerness.

"They were loud. I got bad vibrations so I hid."

"Could you hear what they were saying?"

"High, low? No, that wasn't it. Tidy? Tiny bones, maybe. Tiny bones, tiny bones." It sounded like gibberish to me. Indeed, as Rosie repeated them, they took on a sing-song cadence.

"When did you first see them?" Franklin asked her. A few days ago I would have told him to let me ask the questions. Tonight I figured he'd earned the right to play detective, particularly after drinking that rotgut.

"I was coming down the street, on the same side as that building where I saw her"—she pointed at me—"sitting on the wall. Somebody was arguing. I could hear their voices across the street. They were standing right by that corner where I was going, so I stopped, hopin' they'd go away."

"A man and a woman?" I asked. Perhaps it was the same couple Kevin Franklin had seen, right after he left Ruth's apartment. He hadn't been able to tell either.

"Dunno," Rosie said with an unconcerned shrug. "They was both wearing pants. Tiny bones, tiny bones." She sang the last words to a tune of her own devising.

"Did one of them have long hair?" Rosie shrugged again and yawned. I didn't want to press her too hard on this one point. I might lose her. "Could you hear what they were arguing about?"

Rosie shook her head. "No. Just mad-sounding. One of them hit the car. Smack, like this." She brought her left hand down, open palmed, onto the edge of the shopping cart. "Not the fancy car with chrome, the other one that I scratched."

"What kind of car was it?"

"Dunno. Some of 'em I do because of the gizmo on the hood. But most of 'em look alike."

"Could you tell what color the cars were, the fancy car and the other one?" I asked, without much hope. It had

307

been dark, and the street lamp didn't offer that much illumination.

"Like fire," Rosie said, her face bemused. "A'course, when all the cop cars got there with those red lights, everything looked like fire." She waved the stick at us. "I'm tired. I wanna go to sleep. You go away now."

"Are you sure you told us everything?" I asked her. "It's really important, and we don't want to have to come looking for you again. What happened to those somebodies who were arguing? Did they leave? Or did they belong to the cars you scratched."

She thought about it for a moment, then shook her head. "They walked toward me, so I hid. Between two cars. They didn't see me, though. They went into a building."

"Was it the building where you saw me sitting on the wall?" I was certain that it was, just as I was certain one of Rosie's somebodies had been Sam Raynor.

"Mighta been. I couldn't tell. I was pushing my cart toward my corner. Only I couldn't get it up to the sidewalk 'cuz of those damn cars blocking the curb cuts."

"Before the cop cars came, did someone come out of the building and get into one of the cars and drive away?"

Rosie was past her limit as far as questions. She shook her head and brandished her nail-studded stick. "I don't remember anything else. I'm tired. You go away now. I'm not talking anymore."

"Okay, Rosie, we're leaving now. We really appreciate you talking to us, because it's important." I took one of my business cards from my purse and lay it on the grass in front of me as I got slowly to my feet. "This is a phone number where you can reach me if you remember anything else about that night."

She gave no sign of interest in the card, instead watching our faces as Franklin and I backed away from her campsite. As we retraced our steps toward the cemetery gate, I heard Rosie singing. Tiny bones, tiny bones, over and over again, an eerie mantra borne on the still night air. It means something, I thought. But I couldn't quite figure it out yet.

"The cookies were a great idea," I told Joe Franklin as we reached the cemetery gate.

He favored me with a sidelong glance and a weary grin. "Yeah, I thought so."

"You had more nerve than I did, drinking from that bottle."

"I've had worse. Did we find out anything we could use?"

I didn't answer right away. We left the cemetery the same way we'd entered, and walked along the south side of Piedmont Avenue until we came abreast of my Toyota. I pulled my keys from my pocket.

"I'd like to think that was Sam Raynor she saw, arguing with whoever followed him into your daughter's apartment building and killed him. Too bad she couldn't give us a description."

"But she scratched the car." Franklin kneaded the back of his neck, looking exhausted. "A car that looked like fire, a red car."

I laughed and drummed my fingers on the roof of my blue Toyota. "Just about everybody involved in this case drives a red car, or a variation thereof," I said, thinking of Sam Raynor's bright red Trans-Am, both the Yancys' vehicles, Tiffany Collins's red Subaru, the red Buick that hit Tiffany that night on Howe Street. "Tomorrow I start looking at fenders and paint jobs."

Thirty-six

THE FIRST PAINT JOB I EXAMINED WAS THAT OF SAM Raynor's Trans-Am, now sitting at the Oakland Police Department impound lot, where it had been towed after I found it last Monday on Howe Street. There was no letter R scratched anywhere on the vehicle's finish, but I wasn't surprised. When I'd spotted it, the Trans-Am was parked near the corner, but not close enough to block the curb cut so that Rosie wouldn't be able to get her shopping cart up to the sidewalk.

I thanked the officer who'd let me into the lot this Sunday morning, and eliminated one red car from my list. Then I drove through the Tube to Alameda, heading for the bungalow on Marion Court. Chief Yancy drove a red pickup and he had been on Piedmont Avenue the night Sam Raynor was killed. Did Rosie know the difference between a pickup truck and a car? Or would she have mentioned it?

As I drove through the narrow West Alameda streets, I found myself singing as Rosie had last night. Tiny bones, tiny bones, over and over again, like a song on the radio, now irritatingly enmeshed in my consciousness. It nudged at me, as though I may have heard it before, a piece of the puzzle that had yet to fall into place. I couldn't help thinking tiny bones meant something, if only I could make the connection.

The chief's pickup was nowhere to be seen on the culde-sac, and Yancy didn't answer my knock at the door of the little stucco house. From Marion Court I drove to Dana Albertson's apartment on Santa Clara. I looked for Claudia's burgundy Nissan parked on the street, but didn't see it. As I approached the front walk, Dana and Claudia stepped out onto the porch of the Victorian house. Both wore shorts and sleeveless tops, sandals and sun visors. Dana carried a rectangular Coleman cooler, and the handle of a wicker picnic basket swung from Claudia's arm. I planted myself at the foot of the steps and gazed up at them.

"Now what?" Claudia said with a frown. Dana sighed, set the cooler on the porch and sat on it, glancing from me to Claudia.

"I need to look at your car. Where is it?"

She set the picnic basket on the porch railing and waved

her hand to the right. "Around the corner. Why do you need to look at my car?"

"Humor me." I turned and walked in the direction she'd indicated, with both Claudia and Dana following close behind. "When you went to the movie Saturday night, who drove?"

"I did," Claudia said as we reached the corner.

"Where did you park?"

"Howe Street. It's always easier to find a spot on Howe Street."

"Which cross street?"

"I don't know," Claudia snapped at me.

Dana volunteered the information I needed. "It was up past that church. I don't know the name of the street."

"Ridgeway." I stopped and surveyed Claudia's Nissan sedan, tucked into a space on Caroline Street, its dark wine-red surface covered with a layer of soot and dust. I walked slowly around it, checking for marks. No R. Nothing, other than a ding on the driver's side door. I stepped from the street to the sidewalk and fixed Claudia with a gaze. "You say you and Dana left Fenton's around ten-thirty Saturday night. You mentioned that you saw Harlan Pettibone. Did you by any chance see his car?"

"The one with the stuffed tigers stuck to the window?" Claudia's tone was withering. "I think I would have noticed."

"Did you walk directly to the car?" Both women nodded. That meant they'd crossed Piedmont Avenue and gone up Ridgeway to Howe Street, passing the church. Depending on their pace, it was a short stroll, possibly five or six minutes. Claudia's car had been parked a block above the corner where Ruth's apartment building was located. So they wouldn't have seen the two people arguing near the intersection of Forty-first and Howe.

"Did you see anything at all unusual?" I asked.

Claudia answered with a curt shake of her head, but Dana nodded. "I did, on that cross street. Ridgeway, you called it. I saw a bag lady pushing a shopping cart. Well, I don't know if a bag lady's all that unusual these days, but

311

I noticed because she was pushing that cart right down the middle of the street."

"Thanks."

I left them standing perplexed on the sidewalk and headed back to my own car, frustration and something else nagging at me. At least Dana's sighting of Rosie focused the time the homeless woman arrived at the scene. If she'd been at Ridgeway and Howe just after ten-thirty, she probably traveled the long block from Ridgeway to Forty-first Street in ten minutes, maybe less. So that put her at the construction site about 10:45.

A couple of things concerned me about Rosie's story of the two people she'd seen and heard arguing. First of all, I couldn't be sure that either of the cars she scratched Saturday night had anything to do with the case at hand, although one of them looked "like fire." That description suggested a red car, but it could have been any color, enhanced by Rosie's imagination or her memory of the flashing red lights that arrived on the scene after Sam's murder. Harlan's Chevy Camaro was bright orange, but surely Rosie would have noticed the stuffed tiger embellishments. But maybe not. Rosie's description was as vague as Rosie herself.

I wanted to get a look at Harlan's tiger-festooned Camaro. I drove past the Pacific Avenue apartment he'd shared with Sam Raynor but I didn't see the car. It was probably still parked outside the enlisted club at the Naval Air Station, where Harlan had started the fight with the two Marines last Saturday night.

I left Alameda and drove first to San Leandro. No red Subaru in Tiffany Collins's slot at the Estudillo Avenue building. I headed back to Oakland, for her brother's house on Miles Avenue, but found neither Acey's Harley nor Genevieve's bronze Plymouth. It seemed the whole world was taking Labor Day weekend off—except me. Downtown Oakland looked deserted in the midday sun, as though all its inhabitants had been snatched from the streets and plopped down somewhere else, presumably at a beach or in front of a barbecue grill. I thought again of Mother, the family picnic and my aborted trip to Monterey, part vacation and part obligation. I hadn't returned her phone call from earlier in the week because I didn't want to talk with her. Yet, for all the progress I was making today, I might as well have gone south.

I parked outside my Franklin Street building and went upstairs to my office. When I called Duffy LeBard's office on Treasure Island, the petty officer who answered the phone told me the chief was out and not expected back until Monday. I left both my home and office numbers, along with a message asking Duffy to call me as soon as he returned.

A moment after I hung up the phone it rang and I picked it up before the answering machine clicked into play. "Jeri," Errol Seville said, sounding surprised to find me here. "I just left a message on your machine at home and I thought I'd do the same at this number."

"Well, you got the genuine article instead. Did you find out something about Ruben Padilla?"

"I did indeed," Errol said, sounding as though he were pleased to be doing some detective work again. He'd talked with a contact at the Salinas Police Department. There were a lot of Padillas in Monterey County, but my description of the man who'd barged into my office Friday afternoon had narrowed the field of possibilities.

"Ruben Castor Padilla. Age thirty-one, born and raised in Salinas. Parents Castor and Natividad Padilla, from Oaxaca, Mexico."

"Farm workers?" I asked.

"Originally. Now they own a truck farm and nursery east of town. Ruben is one of seven kids, three boys and four girls. Siblings are all married with families. Ruben and his youngest sister are the only ones who've left the area. She's going to school at U.C. Davis. The others have stayed put. One brother works the farm with the father, one's a dentist in Salinas. Of the sisters, the oldest is a nurse, one's a teacher, and one owns a kids' clothing shop."

"Sounds like your basic middle-class success story," I

commented. "But why does your contact at the Salinas P.D. know so much about the Padilla family?"

"Because Ruben's the kid who was always in trouble. Juvenile stuff in high school, some of it alcohol-related. When he was nineteen, he did some time at Soledad," Errol said, mentioning the state prison south of Salinas. "Assault with a deadly weapon. Again, alcohol-related."

"What was the weapon?"

"A pool cue. Ruben was at a local bar shooting pool and he got into an argument with the other player. He picked up a cue and used it to beat the other guy, who almost died. According to my friend at the P.D., Ruben Padilla was a mean drunk. No hint of trouble since he was paroled, however. Presumably he's cleaned up his act."

He certainly has a temper, even when he's sober, I thought, recalling Padilla's behavior Friday when he burst into my office. I thanked Errol for his help and hung up, staring at the telephone. Ruben Padilla had evidently put his life back together after getting out of prison, what with his marriage to Denise and a baby on the way. When Denise told me how she'd met Ruben, she said he'd been attending meetings at the church where she sang in the choir. Must be AA meetings, I thought. Ruben Padilla had sobered up, walking the straight line in order to stay out of trouble.

Could he be sent over the edge, particularly if something threatened his new life? The unwelcome appearance of Sam Raynor could be just such a catalyst, particularly since Sam had threatened Denise, using as his weapon Scott, the son he hadn't seen since Denise walked out on him years ago. There was something else as well. Ruben Padilla had never answered my request that he explain his presence at the scene of Sam Raynor's murder. Even now as I stared at my phone, I could see his angry face, suffused with red from the flashing lights. Why was he there? It couldn't just be coincidence.

When I considered the possibilities, both Ruben and Denise Padilla had a lot to lose.

* * *

Alex called me at home Sunday afternoon. I was correct in yesterday's guess that he'd had duty. "Let's go to dinner," he said. We met at Nan Yang, a favorite Burmese restaurant in Chinatown.

We hadn't seen each other since the night of the murder. At first our conversation seemed awkward, but I was curious to know how Lieutenant Bruinsma was faring with her *JAG Manual* investigation. And Alex was curious about my own efforts to find out who killed Raynor.

The lieutenant was covering much the same ground as I had. I knew she'd been trying to get in touch with Tiffany Collins earlier in the week. Evidently she'd found out from another sailor about Sam's other girlfriend, Claudia Yancy. This led to a long closed-door session between Lieutenant Bruinsma and Chief Yancy, who looked shaken when it was over.

"Actually, he's looked preoccupied since you talked with him last Tuesday," Alex said, spooning ginger salad onto his plate. "He swears he didn't kill Raynor. Says he was in a bar all night. Have you checked out his alibi?"

"Are you pumping me for information?" I helped myself to Thai garlic noodles and we traded serving bowls.

"Of course I am." He set down the bowl and picked up his chopsticks, a frown creasing his dark face. "Yancy works for me and I'm concerned about him. His wife left him, you think he's a suspect in a coworker's murder. God knows what Lieutenant Bruinsma thinks—she plays it close to the chest. What am I supposed to do, pat Yancy on the shoulder and tell him it'll be all right? Or do I relieve him of his duties, pending arrest?"

I thought about it for a moment as I segregated a fire-hot chile from the rest of the ginger salad on my plate. "Yes, I checked his alibi. It's not completely watertight. The bartender couldn't verify Yancy's every move. But I'm fairly certain the chief's telling the truth. That doesn't mean I've eliminated him from my list of prospects, just that several other people have bumped ahead of him in line."

Satisfied with my answer, Alex now moved the topic from the living to the dead. Lieutenant Bruinsma had taken my advice and talked to Duffy LeBard about Sam Raynor's alleged involvement in transporting and selling drugs on Guam. It also seemed the Navy wasn't thrilled to learn that Raynor had lied about a few things when he joined up, such as the fact that his mother was still living and that he'd been married before.

"So much for the four-oh sailor," I said, referring to the Navy's system of evaluating its enlisted personnel, a four-point system, with four being the highest on the scale. Ruth had told me that Sam's evaluations throughout their marriage had been consistently high, despite the chaotic state of their home life.

"It's not perfect." Alex shrugged. "We're so keyed into job performance. If a sailor does the job he's supposed to do, and does it well, we don't look any further. Unless that sailor gives us a reason to. I don't think it's any different out in the civilian world."

I nodded, thinking of my jobs in law firms and some of the jerks I'd worked with, jerks who ultimately got the job done—but you wouldn't want to have a cup of coffee with any of them.

"Accomplish the mission," he continued, waving chopsticks at me. "That's the first priority, whether it's repairing aircraft, training personnel or completing an audit. There's privacy to consider. We can't pry into people's personal lives."

"Until the personal impacts the professional. Or someone winds up dead. It's a tough call."

We talked of other things as we finished our dinner and lingered over tall glasses of strong coffee sweetened with condensed milk. Then I went home, singing as I drove.

Tiny bones, tiny bones. I laughed out loud as I conjured up a scene of half-pint skeletons jiving across the top of a gravestone.

Monday was Labor Day. I slept in and had a late breakfast as I read the Oakland *Tribune*, thinking about the picnic all my Monterey relatives would be having later in the day.

Duffy LeBard called me shortly before noon, as I was picking ripe tomatoes off my plants on the patio.

"Where've you been?" I asked him.

"Lake Berryessa," Duffy drawled. "Fishin' and foolin' around. Came back this morning so I could beat the traffic. What's on your mind?"

"Harlan Pettibone."

Duffy chuckled. "Good ol' Harlan. The brig is cutting him loose tomorrow. At which point he's supposed to report to the legal center here on T.I. They are finally going to process the little pissant for the bad conduct discharge he so richly deserves. That's an answer to prayer. Get him out of my Navy and let the civilian authorities deal with him. Now, why is Harlan on your mind?"

"A couple of things," I said. "First of all, Harlan's car."

"The tigermobile? What about it?"

"Where is it?"

"Don't know. It's not at his apartment?" Upon hearing my negative response, he continued. "Assumin' he drove to the club, it's probably parked in the lot there, or somewhere in the vicinity. Why?"

"I need to take a look at it, to see if it has some damage."

"Was he in an accident?" Duffy asked.

"Maybe." I didn't want to go into detail about Rosie and her mark.

Duffy said he'd call the air station to see if anyone had spotted the car. "You said there were a couple of things on your mind. What's the other?"

"Harlan's middle initial. T for Texas, T for tiger. What does it really stand for?"

Thirty-seven

    I DROVE TO BENICIA IN THE MIDDLE OF THE AFTER-noon and parked my car on a street in a large new subdivision just off Interstate 780. I was armed with a large bottle of mineral water to counteract the heat, and a paperback mystery as a buffer against the boredom of the stakeout. The house I was watching, directly across the street, was pale blue stucco with a double car garage, and it had a closed-up look because the owners were away for the weekend. I hoped that, like Duffy LeBard, they would come home early, driven by a desire to beat the traffic jams that always developed on the last day of a three-day weekend.

    I was halfway through my mineral water and five chapters into my novel when the garage door of the house I'd been watching began to creep upward. Automatic opener, I realized, as a boxy Jeep Cherokee drove up the street and pulled into the driveway. The vehicle's occupants opened their respective doors and got out, dressed in summery casual clothes that spoke of a carefree holiday weekend. The driver opened the back of the vehicle and removed two large zippered nylon tote bags and a large cardboard carton.

    The Cherokee was red, I noticed as I crossed the street, brighter in hue than the fat round tomatoes in the carton, certainly brighter than the Buick sedan parked in the garage. Ruben Padilla glowered at me as I examined the rear fenders of the Cherokee, searching for Rosie's R. It wasn't there. What I did notice was the bumper sticker, a white strip with red letters reading EASY DOES IT. That phrase was a common sight these days, a dead giveaway that whoever put the sticker on the car was involved in a twelve-step program such as Alcoholics Anonymous, recovering from one or more addictions ranging from alcohol to drugs to gambling. In light of what Errol had discovered about Ruben Padilla's prior record, his problem was—or had been—booze.

Arms akimbo, I looked up at the two adults who had joined me at the back of the Cherokee. Ruben's face was dark with anger at the sight of me. His mouth worked as though he were ready to let fly with an outburst. Denise radiated alarm, her teeth gnawing her lip. Yet neither of them said anything, no doubt because the boy was there.

I examined eight-year-old Scott Raynor, my eyes meeting his curious blue gaze. His mother and stepfather had been hiding him in Salinas since his father showed up earlier in the summer. The boy was wiry and tanned and he was going to be tall. He wore shorts and a T-shirt with an ice cream stain on the front. One knee showed a scab, and when I got close to him, my nose picked up that dusty, sweaty scent children get when they've played hard. With his curly red-gold hair, he looked disturbingly like his father, Sam Raynor, a daily reminder to Denise of her disastrous first marriage.

As if she knew what I was thinking, Denise put a protective arm around her son's shoulders and drew him close into a fierce embrace. The kid squirmed a bit and stared at me, wondering what the heck was bothering all these grown-ups.

"What are you doing here?" Denise asked in a low voice. "How did you find out where we live?"

I walked to the sedan parked in the garage and looked at the rear. No marks marred the dark red finish. Then I checked the front, on the driver's side, and saw the crumpled spot, just where I knew it would be. I turned and looked at the three of them. They had followed me up the driveway and stopped at the entrance to the garage, Ruben and Denise bracketing Scott.

"I got your address from the DMV," I told Denise. "A week ago Saturday night you made a left turn from

MacArthur Boulevard onto Howe Street in Oakland. You hit a red Subaru. The other driver got your license number. She was Sam's current girlfriend, by the way."

Denise's face paled over her mint-green maternity blouse. She plunged one hand into her shoulder bag and pulled out a set of keys, handing them to her son. "Take the bags into the house," she ordered. "And stay there."

"How come?" Scott asked. He knew something was up, but his question netted a stern don't-argue-with-me look from Denise. He sighed and went to fetch the tote bags, hauling them to the door leading from the garage to the house, which he unlocked with the keys Denise had given him.

When he was gone, I folded my arms across my chest. "Both of you were on Piedmont Avenue the night Sam was killed. Why?"

"You were there?" Denise stared at her husband. "What were you doing there? You never said anything."

Ruben's mouth twisted. "You told me the car got hit in the parking lot at the bank. So I guess we're even."

Denise sighed and covered her face with her hands. "I need to sit down."

Ruben strode quickly to the front wall of the garage, where I saw a workbench and shelves displaying an array of tools. He pulled a stool from under the workbench, carried it to the middle of the garage and set it down on the oil-stained concrete. Denise sat down wearily, and Ruben took up a protective position, standing in back of her, his big thick-fingered hands resting on her shoulders. She reached up and patted one hand, then took a deep breath.

"I went to see her. Ruth. But I lost my nerve."

"How did you know where she lived?"

"I did a little detective work of my own." Denise's chin tilted as she flashed a brief smile. "When Mitch Burgett stumbled onto me at the bank, he mentioned that Sam had married again and that he was in the process of getting a divorce. I asked him who Sam's latest victim was. That went right over Mitch's head. He never could see Sam for what

320

he was, even when Sam was beating me." Denise's smile disappeared.

"He said Sam's wife was named Ruth Franklin and she was an admiral's daughter Sam met in Hawaii, but her folks lived here. When Mitch said Franklin, I recognized the name. Her father's that admiral from Alameda that ran for the state senate and got beat in the primary. I remembered seeing him on a television debate on one of the cable access channels. A poker-up-his-ass kind of guy."

I nodded. At one time I may have described Joe Franklin that way myself. "So you got out the phone book and called all the Franklins."

Denise nodded. "It was easy. There aren't that many Franklins in Alameda. I got Mrs. Franklin. On the phone she sounded like a really nice lady. So I lied to her. Said I was in high school with her daughter Ruth and I'd heard Ruth was back in the area and I'd love to see her again. And Mrs. Franklin believed me. She gave me Ruth's address and phone number. Just like that."

I'd used the same technique myself, to obtain information from unsuspecting and trusting people, like Lenore Franklin. "When did you call Mrs. Franklin?"

"About ten days before . . . before Sam was killed. I couldn't make up my mind whether to contact Ruth. If I did it, should I call her on the phone? Or just go visit her? I couldn't decide what to do."

"Why did you want to talk to Ruth?"

"I'm not sure." Denise looked perplexed at her own behavior. "When Mitch found me, it turned my whole world topsy-turvy. Sam showed up and threatened to take Scott. I felt like I was under siege. But not just me. I knew there was this other woman, Ruth, going through the same thing. Maybe I could offer her some comfort. Maybe we could band together and vanquish the dragon."

She slumped tiredly on the stool. Ruben could contain himself no longer, words tumbling from his mouth in a burst of indignation. "You didn't tell me any of this. All I knew is that you were brooding and upset. I could see the tension in your face, feel it in your body. I was worried

321

about you and the baby." He looked up at me. "She had a miscarriage the first year we were married. I was afraid we'd lose this one. It's been like this ever since that creep ex-husband showed up."

"Did you ever meet Sam face-to-face?"

Ruben balled his fists and snarled out the words. "If I had, I'd've taken him apart."

"Like the guy you put in the hospital before you wound up in Soledad?"

Ruben paled. His hands dropped to his sides. "You know about that?"

"That's exactly why I didn't tell you." Denise roused herself and reached for his hand. "I was afraid of what you might do. You've been stressed-out too. I didn't know where you were that night. I was afraid you were in a bar."

His face crumpled. "Damn it, Denise. I wouldn't do that to you. I've been sober since I got out of jail." He looked at me, anguished. "God damn it, things have been out of kilter since the day Raynor walked into the bank and started making threats about Scott. He didn't care anything about that boy. He just wanted to torment Denise. You gotta understand, Denise and Scott are the best things that ever happened to me. I don't want anything to screw that up."

"I do understand," I told him.

"I wasn't in a bar." Ruben looked down at Denise and stroked her shoulder. "I went to an AA meeting here in Benicia, and blew off some steam. When I got home, I saw your car pulling out of the driveway. It was nine-thirty. I got upset again. Where the hell were you going? So I followed you."

"You followed me?" she echoed. "To Oakland?"

"Wait a minute. Back up," I said, feeling as though I were directing traffic. "We're talking about Saturday, the night Sam was killed? Ruben, you went to a meeting. And Denise, you finally decided to go visit Ruth. Why? Why Saturday night?"

"Ruben and I had a fight," Denise said. "During dinner. We've been short with each other ever since this started. Ruben slammed out of the house, steam coming from his ears. And I threw a plate against the wall as I was cleaning up after dinner. That's when I decided I had to talk to Ruth. I had to talk with someone else who'd been through what I had. I called the number her mother had given me but there was no answer. I was really jumpy and restless, and all of a sudden I just wanted out of the house. So I got in my car and drove to Oakland."

"What time did you get there?" I asked. "And what did you do when you arrived?"

"After ten. I found the apartment building. I found her name, R. Franklin, apartment 303. But there wasn't any answer when I pressed the buzzer." Denise sighed and shook her head. "So I got back in my car. I thought about waiting. I thought about going somewhere for a cup of coffee. But I couldn't make up my mind what to do. It was ridiculous. I was paralyzed with indecision. I guess I waited for about five minutes. Then I started up the car and circled the neighborhood a few times. I was on my third pass when I hit that car. At that point I thought, this is insane. I've got to go home. So I did." She glanced up at her husband, her face troubled. "Ruben wasn't here. He didn't come in till much later."

I looked at Ruben and he continued the story. "I saw Denise park in front of that apartment building. I found a spot in a lot across the street. I saw her go up to the door, then leave."

"Did you see anyone else enter or exit the building?" I asked.

Ruben rubbed his chin with one big hand and shrugged. "A couple of minutes after Denise drove away, I saw a man and a woman. The guy was carrying a kid."

Ruth and Kevin, I thought, arriving home with Wendy. So it must have been around ten-thirty. "What did you do then?"

"I walked over to the building to check that board that lists all the tenants. I didn't see any names I recognized. I'm standing there wondering what my wife is doing visiting this apartment in Oakland in the middle of the night. I feel angry again." He balled his right hand into a fist and

323

smacked it into the open palm of his left. "I don't drink anymore but I get these sugar jags, chocolate cravings. So I walked over to the main drag, Piedmont Avenue, and I found a place that had coffee and pastries. Had coffee and some cheesecake with chocolate chips. With all that caffeine and sugar, no wonder I couldn't sleep the rest of the night."

"What time did you leave the dessert place?"

"Don't know. I think it was past eleven. The parking lot was just around the corner but I didn't feel like going home. I walked up Piedmont to MacArthur, then back up Piedmont on the other side of the street. Got all the way to a cemetery before I turned back. I don't know what time it was. When I got to the parking lot, there were flashing red lights everywhere. I walked up to the police line, curious just like everyone else. And I heard a cop, talking into a radio. He said the victim had been shot, and his name was Sam Raynor."

Ruben gave a short laugh and shook his head. "Couldn't believe what I was hearing. Then I thought, good, somebody blew the scumbag away. So I stood there for a while, just watching. You must have seen me then. I hung around for a long time. I don't know how long. It wasn't until I drove home that I thought about Denise being there and wondered if she was in some kind of trouble."

"You think I shot him?" Denise asked, her voice exasperated. "Where would I get a gun? You don't have one. I don't even know how to use one. I'd probably shoot myself."

"It was Ruth's gun." They both looked at me, startled, as though they'd forgotten I was there. "Sam forced his way into her apartment and threatened to take Wendy, just the way he threatened to take Scott. Ruth got her gun. She and Sam struggled and it went off. Sam choked her until she lost consciousness. He was shot outside her apartment, in the hallway. Ruth didn't kill him. Someone accompanied Sam into the building. That's why it's important for me to know whether either of you saw Sam, or saw anyone enter or exit the building."

I took them through Saturday night one more time, enough to confirm that neither of them had seen more than what they'd already told me. "A different question, Denise. When you were married to Sam, how well did you know his relatives?"

"Just the ones in Gilroy," she said, with a barely suppressed shudder. "Sam's mother, his aunt Elva, Mitch and his sister Nancy."

"Did Sam or his family ever mention a cousin Ty, or some Tyrone relatives in Bakersfield?"

"Not that I recall. Or maybe I've blocked it out."

I nodded. "I want you to do something for me, Denise. I need information, the kind of information that's hard for me to get. But you work in a bank, with access to computerized records. I'm going to give you a name and a social security number.

"I think this person has a lot of bank accounts, all over the Bay Area. I want to know how many, where, how much, all the information you can locate."

Denise frowned as she contemplated this blatant breach of banking regulations. "If anyone finds out, I could lose my job."

"You can also help me catch a killer."

Thirty-eight

DUFFY LEBARD CALLED ME LATE TUESDAY MORNING with the answers to my questions. As soon as I got off the phone with him, I called the real estate firm in Gilroy where Nancy Tate worked. She wasn't at the office, but when I told the receptionist it was urgent, she patched me through to Nancy's home phone number. She answered on the third ring.

"Tell me about your cousin Ty," I said.

She did. We were on the phone for half an hour. After I finished that call, I kept looking at the phone, waiting for it to ring, willing Denise Padilla to call me with the information she had promised to obtain.

The phone didn't ring. Its silence was making me crazy so I left the office, heading for the Alameda County Courthouse to do some routine sifting through files at the offices of the county assessor and recorder. That done, I had a late lunch on the way back to my office. When I unlocked my door, I saw that the message light was blinking, but none of the three messages were from Denise. Muttering impatiently under my breath, I returned the calls. Then I switched on my computer and wrote a report for the client who'd requested the information I'd found at the courthouse.

It was nearly four when Denise called. "I've got what you need," she said. "It took me most of the day, but there's a lot. Do you have a fax machine?"

I gazed like a proud mother at my brand new acquisition and gave Denise my fax number. Soon the fax machine hummed and sheets of paper emerged from its maw, confirming my theory. Now it was time to leave the office for the streets.

According to Duffy, Harlan Pettibone was to have been released from the brig by noon today. He had a one o'clock appointment at the Navy Legal Service office on Treasure Island, where he was to be processed for a bad conduct discharge, based on his less-than-sterling record in the Navy. Then, presumably, he was to report to his command, Port Services at the Naval Air Station, Alameda.

Since I couldn't get on the base, my best chance for picking him up was at the Alameda apartment he had shared with Sam Raynor. At twenty minutes to five I parked directly opposite the tired-looking L-shaped structure on Pacific Street. From that vantage point I could see the residents arriving home from work. Judging from the body language of those I saw getting out of their cars, Harlan's neighbors appeared to be as weary as the sagging stucco building where they lived. There's something about the first day back at work after a three-day weekend that does that.

For the next hour or so I watched the evening parade of people check their mail and enter their apartments. So far Harlan hadn't come home. The curtains were drawn at the window of apartment 210, and I didn't see the orange Camaro anywhere in the parking lot. I waited. Mr. and Mrs. Torelli departed the manager's apartment, with Honeybunch in tow. A woman exited the apartment next door to Harlan's, carrying a basket piled high with clothing, and went downstairs to a room at the corner of the L, to what I guessed was the laundry room.

Finally, at six, the orange Camaro roared into the lot and parked near the stairs in back. Harlan Pettibone emerged, wearing a summer white uniform. He hefted a couple of brown paper grocery sacks and climbed the stairs, setting the sacks down outside the door while he unlocked it. He opened the curtains halfway and turned on his stereo, which was tuned to some heavy metal rock station. I could hear it all the way across the street. Evidently the neighbors could hear it more than they cared to, because a man two doors down came out of his apartment and knocked on Harlan's door. After a brief exchange, the man returned to his apartment and the music went down a few notches.

I was about to hazard a trip over to check out the Camaro when Harlan emerged from the apartment, wearing his off-duty uniform of black jeans and an orange T-shirt. Even at this distance he radiated energy, bouncing as he walked barefoot along the upper walkway, then down the stairs to the bank of mailboxes near the manager's apartment. He returned to his apartment with a handful of envelopes. A moment later the music that had poured through the open door stopped in mid-reverb. I saw him framed by the curtains in the front window, left hand to his ear, right hand gesturing, as though he was talking on the phone. Then he disappeared from view.

Minutes ticked by on my dashboard clock. Then Harlan emerged once again, this time wearing his high-topped sneakers. He bounced down the stairs and got into the Camaro. The engine roared to life and Harlan zoomed out of the parking lot, much too fast for a residential street. I followed him down Pacific. He turned right onto Webster Street, and I wondered if he was heading for the bar where I'd first encountered him. But he passed the tavern, driving all the way down Webster till he reached Encinal. He turned left and I followed a few car lengths back, barely making the light before it changed.

Harlan was headed for downtown Alameda. He stayed on Encinal until he reached Park Street. He turned left again, bullying his way into traffic. This time I missed the light, banging my fist against the wheel of my car in frustration as the signal turned red. But luck was with me. Out of the corner of my eye I saw the orange Camaro stop and back into a spot half a block down Park Street. Harlan got out of the car and went into a building. When the light turned green again, I made the left and drove slowly along the street, glancing to my right to see which business Harlan was patronizing.

It was a Mexican restaurant called Juanita's, and the Camaro was parked in front. I passed the restaurant, scanned the street for a parking space, and spotted one near the corner of Park and Central. My dashboard clock read six-fifty. I got out of my car, crossed at the light and walked along the other side of Park Street, looking over four traffic lanes to the plate-glass windows of Juanita's. Evidently Harlan's phone call at the apartment had been to his cronies, to let them know he'd been liberated from the brig, because he was sitting at a table by the window with four or five other guys. They were drinking beer and talking all at once. The orange Camaro was parked right outside the window where Harlan and his buddies sat, less than ten feet from the curb. That was far too close for me to examine the rear bumper for Rosie's R. I'd have to wait until Harlan left the restaurant.

I watched while they ordered a meal from the waitress,

then I doubled back on my side of the street, to a restaurant and coffee bar called the Courtyard. Inside I paid a quick visit to the rest-room facilities at the back, then returned to the counter, where I ordered a caffe latte and a large bran muffin left over from that morning's breakfast trade. I hadn't had any dinner and my stomach was making its displeasure known. The Courtyard had several small tables with chairs outside its Park Street entrance, so I carried my coffee and muffin out the door, grabbing last week's edition of the *East Bay Express* from the basket of newspapers at the entrance. I took a seat at a table on the sidewalk, facing in the direction of Juanita's. From that angle I couldn't see Harlan and his buddies, but I had a relatively unobstructed view of the orange Camaro.

I peeled the paper off my bran muffin, broke it into small chunks and ate it slowly, nursing my caffe latte as well. The muffin was stale but I consumed it anyway. It looked like I had a long evening in front of me. An hour crawled by and the summer day faded into dusk, until I could no longer read the type on the newspaper in front of me. My coffee was now cold dregs and I'd long since finished reading the newspaper. For something to do while I waited, I was reduced to flicking crumbs off the table with my thumb and forefinger.

Finally Harlan and his buddies burst out of Juanita's, Harlan's orange T-shirt a glowing nucleus as the others whirled noisily around him on the sidewalk, with much backslapping and rough-housing. I leapt up and headed for my own car. By the time I crossed Park Street at the light, the others had spun off one by one and Harlan was opening the driver's side door of his Camaro. I heard the engine roar as I unlocked my Toyota. I turned the key on my own engine as he came abreast of me.

Harlan wasn't going home. He made a right onto Central, driving the opposite direction. Keeping my distance, I followed him as he turned right again on Broadway, heading toward the bay, then left onto Otis. We sped past the High Street intersection, around the curve at Fernside and onto the metal-surfaced bridge that separates the main island of Alameda from the Harbor Bay development, on what used to be marshland north of the Oakland International Airport. Harlan steamed through the intersection at Island Drive and continued on Doolittle, headed south, in the direction of the airport. To my right were the lush greens and ponds of the Alameda golf course, barely visible in the gathering dusk. Farther south and east was San Leandro Bay, and for several miles Doolittle ran right along the shoreline of what was known as the airport channel. But Harlan didn't plan on driving that far. He made a right turn onto Harbor Bay Parkway.

Nearly a mile into the parkway the road curved to the right, and widened with the addition of a grassy median strip. Just past this point Harlan pulled the Camaro over to the side of the road and stopped, lights on. Either he knew he was being followed or he was keeping an appointment. I didn't have much choice. I passed him and drove another quarter mile until I reached the nearest intersection, Maitland Drive. I turned right and so did the boundary of the golf course. I parked the Toyota, switched off my lights and got out.

Now that the sun had disappeared behind the hills of San Francisco, there was a slight chill in the air, a breeze blowing off the bay, raising a fine layer of gooseflesh on my bare forearms. I shoved my purse under the seat and locked the car door. I carried only my keys and the tiny flashlight I'd had with me Saturday night, when Joe Franklin and I talked to Rosie in the cemetery. Now I stuck both keys and flash into pockets of my jeans and quickly walked the short distance to the parkway.

I could still see the lights of Harlan's Camaro parked in the distance. If he'd picked up on the fact that I was following him, surely he would have left by now. So I figured my guess that he was meeting someone was correct. I considered my options. If I approached the Camaro from this side of the parkway, he'd see me for sure. I darted across the deserted street. Maitland Drive dead-ended at the airport perimeter. Both sides of the parkway were paved and curbed, landscaped with grass and bushes. The few streetlights arrayed on either side of the street illuminated only their immediate area. Harlan had parked midway between two such lamps. I set out in the direction of the Camaro. I'd only walked a dozen yards when a car turned off Maitland onto the parkway. I dropped and flattened myself on the grass, motionless, as the headlights passed me.

As the vehicle continued down the parkway toward Doolittle Drive, I got to my feet and moved forward slowly, my shoes swishing through the grass. My footsteps sounded loud to me, despite the intermittent roar of jet engines from the airport. I moved in a low crouch as I approached Harlan's Camaro, thankful I'd worn dark clothing. Though an expanse of asphalt and the median strip separated us, I was wary of being seen. I saw Harlan, a shadow sitting behind the wheel of the orange Camaro.

Another car was approaching, this time on Harlan's side of the parkway. The vehicle was long and shiny, white with lots of chrome. It came to a stop a few yards in front of the Camaro, engine running, lights still burning. The driver got out, a tall man in dark pants and a white shirt. He shut the car door and walked back toward the Camaro. Now Harlan got out of his car, but he left the driver's side door open, as though he wanted to be able to slide quickly under the wheel. He stepped around the door and walked forward. The two men met in the space between the cars.

Another car turned off Maitland Drive onto the parkway and approached on my side of the road. After it passed, I moved several yards farther along the parkway until I came to the spot where the median strip ended. Now I was well past the rear of Harlan's car. Harlan and his companion seemed intent on their conversation. I darted across the parkway to the fence that bordered the golf course, then I moved forward, my objective the rear bumper on the passenger side of Harlan's orange Camaro, its red taillights glowing at me.

I wished I had a ditch or some bushes to mask my movements. Instead I had a sidewalk and the inadequate cover of the foliage planted near the fence. As I moved closer to the Camaro I heard voices. Harlan and the tall man seemed in-

331

tent on their conversation. They hadn't budged from their spot between the two cars. Finally I was even with the rear bumper of the Camaro, parked at the curb. I remained crouched for a moment, sheltered by a low-hanging bush with scratchy leaves. Then I moved low and fast, over the grass and the sidewalk to the rear bumper of the Camaro. I pulled the little flash from my pocket, shining its narrow beam on the bright orange finish. And there it was, the spiky R Rosie had scratched deep into the surface with her nail-studded stick, on Saturday night when Harlan Pettibone and Sam Raynor had argued on Howe Street.

"Don't fuck with me, man." I heard Harlan's voice now, in his affected Texas twang, carried back on the breeze as he talked with the man who'd come to meet him. "You had two weeks to turn over the fucking car. I want my money."

The other man's reply was muffled as a jet took off from the Oakland airport. Eager to hear more of the conversation, I risked moving closer, edging up the passenger side of the Camaro, mindful of the red glow of the taillights of the second car, which I now saw was a Cadillac Coupe de Ville. I was unable to tell whether there was anyone else in the Caddy. Now I was close enough to pick up words and phrases.

"I know how much the fucking Mercedes is worth," Harlan was saying. "So don't hand me that bullshit. Only reason I ain't come looking for you before is I've been out of circulation. But I'm here now. And you got your cut. So fork over the goddamn money."

The other man was white, tall and bulky, his features soft and fleshy in the harsh illumination provided by Harlan's lights. He grumbled a bit and reached into his pocket. I tensed, and so did Harlan, but the taller man pulled out a thick roll of bills. He counted out what appeared to be a substantial sum.

Harlan was going to benefit quite nicely from the theft of Tiffany's Mercedes, the one that everyone assumed was warm, if not hot, when Sam bought it. It was even hotter now. No wonder Tiffany swore Sam had been angry when the car was stolen. He'd set up the purchase, loaning Tiffany the cash and arranging a payment schedule, solely as a means of laundering his money. Then his pal Harlan got greedy, saw an opportunity and took it. No doubt that was one reason for their argument the night Sam was killed.

Suddenly the transaction was over. The tall, bulky man strode to his Cadillac, got in and fired up the engine. I memorized the Caddy's plate number so I could check it with the Auto Theft detail at the Oakland Police Department. He pulled out onto the asphalt, headed toward Maitland Drive. Harlan remained standing in front of the left headlight of the Camaro as the Caddy made its U-turn at the intersection and headed back down the parkway toward Doolittle Drive. I froze, tensed, by the car's right front fender. All I had to do was wait until he got into the Camaro. Then I'd make a run for that bush at the golf course fence, staying in its shelter while Harlan drove away, leaving me to double back to where I'd left my Toyota.

I'd been kneeling too long, and when I attempted to straighten my legs, my foot slipped. I swore under my breath as my foot made contact with some gravel, the pebbles pinging against the Camaro's hubcaps. The sound was enough to divert Harlan from counting his money.

"What the fuck?" he said as he moved swiftly from his position near the left front of the Camaro to the right, shoving the cash into his pocket. I stood up to meet him.

"What the fuck?" he said again, staring at me.

"I told you I was going to be all over you, Harlan."

Thirty-nine

"LIKE FLEAS ON A DOG. I REMEMBER."

Harlan grinned. This time he didn't look like the skinny goofy sailor with the crooked nose, who rose to the bait I provided that day in the bar. He looked menacing.

"I remember, honey. You really got me goin'. I went home, told Sam about it. He cussed up one side and down t'other, told me you was a private eye."

I moved forward, away from the Camaro, onto the concrete sidewalk that paralleled the road. "You really have the shitkicker routine honed to a fine edge, Harlan. The cornpone accent, and all that 'T for Texas' bullshit. You play the buffoon, and no one takes you seriously. Not even Sam. He must have been surprised when Cousin Ty blew him away."

Harlan laughed. "Me? Now what makes you think that?"

"Harlan T for Tyrone Pettibone." I moved another step away from the Camaro and he watched me warily. "Not Texas, not tiger. Tyrone. Tiny bones," I said. I'd been singing the phrase in my head for the past few days, and it was an effort not to sing it now. "When you were kids, Sam used to call you tiny bones, because you were short and skinny and it's a play on both your names. Later he shortened it to Ty-Bone, because everyone called you Ty."

"Where'd you get all this stuff?" Harlan asked. He raised his bony shoulders in a shrug, then strolled toward the open driver's side door of his car.

I angled in that direction, stepping off the curb onto the road in front of the Camaro, to see what he was up to, but he merely stood next to the door with both hands visible, resting on the hips of his black jeans.

"I talked to your cousin Nancy down in Gilroy this morning," I said. "She filled me in on the family history. Your mother's maiden name was Tyrone. Lots of Tyrones down in Bakersfield. They came out here from Texas during the Depression. Your mother is Ida, younger sister of Alma Raynor and Elva Burgett. You were born in Bakersfield. You never even got to Texas until your parents split up. Your mother married Ed Coffin and you didn't like him, so you went to live with your father in Lubbock. But you used to come to Gilroy in the summer and stay with your aunt Alma. You and Cousin Sam raised some serious hell."

Harlan blinked his pale eyes and raised his right hand to rub his chin. "Yeah, we did at that. Now, I admit to bein' a hell-raiser. What makes you think I'd kill somebody?"

"Money. That long green stuff you just collected from your partner in the Caddy." I watched him as he stood near the car. Was it my imagination, or had he moved closer, as though he were going to slip behind the wheel? I edged a little farther to my right in an effort to see him clearer. Now I was in the middle of the right lane of the parkway.

"It was always money." My body tensed as I stared at Harlan, ready to move if he did. "That's where I got sidetracked. So many people who had good reasons to hate Sam, whose lives were destroyed or damaged because they came in contact with him. I lost sight of the fact that this whole case was about the money he was hiding from Ruth. Sam wasn't murdered because of all that white-hot passion. The motive was cold hard greed."

Harlan backed up, leaning against the Camaro, just behind the open door. "How do you figure that?" he drawled, still twanging the Texas accent. He even hooked his thumbs on his belt loops for effect.

"I don't have to figure. I've got account numbers and balances. Twelve separate accounts in banks from here to Vacaville, all in your name. All opened with amounts less than ten thousand dollars, so you wouldn't attract any attention. All opened within ten days of Sam closing his account at Wells Fargo in San Jose, the one that received the wire transfer from Guam."

"You're a damn good detective, honey. Don't mind telling you, you had ol' Sam worried."

"Worried enough to want to get his money back from ol' Harlan. But you didn't want to give it up. So you killed him instead."

"I got busted for fighting Saturday night," he protested, raising his open hands in a parody of supplication. "Wasn't anywhere near Sam."

"I've got witnesses who place you at the scene, every step of the way. You were at Fenton's with your buddies at ten-thirty. From there you went to the corner of Forty-first and Howe. You met Sam there, at Sam's request. Sam was pissed off because he figured out it was you who stole the Mercedes. He also told you I was getting too close and he wanted to stash the money somewhere else. You argued about it, in voices loud enough to be heard across the street. One of you even slapped the car."

I watched his face in the light from the nearby street lamp, looking for some reaction, but I saw none. "Sam demanded his money back," I continued, speculating on what those voices actually said. "He gave you an ultimatum. As far as he was concerned, that was that. Then he headed across the street. He wanted to throw a scare into Ruth. You tagged along. Maybe you were still arguing. Maybe you even wanted to keep Sam from doing something stupid to Ruth. Mostly I think you were looking for a chance to hang on to all that money. And you found it."

A jet took off at the airport, and I waited until the roar died away. "You were out in the hallway waiting for Sam. Then you heard Sam and Ruth fighting. You heard the gun go off. When you went into the apartment, Sam had his hands around Ruth's throat. You pulled him off her and shoved him out the door. But the gun was right there, with opportunity written all over it. So you picked it up and followed Sam outside. You shot him in the back, wiped the gun and dropped it down the trash chute. Then you hopped

336

in your Camaro and drove over to the enlisted club at the air station. You walked in looking for a fight, jumped those two Marines and got yourself tossed into the brig. It gave you an alibi and it kept me away from you. Until now."

I could probably prove most of it. Harlan didn't help matters by confirming anything I'd just said. Instead he reached behind the driver's seat of the Camaro and pulled out a shiny metal object. Without a word he launched himself at me.

I hate to admit it, but I'm afraid of being beaten up. I've encountered physical violence before. I've come to blows several times during my tenure as an investigator, though I usually rely on a quick tongue and quick reflexes to avoid getting punched out. But sometimes that isn't enough. A couple of years ago I was pistol-whipped in a parking lot and I wound up in the hospital. It left me with a scar on my forehead and some trepidation about mixing it up. I was several inches taller than Harlan and no doubt outweighed him. But he was flailing at me with vehemence born of desperation.

All these thoughts flashed through my head as the shiny object Harlan held connected with my left shoulder. Now thought flashed into pain. What the hell was that thing? A tire iron, the kind that looks like a large plus sign, used to loosen lug nuts. Harlan swung at me again, this time at my head. I dodged, but the end of the tire iron grazed my head. Was that pain roaring from my cranium, or another jet blasting down the runway?

I moved to the right, kicking at his feet. Then I grabbed the crossbars of the tire iron and we struggled over it, our heads close together, close enough for me to see his ugly little face, contorted with fury, glistening with sweat in the waist-level light from the Camaro's headlamps. We partnered each other in this awkward dance, then I shoved him back against the hood of the Camaro and kneed him hard in the groin.

Harlan bellowed in pain and outrage, but my blow to his scrotum didn't put him out of commission. It just made him madder. I tried to wrench the tire iron away from him, but he sprang forward, his tightly coiled body shoving the tire iron hard into my stomach. I stumbled backward and fell, my butt smacking painfully on the asphalt in front of the Camaro.

I felt gravel on the roadway surface, poking at me through the fabric of my jeans. Harlan moved in for another try, his right foot drawn back to kick me, his right hand holding the tire iron above his head, ready to bring it down on mine. He landed one kick on my hip, painful, but it would have been worse had he not been wearing high-topped sneakers.

I scrambled to my feet, left hand scooping up a handful of gravel. I peppered his face with the rocks. He bellowed and his right arm dropped. Now our struggle over the tire iron took us into the middle of Harbor Bay Parkway, toward the grassy median strip. Where were all those cars that passed us earlier?

I snatched the tire iron from him, but I had little time to savor that victory. Harlan rushed me, knocking me off my feet once more. I fought for balance but my left ankle twisted painfully. I fell onto my left side, landing hard on the pavement at the edge of the median strip, my head just grazing the concrete curb. I lay there for a few seconds, stunned, expecting to ward off another kick. What I got was the roar of the Camaro's engine and the sudden bright flash of the headlights as Harlan jerked the car out onto the parkway.

I scrambled to my feet, ignoring the pain in my hip. I ran along the grassy median toward Maitland Drive, as though I had the defensive line of the 'Niners on my tail. I might have had a better chance with the 'Niners. Harlan Pettibone intended to mow me down and leave me as flat as road kill.

Harlan zoomed the Camaro up onto the median strip, where it bounced and slewed in my wake. He hit something, a bush maybe, that slowed him down for a moment. I ran back across the parkway to the sidewalk that bordered the street and the golf course, gaining some distance. Then I was pinned in the merciless glare of the headlights as he

338

barreled off the median, angling across the roadway toward me.

Suddenly I realized I still clutched the tire iron I had wrenched away from Harlan. I tossed it away and made a running jump for the golf course fence. Harlan aimed the Camaro at the fence and lurched forward, hitting hard as I reached the top. My grip on the steel mesh loosened and I fell, managing to get my feet under me, knees bent to cushion my landing.

I dented the hood of the Camaro when I landed. As I leapt to the ground I spotted the tire iron I had dropped, just a few feet away. I seized it as Harlan threw the Camaro into reverse. But he was stuck. He'd run over a small tree to get to me. Now his wheels spun furiously as the car's rear end backed up against the broken trunk. The Camaro wasn't going anywhere.

"You crazy son of a bitch," I yelled.

I brought the tire iron down hard on the driver's side of the Camaro's windshield and it cracked. Harlan bellowed at this affront to his beloved tigermobile. I hit the glass again, feeling childishly satisfied as the crack widened and deepened. By the time Harlan got the door open I was at his side. I grabbed him by the shoulders, ignoring his flailing fists as I hauled him out of the driver's seat. I shoved him back against the car and drove my fist into his stomach. That knocked sufficient wind out of him so that I could hold him pinned with my right hand while my left quickly reached for the keys, killing the Camaro's engine. Then I pulled him away from the car, bent his arms behind him and frog-marched him toward the road.

When we reached the sidewalk under the nearest streetlight, I kicked his high-tops out from under him. He was sprawled belly down on the concrete as I knelt on his back. My adrenaline rush had faded. My aches and bruises were in full cry as I wondered what to do with him.

I saw lights and looked up. A car drove toward us, big and sleek and boxy. It came to a stop beside us and I heard soft music as a window rolled down. In the yellow street-lamp glare the woman's face was round and middle-aged. She looked quite appalled at what she saw.

"Here now, you leave that man alone," she warned. "I'm going to call the police."

"That sounds like a wonderful idea," I told her, with a weary grin.

Forty

"DON'T LET HER STAY TOO LONG," I TOLD JOE Franklin.

We were on the patio in back of the Franklins' home in Alameda. It was the second Saturday in September, late in the afternoon on a sun-splashed day with a clear blue sky, the kind of day we Bay Area residents have in mind when we tell visitors that the best weather is in September and October.

I sat in a lawn chair, sipping a cold beer while Joe examined the coals on his barbecue grill. Judging them to be ready, he removed the lid from a plastic container. With a spatula, he arranged fat red hamburger patties on the surface of the metal grill.

I looked across the yard to where Ruth sat by herself, cross-legged on the lawn. Her back was to us, her head down as though she were examining the blades of grass before her.

The Raynor case was still pending, only the suspects had changed. Wednesday morning I met with the Oakland police and the District Attorney to outline Harlan Pettibone's movements the night of the murder. I also turned over the evidence against him. The paper trail that led from Sam Raynor's bank accounts on Guam and in San Jose to Harlan's multiple accounts provided ample motive, and the D.A. agreed.

Serendipity provided some physical evidence placing Harlan at the murder scene. It was a tiny scrap of a partial print, lifted from the underside of the handle of the trash chute at Ruth's apartment building. The partial matched Harlan's left index finger. By Friday he'd been charged with Sam's murder.

Meanwhile, the charge against Ruth had been dropped and Bill Stanley had moved on to his next case. If Harlan had asked for the criminal lawyer's services, I'm sure Bill would have obliged. But Harlan would have to avail himself of the public defender. Bill Stanley had been retained by a wealthy Piedmont entrepreneur charged with shooting his partner, a high-profile, high-drama case involving embezzlement, infidelity, and junk bonds, splashed all over the past few days' editions of the Oakland *Tribune*. Bill called me late Friday to inquire whether I was available to do some investigating, but I had other plans.

For Ruth, the Raynor case should have been over, but it wasn't. The scars remained. Whether they were permanent scars would only be revealed in time.

"It was her idea." Joe sighed. He glanced across the yard at his daughter, then used the spatula to lift one of the burgers, examining it for doneness.

Ruth quit her job at Kaiser. She'd given up the apartment on Howe Street and moved back into her parents' house, to live in that pink and white bedroom that looked the same as it had when she was in high school. If Joe and Lenore weren't careful, Ruth would stay there, fearing to venture out into the world again.

"I know it was her idea. It's a normal reaction. She's shell-shocked, frightened. Ruth's been through a lot. But she can't hide in that bedroom forever. She has to get out eventually and go on, for Wendy and for herself."

"I agree." Joe reached for his beer and gave me a sideways half smile. "When it's time, I'll boot her out."

He pressed each burger against the grill before flipping it

341

over. The sizzle and smell of roasting meat made my mouth water.

"You want yours plain or with cheese?" he asked.

"Cheese." I got up and handed him a plate piled with sharp cheddar, and he dealt slices onto the sizzling burgers. As the heat of the coals melted the edges of the cheese, I reached into a bag of buns, separating each one and placing the bottom half on each burger.

The back door opened and Kevin came out onto the patio. He carried a large tray loaded with dishes, cutlery, and glasses, and Wendy followed him, bearing bottles of mustard and ketchup. Kevin set the tray on one end of the red-and-white-checked cloth that covered the picnic table. Then he stepped past Wendy, headed back inside for another load, just as Lenore came out of the kitchen with a big pitcher of iced tea in one hand, the other carrying a large bowl filled with potato chips.

Wendy reached up and set the bottles she carried on the corner of the table. Then she walked to the edge of the patio and stared at her mother. I still thought the child looked more solemn than any four-year-old should normally be. Perhaps my contribution to dinner, a half gallon of chocolate chocolate chip ice cream, would help me coax a smile from her, as I'd done that Friday afternoon before the murder.

"Mommy, come help set the table."

Wendy's voice piped like a reed. Ruth gave no sign she'd heard. I saw Lenore and Joe exchange glances. Wendy called to her mother again, and I thought I saw Ruth's head move. Then Wendy set out across the lawn, propelled by determination. She took her mother's right hand and tugged insistently. "Mommy, burgers almost ready. Come help set the table."

Ruth slowly got to her feet. Her right hand still held Wendy's, and with her left she stroked the little girl's fluffy red-gold hair. All of us watched in silence as Ruth and her daughter walked together to the patio. When they reached the picnic table, Ruth picked up the stack of plates and set five places. Wendy climbed onto the bench and began sorting out the cutlery, handing her mother a fistful of forks.

Kevin bustled out of the kitchen with another tray, this one with bowls of sliced tomatoes, onions, lettuce, pickles, and relish. He set down the tray and reached for a handful of chips.

"Don't let the burgers burn, Dad," he warned Joe, whose attention had been on Ruth instead of the grill.

The Admiral harrumphed as he turned back to his duties. "I'm not going to let the burgers burn. I never do. In fact, they're ready. Jeri, I've got one here that's medium rare."

"I'll take it." I picked up one of the plates and met him halfway as he lifted the hamburger from the grill.

I returned to my apartment later Saturday night, replete with cheeseburgers, chips, and ice cream, a full stomach making me drowsy and content. Abigail greeted me at the door, tail up and in full cry, so I spooned up a bowl of cat tuna and filled her water dish. Then I stripped off my clothes and got ready for bed. I was propped up against the pillows, book in hand, when Alex called.

"I got orders. The Pentagon. It's a terrific job, a real career-enhancer. I leave in January."

"Congratulations," I said, and meant it. Alex's career was as important to him as mine to me. I suspected he harbored ambitions to be the first Filipino-American admiral. "I know you'll do well. We'll have to make the most of the next three months. Any plays or movies you want to see?"

"That's the other reason I called. You ever been to the Asian-American Theater Company, over in San Francisco?" When I answered in the affirmative, Alex continued. "This guy I went to school with, he wrote a play. About Filipino immigrants. This company is putting it on. It opens next week. He sent me a pair of tickets to opening night. Want to come with me?"

"I'd love to. My calendar's still clear, this week. After that I'm going to Monterey."

"Aha," he said, chuckling. "You're finally going to see your mother."

343

"I'm going to see family. And friends."

"You always qualify it. Why can't you just admit you're going to see your mother?"

"Alex, don't start."

I ran my fingers through my hair and stretched one leg out under the sheet, poking a toe at my cat, who had joined me on the bed. She'd washed herself from ears to tail and was now settling in for the night. Abigail opened one eye, then shut it and tucked her nose under her paws. Alex wisely didn't start what he couldn't finish. Instead we talked about where we'd have dinner before attending the play.

I called Monterey Sunday morning. I was having coffee and bagels along with my Sunday comics, but Mother was still in bed. Her voice sounded sleep-fuzzed but it sharpened when she recognized mine.

"Well, after three tries, I'd given up on you."

"I was busy."

I spread cream cheese on half an onion bagel. I'd also splurged on some lox, but if I didn't keep an eye on that plate, Abigail intended to steal it from under my very nose. In fact, she'd abandoned her favorite toy, the yellow yarn mouse, and her round tabby body was perched on one of the dining room chairs. Out of the corner of my eye I saw a pair of ears rise slowly and a set of whiskers twitch. I reached for the plate and moved it out of paw range. Then I added salmon to the bagel and took a bite. Pure heaven.

"Yes, I thought as much," Mother said. "The murder investigation, right?"

"That's all wrapped up, as of Friday." I didn't go into any detail and she didn't ask.

"We had quite a picnic on Labor Day. Everyone missed you. I guess I should fill you in on all the family gossip."

"Save it until I get there." I wiped a bit of cream cheese from my lips. Abigail made her move, up onto the table, feinting for the lox, and I swatted her paw. She retreated to the chair.

"You're coming to Monterey after all?"

344

"If I'm still invited."

"Of course you're still invited. You're always welcome, Jeri. When can I expect you?"

"I'm having dinner with Dad next Saturday," I told her, "so I'll drive down the following week. I don't know how long I can stay."

"Stay as long as you like." Now Mother's voice sounded wide-awake and cheerful. "It'll be good to see you."

After I hung up the phone, I toasted the other bagel half and reached for the cream cheese. As I spread on a thick layer, Abigail stared at the lox.

"Do you know how much this stuff costs?" I pointed the knife at the salmon. "More than a can of kitty tuna, that's for sure." I layered salmon on my bagel. "It's too rich for you. The vet says you're too fat. You're spoiled rotten."

Abigail twitched her whiskers and stared at the last piece. Then she stared at me and brought forth a pitiful quavering meow.

"And I'm a pushover," I said. I cut the remaining salmon into tiny pieces and set the plate on the floor.

Coming to bookstores everywhere
in November 1994.

DON'T TURN
YOUR BACK
ON THE OCEAN

by Janet Dawson

Published in hardcover by Fawcett Columbine.

Read on for the intriguing opening pages from
DON'T TURN YOUR
BACK ON THE OCEAN . . .

Chapter 1

ON LAND, THE BROWN PELICAN LOOKED BIG AND UN-
gainly. This one perched on a fence near the end of the
Coast Guard jetty, a bundle of gray-brown feathers dwarfed
by its huge dark bill and the loose dark brown throat pouch
beneath. The pelican stared at me with one round unblink-
ing eye, set high in its white-feathered head, then spread its
powerful wings and took flight. I marveled at the bird's unexpected grace as it glided with military precision between
the turquoise water of Monterey Bay and the clear blue
September sky.

Suddenly the pelican altered course and plunged some
twenty feet into the water, breaking the smooth glassy surface. I counted the seconds until the bird emerged from the
water, a silvery fish wriggling in its beak. The bird straightened its S-shaped neck and swallowed its prey.

"We've got some sicko at it again," Donna Doyle said,
joining me near the fence. "Just like back in 1984 and
1987. The creep catches the pelicans, cuts off their beaks or
slashes their pouches. Or both. Then he releases them. Pelicans can't fish without their beaks, so the birds starve to
death.

I shuddered at the image, chilled despite the warm late-
September sun. I turned to look at my cousin. As a private
investigator, I'm well aware that there are a great many evil
people loose in the world. Quite often they treat their fellow human beings the way they treat animals.

"Who's involved in the investigation this time?" I asked.

"We are of course." In this case, *we* meant the California
Department of Fish and Game. My cousin is a biologist

349

who studies and monitors seabirds, specifically the brown pelican, a thirty-million-year-old species that is on the endangered list. Blame DDT and a host of other pollutants.

Donna grasped the mesh of the chain-link fence separating us and other human observers from the rocks that formed the breakwater at the end of the jetty. Dozens of California sea lions sprawled unconcernedly in the early-afternoon sun, their companions an assortment of seagulls, cormorants, and pelicans.

"Also the Monterey County SPCA and the National Marine Fisheries Service, since pelicans are protected. But I thought maybe you could help."

"Me?" I stared at my cousin. She was three years older than me, thirty-six, and a few inches shorter than my own five feet eight inches. Her round fair face was full of freckles, splashed across a snub nose. "What makes you think a private investigator from Oakland can help?"

"The outside observer," Donna said. She ran a hand through her short unruly blond hair. "Another pair of eyes that might see something we've missed. These incidents are similar to the earlier ones, but there are some differences, too. Think about it. I have to talk to someone."

Earlier I'd wondered why my cousin had asked me to meet her here. Now she walked toward the inward side of the jetty, where the vessels of Coast Guard Group Monterey were tied up. Donna went through the gate and boarded the gleaming white cutter. I took a seat on the low concrete wall on the bay side of the jetty, just to the right of two elderly men who'd cast fishing lines into the blue water.

I heard sea lions barking in the distance, beyond the end of the jetty. The creatures congregated under Commercial Wharf Two, farther to the east, where the fishing boats unloaded their day's catch. Fisherman's Wharf was closer, several hundred yards distant. The wharf jutted over the water, buildings and planks balanced on a forest of thick pilings pounded into the bay floor. A number of small boats road the water in between, at anchor, a picturesque sight for the customers of the restaurants whose broad glass windows sparkled in the afternoon sun.

I shifted, tucking my blue-jean-clad knees under my chin, and gazed out at Monterey Bay, a marvelous sight on this clear autumn day. As the bay curved to the east toward the coastal hills, it was edged by the smooth sand of Del Monte Beach and the mounded dunes along Highway 1, where huge breakers rolled foaming onto the beach. Farther north, past the Salinas River and Castroville, the self-proclaimed artichoke capital of the world, I saw the tower of the Pacific Gas & Electric generating plant at Moss Landing. Beyond that, distance and haze made the shoreline and the coastal hills indistinct as they circled north, then west, past Watsonville, Capitola, and Santa Cruz.

The blue-green water glittered like a jewel, dotted here and there with white foam and froth, moving with tide and current, waves and backwash from the boats that rode its surface. The bay was alive with fish and slick black sea otters, barking sea lions and harbor seals, white seagulls, brown pelicans, the darker cormorants. Beneath the water's surface kelp drifted gently, hiding place for octopus, squid and rays, schools of fish and thousands of tiny sea creatures, all depending on one another for survival.

The first whale I ever saw was in Monterey Bay. I was five years old, walking hand in hand with my grandfather on the bluff overlooking the rocky shore at Lovers' Point. Suddenly Grandpa pointed at the water. My eyes followed the direction of his hand and I saw a whale breach, close to shore. The creature's enormous gray bulk lifted impossibly high, majestic in slow motion. Then it returned to the mother ocean with a mighty splash as I stood openmouthed, awed, entranced, clinging to Grandpa's hand.

"Well that was a deadend." Donna tapped me on the shoulder and brought me to the present. "I thought one of the Coasties had a lead, but it didn't pan out. Did you think about what I said?"

"No," I admitted. I'd been drowsing in the sun, and Donna's mutilated pelicans had been far from my mind. "I'm on vacation. I'm here to loll about on Mother's deck, with a can of beer and a paperback, soaking up the sun. A week's respite from personal injury cases and digging information out of tax records at the assessor's office. Even private investigators take vacations."

Not very often, though. I was the sole owner of J. Howard Investigations. If I took time off, J. Howard didn't get paid. It was different from my five years as an operative for the Errol Seville Agency. Back then I had health and dental insurance provided by the company. But Errol had retired to Carmel eighteen months ago, sidelined by health and age, so I set out on my own.

My cousin tilted her head to one side, a challenge in her blue eyes. "Come on, Jerri you know you can't resist a puzzle. Meet me this afternoon at the SPCA and talk to my friend Marsha. She's their investigator."

"Okay, okay. Now can we get some lunch? I'm hungry."

"Well . . ." Donna's voice trailed off as we continued up the jetty, to where it intersected Cannery Row. Now we walked along the paved Recreation Trail that edged the bay, all the way from Del Monte Beach to the Point Pinos at the tip of the Monterey peninsula. The Rec Trail was crowded with people, though it was a weekday, people walking, running, roller-skating, on bikes, or pedaling one of the two-seater jitneys tourists rented down on the Row.

Something else was on Donna's mind, something other than the most recent spate of pelican mutilations. I'd known her all my life and I could pick up on her moods. More than relatives, she and I were friends, similar in age, temperament, and personality. Her father and my mother are siblings, so she is my first cousin, one twig on my extensive maternal family tree. The tree is quite large, with lots of roots here on the peninsula.

I guessed Donna would tell me what was bothering her, in her own good time. "Where are we going for lunch?" I asked.

"The wharf. Racella's."

"Got the urge for squid. I know you. Fine with me. I just got here yesterday, so I haven't seen Nick or Tina yet."

My family, on my mother's side, is Irish and Italian. Grandpa Dennis Doyle was a big black-haired, blue-eyed Irishman from County Mayo, a fiddle-footed fellow who

352

wandered from Ireland all the way across America, finally lured to Monterey by the work offered by the canneries. He married Angelina Ravella, daughter of a Sicilian who'd been fishing the bay since the turn of the century. And so my families were linked.

The Ravellas were additional and numerous branches on the family tree. Granny Doyle's brother Dominic and Dom's sons Nick and Sal carried on the Ravella fishing tradition. Nick was now retired from the fishing fleet. He and his wife Tina operated Ravella's Fish Market, a fixture on the wharf almost as long as there has been a wharf.

A man and a woman pedaled towards us in a jitney, weaving from one side of the Rec Trail to the other. A little towheaded boy sat in front of them in the bike's basket, his face beaming in the sunshine. We got out of their way, then Donna stepped off the path, heading for a bluff overlooking this sheltered part of the harbor between the wharf and the shore, where an unoccupied picnic table stood under the shade of a Monterey pine. Below us a sea otter did what otters seem to do best, eating as it floated on its back, oblivious to all but the sun and the water. The otter was close enough to shore that I heard the sound it made as it broke a clamshell on the rock resting on its chest.

"I need to talk with you," Donna said, "before we get to Ravella's."

I turned my gaze from the otter to my cousin's face. Her sandy eyebrows were drawn together, emphasizing her frown. "What else is going on besides these pelican mutilations?" Now I frowned. "Is it family stuff?"

Donna nodded. "Cousin Bobby."

"Of course. Cousin Bobby. In trouble again?"

"Actually he's cleaned up his act. Hasn't been in trouble for a while. Until now."

We stood in silence as the otter below us submerged and swam toward the wharf, the tip of its head visible above the water. Bobby was the youngest of Nick Ravella's brood, the only boy, preceded by three girls. He was twenty-nine, the same age as my own brother Brian. I pictured Bobby, seeing a tough wiry body honed by years of hard work

353

aboard his father's fishing boat, a head of curly black hair atop a lean brown face. He had big brown eyes curtained by long lashes, and a cheeky infectious grin that made sure he never lacked for female companionship.

Bobby was a charmer, all right. He also drank too much, and his reputation as a hell-raiser was legendary. When he had a snootful he got belligerent and argumentative and got into fights. Even worse, he sometimes climbed into the driver's seat of the lovingly restored classic 1957 T-bird that had once been Nick's, and drove while drunk. As a result he had a couple of DWIs on his driving record and the attention of law enforcement all over Monterey County.

"How and why has Bobby cleaned up his act?" I asked Donna. She and Bobby had always been close, despite the difference in their ages, so she'd certainly be in a position to know.

"The how is AA. He's been going to meetings and staying sober." Donna stepped away from the edge of the bluff. We climbed back up the slope and rejoined the walkers and roller skaters on the Rec Trail. "The why is Ariel Logan."

"A woman," I said. It wouldn't be the first time someone was redeemed by another person's faith. "She must be special."

"Yes. I introduced them, so I feel rather proprietary about the whole thing. It was just over a year ago, last August. She was buying fish at Ravella's. Bobby and I were there. They looked at each other—sparks."

"How did you know Ariel?"

"Her family lives in Carmel. She's a grad student at Cal Poly in San Luis Obispo, studying environmental engineering. She toured our marine pollution lab down at Granite Canyon that summer, so that's how I met her. All this past year Ariel and Bobby were seeing a lot of each other. I know she was bothered by his drinking, because she mentioned it to me. I think she gave him an ultimatum of some sort, last spring. Whatever happened, it took. All of a sudden Bobby straightened out. He's made a real change for the better. I've noticed it. So have his parents. Even his ex-wife noticed it."

354

"So what's wrong now? You're walking so slow I know you want to tell me before we get to Ravella's."

Donna turned and faced me, her frown deepening. "Ariel Logan is missing."

Chapter 2

NEAR FISHERMAN'S WHARF A TREE-SHADED CLEARing held a statue of Santa Rosalia, patron saint of Italian fishermen. A woman in long flowing robes, she stood looking out at the harbor, her hands outstretched, all smooth curving lines. Donna and I stopped near the statue and looked down at the water, washing onto the sandy sliver of beach edging this portion of the shoreline. A young couple had staked out a spot on the beach. They were eating sandwiches and fending off bold seagulls who aimed to part them from their lunch.

I spotted a bench under the stand of Monterey pines and claimed it. Once seated, I stretched my legs out in front of me, staring at the dusty toes of my formerly white athletic shoes. Then I raised my eyes and looked out toward the Coast Guard jetty, watching the progress of a man and a large dog in a dinghy, threading through the larger boats.

"Everyone around here knows I'm Bobby's cousin," Donna said. "I got a call yesterday from someone I know at the sheriff's department. They want to question Bobby."

"Why?"

"Bobby and Ariel quarreled at the Rose and Crown on Alvarado Street, last Friday afternoon. The barmaid and several customers saw them." Donna's hand clawed at her blond curls. "No one has seen Ariel Logan since. Or at least no one will admit to it."

355

"There must be more to it than that. What else did your source at the sheriff's department tell you?"

"Our old friend the anonymous telephone caller. Something along the lines of, 'If you want to know what happened to Ariel Logan, ask Bobby Ravella.' "

"Could be some wiseass who saw the argument and is trying to be funny."

"Or it could be more serious than that. My friend Marsha at the SPCA has been getting anonymous calls about the pelicans, too. With much the same message."

I sat up straight. "Implicating Bobby in the pelican mutilations? I can't believe that. Not Bobby. He's a fisherman. He loves the sea—and everything about it."

"You and I know that. The fishermen watch the seabirds to find out where the fish are. During the last run of the pelican mutilations several years ago, the fishermen formed a coalition to find out who was doing it. They didn't want to be tarred by that brush. Trouble is, when something like this happens people are quick to point the finger at the fleet." Donna shook her head.

"Now and then we have an incident, someone shooting at sea lions and otters. Fishermen know the animals are protected but they can get exemptions from the Marine Mammals Protection Act. If a sea lion is after a fisherman's catch, he's allowed to use reasonable means to protect it. I don't know that anyone has defined *reasonable means*. Depending on the circumstances, the fisherman can shoot at a sea lion."

"Bobby wouldn't do that," I repeated. "I've been aboard the boat. He uses those noisemakers, those sea-lion bombs, to scare the critters off."

"Right. But he also has a thirty-caliber rifle aboard, just in case." Donna sat beside me on the bench.

I stared out at the water, thinking about my cousin Bobby. He didn't strike me as a guy with a mean streak. He was rowdy, but he had charm and kindness and his grin was quick and ever-present. On the job he was serious and capable. Alcohol was the kicker here, the drug that could change a human being into a monster. His misadventures with alcohol seemed confined to weekends, that period from Friday night to Sunday, when Bobby wasn't out fishing, when he was likely to hoist a few with the guys. It occured to me now that it had been a while since I'd seen my cousin. I didn't know whether he was caught in the grip of alcoholism, or just a guy who had too many beers on a Saturday night. When does a person cross that boundary?

"There's a line between shooting at a sea lion to scare it away from the catch and someone catching and mutilating pelicans. It takes planning and deliberate cruelty to catch a seabird and cut off its beak. I can't believe Bobby would do that."

Donna shook her head. "Neither can I. Even at his worst. It's just these damned anonymous calls about the pelicans and now Ariel. I don't know what to think, Jeri."

"I think someone's making a big effort to get Cousin Bobby in trouble. When was Ariel reported missing? By whom?"

"Her parents filed the report. They'd been in Europe, didn't get home till Sunday evening. The sheriff's department put out an APB for her car. They found it yesterday, in the parking lot of the Rocky Point Restaurant, down on Highway One."

I watched the couple on the beach below us toss bread crusts to the seagulls. One big white gull caught a crust and took to the air, with his compatriots in pursuit. "You say Ariel's a student at Cal Poly. It's the last week in September. Surely the fall term has started."

Donna nodded. "She should have been in class Friday. Ariel's college roommate says she left San Luis Obispo early Friday morning.. The roommate's the one who alerted the Logans that Ariel wasn't where she was supposed to be."

"She cut classes to come up to Monterey," I said, "to see Bobby or for something else. I wonder if she left here on Sunday, on her way back to school. Maybe she was taking the scenic route."

There are two ways to drive from Monterey to San Luis Obispo, a central coast city a hundred and fifty miles farther south, known to its residents as "SLO," an accurate description of the pleasant, unhurried pace of life. If Ariel Logan had been returning to her classes at California Polytechnic University, the faster route would have been to take California 68 northeast from Monterey to Salinas. There she could connect with U.S. 101, a four-lane freeway that ran the length of California, approximating the route of El Camino Real, the King's Highway of the days when California was an outpost of Spain. Depending on how leadfooted she was, and how many stops she made on her way south, Ariel Logan could have made the trip in three hours or less.

The scenic route was down Highway 1, also known as the Coast or Cabrillo Highway. The two-lane road hugged the rocky cliffs and headlands where California crashed into the Pacific Ocean, past some of the most spectacular scenery found anywhere in the world. It was a beautiful drive, good for the soul, a drive a young woman might want to take if she'd had a quarrel with the man in her life. But it was much slower. The narrow two-lane road is popular with tourists in all but winter months, so traffic on Highway 1 usually moves at a glacial pace, which is wise, given the curves. Again, depending on the number of pit stops, Ariel Logan could have made it to SLO in five or six hours. But she never got there.

"What was she doing at the Rocky Point Restaurant?" I wondered aloud. The site where Ariel's car had been found was about ten or eleven miles south of Carmel. The restaurant itself was about half a mile off the road, down a drive leading to the edge of the headland.

"I don't know," Donna said. "Maybe Ariel wasn't on her way back to SLO, Jeri. Which means she could have driven down to Rocky Point anytime after she left Bobby on Alvarado Street."

"Maybe she just needed to stare at the ocean for a while, to sort out that argument with Bobby. There's a beautiful view from the bar, or anywhere on the point. Would she have gone walking on those headlands?"

"I hope not." Donna looked grim. "It's dangerous on this

358

coast. You just don't turn your back on the ocean, not around here. Even when you think you're a safe distance away, one of those waves can suddenly leap up and snatch you right off the face of the earth."

I nodded, recalling something that happened several years ago, when two local women went walking on the ocean's edge, accompanied by a dog. A wave must have swept them out into the Pacific, which doesn't often live up to its name. The dog—or what was left of it—washed ashore several weeks later. I don't think anyone ever found the remains of the women.

Sometimes the ocean lulls you into a false sense of security, even on a broad sandy sweep, like Monastery Beach just south of Carmel. The locals call it Mortuary Beach, with good reason. Here on the Pacific side, the continent ends abruptly. The ocean floor doesn't deepen gradually, like it does on Atlantic beaches. Just under the surface of all that lovely blue-green water is a vicious undertow and an undersea cliff that plunges suddenly deep. Mortuary Beach has claimed its share of victims.

"I hate talking about Ariel in the past tense," Donna said, her voice quiet. "But I'm afraid she went into the water."

"What if she was meeting someone at Rocky Point? Does anyone at the restaurant recall seeing her?"

"I would hope that the sheriff's department has asked that question. Whether they've gotten any answers, I don't know."

"I assume you have a reason for telling me all this. What do you want me to do?"

Donna fixed me with a gaze from her blue eyes. "Talk to Bobby. After my friend at the sheriff's department called yesterday, I went to see Bobby. He seemed surprised, shocked, upset. He didn't know Ariel was missing. He'd tried to call her at her parents' house several times over the weekend and kept getting the answering machine. So he figured she'd gone back to school. He tried to reach at her apartment down there, with no luck. Couldn't even get Ariel's roommate. Bobby says he hadn't seen or talked with

Ariel since Friday, when they had the argument. But he wouldn't say what they were arguing about."

"You and Bobby have always been close. If he won't tell you, what makes you think he'll tell me?"

"I figure if we both work on him, maybe one of us will get him to talk." Donna shrugged. "You know how stubborn he can be. Tuesday it was just Ariel missing. But those phone calls give me a bad feeling. Anyone could have seen Bobby and Ariel arguing at the Rose and Crown. Obviously whoever is making those anonymous calls did."

I got to my feet and stepped back onto the Rec Trail. "Okay, I'll talk to him. Is he likely to be at Ravella's this afternoon?"

"Why do you think I suggested a late lunch there?" Donna said as she joined me on the path.

I grinned. "I thought it was a sudden urge for squid and chips."

"Nick and Tina don't know anything about this," she warned as we walked toward Fisherman's Wharf. "At least not yet. But they will soon. The rumor mill is already working overtime. You can't keep a secret in a small town. And despite the population figures and the big-city pretensions, Monterey's a small town.

More novels starring Jeri Howard, the tough
and fiesty female private investigator,
created by

JANET DAWSON